S0-BNE-489

BOOKS BY JOHN WHEATCROFT

FICTION

Edie Tells
Catherine, Her Book
The Beholder's Eye
Killer Swan
Mother of All Loves
Trio with Four players
The Education of Malcom Palmer
Slow Exposures
Answering Fire

POETRY

Death of a Clown
Prodigal Son
A Voice from the Hump
Ordering Demons
The Stare on the Donkey's Face
Random Necessities
Gowpen: A Double Handful of Poems, with Karl Patten, (limited edition)
Declaring Generations, with Peter Balakian (limited edition)
The Fugitive Self: New and Selected Poems

DRAMA

Ofoti, a play for stage and television
A Fourteenth-Century Poet's Vision of Christ, a poetic drama for voices and instruments, music by Thomas Beversdorf

INTERVIEWS

Our Other Voices: Nine Poets Speaking

TELLING TALES

John Wheatcroft

The Wessex Collective, 2010

Telling Tales © 2010 by John Wheatcroft

ISBN-13: 978-0-9797516-7-7
ISBN-10: 0-9797516-7-5

Published by The Wessex Collective
P.O. Box 1088
Nederland, CO 80466-1088

Web: http://www.thewessexcollective.com
contact: sansan542000@yahoo.com

Acknowledgments

Four of these stories, some in slightly different forms, have appeared *The Ohio Review*, *The Long Story*, *The Alembic*, and *Cold Drill*. The novella *Anwering Fire* was published, with a long story, in paperback by Lunar Offensive Press.

I am most grateful to R. P. Burnham, David Fletcher, Steven Fried, Eve Granick, John Murphy, and Paul Susman for their encouragement, commitment and editorial help.

cover graphic: Max Beckmann, "The Street" [*Die Straße*], Plate 2 of the graphic work, *Die Hölle*, 1919

The Wessex Collective, publisher of progressive books:

If literary fiction (story telling) is the way that human beings can understand and describe what history feels like, we believe it should be relevant to universal and historic human experience. We believe also that literary fiction provides an opportunity to recognize, with significant impact, the problems of societies as well as individuals. At The Wessex Collective we are publishing books that demonstrate an empathy for human vulnerability and an understanding of how that is important to the larger society.

Contents

For my grandchildren,
David, Kate, and Hannah

B/WILL/IAM/IE AND AL AND MAX AND YOU AND I

Willie was expecting to meet Al and Max. Well, not exactly to meet. More precisely, to be met by. "To meet" and "to be met" are not the same. Saying it wrong, then getting it right, or as close to right as you can come with words, is part of the story. Not the most important part, perhaps, but important. Important for the I in the story and the you. The Willie, Billie, Bill, William, Will, and the Al and Max couldn't care less, as the saying goes. You'll see what I mean as the story progresses.

If this were a story only about a Willie, a Billie, a Bill a William, a Will, and an Al and Max, the first two paragraphs could have been left out. The story would start moving more quickly were it to begin with the third paragraph, which is coming up. But if an I weren't in this story, there would no one to tell it. And if a you weren't in this story, there would be no one to tell it to. In that case this story wouldn't be.

Let's start over again. Willie was expecting to be met by Al and Max. After the game Sunday afternoon he'd slowly walked the gauntlet of celebrating fans outside the chain link fence that separated the stadium from the parking lots. Scores of hands had been giving high fives and holding out programs and pens. "Hey, Willie babe, sign my progrum, come on" "Get anotha one next Sundy." "You my boy, Willie." "How bout ya signacha, right heah, Willie." Where Willie's Mercedes SL350 had been parked in one of spots reserved for players' cars, arc lights on tall stanchions were throwing cones of blue-white into the dusk. Willie had not been expecting to be met by Al and Max at that time in that place.

Nor was Willie expecting to be met by Al and Max Tuesday or Wednesday—after a win, Monday was always a day off—as he crossed the almost empty parking lot after practice. They'd want to give him time to sweat it. By "they" I don't mean Al and Max, who would be meeting him either today, Thursday, or tomorrow, before the upcoming Sunday game. Saturday also was a day off. "Meet" here doesn't mean "run across" or "greet." It's a euphemism for something I'd rather not say and Willie would rather not think about.

As Willie, gimp from a cheap shot he'd taken from that bastard Morelli, who was trying to bump Howard as starting tight end, headed for his car, he knew it would make no difference that McKinley and Kolanko were flanking him. If it were a matter of size, strength and athleticism, Al and Max would never be sent to meet him. But adding McKinley's 290 and Kolanko's 275 to Willie's 215 pounds of muscle would mean nothing to Al and Max. They'd likely be twenty years older than Willie. For sure they'd never be able to stay with Clifton thirty yards downfield as he faked outside and cut back in, then at the last second reached in front of him, got some fingers on Kish's almost perfectly thrown bomb, and batted it out of Clifton's outstretched hands. Al and Max possessed a different kind of proficiency with another kind of missile than a football.

Had that play last Sunday ended there, Willie wouldn't be expecting to be met by Al and Max. After the incomplete pass Kish would have run out of downs. The "o" would have taken over, Gronowski would have gone on a long count, then put down his knee after the next couple of snaps to use up the less than a minute left on the clock. The score would have remained the same, preserving the win but staying within the three-point spread given on the game by the wire service.

Would have. Although he'd done a hell of a lot better at football than academics at State, where he'd dropped out and entered the draft after the last game of his red-shirted eligibility, Willie wasn't stupid. But he just couldn't figure out what had made him, after batting the ball out of Clifton's hands, swoop under it as Clifton went sprawling behind him, scoop up the ball with the fingertips of his left hand just before it hit the artificial turf, then draw it against his ribs, and streak down the sideline, faking Kish out of his socks and outrunning Raines, who was supposed to have 9.4 speed. Even if, after making the interception, Willie had let Kish shove him out of bounds or let Raines bring him down from behind, the score would have stayed where "they" wanted it. With the win in his pocket, Coach still would have had Gronowski kneel a couple of times rather than risk a turnover by trying for six or a field goal with a possible fumble recovery and runback for a TD. Any additional points would be meaningless. Except to "them."

When Al and Max would meet Willie, they'd sidle up to him as whores and dope peddlers on the streets do, then would reverse direction and fall in with him, Al on one side, Max on the other. McKinley and Kolanko, who knew what it meant not to play by the rules, would recognize not Al and Max but what they were. Too smart to take on trouble on behalf of a teammate with whom off the field they weren't brotherly friendly, McKinley and Kolanko would casually and wordlessly give way as Al and Max took their places, then without looking around would veer off toward their own cars. Al and Max would escort Willie not to his cream-colored SL350, but to a black Cadillac sedan parked nearby.

Al and Max, as you might or might not know, are a pair of characters in a famous story by Ernest Hemingway called "The Killers." The sentence I've just put down and you've just read is not a perfectly coherent sentence grammatically. Ernest Hemingway isn't called "The Killers," as the sentence says he is. Had I phrased it, "Al and Max, as you might or might not know, are two characters in a famous story called 'The Killers' by Ernest Hemingway," the sentence would be grammatically coherent but stupid. It would make a point of the fact that Ernest Hemingway was the one to call his story "The Killers." True, he was. But there's not much point in making a point of it. Writing does present problems.

Even though it is self-evident that Ernest Hemingway called his famous story with Al and Max in it "The Killers," the matter does bear some looking into. Almost always the writer is the one to call the story what it's called. True, sometimes a lover or friend or an acquaintance or editor or someone the writer doesn't know, just overhears, will provide the title the writer puts on his or her story. Even someone the writer despises or hates, an enemy, may inadvertently supply a title for a story, a very fine title, one that's better than any the author her or himself might have come up with. Still another possibility is that the writer may read the word or phrase she or he uses for a title. Lifting titles is not an uncommon practice. It's an art, though a minor one. But no matter where the title comes from it's the writer who places it above where the story begins.

The name of the story you're reading, if you still are, is "B/Will/iam/ie and Al and Max and You and I." This title was not stolen. Nor suggested by anyone I know or love or like or dislike or despise. I made up the title. It's the thirteenth title I tried on the story. The only one to fit, though the first part of it is rather hard to pronounce.

It's possible that Ernest Hemingway tried a number of titles on his story before he settled on "The Killers." One title you can be pretty sure he didn't consider is "Nick Adams Learns a Lesson." Like Al and Max, Nick Adams is a character in "The Killers." And in the story he does come to a realization, a very important realization about life. And death. This turns him from a boy to a man. Saying in the title that he came to an important realization and that he grew up would have been simplistic and klutzy. Ernest Hemingway was neither a simpleton nor a klutz.

Instead of telling you in the title, Ernest Hemingway wants you to discover in his story that Nick Adams comes to an important realization and becomes a man. He wants you to come to the realization in the way that Nick Adams does, not by being told but by experiencing. Well, not exactly in the way Nick Adams does. He comes to the realization by experiencing it the story. Since there's no you in that story, as there is in this story, you can't come to the realization by experiencing it the story. You're supposed to experience the realization about Nick Adams experiencing the realization by experiencing the story about Nick Adams experiencing. The experience involves being met by Al and Max. In a minute you'll be seeing more of Al and Max.

A more likely sort of title Ernest Hemingway might have put on his story before he put "The Killers" on it is a phrase like "with a towel in his mouth." In the story the narrator, who is and isn't Ernest Hemingway, writes the sentence "He never had a towel in his mouth before." That would not be a simplistic or klutzy title. It would be okay. If you were to read "The Killers" while on the lookout, you could probably find some other phrases that would be okay titles. As a writer, though, Ernest Hemingway, who put the title "The Killers" on the story, was more than okay.

Billie was expecting to be met by Al and Max. Not as she stepped out the side door onto the street. Over the door a globe the size of a human head hung from the end of a pipe shaped like a question mark. The lit bulb inside the globe, which was grimy, threw a circle of gray light that made little impression on the darkness.

To reach the parking lot Billie had to walk a couple of dozen steps along a brick wall, past the window of the office where with the place closed up Frankie would be working at his desk. Edging the drawn shade in the window were slivers of light. In the third stall of the parking lot behind the building stood Billie's' Taurus. The cinder parking lot was dimly illuminated by a light on a telephone pole that Frankie'd had hung there. In the darkness, along the wall, before she'd reach the parking lot, Billie was expecting to be met by Al and Max. That's where they'd met her before. Only the plick plick plick plick of her stiletto heels on the concrete sidewalk broke the early morning silence.

Billie could have asked Frankie to have Bugs escort her to her car. But she didn't want to get Frankie, who had a good thing going and always kept his nose clean, involved. Ever since she'd started working at Frankie D's place two years ago she'd been leaving at about two thirty every morning except Monday and Tuesday, her days off, and walking to the parking lot alone. Everybody in the neighborhood, even sickos, who might try to mess with a girl by herself on the street at such an hour knew better than to try anything like that outside Frankie D's Place. So all at once to want Frankie to have Bugs see her to her car would let Frankie know Joe Blackie was in deep trouble.

Besides, being big and strong and tough as Bugs was, enough so to see to it that whoever came into Frankie D's Place behaved and when somebody didn't, as happened every so often with some smart ass or busthead, to put them in their place or heave them out, and small as Al and Max were, what with their being sent by who they were, it wouldn't help one damn bit.

Thick as he was in the attic, Bugs would right off figure what Al and Max were there for. So after a joke about their taking "good care of the little lady," he'd turn her over to them, then lumber back and tell Frankie the heat was on Billie over Joe Blackie, of whom because he smelled of trouble Frankie had never been particularly fond to begin with. Which might even cost Billie her spot, since Frankie, feeling where the heat was coming from, would never want to give any such source a reason to turn any heat on him. Some nights in Frankie D's Place Billie picked up over two hundred clams in tips.

Billy wasn't too much scared that Al and Max would really do anything to her besides letting her know they were for real. Like crowding her, maybe, like they had the time they'd met her last week, so their hips and elbows bumped her side as they'd crossed the parking lot to where their black Cadillac stood between her Taurus, which looked a whore's purple in the dim light, and Frankie's' white Continental, which looked dirty gray. For sure they'd put the fear of God in her by throwing things at her like "Sista, ya betta come clean wid us er ya know wheah ya'll end up—in the Goddamn dump," this from froggy Al, or was it Max, while the other with the skinny voice, like his lungs were giving out, lied between his teeth, whispering "Shet up, dumb ass, er yer gonna give th liddle lady the wrong idear when we jes wanna have a friendly convasayshun wid her pal Joe Blackie about a bizness mattah." Which was even scarier than the up-front talk.

It was true, though, while the one that sounded friendly-like but lied opened the door of her Taurus after she'd unlocked it, the one that had talked straight out did give her arm a pretty hard twist that made her wince and yell "ouch!" which broke the early morning quiet like a scream, as she'd slid in. Before the nice sounding one slammed the door, she'd tried to talk as scared as she could, talking scared not being hard when she thought not just about herself who she thought Al and Max wouldn't hurt too much, but about what was going to happen to Joe Blackie unless he'd manage to get to some place like Australia.

"I sweah ta God I ain't seen Joe fa ova a month, I sweah ta God he moved all his stuff outa my place, afta we had this terrific fight ova a customa he thought I wuz playin up ta fer real when I wuz jes doin whad Frankie tells us is pata the job 'n I ain't seen nuthin a Joe since, not even his shadda, I sweah ta God I ain't even hud from im n don't have no idea wheah he's hangin out now."

Some of which was true. Not too long before Joe Blackie took off they had a humongous fight over a guy that had his hand practically on her pussy, which did have black panty hose over it, though. Joe Blackie had taken in the scene in the mirror behind the bar, where he was sitting drinking by himself. Back at her place he'd hung one on her right eye so hard even a couple of thick coats of makeup and eye shadow as heavy as what football players put on against the sun didn't cover up the black and blue, then the green and yellow for a week or so. The first two nights her eyelid was so swollen it looked like she was squinting and she couldn't get the false eyelash on. Since she couldn't have one eye with an eyelash and one without, she had to leave both off. Which made her look as if she'd been singed. Thank God Frankie didn't ask any questions. Right after Joe Blackie had socked her they'd made up in bed where he really was super.

It *was* true that Joe Blackie was gone. But it wasn't true about his stuff. Because he went in such a hurry he left all his shirts and suits and neckties and socks and underwear and shaving gear behind at her place, which she hoped they had no way of checking out. It was also true that Joe Blackie never told her where he was going or even that he was. And she hadn't heard a word from him. Which in one way made her sad because she missed him. Still she had to admit she was relieved because she didn't want to get involved with who sent Al and Max to meet her any more than Frankie did. And somebody else would come along, in fact had, though he wasn't the stud Joe Blackie was.

So mostly what Billie would tell Al and Max when they came back to meet her behind Frankie D's Place as she knew they would one of these a.m.'s would be true.

Al and Max, I'm sure you recall, are two characters in a famous story by Ernest Hemingway, which he didn't call "With a Towel in His Mouth," but did call "The Killers." One reason "With a Towel in His Mouth" would have been an okay title for the story is that a towel is an everyday object. In his story Ernest Hemingway makes towels important. He uses towels in an uncommon though not unknown way. The towel business is very plausible because towels are found in lunchrooms like the one in Ernest Hemingway's story. Towels are used for drying dishes and utensils, of which in an eating establishment there are plenty. Dishes and utensils are, or at least should be, frequently washed and dried.

In restaurants towels are also used for drying the hands after they've been washed. Often in the toilets of lunchrooms, diners and the lesser sort of eating places, signs are posted declaring that the law requires employees to wash their hands after relieving themselves. If employees in such eateries do wash their hands, normally they dry them on a towel. The same goes for customers, although there's no law requiring them to wash their hands after relieving themselves in the toilets of these places.

In his story Ernest Hemingway never has the narrator tell the reader where the towels come from, whether they're dish towels or hand towels of ordinary size or long towels on a roller, what kind of cloth the towels are made of, whether they're clean or dirty, what color they are, whether there are patterns in the cloth, whether the towel put in the mouth of Nick Adams and the towel put in the mouth of Sam the cook, another character in the story, are a matched pair to balance the way, according to the narrator, Al and Max are dressed like twins. All we're told is that in the kitchen of Henry's lunchroom Nick Adams and Sam the cook are "back to back in the corner, a towel tied in each of their mouths."

The way Ernest Hemingway has his narrator say it, it sounds as if Nick Adams and Sam the cook have more than one mouth each, which is absurd. Even cows, which have two stomachs, have only one mouth. If

Ernest Hemingway had had his narrator say, "Nick Adams and Sam the cook had a towel tied in their mouth," it would seem that Nick Adams and Sam the cook had only one mouth between them, which is equally absurd as each having more than one mouth. What Ernest Hemingway might have had his narrator say is "Nick Adams had a towel tied in his mouth, and Sam the cook had a towel tied in his mouth." Although that construction is grammatically correct and perfectly clear, it doesn't read as well as what Ernest Hemingway has his narrator say. Ernest Hemingway was no pedant.

In Ernest Hemingway's story there's no mention of the toilet where there well may be jack towels. Notice what Ernest Hemingway has his narrator leave out of his story. Almost surely Henry's lunchroom would have a toilet, or rest room, as we euphemistically call it, perhaps two, one for Men, Georges, Jiggses, Steers, Buoys and one for Women, Marthas, Maggies, Heifers, Gulls. If there were two, there would be two roller towels, one for Nick Adams' mouth and one for Sam the cook's.

In most eating places people like Sam the cook and George the counterman, another character in the story, work eight-hour shifts. Most human beings need to relieve themselves at least once within eight hours. Nowadays, too, most often a law requires a sit-down eating establishment to provide a rest room for its patrons. Whether such laws existed when Ernest Hemingway wrote "The Killers" I really can't tell you. I suppose I could find out, but it wouldn't be worth the effort. If most localities then did have such an ordinance, there's no way of knowing whether the localities of Henry's lunchroom was one of these.

As a matter of fact, there's no way of knowing where Henry's lunchroom is located. Reading the story, you have a sense you're not in the Deep South or Southwest or up in the Rockies or out on the prairies. The atmosphere and what happens suggest the North. The way Al and Max put down the town Henry's lunchroom is situated in lets you know it's not in a metropolis.

The name of the town, we do know, is Summit. George the counterman tells Al or Max that when he asks what "they call" the town. It does seem strange that neither Al nor Max knows the name of the town they've been sent to in order to meet a certain person who is living there. You have to wonder how they found the place, even whether they've got the right town. It is possible that Al and Max really do know the name of the town even though they seem not to. Al and Max are actors, of a sort. Bad actors, you have to say.

That I know of there's a Summit in New Jersey and a Summit in Illinois. There are probably a number of other Summits, as well. I believe the Summit in Illinois, being close to Chicago, a city known for gangsters during the time Ernest Hemingway wrote his story, is a likely locale. Since he came from Oak Park, which is only a few miles from Summit, Illinois, Ernest Hemingway should have a pretty good sense of what can plausibly go on there.

Actually, though, Ernest Hemingway used the name Summit not so you would look it up in an Atlas, as I have, and perhaps go there looking for Henry's lunchroom. Or that you could find out whether there was a law in Summit at the time he wrote the story requiring sit-down eating places to provide toilets for its patrons. It seems likely that Ernest Hemingway, who often makes subtle suggestions and implications in his stories, decided to use the place name Summit because, referring to a topographical feature, as do Mountaintop, White Plains and Pleasant Valley, summit designates the highest point, the spot from which you can't go on up as you climb the hills of the world. A character in Ernest Hemingway's story named Ole Andreson has reached the highest point of his life, which is also the lowest, an irony of the sort Ernest Hemingway peppers his stories with. Al and Max have come to Summit to meet Ole Andreson, who is a Swede.

Except for one, I'm not going to tell you the names of the places where my story "B/Will/iam/ie and Al and Max and You and I" takes place. By the end you'll know where you are. Maybe.

Bill was expecting to be met by Al and Max. Having been met by them once, he didn't relish the prospect. Another such meeting might well destroy his marriage and jeopardize his career as an architect. Through circumstances so unlikely it was most improbable they would fall out that way a second time, he'd been most fortunate to have survived relatively unscathed.

On that occasion he'd parked the Accord in the carport, picked up his attaché case from the seat, walked over to the stanchion, flicked the switch that turned on the bulb in the middle of the vinyl roof of the breezeway, taken two or three steps toward the door of the den. He'd been mulling over some problems in the Heather Hills project. Even if Denise and the suspicions he'd had of late had been at the front of his mind, it would never have occurred to him that someone might be crouching behind the arbor vitae planted between the carport and the breezeway.

Suddenly he felt an arm, Al's or Max's, go around his throat, smashing into his windpipe so he couldn't cry out. A knee hit him hard in the back, between his kidneys. As a pair of fists, belonging to Max or Al, commenced punching his face, a voice hissed at him, "Fuck around with our pal's wife, will ya." Another voice croaked, "Know whad we're gonna do? We're gonna cut off yer prick and ram it down yer throat, thass whad we're gonna do?"

Feeling himself falling backward onto the knee rammed into his spine, Bill in his terror snapped himself forward with such force that he broke loose from the stranglehold of Al or Max. Blindly swinging his attaché case, he went crashing into the body the fist belonged to, knocking either Max or Al over backward. Momentum projected Bill toward the house. All in a single motion he kicked Al or Max, stumblingly high-stepped over that sprawled body, then sprinted the five or so yards he was from the den, where he grabbed and turned the doorknob, fortunately unlocked, shoved open the door, lurched into the den, slammed the door closed, and threw the deadlock as he landed staggering inside. Half leaning, half slumped against the inside of the door, he felt his knees buckle. But he didn't go down.

"That you, Bill?" Linda called from the kitchen at the other end of the ranch house. Sounding normal while he was in panic, his wife's voice startled him.

"Uh huh," he managed to get out between heaves of breath. Then, trying to sound casual, he added, "Be there in a minute, hon."

Ear against the door, he listened. Heard nothing. Using the wall for support, he slid toward the picture window beside the entrance, poked half of his face beyond the drapery, and peeked out. Saw only the orange light in breezeway. Although he couldn't find a car parked anywhere along Acacia Drive, he did hear an engine turn over not too far off, then roar, then fade. All at once he became aware that he was squeezing the handle of his attaché case so hard that his hand hurt. He relaxed his grip.

Still short-breathed enough to feel and hear the suck and blow of his lungs and sensing the pounding of his heart, he wobbled to the mirror hanging above the candle table on the other side of the doorway, then snapped on the lamp. The full realization of what having been met by Al and Max meant, unsatisfactory as it had to be for them, had begun settling weightily on him as he felt the subsidence of adrenaline. In the mirror his left eye showed redness and puffiness. No other mark that he could see. Immediately he decided he'd tell Linda he'd bumped into something. Not the proverbial door. Rather, the towel holder in the john of the Carstone and Dambrowski suite. Preoccupied by the Heather Hills project, he'd walked in without switching on the light.

In the three days since that meeting with Al and Max, Bill had not got in touch with Denise. Nor had she telephoned or left a message, in the code they'd devised, at his office. He wondered whether Curtis had confronted her and if so whether she'd confessed. Surely Curtis wouldn't have hired a couple of thugs to work his wife over, no matter what. For not having been more wary, Bill cursed himself.

The time before last, while Denise was driving them to Laguna, a suspicion they were being followed had invaded his mind. A number of times he turned and looked behind. If Denise noticed the black Cadillac sedan in the rearview mirror, she didn't say anything. When the Cadillac kept on as Denise swung into the motel, he dismissed his misgiving as jittery nerves.

Their next time, as he'd driven them toward a lodge on the far side of San Juan Capistrano, he'd picked up what he thought was the same Cadillac in the rearview mirror. Afterward, sitting on a private little balcony, sipping perfect Manhattans Denise had brought in a flask, he told her about his apprehensions. She expressed doubt that Curtis would do anything like hire an "eye," he trusted her so. Besides, he had too much ego to be jealous. But Bill detected a whiff of alarm in her assurance. Because she hadn't asked about their next rendezvous when he hadn't asked her, he'd had to conclude she too was worried and thought it best to cool it for a spell.

Thinking back about Al and Max, as he found himself continually doing, Bill had told himself they weren't the size you'd expect. Nor had they been adept at their business. Yet he doubted that Curtis would call them off. No matter that they'd bungled and would lie about the damage they'd inflicted, Curtis, seeing Bill on his feet next morning with only a mouse under his left eye, would want to work Bill's nerves. In the office Bill accounted for the mouse by saying he'd been hit by the ball while playing squash, which he did every Wednesday evening. Only Curtis knew differently, and he was hardly in a position to acknowledge what he knew.

To avoid giving Linda, whom he did love, any reason to wonder and worry about what was going on and in the hope of finessing whatever might happen, Bill had rejected the possibility of involving the police. While he shrank at the thought that someone, maybe Bill himself, might end up a corpse if he were to start carrying a pistol, the next afternoon he found a sleazy pawnshop just off Pershing Square and paid outrageously for a pair of knuckle-dusters and a blackjack. If Linda or a passerby were to happen on some violence in the breezeway, he'd offer the speculation that Al and Max were a couple of muggers who'd wandered out of their territory. Then, if the police were brought into it, attempted mugging would be his story.

For two evenings now Bill had slipped the fingers of his left hand through the holes of the knuckle-dusters, then wrapped them over the brass before picking up his attaché case as he got out of the Accord in the carport. Awkward as it was to grasp the handle, he was ready to let go of it on the instant. Slamming the door behind him, he slipped the fingers of his right hand inside the strap of the blackjack lying in the pocket of his jacket and gripped the leather-covered shaft. Tight.

By entitling his story in which Al and Max appear "The Killers," Ernest Hemingway was subtle and devious, two desirable qualities in politicians, lawyers, racketeers, and writers of stories. That title doesn't give away that the story is mainly about Nick Adams, who at first as you're reading you don't even notice happens to be sitting at the counter in Henry's lunchroom, where the story begins. That's subtle.

The title "The Killers" leads, or I should say misleads you to believe the story is about a pair of bloodhounds named Al and Max, who come into Henry's lunchroom just as the story starts. While they are very prominent in the first part of the story, which takes place in Henry's lunchroom—and by the way, Henry never appears—they're not in the second part at all, except in people's minds. Where Al and Max go off to, the narrator of the story never tells us. Maybe even Ernest Hemingway doesn't know. Or care.

On the other hand, though, since the writer can do whatever he wants with the characters in his story—including you in my story "B/Will/iam/ie and Al and Max and You and I," as you'll see later—he can be held responsible for what happens to them. Following this line of storytelling-thought, you might fairly conclude that Ernest Hemingway just disappears Al and Max, "disappears" like "meet" and "met by," being a euphemism, which while anachronistic with regard to the time Ernest Hemingway wrote "The Killers," you certainly understand. Ernest Hemingway can get away with disappearing Al and Max because in themselves Al and Max are not important in the story. Disappearing somebody is not what "The Killers" is about, unless you call Ernest Hemingway's disappearing Al and Max eight-thirteenths of the way through the story the main event, so to speak. That would make the remaining five-thirteenths of the story an excrescence, which Ernest Hemingway, whose father was a surgeon, would surely have known to remove.

Al and Max find themselves in the town of Summit, which would seem to be off their beat, because they've been sent to meet someone who regularly eats in Henry's lunchroom. The sending and the reason for it are not part of the story. The sending was done by a character or characters who live in Ernest Hemingway's head. He chooses not to bring them out for anybody to see, which he has a perfect right not to do. You might look at it this way—what Ernest Hemingway didn't put in his story "The Killers" makes what he did put in so interesting.

Al and Max were always at William's heels, dogging him. When he'd wheel around suddenly on the street, something he'd formed the habit of doing, he'd catch a glimpse of the black leather glove or black leather shoe of either Al or Max as he ducked into a doorway or behind a kiosk or into the entrance of the subway.

Every morning immediately after getting out of bed, before urinating, and each night after urinating just before climbing into bed and a number of times a day before leaving his apartment and another half dozen after returning, William would look down from his fifth floor window. Al and Max would be standing on the sidewalk across the street staring up at him. Or pretending not to be staring at him. Or just starting to walk off as it they hadn't stopped. Or walking by as if they weren't about to stop. Sometimes he'd see a black Cadillac sedan standing in the NO PARKING zone in front of the entrance of his apartment building. William had no doubt who were inside.

At his desk at work William would open the door of his cubicle and peer out at the "gawks," as to himself he called museum-goers, when Al and Max had stopped in front of or were walking away from the Kwakiutl totems across the corridor. Often he would spot them sauntering into the area, or loitering, or just leaving. Imagine, their pretending to have any interest in Kwakiutl totems!

When William ate lunch sitting at the counter in the narrow delicatessen, just a short walk from the museum, he would often pick up Al and Max in the mirror in front of him as they'd be sitting at a table against the wall behind him. All he'd be able to see were their profiles, because always they'd be pretending to be looking across the table at each other instead of watching his back on the stool. Sometimes, though, he'd catch them when they'd sneak a look at him in the mirror in which he was eyeing them.

If William were sitting at one of the tables against the wall, Al and Max, their backs hunched, would be perched on stools at the counter. They'd pretend to be sipping coffee. When he'd shoot a furtive glance at the mirror they were facing, he'd catch a glimpse of their eyes under the snapped-down brims of the homburgs they always kept on while inside the delicatessen. Al and Max never talked to each other.

When William rode the subway, Al and Max would enter the car he did through another door, then sit close to him behind newspapers they'd feign reading. In the theater where he'd be seeing a play or a film or hearing a concert or recital or taking in dance, Al and Max would be sitting a couple of rows behind him, across the aisle. How naïve did they imagine he was to think they could make him believe they had an interest in art, drama, film, music, dance?

In gentlemen's rooms Al and Max would position themselves at urinals close to the one William was using. While pretending to be looking up at the ceiling or in front of themselves at the handle of the flusher or down at the business they were, or were not, doing, they'd eye him peripherally. If he would go into a stall, not because he had to but to be out of view, they'd enter stalls on either side of him. If his were an end stall, either Al or Max would enter the one next to his and, as William emerged, Max or Al would be standing there as if waiting for the stall to be unoccupied.

While William was inside a stall, he was certain they were watching his feet beneath the door to see which way they were pointing. Afterward, they'd wash their hands at basin near the one he was using and would sneak glances at him in the mirror. If there were paper towels, they'd pull one out of the holder just after he did. If there were a blower, they'd dry their hands in the hot air it exhausted just after he had.

Sooner or later, William knew, Al and Max would come at him from the front. That time was approaching, William was more certain than ever, when, returning from work one evening, he unlocked the door to the foyer of his building to find Al and Max inside. They'd positioned themselves in front of the two elevator shafts. Both cars were waiting with their doors open. Al and Max weren't entering either car.

Without breaking stride or glancing at them, William strode into the car to his right. As the door began to close itself, Al and Max gradually passed out of sight. Just before the door of his car had shut itself completely, William heard the door of the other car start to close. When his car arrived at the fifth floor, before the door could open itself, he held down the CLOSE button, then pushed the FOYER button. While the machinery beside him settle to a stop beside his. As his car began to descend, he heard the door of the other car opening itself.

When his car opened its door onto the foyer, William found himself face to face with a woman who obviously was waiting to enter. She had on a green cloth coat with a ratty looking fur collar and a purple cloche hat—in June! On a number of occasions since he'd moved into the building a little over a year before, when the woman and William had been riding up in the same car, she'd asked him to push button 7. On a number of occasions she'd already been on the descending car when it stopped at floor 5 to pick up William. She and he would ride to the foyer in silence. Ancient as she was, her face was made up startlingly, with thick white power, circles of crimson rouge, thick crimson lipstick, and violet eye shadow. Beneath the edge of her helmet-shaped hat, a fringe of gold-colored strings covered her forehead all the way to her penciled eyebrows. The woman waited for William to step from the car.

"Please," he threw out, forcing a smile as his hand swept the space between them like a courtier's ushering in a duchess. "I pushed the foyer button by mistake. I'm going up too."

No sooner were the words out than William realized that if the woman had been watching the indicator arrow, as seemed probable, she'd be aware he'd just descended. But she returned his smile without wrinkling her forehead or knitting her brows questioningly, then tottered into the car.

"Would you mind pushing number seven?" The woman's voice sounded like a small piece of rusty machinery. William pushed 7, and they ascended in their customary silence.

When the car had passed floor 5, which William knew the woman was aware was his floor, she rasped, "You're so much the gentleman," and flashed him a ghoulish smile. Never before had he offered this little gallantry. As the doors at floor 7 closed themselves behind the shambling woman, William pushed button 5. When the car stopped and the doors opened themselves, he was expecting to be met by Al and Max. The hallway in front of the elevator shafts was empty. As was the corridor all the way to his apartment.

A certain Ole Andreson, whom Ernest Hemingway has the narrator in his story "The Killers" call "the Swede," is the person Al and Max have been sent to Summit to meet. The Swede finally shows up toward the end of the story. By this time Al and Max have been disappeared by Ernest

Hemingway. Since the story's not about Al and Max, it doesn't matter that they've vanished. In fact, you might make the case that it's altogether proper that Ernest Hemingway has got them off the page. After the way they treat Sam the cook and George the counterman and Nick Adams in Henry's lunchroom and the way they intend to treat the Swede if he'd have bopped in for dinner, they deserve to be disappeared from the story.

The first and last we see of Ole Andreson he's lying in bed with all his clothes on, facing the wall in an upstairs bedroom at the back end of a corridor in Mrs. Hirsch's rooming house. These are not good signs. A Mrs. Bell—like Henry, who presumably owns Henry's lunchroom, Mrs. Hirsch never puts in an appearance in the story—looks after the rooming house for Mrs. Hirsch. Mrs. Bell's name is what's rung to signify the end of a round in a prizefight, making a sound that Ole Andreson, who according to what Mrs. Bell tells Nick Adams— "He was in the ring, you know"—must have heard on a number of occasions.

Mrs. Bell apparently doesn't connect her name with the sound Ole Andreson probably remembers hearing as he lies in bed, facing a wall he has been talking to. She believes Ole Andreson, whom she characterizes as "an awfully nice man," ought "to go out and take a walk on a nice fall day like this," and perhaps meet someone, which Ole Andreson "didn't feel like" doing. Mrs. Bell feels sorry for Ole Andreson. For the wrong reason. Since Ernest Hemingway ends the story with the Swede's never having been met by Al and Max, Ole Andreson will always be waiting to be met by Al and Max.

What kind of a note Ernest Hemingway ends the story on for Ole Andreson isn't the point of it, though, unless you're a kind and sympathetic soul like Mrs. Bell. Or squeamish. If you are, you can thank goodness Ernest Hemingway ended the story when and where he did or we'd have blood all over the page. But Ernest Hemingway's story isn't any more about what happens or doesn't happen to Ole Andreson than it is about what Al and Max do or don't do. Ole Andreson is in the story much less than Al and Max are, only from about ten-thirteenths to their twelve-thirteenths. That amounts to just about two-thirteenths for Ole.

Ole Andreson's being in just two-thirteenths of the story, though, isn't the reason "The Killers' isn't about him. To have a story be about you, you have to have some choices. Ole Andreson doesn't have any more choices than Al and Max have. Like them, he's done all his choosing in Ernest Hemingway's head, before the story begins. Unless you call deciding not to do anything but lie in bed with all your clothes on facing a wall in an upstairs room at the back end of a corridor in a rooming house is a choice. Which I guess it really is if you know a couple of torpedoes you have no desire to collide with have come to town to zero in on you. Ole Andreson's choosing to lie in bed with all his clothes on does have a good side to it—it saves the undertaker the trouble of dressing a corpse, surely one of the most uninviting duties of an unappealing occupation. That kind of choosing, however, isn't the kind that would make Ole Andreson the character Ernest Hemingway's "The Killers" is about.

The only person who's in thirteen-thirteenths of the story is Nick Adams. That's the whole story. Then, too, Nick Adams is met by Al and Max and therefore he has to make choices that matter. Most importantly, he has to choose whether to go from Henry's lunchroom to Mrs. Hirsch's rooming house and see Ole Andreson as he lies in bed with all his clothes on staring at the wall in an upstairs room at the back end of the corridor. Of course Nick Adams could choose not to go. Which would also be making a choice.

Although Ernest Hemingway doesn't have his narrator tell us so, we can imagine that as Nick Adams goes to see, "see" being rather different from "meet," Ole Andreson, he has an ache in his gut and a foul taste in his mouth. Since he's a very young man, he might also feel that he's going to pee his pants. In one way it's too bad that Nick Adams doesn't know there's no reason for him to be all clutched up. He's perfectly safe. Ernest Hemingway, who's strong on endings, is going to have "The Killers" end without Al and Max ever finding out that Nick Adams has gone to see Ole Andreson.

This is ironic. It's also ironic that, although it's very hard and very brave for Nick Adams to go see Ole Andreson, he doesn't tell him anything important that Ole Andreson doesn't already know. All that Ole Andreson doesn't know is something that Nick Adams and George the counterman and Sam the cook got to know—the names of those who came to meet Ole Andreson are Al and Max. You and I know it too. Knowing or not knowing this doesn't mean beans to Ole Andreson. Ernest Hemingway is also strong on irony.

Will was expecting to be met by Al and Max. Well, not exactly to be met by. In his mind it was to meet. As I count on you remembering, "to be met" and "to meet" are not the same. Also at this point you ought to know that getting it as close to right as you can come with words is an important part of the story. Will could be quite certain about much time Al and Max would allow themselves between arriving at the parking lot and meeting him, as they'd believe, in the bar of the terminal at fifteen past five. They never just killed time. So to provide himself a safe margin, he intended to reach the airport well before they would. He'd park appropriately in short-term parking, choosing the closest empty stall to the terminal. In the sulfurous fog that would be hanging over the airport in early evening, the lights on the tall stanchions on the parking lot would glow like cats' eyes. Will would sit in his sapphire-blue Jaguar until Al and Max would come driving in.

When the black Cadillac sedan would also pull into short-term parking, Will would have to hope that between the time he'd parked and the arrival of Al and Max no stalls between the one he was occupying and the terminal would be vacated. He would want to be facing Al and Max, not to come up behind them, as they would be proceeding to the terminal. At that hour, when commuter traffic was heavy, it would probably be as Will hoped. If not, he'd be forced to improvise. Improvisation makes for uncertainty. Time and space contingencies have to be allowed for. Will wanted the meeting to go as he'd planned, with every movement thought through in advance.

When he'd see the black Cadillac sedan cut into an empty parking stall, Will would begin to get out of his Jaguar. As the Cadillac braked to a stop, Will would start toward it, walking slowly, giving Al and Max time. As they emerged from their car, Al from the driver's side, Max from the passenger's (or would it be Max who was driving?), Will would pick up his pace. Al and Max, after strutting down the length of the Cadillac on their different sides, would swagger shoulder to shoulder through the pale yellow light thrown by the glowing cat eyes, across the macadam parking lot toward the terminal. Al and Max would be expecting to meet Will inside, at the bar.

At this juncture Will would be able to see that Al and Max, shadowy forms in the dusk, would be wearing black homburgs and tight-fitting black chesterfields, into the pockets of which both had plunged their hands. Glancing at them, you might take them for twins their mother had dressed identically. Which would be absurd for two middle-aged men. Were you to draw close, you would discover that their features were quite different. Both faces, though, would be pinched expressionless, making them seem similar. Will would have on a Burberry gabardine raincoat, tan, and a pearl-gray fedora. Inside the deep pocket of the raincoat, Will's right hand would be clutching the butt of a Smith and Wesson .45, inherited from his paternal grandfather. His forefinger would be inside the guard, hooked on the crescent-shaped trigger. His hand would feel clammy.

When he was certain that Al and Max were close enough to see him distinctly through their narrowed eyes, Will would draw the pistol from the pocket of his raincoat, would lift it shoulder-high, and with his arm stretched full-length and kept stiff at the elbow, he would point the mouth of the weapon at either Al or Max. Although he would have no way of knowing which was targeted, it would make no difference.

Seeing the barrel of a pistol in a hand on an outstretched arm pointing at one of them, both Al and Max, without consulting, would know what to do. They would not take time to draw their hands from the pockets of their chesterfields. Will would have no intention of squeezing the trigger of the Smith and Wesson he was aiming at either Al or Max. It would make no difference if he would have, because the chamber was empty.

At a few minutes past four Will had been sitting at the walnut desk in his spacious office, with ETAVIRP in gold letters on the door of the suite of Pemberly, Curtin, McSorley, Altshire, and Green, on the thirty-first floor of the Met-Plaza Building. Having reviewed the materials one last time, he lacked the courage to walk over to the window, which on a clear day offered a splendid view of the city and river below but which on this foggy afternoon was just am empty gray. Instead, Will removed a Smith and Wesson .45 from the middle drawer of his desk. Slowly he'd raised the pistol, then put its mouth into his mouth and hooked his forefinger on the quarter-moon trigger. On his feverish lips the metal felt icy. Broken in fortune and spirit, exposed, disgraced, with only a shred of pride remaining to cover his ugly nakedness, he knew he was already signed, sealed and delivered, as they say. Unfortunately, though, he had not yet become an inert piece of goods. Or bads.

Before Will could bring himself to squeeze the trigger, there came to him what might be called, were he a religious man, a vision. Had he been a writer of fiction, it might be called a scenario. Will saw Al and Max. Having been met by them three days before, he knew exactly what they looked like. Will also saw himself, not as if he were inside himself looking at himself in a mirror, but as if he were inside the mirror looking out at himself, sitting at his desk with the barrel of a pistol in his mouth.

Will saw himself remove the pistol from between his lips and lay it on the desk top, watched himself dial his telephone, heard the ring of a telephone in the receiver, then a grunt when it stopped ringing, listened to himself arrange to meet Al and Max in the bar of the airport terminal at 5:45. He beheld himself get up from his desk, push his Burgundy leather desk chair into the kneehole of his desk, remove the cartridges from the pistol, flick off his desk lamp, cross to the closet, put on his Burberry raincoat, stash the Smith and Wesson in the right-hand pocket, leave the office, taking care not to lock the door. As he watched himself pass Cora at her desk, he heard himself tell her there was no need to stay and finish the Amtech report, which just as well could be done first thing in the morning.

Then Will watched himself descend in the elevator, stride into the underground garage, climb into the Jaguar, drive through the thickening late afternoon fog to the airport, park in the closest stall to the terminal in short-term parking, and sit and wait. As if time were compressed, almost immediately he spied the black Cadillac pull into a stall beyond where he was sitting and stop. He saw Al and Max get out, watched himself climb from the Jaguar and walk slowly toward his meeting with Al and Max. Watched the pistol come out of the pocket of his raincoat, watched himself raise the arm whose hand was grasping the pistol until it was leveled at Al or Max. At this critical moment the vision or scenario had dissolved into the blank grayness of the world beneath his office.

Before Bill had stirred in his desk chair, a confirming gratification hit him. Were his vision or scenario to be acted out, no one could say he had placed the mouth of the pistol into his mouth and pulled the trigger. No, the first horrified person or persons who happened on the spot where he would have just met Al and Max couldn't say that. Nor could airport security, who would arrive on the scene with what seemed prescient promptness. Nor could the meticulous homicide investigator or the forensics expert or the hack obituary writer or the unctuous Reverend T. Newton Parkinson, rector of All Saints' Episcopal Church. Nor could fork-tongued Al Green or that crooked son of a bitch Everett Altshire. Nor could Will's doddering Uncle Nathaniel or his close sister Amanda or his distant sister Vanessa. Nor could his stonyhearted wife or troubled Will junior or, most important of all, wild, beautiful teenage Lizzie.

Lowering the pistol, Will emptied it, arose from his desk, turned off the desk lamp, walked to the closet beside his private john, opened the closet door, put on his raincoat, hanging like a suspended body, and the pearl-gray fedora, and slid the Smith and Wesson into the right-hand pocket. He'd closed the closet door. Then he'd stridden back to his desk, picked up the telephone and punched seven buttons.

Will was confident he'd soon be meeting Al and Max.

Al and Max, as you sure as shootin' ought to know by now, are a pair of characters in a story called "The Killers." Ernest Hemingway wrote the story, most likely, before you and I were born. In case you haven't or have noticed, I might as well acknowledge I'm possessed by that story. I might as well also acknowledge that I stole Al and Max in the story you're reading from Ernest Hemingway. You might say I thugnapped them.

As you also ought to know by now, in my story a Willie, a Billie, a Bill, a William, and a Will are anticipating a meeting with Al and Max. Although to give away the ending is, or used to be, considered bad form in story-writing, let me assure you that just as Ole Andreson in Ernest Hemingway's story never meets or is met by Al and Max, in this story, Willie, Billie, Bill, William, and Will will also be forever waiting to meet or be met by Al and Max. Had I let the "ills" and Al and Max meet, my story would be over before it's finished, a patent absurdity.

Although I stole Al and Max and cribbed the idea of not meeting from Ernest Hemingway, there are differences between his story "The Killers" and mine. As my title, which I concede is not subtle or devious, indicates, there is an I in my story. There is no I in Ernest Hemingway's story. There is, though, a storyteller who although not Ernest Hemingway in the story of his life, stands in for Ernest Hemingway. Whereas in this story I am sometimes conspicuous, like right now, the narrator Ernest Hemingway is always inconspicuous.

There's a flip side to this I/storyteller business, too. Just as there is an Ernest Hemingway in the story of his life, as well as an Ernest Hemingway narrator of his story "The Killers," there is an I in the story of my life as well as an I in my story "B/Will/iam/ie and Al and Max and You and I." The two I's have some things in common but are not identical. Unlike Ernest Hemingway in the story of his life, I in the story of my life am pretty inconspicuous. I qualify "inconspicuous" because one thing about the I in the story of my life is self-evident: I am writing a story called "B/Will/iam/ie and Al and Max and You and I," in which I'm telling a story that I am in. You get the self-reflecting ad infinitum two-mirrors picture don't you?

Were you to read Ernest Hemingway's famous story "The Killers," something I earnestly—don't miss the fortuitous pun—recommend, or, if having read it, you remember it, you might notice another difference between it and my story. Because Ernest Hemingway must choose where to begin and end, what to put in and what not put in, whose story to make it, which words to use, which title of the few fitting titles is must subtle and devious, he as the storyteller does not go into a funk. While in all probability he wishes that necessity did not bear down on him so hard and while he can't be altogether happy with the only choices open to him, he does what he must with a grudging sort of acquiescence. You might say he not altogether accidentally resembles the character in his story named Nick Adams. Although Nick Adams is not an Odysseus or an Aeneas or a Beowulf, he proves himself to be almost heroic in the choice he makes after having been met by Al and Max. While not a Homer or Virgil or an anonymous Anglo-Saxon scop, all of whom knew how to tell a whale of a tale—let's not forget Herman Melville—Ernest Hemingway is almost heroic when it comes to writing stories.

As did Ernest Hemingway, the storyteller of "The Killers," I, in writing my story "B/Will/iam/ie and Al and Max and You and I," have had to make choices. Unless you're a literary moron, you must have noticed that the I in my story is not a heroic character. To have called my story the "I-ey" or the "I-id"—forget about Freud right now—or just plain "I", would have been pretentious as well as silly. The sad truth is that, when it comes to making choices in my story, I, unlike Ernest Hemingway, am anything but almost courageous. If you find the I in my story to be a klutzy coward, I certainly won't disagree.

As for the I in the story of my life—well, now, that's a different story, isn't it. The less said about him here, the better. The only thing about him that matters is that he's writing this story.

As for Ernest Hemingway in the story of his life, I think it more than likely that he wrote the story called "The Killers" in the hope of keeping Al and Max *in* the story and *out of* his life. He wanted to prevent them from discovering where sometime, like Ole Andreson, he'd be holing up. He hoped to make it impossible for them to track him down and meet him. Don't most writers write their stories for some such reason?

Unfortunately Ernest Hemingway, while he wrote one hell of a story for us to read, was not successful in warding off Al and Max. After years of searching, Al and Max, who, whatever else they may or may not be, are relentless, caught up with Ernest Hemingway in Ketchum, Sun Valley, Idaho. No doubt they had it in for Ernest Hemingway for disappearing them from his story "The Killers" before they were able to meet Ole Andreson, whom they'd been sent to meet in the town of Summit, where, as would Ernest Hemingway in Ketchum, he was holing up. Al and Max's meeting with Ernest Hemingway in the story of his life was for real.

There are some ironies here. Whenever Ernest Hemingway is

involved, you can bet your bottom dollar or your life, depending on your "values," as they call them these days, that ironies are lurking somewhere close by. For one thing, it's ironic that the name of the place where Ernest Hemingway in the story of his life is caught up with by Al and Max is Ketchum, Sun Valley. Ketchum, if your ear hasn't already told you, is a slurred phonetic spelling of "catch him." Then, too, to have things end in a valley is quite different from having them end on a summit. And I'm afraid that when Al and Max showed up they hardly brought sunshine. While appropriate, these ironies may be taken as happenstance. I wonder.

A more significant irony is one that's willed. As a character named Will, of all possible names, would do if he could but can't because I disappear him too soon from the story I in the story of my life am trying to get written, Ernest Hemingway in the story of his life did finesse Al and Max. Realizing that somehow they had managed to get out of his story "The Killers" and to catch up with him in Sun Valley, Idaho, Ernest Hemingway in the story of his life made up his mind not to end that story like Ole Andreson, who to this day is lying in bed with his clothes on, facing a wall in an upstairs room at the back end of a corridor in a rooming house in the town of Summit, waiting to be met by Al and Max. Just as he knew when he'd reached the place and arrived at the time to stop writing his story "The Killers," Ernest Hemingway knew when he'd come to the place and the time to stop writing the story of his life.

I in the story of my life am still writing away at the story called "B/Will/iam/ie and Al and Max and You and I." Whenever I choose to, I can stop. And I'm sorely tempted to end the whole sorry mess here and now. But I won't. Because the story isn't finished. Ending something and finishing something are not the same. Willie, Billie, Bill, William, Will, and Al and Max and I in the story have been taken care. That leaves you, doesn't it.

Even though I in the story of my life, being of an old-fashioned, well-brought up ilk, for the sake of politeness placed you ahead of the I in the title "B/Will/iam/ie and Al and Max and You and I," I've saved you for last. Along the same line, you might have noticed that, while all the letters designating the "ill"—another ironic pun, I'm afraid—characters reside in that first alphabet-soup word of the title, the characters themselves don't appear in the same order in which their names can be extracted from that scramble of letters.

Well, that gives *you* something to do and is reason enough for you to be in my story—you can fish those letters out and properly arrange them.

While you're at it, you might even be able to rearrange the letters into a less klutzy, more subtle and devious title. And there's still more for you to do. You can neaten other things up and you can find words that come closer to being right than are the words I've settled for.

Your potential for improving things is not all that's concerned with you. In addition to being a character in my story, you too are a character in the story of your life. Most probably, like the two I's and the two Hemingways, the two you's are almost but not quite the same. All that I know about you in the story of your life is that at this instant you are reading a story about the you who is a character in a story some I is writing. Frankly that's enough.

You, on the other hand, must wonder about you. I mean the you in the story of your life must wonder about the you in my story. For example, you must wonder why since I've given you equal billing with Willie, Billie, Bill, William, Al and Max and I in the title, yet you aren't in the story more. Also why you aren't more in the story. Those two are different wonders. Both are expressed in the same words, but the words are not in the same order, which changes their meaning. By now you've caught on to this sort of stuff, I'm sure.

Still another wonder you might have is, when I put you in my story without your permission, maybe against your wish and will, why then couldn't I have been gracious enough to make you heroic, like Odysseus in the *Odyssey* or Aeneas in the *Aeneid*, or Beowulf in *Beowulf*. Had I done so, you might point out, I could have called my story the *You-ey* or the *You-id* or just plain *You*, all of which would be shorter, less awkward, and not as off-putting titles than the one I've chosen to go with. Or you might wonder why I wasn't willing to make you at least almost heroic, like Nick Adams in the story "The Killers" and Ernest Hemingway, the teller of that tale. Had I done so, it might occur to you that I could have called my story "The Killers Redux," a title in which the Latin would add a touch of much needed class. "Redux" seems to have caught people's fancy in the last few decades.

To be up front with you, let me tell you I've devoted a considerable amount of thought to heroism. And, alas, I've come to a melancholy conclusion: in this our time during which *the* bomb has been dropped and more bombs are standing ready to be let go and missiles are being launched day in and day out, I'm afraid—I use the phrase as more than a verbal mannerism—I haven't been able to hit upon a jot of antique heroism or a tittle of Lost Generation almost heroism anywhere around my neck of the woods of the world to invest in you or any other character in my story. I concede that apprising you of how necessary you in the story of your life are to my story and of how vulnerable you in my story are to the way I choose, no, really must make use of you, provides you scant consolation.

Despite whatever wishes, wonderings, complaints, resentments, reproaches, angers, grudges, etc. you in the story of your life might be nursing because of my treatment of you in my story "B/Will/iam/ie and Al and Max and You and I," I'm not going to let you in the story of your life off the hook. Not quite yet. Not before my story is finished. And my story won't be finished until the you in my story ask the you in the story of your life a question. What that question is, I in my story am not going to tell you. In fact, I in the story of my life can't. Which is why I had to write this story.

See, you're in my story lots. And there's lots of you in my story. Maybe you'll never get out.

"BARE RUINED CHOIRS WHERE LATE THE SWEET BIRDS SANG"

Père Patou couldn't stomach the omelet with mushrooms Esther had whipped up for him. After all these years you'd think the woman would concede that a few bites of the baguette M. Jabot had baked early that morning, dipped in black coffee, made all the breakfast he wanted. Of course she couldn't be expected to understand he had little appetite for food at this hour because the taste of the body and blood of our Lord was still on his tongue. Then again, it might be that she wanted Père Patou to have something substantial in his belly on this particular morning since, without knowing what it was about, she'd found out he was to attend a meeting of the village council. His apprehension regarding the outcome gave him even less desire for food than usual.

Returning to bed after using the commode—at fifteen before two, it turned out—he'd lain awake listening for the bells. When he'd heard the first of the three double strokes, *dindelles* they were called, he hadn't been certain what the hour was. Rather than twist the switch on the bedside lamp to provide light for him to read the face of the nickel-plated alarm clock, on three milking-stool legs with a silver beret on top, he'd waited until he'd heard the chiming of two o'clock to learn how much of the night was yet to come. After that he'd merely dozed.

When the three *dindelles* had struck at fifteen minutes before five, Père Patou had pushed up his bones, pulled himself to a sitting position on the side of the bed, and crossed himself. Then he'd knelt and said aloud his morning devotions, first the Paternoster, next *Je vous salue, Marie*, finally a prayer to St. Francis de Sales. After flicking on the lamp, he'd switched off the alarm. Although he'd had more than ample time to get himself ready to say Mass, he'd decided it was senseless to go back to bed only to lie awake for another half hour.

Neither the bells nor the crowing of M. Grenier's cocks had awakened him. The need to relieve himself had. And during the night the striking of bells had not kept him from sleep. That was the point, the very point. And it wasn't that he was without any hearing. His ears still took in the barking of the village dogs, sometimes even the mewing of the doves that roosted in the cupola on the old tithe barn, now used for storing deconsecrated statues, cracked fonts, and broken church vases. When the wind was brisk and from the south, he could also pick up the clanging of the bells on the cows and goats in the pastures of M. Leschemell and the crying of the ewes of M. Constans when their kids were taken from them, in the adjoining meadow, just below the village.

But it was true that for some time now the cheeping of the chaffinches that flew into the presbytery garden to feed on the bread crumbs he scattered every morning after breakfast were growing fainter and fainter. And to himself he acknowledged that when a mere handful of parishioners attended Mass, the responses were so indistinct that he was timing his leading of the liturgy to the length of time he knew it took worshipers to give each response. Still and all, M. Le Tourneau had been wrong to argue that only because he was going deaf Père Patou was not kept awake by the ringing of church bells throughout the night.

And if M. Le Tourneau was hearing the bells in his sleep, as he insisted, well then? Since he wasn't awake to know he was hearing them, what matter? No, no, Père Patou refused to believe the bells were affecting M. Le Tourneau's sleep. Nor had they been an annoyance to anyone in the village until the businessmen had begun patronizing the Hotel Le Tourneau after the hotelier had converted the old *relai*s into a fashionable establishment. Yes, they were the only ones to complain, outsiders. Everyone in the village, having heard the bells ring day and night within minutes of birth, was so accustomed to the sound that it would never occur to anyone to think of the bells as a nuisance.

Such had been Père Patou's reply to M. Le Tourneau when he'd asked to be told how the priest could be so certain the bells were not a nightly disturbance. "In any case," M. Le Tourneau had then thrown back at him, "I'm talking about *now*, *modern* times, *other* people." "Ah, *monsieur*," Père Patou had responded, vigorously holding to his point, "truly, those to whom the village belongs would be lost without the ringing of the bells at all times." "That remains to be seen, *mon père*," the hotelier had retorted, as he'd shown the priest his stoop-shouldered back and walked out of the presbytery with his nose in the air. "And then will you cut the throats of M. Grenier's cocks?" Père Patou had flung at his heels. M. Le Tourneau was thirty years younger than his pastor.

For more than four hundred years the bells, which had been cast while Savoie's own St. Francis de Sales was still on this earth, had been striking every quarter hour and had been ringing the Angelus morning, noon and evening, as well as summoning the village to the church. How sweet and mellow those bells were! As Père Patou had pointed out to M. Le Tourneau, even though he'd known the hotelier would brush it aside, inscribed on the shoulder of each bell was WEGHEVENS, MECHLIN, ANNO DNI, 1583. And who could say that for many years before those bells had been carried by wagon all they way from Belgium a more primitive clock had not been chiming time in the village?

Between bites of coffee-soaked bread, Père Patou forced himself to swallow a few forkfuls of omelet in hope that this morning, when he needed to rally his forces for what lay ahead, Esther would not light into him for not eating. With all her virtues and good intentions, the woman was a trial, a burden he'd been given to bear to the end. Not only did she take it on herself to decide what he was to eat, but she also assumed the office of mistress of his wardrobe, such as it was.

As evidence of her daily scrubbing on a washboard over a tub, which had her always smelling of lye, Esther placed clean linen undergarments on Père Patou's bed daily, while he was saying the evening service. Every Saturday a freshly laundered cassock was in the pile, and he had to surrender to her rough red hands the cassock he'd been wearing. Constrained by his self-prohibition against ever offending his housekeeper, who had suffered unspeakable adversity in her life, he had never let her know that he preferred the feel of clothing he'd been wearing to cloth that, freshly laundered, seemed like new. Just as he didn't mind a bit of fray on his cassock, he was perfectly comfortable with a few spots and stains, reminders of the faults of the flesh.

Without a word of remonstrance, Père Patou put up with the woman's taking it upon herself to decide when to remove an article of clothing from the chiffonier or closet of his bedroom, without informing him. Something would simply be gone. Then he'd have to go through the annoyance of ordering new linen or a new cassock through M. Fouchet and to wear it with discomfort until it was broken in. Esther even pestered him about his well-worn brogans. Though she didn't dare confiscate and dispose of them, she regularly covered the scuff marks with polish while reproaching him for not ordering a new pair from the shoemaker in Cruseilles. Père Patou had unusually large feet and it was hard to come up with shoes that didn't pinch.

Only over his liturgical vestments was he the master. During the half century Esther had been his housekeeper, she'd never put a foot inside the church. A couple of times in the first year or so she'd been in the village, a sixteen year-old then, he'd caught sight of her peering in through the fluted arch whose iron-stropped door was standing open. The way she'd hung there suggested she feared that the God Whose home the church was would strike her dead if she so much as breathed the air inside the sacred building. Yet was not God also her and her people's God? Still, he couldn't be sorry that her inhibition put the seedy garments in the presbytery beyond her reach.

So it would appear he'd eaten more of the omelet than he had, Père Patou chopped all that was left into little pieces that he then scraped to one side of his plate and covered with a hunk of bread. He made use of this childish subterfuge fatalistically, realizing Esther surely would discover how much of the omelet she'd prepared lay beneath the bread and would charge him with starving himself. Maybe this constant fear of hers was a legacy of her deprivation as a child. This morning he was willing to buy time before being reproached.

While sipping what remained of coffee in his mug, Père Patou withdrew from the pocket of his cassock the letter M. Meunier, the village postman, had delivered to the rectory first thing in the morning. Unfolding it, he read it for the third time. Although he knew it was superstition, for God no longer spoke to men in such ways, he couldn't rid himself of the feeling the letter was an ill omen. To think—when he'd written to the bishop six weeks ago, immediately after the threatening visit from M. Le Tourneau, no reply had come until this very day. In the intervening time, hearing nothing more from M. Le Tourneau and concluding that the hotelier had decided to drop the matter, Père Patou had thought it best to let sleeping dogs lie. He'd said nothing with his mouth closed to anyone in the village about M. Le Tourneau's complaint. Then just yesterday afternoon to receive a request to meet this morning with the mayor and the village council concerning "the matter of the bells!"

Now that it had turned out M. Le Tourneau, rather than giving up, had been carrying on his effort to have the bells silenced at night, the curt formality of the dismissal of his plea for help from above, conveyed not by the bishop himself, or by his suffragan or even by his coadjutor, but by the secretary to the rural dean, was a needle in Père Patou's heart. The oldest active priest in the diocese, he had served as curè in this village for more than half a century.

1 August 1995

My dear Père Patou:

His Excellency has asked that I make reply to yours of 14 June. Although the Bishop appreciates your calling to his attention the matter your letter speaks to, it is his policy not to intervene in such affairs when the concern is not palpably ecclesiastical.

Confident of your ability to resolve the difference that has arisen, without compromising the diocese while satisfying the parish, his Excellency wishes me to convey his personal respects to you.

I am yours truly,

Herbert Barres
Secretary to the Rural Dean

Mindful of the indifference of the incumbent bishop to the villages under his jurisdiction, Père Patou acknowledged to himself that such laissez-faire did have its fortunate side. Despite regularly dispatched diocesan letters reminding priests to see to it that women of the parish participate in the celebration of the Mass by having them serve as lay readers, Père Patou had not done so. His noncompliance, he reasoned, was not willful disobedience, in that he was certain no woman in the village would be willing to stand behind the lectern and present the epistle. And should one have considered volunteering, she would have been unable to read the Holy Scriptures, for in violation of the edict of *le Saint Père*, Père Patou was still conducting Mass in Latin.

When the decree to use the translation into the native tongue had been issued, Père Patou had dutifully attempted to memorize the authorized French translation of the liturgy. It had sounded strange, downright unholy, to his ear. Yet he had persisted. Until he would have felt secure saying the Mass in the vernacular, however, he considered himself justified in delaying such a radical innovation in his parish. Therefore he continued to use the Latin he'd known from the time of his catechesis as a boy. Never had he succeeded in reaching the point of confidence in proceeding in French. And even if he had, he told himself, his flock would have been unable to give any responses in any language but the Latin they too had memorized as children. Without much understanding of what they were repeating, still they were spiritually fortified by uttering it.

Père Patou had thought of asking M. du Praz, the schoolmaster, to help him teach the villagers and farm families in the parish the liturgy in their own tongue. But considering that he himself had been unable to gain the assurance needed to lead his parishioners in the vernacular, he concluded it would be preferable to the ear of God that the Mass be said in Latin, with the participation of the people and the security of the priest. If the bishop had been informed of his curé's failure to comply with the papal edict, he'd taken no measures to enforce it. Père Patou, even though in his heart he believed he was justified in violating these new ordinances of Mother Church, regularly confessed his pastoral dereliction to Père Girard in the neighboring village of Champagne.

When he would be staying close to home, as ordinarily he did after breakfast, Père Patou would pour himself a second cup of coffee from the pot that Esther would leave on the fender of the stove. This morning he particularly wanted that second cup. But having no idea how long the meeting would go on, he worried that he wouldn't be able to make it through without feeling the need to relieve himself. Not wishing to contend with the discomfort of trying to hold out nor with the embarrassment of having to excuse himself, perhaps at a critical juncture, after refolding the letter and tucking it back in his cassock, he carried his dish, utensils and mug to the kitchen sink. He was disappointed in his hope that Esther would have gone out to her *jardin potager* to fetch herbs, so that he might scrape the uneaten omelet into the garbage pail and bury it under the slops. After staring first at the incriminating evidence, then at him, Esther didn't make a sound. Was it, he wondered, that, able to read the state of his mind, the woman realized he was deeply troubled and so decided to spare him from her tongue?

He was to be at the meeting, M. Burnier, the council clerk, had informed him, at nine fifteen. As Père Patuou was about to wriggle his old railroad watch out of the pocket of his cassock, the bells rang three quarters past the hour of eight. So unaware consciously was he of the punctuation of time every quarter hour that he hadn't noticed the striking of fifteen and thirty past while he was having breakfast. In order to relieve himself before setting off for the *Hotel de ville*, he went into the toilet. Though he waited and strained, nothing would come.

"Ah, yes, that's old age," Père Patou mumbled. "Not being able when you want to. And then it will be having to when I don't want to."

Immediately reprimanding himself for muttering what God's ear might hear as a murmur against His way for His children and His will for one of His servants, he prevented himself from wording a thought he couldn't keep from darting into his head—likewise, never again to hear the beautiful songs of the shy warblers and larks in the woodlands belonging to M. Constans, while having to hear the squawking of the crows that haunted the graveyard beside the church, like the restless souls of sinners. But then, he went on with himself, doesn't God, Who made the crows, also love *them*?

Giving up at the toilet, Père Patou saw through the casement window that Esther was now in her garden, bent over, snipping. Tiptoe he hurried back into the kitchen and ran a finger of water into a tumbler. Then he scurried into the pantry and poured three fingers of Pernod in with the water. After shaking the tumbler, he drained it in two gulps and smacked his lips over the taste of anise and licorice. He felt a warmth in his belly, even though the water, drawn from what he liked to think of as one of the deep wells of salvation the prophet Isaiah told of, was cool. Before leaving the rectory, he stole into the kitchen again, rinsed the tumbler, dried it and replaced it on its shelf in the cupboard.

After scattering the bread crumbs, which he'd saved from his breakfast, in the presbytery garden, Père Patou headed up the high street of the village. Seven years ago the surface had been macadamized. The smell of fresh cut hay told him that M. Grenier, who still wore sabots in the fields, had been mowing the meadow nearest to the churchyard since shortly after the angelus had rung. When the noon angelus would chime, M. Grenier would be washing down his baguette and cheese with M. Giardi's wine, as he sat leaning his back against the wheel of his cart. And when the angelus would ring at six in the evening, M. Grenier would head home.

Directly across the street from the rectory stood a higgledy-piggledy cluster of buildings. In the farmhouse on the corner, where the street became a dirt road and turned sharply south, M. Grenier lived with his wife and a dull-witted daughter. His two sons had left the region some years ago, breaking their mother's heart, successful though they'd become in business together in Aix-en-Provence. Like the church, the rectory, the old *relais,* and *the* other couple of dozen houses that made up the village, M. Grenier's home was constructed of local stone, covered with whitewashed stucco. Beyond its red tile roof, on this sparkling clear morning, Père Patou could see the gray-blue mass of Mont Blanc, some sixty kilometers to the east.

Adjoining M. Grenier's farmhouse were a bakehouse, barn, and cart shed, with a louvered dovecot on top, all of whose surfaces were undressed quarry stone. In the loft of the barn, which M. Grenier had converted to a pied-à-terre, Esther lived, with half a dozen cats. Carved into the lintel above the oak door that opened onto a flight of rickety steps was that date 1590. This was the extent of Père Patou's acquaintance with the lodging he'd found for Esther when she'd suddenly appeared in the village during the early days of the war.

Lichen and moss grew along the foundation stones of the bakehouse. Against the wall of the barn leaned a manure spreader. Through the doors of the cart shed, which stood open to the street outside and to the courtyard inside, Père Patou caught a glimpse of Mme. Grenier, a stumpy woman in her late sixties, sawing wood on a sawhorse. Hanging on the back of one door was a harness, on the other a yoke and a seine. At the end of M. Grenier's property, running along the back wall of the cart shed, grew tangles of bramble, nettle and blackberry.

Lying in the shade of the gnarled plane tree at the corner of the shed was M. Grenier's big mongrel. Her shaggy brown-white coat and long nose suggested she was predominately shepherd. The contentment the dog's posture bespoke served as a passing reproach to the priest for the grumbling and anxiety he'd allowed to take possession of him this morning. "*Considerate lilia agri quomodo crescunt; non laborant, neque nent,*" he recited aloud to himself. And, ah yes, he reminded himself, before uttering these words Christ had asked, "*Et de vestimento quid solliciti estis?*"—a question Père Patou would like to put to Esther but didn't dare. Recognizing the curè as an old friend, the shepherd gave the earth a slap with her thick tail.

Père Patou was approaching the first of the tall green lampposts situated between the cruelly pollarded lime trees standing in a rank in front of the Hotel Le Tourneau. With their squares of panes, these streetlights—the only ones in the village—were designed in imitation of the nineteenth-century gas lamps Père Patou remembered from his childhood in Chambéry. Here came Mme. Renard's fluffy poodle, lifting his feet like a trotting show pony, as he pranced down the middle of the street from the far end of the village. He passed Père Patou, who stopped and turned to watch him, without paying him the least heed. A couple of meters from M. Grenier's shepherd, whom for years he'd been treating as an enemy, he pulled up short, eyed her, then let go a volley of yips directly at her, sharply piercing the silence enfolding the village. Stretched on the ground, the shepherd still was taller than the poodle. And she weighed many times as much.

So intensely was the small dog yelping that Père Patou could catch glimpses of his needlelike teeth. The big dog never stirred, except to turn her muzzle away from the yapper in what Père Patou construed as a gesture of disdain. As abruptly as he'd interrupted his prance through the village to reprobate the shepherd, the poodle reversed direction and paraded off the way he'd come. The laugh that escaped Père Patou left him feeling less discontented and fretful. Whatever would happen God was permitting.

Before walking on, he glanced up at the bell tower of the church. The weathervane goat on top was pointing his tail toward Dijon, his horns toward Mont Blanc. Since time was measured in the village by the striking of bells, what did it matter that there was no clock dial, as there was in the steeples of churches in Crusseilles and Frangy? How dear the village bells were to the priest—just as were the surrounding mountains, Jura to the north and the great Mont Blanc to the east—not merely delighting his senses but also nurturing his spirit. In the same way that the mountains took his eye close to the feet of Heaven, the bells let him hear God's voice speaking to his legions of angels. And while the ringing of time reminded him of the temporality of his body, it also assured him of the immortality of his soul.

In harmony with his willed acceptance of the inevitable was Père Patou's gratitude that, although at eighty-three of course he wasn't the big powerful fellow he'd been when at twenty-seven he'd come to the village, God had kept him essentially sound. True, like his hearing, his eyesight had diminished a bit, though not so much as to inhibit his reading the Scriptures. And he still had a keen enough nose to relish the odor of manure as well as the sweetness of new-mown hay and the heady perfume of honeysuckle. Half a dozen of his teeth were gone, but declining to have the dentist in Cruseilles replace them with false ones on a plate, he was perfectly able to bite off bread and munch his food. His tongue savored coffee and Pernod and M. Giardi's good wine as much as ever, maybe more. Although his hair, which had frosted when he was in his mid-fifties and turned luminous silver before he was sixty, had thinned, still it covered most of his high-domed head.

As for bone aches—arthritis the doctor in Dijon had told him—they were tolerable. He did, though, catch himself wincing when he kneeled, then rose, when he shifted positions after sitting or lying for a spell, when he roused himself to use the commode, as he had to two or three times a night, and when he pushed himself up and out of bed for good at five fifteen each morning. But once he was up and going, the aching diminished. He still rode his bicycle to visit the shut-ins and sick in the outlying farms of his long narrow parish.

Yes, most of all, the bells proved that God had preserved the strength and vigor His servant, Père Patou, needed to carry on as priest and shepherd. To keep the bells ringing was one of the functions of Jacques Tricquet, the fifty-some year-old sexton, a thick-set muscular man with a bull neck, a slightly hunched back, and a left leg that was shorter than the right. Even wearing a specially made shoe, whose platform sole was an inch or so high, he listed and bobbed, like a sailboat in choppy water on a windy day, as he made his way, cigarette rolled in brown paper pasted on his turned-down lower lip.

Without fail, at six in the morning, at noon, and at six in the evening Jacques Tricquet would limp to the rear of the nave and ring the angelus by pulling the rope attached to the *campane*. Sunday mornings he would ring the call to church. Every other day it was his function to hoist the great deadweights up to their pulleys in the belfry by tugging hand over hand on the ropes that hung from the tower. The slow descent of these iron pigs, controlled by a mechanism of wheels, barrels and trip pins, caused the bells to be struck by a hammer the proper number of times every quarter of an hour. The working of the ancient contraption was a wonderment to Père Patou.

Every once in a while the *dupla*, the machinery that kept clock time, would become impish. Either the hammer would refuse to strike or it would perform such devilments as ring every nine minutes or sound seven times at three in the morning. Then the sacristan would have to clamber up to where the rooks roosted in with the bells and set things to rights.

Although Jacques Triquet was generally healthy enough to slam the door in the doctor's face, there *were* those occasions when he was too ill for hard work. Then the priest would have to assume the office of sexton. Just last winter Jacques Tricquet had been down with painful lumbago. For the month of February Père Patou had done God's work by hoisting the iron weights. While pulling, he often thought of how many hands had grasped and yanked on the frayed hemp, wondered how old the rope was, wondered how many ropes had served before it.

At first the muscles in his arms and shoulders, and most severely in his calves, though scarcely in his back, God be thanked, had ached to the point of pain. But after two weeks of pulling he felt almost no discomfort. Even when at first he had hurt, that had been easier to put up with than the scoldings Esther had flung at him, with warnings of apoplexy and prophecies of invalidism and death, while clicking her tongue and shaking her head.

Père Patou was making his way along the two-story addition M. Le Tourneau had had built onto the old *relais* two years ago. Originally a large farmhouse had been converted into the relais. When the railway replaced the stage coaches that had fed the posting houses, tracks had never brought a train into the village. After the road that passed through as the high street had finally been macadamized, it *had* brought the automobiles.

Père Patou looked for signs of life in the hotel. Above the green window boxes, planted with geraniums and variegated petunias, the wooden shutters over most of the windows were closed. This suggested that the Hotel Le Tourneau had at least a dozen guests who were sleeping, despite the striking of the clock bells through the night and the ringing of the angelus at six a.m. And, Père Patou surmised, guests must also be in some rooms whose shutters were open and others in the eight or ten rooms in the old *relais.* He'd make this observation to the village council, citing it as evidence that contradicted M. Le Tourneau's contention that the ringing of the bells was keeping his guests from sleep and thus hurting his trade.

To find so many of the red shutters—the shutters on all the dwellings in the village, including the rectory, were painted green—closed when half the morning was gone, confirmed Père Patou's conviction that the clientele attracted to the Hotel Le Tourneau lived by a different sense of time from that which governed the life of the village. How different were the businessmen, in suits and ties, and the women, in fashionable dresses, silk stockings and high-heeled shoes, from the farmers, in freshly laundered work clothes and the shopkeepers in brown corduroy, who made up the former clientele! Those men never had women with them. The women who now frequented the hotel would stroll through the village in broad daylight wearing shorts and culottes, as if on holiday in a German spa or an Italian resort. When Père Patou would drop into the bistro of the old *relais* to sip a glass of wine in late afternoon before the addition had been constructed, the patrons would be smoking clay pipes while chatting about rain, the size of crops, the prices of grain and fruit and wine, of supplies and commodities.

Although he never ventured near that place since it had become the Hotel Le Tourneau, word of its transformation had reached Père Patou's ear. The bistro now was a cocktail lounge where women, smoking not only cigarettes but also cigars, and men stayed up half the night drinking whiskey and gin. Was there any wonder the shutters on the windows of the rooms they finally went to bed in were still closed at nine o'clock in the morning?

In what had been an English garden, a swimming pool and a tennis court now stood. The clientele attracted to the modern Hotel Le Tourneau arrived from the airport at Genève in rented Citroëns, Mercedes Benzes and BMW's. No doubt at that very moment a dozen or so were standing on the tarmac parking lot, which was not visible from the road. To make place for parking, the henhouse behind the old *relais* had been torn down. Just as the addition was constructed of a brick façade over cinder block, rather than stucco over stone, so a parking lot had replaced a farm building and macadam had displaced soil and grass.

The clientele of the Hotel Le Tourneau consisted of many foreigners, almost as many Swiss, Germans, English, and even Americans, as French. M. Le Tourneau had informed Père Patou that these were important international businessmen, who chose his establishment because it lay conveniently close to a major international airport, less than an hour's driving time away, yet far enough from the busy city of Genève to be restful. Thanks to the mountains and prevailing winds, the peace and quiet of the village were rarely disturbed by the roar of low-flying planes. According to the hotelier, all that was preventing his hotel from becoming a world-renowned establishment was the striking of church bells during the hours of sleep.

M. Le Tourneau asserted that his clientele came to hold meetings and transact business while also being able to make use of the recreational facilities his hotel offered. For his part, Père Patou had no doubt there was a darker reason for the desirability of the Hotel Le Tourneau, one which its proprietor was perfectly aware of but would never acknowledge. At once accessible and remote, it was situated to serve as a rendezvous for those engaged in *affaires de coeur clandestine.* Many of those who stayed at the Hotel Le Tourneau did not go to sleep with M. Constans' lambs and get up with M. Gernier's cocks. To think of what the shutters on those bedrooms, still closed when the sun was halfway up the sky above Mont Blanc, were concealing made Père Patou cross himself as he walked by.

Having to pass the main entrance, which was still located in the old *relais*, he hoped he would not encounter M. Le Tourneau, who maintained an apartment for himself and his wife—the Le Tourneaus were childless—in the original building, as he would be leaving for the meeting of the council. Above the undressed stone lintel was fixed a bronze plaque, badly tarnished but still legible:

ALEXANDRE LE TOURNEAU
1886-1938
FILS DE HEROIQUE DE LA FRANCE
LA GRANDE GUERRE
1914-1918

Alexandre Le Tourneau, who had died the year before Père Patou had been assigned to the village parish, was the father of Gustave Le Tourneau, to whom the priest had administered extreme unction and for whom he had said the burial Mass twenty years ago. Edouard Le Tourneau, the present owner of the *relais* turned hotel, was the old war hero's grandson.

The family Le Tourneau was one of the most ancient in the neighborhood. Its recorded genealogy went back to a free farmer during the reign of Louis XII. This forebear had occupied the farmhouse and cultivated the land that shortly after *Le Revolution* had become the *relai*s. Although Père Patou had been curé in the village for more than half a century, he was fully aware that neither his longevity nor his cassock carried the weight that Edouard Le Tourneau's family name did.

Without having run into the hotelier, Père Patou crossed the road. As he approached the village green, which was bordered by bushes whose rose blooms were gone but in which the oval beds of hydrangea, gladiola and buddleia were blooming in the deep colors of late summer, suddenly he heard M. Le Tourneau's throaty rasp inside his head. "That remains to be seen, *mon pèr*e." Voices had been raised in the presbytery after the priest had scornfully refused the hotelier's bribe of paying for the installation of an electronic apparatus that would replace the ancient mechanism in the bell tower, with its barrels and wheels and trip pins, and would dispense with weights and pulleys and rope.

Turning onto the slate walk that cut through the center of the green and formed a circle around back-to-back granite monuments, Père Patou paused to read the legends on these memorials of the two great wars of the twentieth century.

AUX ENFANTS
DE LE HAUTE-SAVOIE
MORTS
POUR LA FRANCE
1914-1918

was incised on the face of the more massive of the two. The names of eighteen men were incised on the other side of the column. Carved in the face of the less imposing stone was

1939-1945
AUX HEROS
DE LA COMMUNE
MORTS POUR
LA LIBERATION
DE LA FRANCE

On the back of this column the names of twenty men were inscribed. For the dead patriots of both wars the priest said a *Kyrie*, which succeeded in driving from his head the refrain "That remains to be seen, *mon père*." Without being aware of it, Père Patou had been repeating M. Le Tourneau's words half aloud.

Standing directly across the green from the Hotel Le Tourneau, the one-story *Hôtel de ville* housed the village school and the offices of the mayor and the council. Affixed to a stone between the separate entrances to the two sides of the building was another bronze plaque, which bore the inscription

ROLAND LESCHEMELL
PIONNIER DE LA RESISTANCE
19-1-1899
13-12-1944

Roland Leschemell's son, Gaston Leschemell, a man in his late fifties, was the present mayor of the village. Above the entrance to the school drooped the Tricolor. Hanging limp over the doorway to the village offices was the flag of Savoie, a white cross in a crimson field.

Flashing into the eye of Père Patou's memory was the façade of this building with a single ensign, a blood-red field in whose center was a white circle in which were spread the four legs of a black spider. Even though the village lay almost forty kilometers beyond the border that had separated Vichy from occupied France, the Nazis had hauled down the Tricolor and hoisted the swastika the day after the Free French, joined by the British and Americans, had invaded Algeria.

That had been a dark time for the sword of France and the Cross of Christ. During those years of pain and humiliation, the *relais* had been commandeered by a unit of military police of the *Wehrmacht*. It had moved in on the village after the local Maquis had carried out a number of sorties, disrupting supply lines for matériel headed south to Italy and Marseilles. One of the German soldiers, a mere boy, had been a devout Catholic.

As inconspicuously as possible, this young man had made his way to the church to receive the Sacraments. Even though the youth, with his liquid blue eyes and beardless face, seemed too innocent to be held accountable for the crimes committed by his government, hearing his confession and granting him absolution with no heavier penance than he would have imposed on a village lad—"*Penitence Légère,*" was the curé's sobriquet among his flock—and then administering to him, his mortal enemy, the saving blood and body of Christ, had tried Pére Patou's adherence to his priestly vow to the breaking point. He had, however kept faith with God. And, though it had taken him some time to bring himself to it, after the boy-soldier had been killed in an ambush, the priest had lit a candle for him in the church and had offered a prayer for his immortal soul.

During those terrible days Père Patou had lived in constant fear that Esther would be discovered by the military police and taken away to…at the time he hadn't known, except that it would have been contrary to her will and well-being. After the war he'd learned with retrospective horror that her fate would have been unimaginably worse than he'd feared. While trying not to alarm her, he'd devised tactics for the two of them that had made her virtually invisible in the village. He himself did the errands necessary to keep the rectory going. Because Esther's features might be seen as Semitic, for the few minutes each day she had to be outside, he had her always wear a shawl or scarf over her head, covering all her face save her eyes, as though she were a veiled sister in a cloister.

It was established that she would cross the road from M. Grenier's just before daylight, then return after dark. Moving his store of grain into the bakehouse, M. Grenier had agreed to secure Esther, who one evening had suddenly appeared at the door of the rectory, in the loft of the barn, which gradually had been turned into a livable space. Her history was shadowy, mysterious. After somehow, miraculously it seemed, having escaped from Krakow the night her grandparents, parents and two older brothers had been carried off, Esther, in one way or another, had made her way, or been led, across Czechoslovakia and Austria into Switzerland.

A few days before Marshall Pétain had surrendered France to the Nazis, 22 June 1940, she had been brought from Sion, just over the Swiss border, by a priest who seemed so ghostly in the twilight he might have been a divine messenger. Speaking grammatical but unidiomatic French, with an accent Père Patou couldn't identify, the strange priest had said he'd been told to deliver Esther to the village curé. Immediately after leaving Esther in the hands of Père Patou, who'd been in the village less than a year, the strange priest had disappeared. Even after she'd learned some rudimentary French, never had Esther been able to provide an intelligible account of how she'd become Père Patou's charge. And despite the inquiries he'd made throughout the diocese, Père Patou hadn't succeeded in finding a trace of the foreign priest, or blessed spirit.

How different the stocky, club-armed, stump-shanked woman with short-cropped grizzled hair, a black mustache, and a face scored like a walnut shell, from that adolescent girl, so fleshless she looked to be on the verge of starvation, whose eyes shone in their deep sockets like wet grapes, and whose black hair was so long it appeared never to have known the blades of scissors. As Esther's flesh had thickened and her skin had wrinkled, her voice had grown hoarse and manlike.

During *l'occupation* her tongue would have given her away in an instant. To this day her French was French words pronounced in an accent Père Patou had difficulty understanding, more so than ever as his hearing was going. In that precarious time he'd constantly warned Esther never to open her mouth so as to be heard by anyone he could not be sure of, as he could of the Greniers, the Constanses, the Giardis, and the Tricquets, with whose deformed son, when years later he'd become sexton, she'd constantly scrap over the rectory gardens.

Sometimes back in those days Père Patou wondered whether he was needlessly cramping the daily existence of a young woman whose life already had been grotesquely misshapen. Even while he would tell himself he should think of her as a sister who was regulated by holy orders, he realized she had to be feeling she'd been imprisoned. As it turned out, all his precautions had been justified. Not every man in the village, he came to discover, had been a loyal son of Free France, the only France, and an enemy of his country's enemies and occupiers.

Climbing the three steps and crossing the narrow portico of the town hall, Père Patou glanced at the door to the school. How few children in the village now, compared to the number in the forties, fifties and sixties! In the seventies the young had begun leaving to find work in towns and cities for wages they could never hope to earn at home. Aging as they were, the women of the village bore fewer and fewer. It seemed quite possible the national government would soon declare the school redundant.

That would be hard on M. du Praz, the schoolmaster. Barely would his pension suffice to keep body and soul together. In fact, his body would fare better than his soul. For M. Giardi asked M. du Praz only sous for the little apartment adjoining his house, built for his mother-in-law, who had died seven years ago. And the farmers' wives saw to it that the schoolmaster, like the cure, was provided with bread and cheese, vegetables and fruit, and every so often a leg or shoulder of lamb. M. Giardi kept M. du Praz supplied with wine, as he did Père Patou, who like the schoolmaster at times enjoyed a bit too much of the gift.

As for M. du Praz's soul, it was too old and worn to tolerate a move to another village as schoolmaster, in the unlikely event he should be invited to serve elsewhere. So long had M. du Praz been in place that it seemed certain he would never leave the village before his body, separated from his soul for eternity, would be carted off by M. Pelletier, the undertaker.

Père Patou was aware his situation was not dissimilar to the schoolmaster's. For every wedding, baptism and confirmation he performed, he said two Masses for the dead. No more than three or four children at a time attended his catechism classes, which, he confessed to himself with shame, was a relief. He was having trouble catching the words carried by shrill young voices, and he had even more difficulty keeping these modern children in order. It grieved the priest that for more than a decade not a single young man from the village had taken holy orders. Only one young woman had chosen to put on the veil.

Like M. Praz, Père Patou would never be appointed to serve in another village. And he would no more relish the prospect of such an uprooting and transplanting than would the schoolmaster. More fortunate than M. du Praz, however, he did have a place of refuge, grieved as he'd be were it necessary for him to resort to it. Yet should the council side with M

Le Tourneau and decree that the bells be silenced between midnight and eight a.m., Père Patou would have to resign himself to enter the house for aged priests, a red brick building that looked like a prison, in Lyon. What then would become of Esther?

From the evening of her arrival in the village, the priest had prayed for Esther's soul, its eternal destiny. Now that she and he, after all these years together, were approaching the end of their earthly lives, he'd increased the attention he devoted to her in his daily prayers. While sometimes he did smart and chafe under her petty tyranny, he knew that she was a pure woman, grateful to him for receiving her and preserving her when the Nazis were in the village. And there was no gainsaying the dedication with which she cared for his needs.

As fervently as he wished that Esther would become a daughter of Mother Church, Père Patou had forborne attempting to convert her. In that she, born a Jew by the will of the Almighty, was the only non-Catholic in the village and was beholden to the diocese for her food and shelter, he felt that to press her would be to take advantage of her. And, to tell the truth, though he didn't consider himself any more cowardly than the next man, he went a little in awe of Esther, not merely because she ordered his domestic life and bullied him, but also on account of the mysterious way in which she had been delivered to him.

Besides, even had she signaled a willingness to receive instruction in the faith, Père Patou foresaw difficulties that amounted almost to impossibility. Though Esther was by no means stupid, was in some ways quite clever, her mind, he judged, was simple. So entirely was it taken up with meat and vegetables and herbs and wine and bread and cheese and sweets and dishes and cups and saucers and mugs and utensils and pots and pans and linens and cotton and leather and polish and washtubs and soap and water and brooms and mops and dustbins and garbage and trash and compost and commodes that he had to doubt whether any room was left for the most elementary explanations of things, let alone for doctrine and religious belief.

Virtually illiterate as she was in French—Père Patou had no idea whether she could read and write in Polish or in whatever the Jewish language she'd learned to speak might be—Esther couldn't possibly be taught the catechism, could she? Nor could she memorize the responses and the *Angelus Dimini nuntiavit Mariae.* And yet Père Patou believed that his failure to attempt to secure Esther in the faith was a sin of omission for a priest. Regularly he confessed it to Père Girard.

Esther's limitations, along with her tragic history, did, however, allow Père Patou a hope he resolutely held out for her. It was supported by his mindfulness that *Pape Grêgoire le Grand* was plunged into such sorrow at the thought that Trajan, the most virtuous of pagans, was to be denied eternity with the Divine Father in Heaven that he prayed and wept continually for the Roman emperor's posthumous redemption. God, for whom time with a finished past does not exist, just as the future is not yet to come—which makes the human concept of progress an absurdity—finally was moved by St. Gregory's pleas. So that Trajan's soul might be released from Limbo and enter Purgatory, the way to the Heavenly Paradise, at the instant of his death, which was a past event for the world but not for God, God performed, unseeable to the eye of man, an extraordinary baptism of fire.

In his prayers to Almighty God and to the Holy Mother for Her intercession, Père Patou petitioned that consideration be given to Esther's essential goodness, as well as to her simplicity and ignorance. He pleaded that the persecution of her people, including her own family, who after all were God's chosen, her miraculous preservation through the angel-of-mercy priest, which might be taken as a sign that a special grace was intended for Esther, and her long service to one of God's vicars—that all these matters be taken into account.

Praying that she not be denied entrance to the Celestial Paradise and that she not be kept from the eternal Light and Love of the Father Who had created her, he besought God to make use of His omnipotent compassion, or was it His compassionate omnipotence? No, it was omnipotence and compassion in one, for both were infinite attributes of the Deity. Once, Père Patou remembered, when he'd taken a few drops too many of M. Giardi's wine, he'd half-joked with God by asking, if my housekeeper is not in Heaven, who then will take care of me—an angel with a deep voice and mustache?

As he entered the door to the village offices, Père Patou sighed heavily. While he was gratified not to have encountered M. Le Tourneau on the way, he found himself wondering why he hadn't come across any of the other councilmen or M. Leschemell or M. Burnier on their way to the meeting. Remembering having heard the bells strike nine, he glanced at his watch. Seven past the hour. Nine fifteen was the time M. Burnier had told him to appear, he was certain. Deciding to try to relieve himself one more time before the council would assemble, he headed for the toilet at the end of the corridor. On the way he saw that the door of the meeting room was closed. While standing at the pissoir, again he ran over in his mind the likely position each councilman would take on "the matter of the bells."

Since yesterday afternoon, when M. Burier had surprised him by requesting in the name of M. Leschemell that he attend the meeting of the council, Père Patou had wearied his brain by dwelling on the eventuality. The arithmetic was always the same. With certainty he knew he could depend on the loyalty of M. Constans, a substantial and widely respected farmer, who kept sheep and cultivated land that had been in his family's possession for generations. Also of M. Giardi, the vintner, whose roots in the soil of Haute-Savoie were deep and strong, and whose wine was pressed from grapes he tended and harvested with his brother. Almost as certain was Mlle. Châtaigne, the village midwife, who with less and less occasion to practice her occupation, concocted and dispensed tonics and elixirs. Whispers had reached Père Patou's ear that she also cured by casting spells and for a few sous would call down curses and maledictions. But since she was one of the few who attended Mass daily and always showed deference to her priest, he was disinclined to credit such rumor.

On the opposing side, of course, would be M. Le Tourneau, who had stopped touching his hat to the curé when he passed him on the high street. Because he was the instigator and self-evidently an interested party, it was most unfortunate that he was a member of the council. Joining him, with little doubt, would be M. Renard, who dressed in an English-cut suit, spent many an evening in the cocktail lounge of the Hotel Le Tourneau, mixing with outsiders and foreign guests. M. Renard prospered by cutting limestone in the quarry on his land and selling it to builders, who carried if off in huge trucks. And virtually sure to take a position on the side of what was being called progress was M. Basin. He rented his land, along with the modern machinery he'd bought—not just big tractors, but also a monstrous gasoline-powered harvester and binder in one—to tenant farmers. He was also cutting and selling for lumber the great oaks and walnuts and beeches in the woods he owned on this side of the ravine, through which the Rhone flowed out from Lac Léman at Genève.

Although he felt the urge to urinate, Père Patou stood straining at the *pissoir* without being able to. Silently he said a quick *Je vous salue, Marie* for help. Nothing came. No, no, there was no getting around it—the council would be evenly divided. That meant that the mayor, M. Leschemell, as *Monsieur le Président*, would cast the deciding vote.

M. Leschemell was a well-to-do dairy farmer, with herds of cows and goats, who processed milk, cheese and butter. But instead of wearing a blue smock and cotton pants he dressed in corduroy. And wore a beret, not the straw hat farmers of the region wore in the field nor the cap they wore in the village.

The antiquity of the Leschemells rivaled that of the Le Tourneaus. And whereas Alexandre Le Tourneau, the grandfather of Edouard Le Tourneau, the hotelier, had been the village hero of the first Great War, Roland Leschemell, the father of Gaston Leschemell, the present mayor, as the leader of the Haute-Savoie maquis, had been a martyr for France during the Second. Exhibiting unimaginable daring and courage, he and his men had again and again caused serious disruption of the Wehrmacht's supply lines. Most spectacularly, in December 1944 when in desperation German troops and matériel were being routed across central France to Normandy, a huge supply convoy had been blown up, killing a number of the military police on guard as it had passed on the track a few miles northwest of the village. One of these had been the devout boy-soldier.

Within hours twenty men from the village and nearby hamlets and farms had been seized. In front of the World War I memorial on the village green, they had been summarily executed by a firing squad. Roland Leschemell, who almost surely had been tortured, had been shot separately, after having been made to witness the killing of his comrades. The German commanding officer had it promulgated that Leschemell had been the leader of the local Communist guerrillas. Père Patou had been convinced immediately that someone in the village had betrayed his country by informing, although at the time he had had no idea who it might have been.

That afternoon every shutter in the village had been closed. Hearing the volley of shots break the silence—fading as his hearing was, Père Patou could still hear that crackle in his inner ear—the priest had run into the sanctuary of the church, had knelt before the Cross, and begun praying. When silence had again reigned over the village, he had stridden to the back of the nave and pulled the rope that swung the *campane* on its cannons twenty times, as if he were ringing the angelus or summoning the people to Mass. Though no one had dared to come that day, the bell had tolled for the dead, some of them heroes, some innocent victims. Then, violating a provision of martial law the German commandant had proclaimed, Père Patou had said the burial service in the empty church.

Yes, this was the bell, along with the clock chimes in the night and early morning, that M. Le Tourneau was contriving to have silenced. Recalling the impudence with which the hotelier had pointed out to his priest that the angelus still would be permitted to be rung at noon and in the evening, Père Patou experienced a flash of fresh anger. By offering such a sop, the man had exposed his crassness and profaneness.

Given their family histories and the prominence they themselves enjoyed, Edouard Le Tourneau and Gaston Leschemell were the two most influential men in the village. In that M. Leschemell was the more congenial and was thought to be less concerned with advancing his own fortunes and was more devoted to the welfare of the whole community than was the hotelier, he had repeatedly been elected mayor. There was, however, no feud or bad will between the two men. They remained on good terms, though M. Leschemell did not frequent the cocktail lounge of the Hotel Le Tourneau, as did M. Renard.

To the dismay of the priest, nevertheless, M. Leschemell, in contrast to M. Constans and M. Giradi and his brother and M. Grenier, who declined to serve any longer after having been a councilor for many years, M. Leschemell stood with M. Le Tourneau as an advocate of "*le progrès*." Père Patou had heard from his lips the very sorts of phrases with which M. Le Tourneau had bombarded the priest—"change cannot be resisted," "the village must look to the future, not the past," "we must marry time or be jilted by it."

Unable to relieve himself, Père Patou hoisted his shoulders, ducked his head, and shook it fiercely, as if both protecting and empowering himself, while summoning all his will to vanquish a potent temptation, one that would lead him to commit a mortal sin. If there were anything that would win M. Leschemell's decisive vote, it would not be an appeal to his loyalty to the ancient tradition of bells chiming the quarter hour without cessation and to the ringing of the angelus thrice daily. No, no, the fact that the striking of the church bells rang the life of the village would carry no weight with the progressive mayor.

Nor would he be swayed by the argument that silencing the bells at night would be a capitulation to commerce and sinful pleasure, a surrender of the way of life of the village to the way of the world. Certainly M. Leschemell would not be persuaded by theological ideas, such as that in their relentless measuring of mortal time the bells were a memento mori, a reminder of transience and of the mutability and impermanence of all that is not divine. Or such as that the chimes mark the recording in the mind of God, in which nothing is ever lost, of everything that happens in the village. To ask M. Leschemell what God thinks of man's notion of progress would be pointless.

These ideas and arguments Père Patou had been formulating and rehearsing to himself in order to be able, as their priest, to impress them on the council and the mayor. But at his moment he forced himself to face the fact that all such considerations would surely be swept aside. Nothing he might say would touch the souls and change the minds of half the councilors. As for M. Leschemelle, Père Patou now realized that the only way he could be brought to understand the dark forces that were at work to silence the bells of the village church would be to invalidate the family name of that champion of progress, M. Le Tourneau.

Père Patou shuddered. Just as strenuously as he'd been endeavoring to relieve himself, he was struggling to unknow what he couldn't help knowing. The dreadful truth, which had been revealed to him in the deathbed confession of a guilt-ridden, terrified human being, he was not permitted to know he knew. It had come to him not as a man but as a priest, as the ear of God but not His tongue. So compelling was this secret and awful knowledge, which belonged to God alone, that if at that very instant he had not expunged it from his mind by a violent sweep of his right hand across his clamped lips, he would have shouted out, loud enough to be heard through the plasterboard of the toilet by anyone inside the village hall, the name that had leaped to the tip of his tongue. As he swallowed it with a choke, only the words "*le traître*" escaped his lips.

Mumbling a Paternoster, Père Patou stuffed himself back into the underclothing beneath his cassock. Trying to think his mind as clean as the slate a schoolboy has just sponged spotless, he crossed himself, left the toilet, and plodded up the passageway. The church bell began tolling nine fifteen as he was opening the door of the meeting room.

To his surprise all six councilors, the mayor and the village clerk were already in place at the green baize table. As though their throats had been cut in mid-sentence, voices went silent. At the foot of the table, opposite M. Leschemelle, sitting at the head, stood an empty chair. To the right of that chair sat M. Constans, to the left M. Le Tourneau. All eyes went onto the priest.

THE BLACK SUN

When he opened the door at the top of the basement stairs, the landlady was lying in wait in the vestibule. Her eyebrows, hairy as caterpillars, met above her nose, which was flat as a platypus', quite a contrast to his proboscis. With her elephantine bulk positioned between him and the front door, clearly she had no intention of letting him pass without a parley.

"The gentleman I mentioned that's wanting to engage the room you're in is after me to let him know when it'll be available. You told me you'd only be staying for a couple of nights, remember? Well, if I know how to count, tonight'll be your seventh. I don't mind telling you I have to keep rented up and the other gentleman's willing to back up his word with cash. So if you're planning on staying I'd like to see the color of your money."

In the close quarters, he smelled stale cigarette smoke, on the landlady's breath, whiskey. Her voice came from the worn reed of a saxophone. Three twenties and a ten settled the matter. His satchel was already packed, he informed her.

Outside, pellets of rain, almost ice bullets, stung his face. Squinting, he turned up the collar of his raincoat, then jammed his hands into his pockets. He never wore a hat. By the time he'd walked a block, his hair was a wet mop. The sky hung so close it seemed he'd bump into it before reaching the museum, a thirteen-minute slog.

Since arriving, he'd caught only a glimpse of the sun. For a very brief time late on the third afternoon, he'd been able to make out a white-gold ring in the smutty sky, a halo without a saint. Otherwise, rain, rain, rain.

The room he'd rented was located in the rear of the English basement in a brownstone, built in what had been a fashionable neighborhood, now a slum. Returning to the room was like entering a public toilet. He'd shake himself as wet dogs do, then rub his face and hair with the towel the landlady provided, a scrap of muslin, always damp. So clammy were the sheets on the bed, really a cot, that he'd taken to sleeping in his shorts and tee-shirt. Ordinarily he went to bed naked.

Happenstance had brought him to this city. In a bookstall beside the Thai restaurant in which he sometimes ate, in the town where he'd been living for a while now—though meticulous about hours and minutes, he'd given up keeping track of months and years—while leafing through a volume of reproductions of paintings, he'd been arrested by one that puzzled him. Even when he wasn't having dinner next door, often he'd find himself back, staring at the print. One evening he realized he'd have no peace of mind until he'd be able to account for what kept attracting him, against his will, it seemed. The next morning he was on his way to this city, in which the museum where the original painting hung, was situated.

For the past six afternoons at four thirty, he'd positioned himself in front of the canvas. Eyeing it for fifteen minutes was all he could manage without becoming light-headed, feeling on the verge of vertigo. He had the room the painting was hanging in pretty much to himself.

The reproduction hadn't prepared him for the real thing. At once he realized he'd been misled by the low quality of the photographic process used to produce the volume in which he'd found the glossy print. In the original, pigments were subtly muted. Also, he'd been expecting the canvas to be, much larger than the book page. It turned out to be smaller, at most 7"x7", inside a thin gilt frame.

Rather than being released by viewing the actual painting, he'd become more perplexed. Shapes that didn't conform to what they purported to be occupied space in a field variously blue-toned, here and there flushed with pink. Objects were disproportionately scaled, making their locations vague, their relationships indeterminate. His inability to find a definable perspective was disorienting.

In an effort to come to some understanding of what the painting intended to say, or was asking of him, he'd decided to concentrate, one at a time, on particulars during each successive visit. First, because most conspicuous, on a large sunflower, a mottled ocher-yellow eye, inside a green rim within a wheel of white spokes. It was growing, blossom-down, on a long stalk that hung from the middle of the top edge of the canvas, like the cord and pull of a window shade.

The following afternoon, staying with what was organic, he'd fixed on some coconut palms, which grew in the same geographical zone as northern conifers. Next afternoon it was a giant cactus, which opened its fleshy, spiny arms to a single delicate rosebud, yellow. And a ghostly plant, silver-gray, out of whose thick stalk grew three symmetrical pairs of hairy scrolls. It resembled no species of vegetation he'd ever seen, living or painted.

On his fourth visit he'd moved to a red towerlike structure, rising midway up the canvas from the bottom edge. A jalousie door on the second of two stories hung open, as if someone had just stepped out into the blue and vanished. An equilateral triangle on top might have passed for a dome, had the painter employed foreshortening. As it stood, the structure looked like a rocket in a cartoon about to blast off.

Day five he fixed on another man-made object, half the height of the red tower. Its façade was the blue-green of glass characteristic of art deco. Obviously the building was designed as a pleasance. It looked fragile.

Yesterday afternoon he'd focused on a slice of an orange, hanging in the same sector of the sky as the sun. For the moon to be visible while standing so close to the sun was an astronomical absurdity.

§

He shook, then brushed rain from his hair with his fingers as he passed between the two central columns on the portico of the museum. Still he felt drops running down his neck. Heading for the room in which the painting hung, he fussed with the belt of his raincoat, in order to open the front and expose his body to dry warmth. The first joints of his fingers were greenish white and he shivered.

Each time he'd walked through the doorway leading to the room of the painting on his previous visits, a guard had been leaning against the jamb, seemingly half asleep. The man was short-shanked. With cuffs that covered his knuckles, his uniform, gray with crimson trim, bagged on him like a hand-me-down from an older brother. This afternoon the guard wasn't at his post.

Reconnoitering, he spotted him at the far end of an adjoining room. On tiptoe he was wagging his finger at the nose of a woman, wearing a green beret, who was half a head taller than he was. Evidently he was reprimanding her, perhaps for permitting the child whose hand she was holding to step across the red line in front of a huge painting of a nude. Out of earshot, the guard resembled a clown mimicking a scolding schoolteacher. He himself had allowed the tip of his brogans to touch the outer edge of the red line, but he'd taken care not to cross it.

When he'd first gazed at the upside-down sunflower, he'd had to resist an urge to step across the prohibitive line, to lift the frame from its fixture, turn the painting a hundred and eighty degrees, and rehang it. The guard had seemed no more alert than a caryatid. But he'd noticed a man in a black raincoat standing in front of a painting on the other side of the room. Then, too, it had occurred to him, a tool of some kind might be needed to release the frame from its fixture. Besides which, he'd suddenly realized, righting the direction in which the sunflower was growing would turn every other object on the canvas upside down.

When he arrived for his final session with the painting, which he was determined to make decisive, there was the same man, or another in a black raincoat, back to him as he faced a picture on the opposite wall. After taking his usual stance, he glanced at his feet. On the parquet floor a little puddle was forming around his brogans, as if he'd had a bladder accident and were standing in his own urine. He watched the water creep toward the red line, touch, then spread over it. No longer chilled, he felt flushed with fever. Closing himself off from the outside world and abstracting himself from all sensation but sight, he fixed his eye on the sun, floating a bit off center in the deepest blue of the sky. Its dense blackness suggested a mass of force. Though only about the size of a shirt button, within the dimensions of the canvas it hung like a gigantic wrecking ball. Were it to lurch into motion it would annihilate whatever stood in its path. Yet never could it break free. If in some way it were to pass out of the picture, the painting would collapse and undo itself. Such a possibility was beyond imagining.

Leaning forward and peering closely he noticed purple currents emanating from the sun's left hemisphere. Taking care to keep his toes from encroaching on the red line as he bent over it, he detected six white specks, scattered like stars inside the ball of blackness. Sunspots, surely—the source of the constant energy being radiated to hold things in place, as well as of the latent power to destroy.

Without doubt the black sun was the asymmetrical center of the world of the painting. No tree, plant or flower would ever grow or decay, no man-made structure would ever be put to use or be demolished, nor would the slice of a moon ever wax into a whole orange or wane into nothingness. All were eternally subject to the black sun's force.

A shock, as if he'd grabbed hold of a naked wire with current surging through it, jolted him. Power, real and potential, holding it all together—that was the secret. The room was spinning and pitching around him. Sensing he was about to tumble over the red line, he struggled to regain equilibrium. As the canvas came leaping toward him, he flung out his hands. The wall, which his palms smashed into, kept him from going down. Uncertain whether inside or out- side his head, a bell was ringing. Coming from behind, a pair of hands embraced him around the waist, providing support. Beside his ear, a husky voice shouted, "Help, guard, help!"

"I'm quite all right now, thank you," he heard himself murmur as he endeavored to move his arms and break loose. When he went on to explain, his voice, though calm, sounded remote. "Just some passing dizziness I'm subject to."

"Guard," the voice behind him yelled again, insistently. "Help! I've got him."

As he tried more vigorously to wrestle free, elbows pinned his arms against the bottom of his rib cage. Twisting his head to discover whose they were, he caught sight of the short-shanked guard waddling toward him. He looked as if he were trying to run on his knees. From somewhere a tall guard came sprinting, followed by another, a burly fellow. When the tall guard pulled up and positioned himself between him and the wall, he gave up the struggle to release himself.

"He cut that painting out of its frame." The voice, so hoarse it sounded disembodied, was emphatically accusatory. Lips were close enough to his ear for him to feel the breath carrying the words, along with a spray of spit he wished he had a free hand to wipe off. "I caught him in the act. It must be somewhere in his raincoat." The three guards positioned themselves so they were hemming him in.

Beyond the rosette on the shoulder of the tall guard's uniform, he could see the sun, a black dot in a field of oyster gray inside the gilt frame. Then the clasping hands let go, pinioning arms fell away. Out of the corner of his eye he saw a forefinger pointing at the wall. Its hand issued from a black cuff. The tall guard grabbed his right wrist and wrenched it hard enough to make him wince. He didn't cry out in protest.

"Let's go, you," the tall guard snapped, jerking his arm up behind his back and jostling him forward. "March!" His voice was a deep growl.

From other rooms people were gravitating toward the little procession. He had to tell his feet to move.

"Stand back!" the burly guard snarled, "all of you get back." Gesturing with their palms, he and the short-shanked guard herded the curious crowd toward another room. Beneath the ringing of the bell, which continued, he could hear a low murmur.

Keeping him in a hammerlock, the tall guard steered him through the doorway. At the pace he was being propelled, he was having trouble staying upright. Wobbling along, he wondered whether he might be thought to be drunk. As he was hustled across three more rooms, which he'd passed through on his way in, the bell continued to ring. In the grand court inside the great bronze doors that opened onto the portico, he was turned left and maneuvered through a scattering of people. All eyes were following him, he could tell.

All at once the tall guard stopped, yanking his arm so that pain shot up into his shoulder. With his free hand the guard threw open a door with a frosted pane, then thrust him into a small office. The tall guard and the burly guard entered behind him. After the burly guard slammed the door closed, the tall guard relinquished his hold on him with a shove. Again a wall prevented him from going down.

"Kill the goddamn alarm," the tall guard growled. The burly guard scurried to a fixture behind a desk. The instant the ringing stopped, he heard buzzing in his ears.

"You," the tall guard commanded, "take off that coat."

Feet astride, the man was standing close enough for him to smell garlic on his breath. His left eye was hazel, his right brown. Pockmarks covered his cheeks.

"I don't know why you've brought me here. I've done nothing wrong." He heard his voice as an echo. The ceiling, he noticed, was very high.

"You take off the coat or we'll take it off for you." The tall guard didn't raise his voice but it was full of menace.

When he tried to slip out of the raincoat, to his surprise he couldn't. The belt was tied. Distinctly he remembered opening the coat to allow air inside the museum to warm him after his walk through the cold rain. Fumbling, he worked the knot in the belt loose, reached up behind with his left hand, and lifted the coat by the collar. As he dropped his right shoulder, he wriggled that arm free. The coat swung down behind him.

While he was wrestling his left arm out of its sleeve, a rolled-up canvas fell to the parquet floor. Holding the coat in front of him, right hand grasping the left cuff, fingers of his left hand pinching the middle of the collar, he visualized himself as a magician about to wave his cape and make a rabbit disappear. In wonderment he stared at the canvas.

The burly guard squatted, as though to defecate, then reached around the bulge of his belly. Lifting the canvas by its edges with his fingertips and holding it at arm's length, as though it were noxious or stank, he let it unfurl. From the right-side-up sunflower he could tell the painting was hanging upside down. There in the blue floated the black sun. The burly guard stretched the canvas flat on the desktop. His fingers were plump sausages.

"Let me have that coat," the tall guard demanded, thrusting out his opened right hand. His fingers were very long.

He surrendered his coat. Draping it over his right forearm, the tall guard wormed his left hand into one of the pockets. To watch someone else's fingers poking around inside what was *his* raincoat made him feel he was being violated. The hand came out empty.

Slinging the coat over his left forearm, the tall guard plunged his right hand into the other pocket. After fishing for a few seconds, his fingers emerged holding an object. The guard flung the raincoat on the chair behind the desk, as if he were disgusted by it.

"I suppose this box cutter isn't yours." The tall guard jabbed the point of the blade at him.

The mottled gray handle the man was clutching was similar to that of an implement he had at home, but he was certain he hadn't brought that to this city. Besides, he recalled, while his hands had been jammed in as he'd been walking from the rooming house to the museum, both pockets of the raincoat were empty.

"No. That tool does not belong to me."

Fluttering his blubbery lips, the burly guard made an obscene noise. The tall guard banged the box cutter down on the desk beside the canvas.

Just as he was about to add that he couldn't account for the cutting tool's being in the pocket of his raincoat, the short-shanked guard came huffing into the office.

If it hadn't been for the interruption, he'd have gone on to honestly say, he hadn't seen anyone, perhaps the man in the black raincoat, who so far as he knew had been the only other person in the room, slit the canvas and remove it from its frame. Nor, he'd have acknowledged, could he claim to have felt someone, most likely the same person who had clasped him from behind, slide the rolled canvas up his sleeve and slip the box cutter into the pocket of *his* raincoat. Now that man, his accuser, was nowhere to be seen.

Before he was able to throw off a weariness that had seized him and find the words he wanted, the short-shanked guard began to whine in the voice of a prepubescent boy.

"Every afternoon the past coupla weeks he's been showing up around four and just stares at that picture till closing. It's the only goddamn thing in the whole place he ever looks at. I been keeping my eye on him."

Striding behind the desk, the tall guard plumped himself down on the raincoat, whose skirt was trailing on the floor. Then he snatched the telephone from its cradle and began punching numbers. While he was waiting to hear the tall guard's voice, it struck him. This unfortunate contretemps might keep him from his own work for a considerable period of time. But when he did get back to it...

IT

As new members of the club, he and his partner had to settle for a six a.m. slot. Though hardly a desirable hour, it did allow him to get to the office by eight thirty. While caught up in the game, he hadn't noticed it. Of course, two torsos in tee-shirts, two sets of privates in jockstraps, four feet in sweat socks and gym shoes, running, stopping, pivoting, lunging, whacking a ball for an hour and a half inside a 20 x 34 x 16 foot court had to be pouring out sweat. The damp heat generated by their stoked-up bodies created a fertile atmosphere for rancid bacteria.

The instant he left the court it hit him. As he showered, it wasn't neutralized by the powerful disinfectant the custodian used. Nor by the commercial-strength detergent in the towel the club provided. Nor by the clean shorts, undershirt and socks he put on. Even if the air of the city didn't carry the sweetness of new-mown grass, the outdoors ought to have seemed fresh after he'd left the locker room. So when he stepped outside, he was expecting to leave it behind. It went with him. As if the gym bag dangling at his side were filled with rotting mushrooms.

When he slammed the door of his Porsche closed, as he sat behind the wheel, it didn't diminish. After starting the engine, he quickly lowered his window. While driving across the parking lot, he pressed the button that dropped the window on the passenger side, to let in some fresh air. That did nothing to counter the odor. At the stop sign he tossed the gym bag, which he'd thrown on the seat beside him, into the back. Just beyond the first traffic light, he pulled to the curb, reached around, snatched the bag, and got out. Walking to the trunk, which he opened, he flung in the bag and slammed the lid closed.

Gunning the engine, he shot off as if he were being chased. Though implausible, it seemed to be penetrating the metal and upholstery between the trunk and the car's interior, as well as the canvas of the gym bag. Either it was increasing or he was finding it more and more offensive. Certainly he wasn't imaging it.

Instead of heading up the ramp and crossing the bridge leading to the avenue on which his office building was located, he turned right on River Street and parked. Getting out and opening the trunk, he grabbed the bag and strode to the end of the bandstand pier. Pivoting like a discus thrower, he whirled the bag, then let it go. He watched it sail through the air and splash in the river.

When he drove on, it went with him.

§

"Oh damn," she said out loud, as she pushed off the snooze button, "my period's starting." That evening she had a date with Zach. The curse was more than a week early, and she hadn't had the usual two days of cramps. In the bathroom she discovered it hadn't begun after all. Worried it was about to, she put on a pad that she'd sprinkled with deodorant powder when she'd finished her shower.

All morning she was aware of it. It seemed so much stronger than usual that she was afraid she might be offending, especially in closed spaces—on the bus, in the elevator car, in the coffee lounge, which she hurried into and out of. To discover whether it had yet begun, she made two visits to the WOMAN's. It hadn't. As an excuse for not lunching with Ashly, Jerry and Josh in the deli around the corner, always jam-packed at noon, she pleaded some necessary shopping.

And she did shop—bought a "new and improved" maxi-strength powder at the cut-rate next to McDonald's. Then she picked up a burger and a Coke to lunch on at her desk with everyone else gone from the office. After eating, she checked herself again. Still no period. She applied the maximum-strength powder generously. All afternoon she avoided her co-workers as much as possible.

Back in her flat, while a TV dinner was heating in the microwave, she phoned Zach. Much as she'd been looking forward to the film, then making love after they'd return to her place, she begged off. She was coming down with a migraine, she told Zach.

While she was washing, drying and putting away her tableware, she filled the bathtub with warm water. After undressing, she poured in scented bath salts, then soaked for half an hour or so. Before climbing out, she washed all over with deodorant soap. After drying, she massaged herself with body lotion. She checked herself again as she was about to go to bed. No period.

When the alarm woke her at seven, it greeted her again. Anxious to find out, she didn't push the snooze button and did hurry into the bathroom. No other indication of her period. She showered, then massaged herself with a fragrant natural oil. In addition to dousing the pad with maxi-strength powder, she gave both armpits half a dozen shots of antiperspirant spray. Contrary to her custom of not wearing perfume to the office, she applied profuse amounts of the least subtle stuff she had—strong and fragrant as cider. The faceted bottle containing it had been a present from Lew, the man in her life before Zach.

All that day she made contact with people only when necessary and stayed in proximity as briefly as possible. Finding it even more offensive than it had been the day before, she hoped to goodness she was covering it up.

Still no sign of her period.

§

Ours is a residential section of the city. Most often the prevailing wind carries the effluence from the industries to the east away from us. When the wind does shift, however, we West Enders are reminded that the factories are there, belching out noxious fumes. Occasionally a wind from the east will set in, and the nuisance will last two or three days.

But this was different. First of all in intensity—to such a degree that you wanted to pinch your nostrils closed and breathe through your mouth. Then too it didn't seem to be coming from the east. Or for that matter, from any direction. When we awoke that morning, there it was, apparently having descend on us while we slept. It seemed almost tangible, as if you might grab handfuls of it from the air, pat them with your palms, and toss them like snowballs. Which is preposterous, of course.

On the other hand, you might say it had risen from the earth beneath us. And while seeming dense enough to be grasped, it also was rare enough, in the chemical sense, to pervade whatever we might use to try to protect ourselves from it. As though our city were standing on top of a vast vat filled with some putrefied byproduct and the vat had sprung a massive leak.

There was still another difference. The way it seemed to infiltrate our person, permeating clothing, hair, even skin, suggested it was something more than a chance visitation by some errant air currents. The fact is there has never been any perceptible movement of air during this time.

When it struck we were annoyed by what we took as a passing nuisance. No one imagined it would persist until it would become a threat to the existence of our city. After the fourth or fifth day, only someone whose olfactory receptors had gone dead could have failed to realize it was ominously intensifying.

Yet well into the second week our elected officials, while offering groundless assurances, refused to acknowledge the facts. "There's no cause for concern," "it will soon pass" "just be patient and put with it," we were told. We, by which I mean an ad hoc citizens emergency committee (CEC, we call ourselves), had to force the release of the truth: no scientifically credible explanation could be found. At that point had to insist that outside experts be consulted. We had to demand that an appeal for aid be made to both our state and the federal governments—aid for which I might say we're still waiting And yet, after we'd compelled those in positions of authority to take such steps, all that we've learned is that instrumentation has confirmed what any normally functioning sense of smell can detect.

The consequences for our citizenry have been profound. On morning one, imagining it would soon dissipate, most of us merely ignored it. With those with whom we weren't intimately acquainted we chose not to acknowledge its existence. By the second day people had begun avoiding one another. When contact was inescapable, we would discreetly turn our heads, as if we were looking at and speaking with someone who was not present. On day three it became the talk of the town. By the hour, it seemed, mutual distaste—to mix the senses metaphorically, although it is a scientific fact that the two senses involved are inextricably connected—was increasing. Before the first week had ended, the desire to be isolated had begun to manifest itself. Progressively, when separation was impossible, tension, anger, conflict, in some instances physical violence ensued.

To this point, at which citizens still hadn't fully comprehended the gravity of what was happening, only those whose lives intertwined were permanently affected. Supposedly unbreakable families and lovers thought to be inseparable were falling apart. Gradually it began to take a toll on all those who worked, played, were schooled, and worshipped together.

Before long law and order commenced collapsing. Along with the already unruly East End, the whole of our city was fast becoming a disintegrating community.

When our elected officials showed themselves to be ineffectual, naturally more and more citizens took measures of their own. Supplies of perfume, deodorants, and disinfectants were rapidly exhausted. Additional quantities couldn't be shipped in quickly enough. Those whose responsibility it was to devise a system of equitable rationing adamantly refused to do so, asserting that supply and demand would provide the most efficacious and fair system of distribution. The issue, however, is moot. Such products, it turns out, offer only minimal short-term relief. Those still carrying perfume and deodorant kits and regularly dousing themselves provide protection only from themselves.

More sophisticated expedients have proved to be no more effective. Nose filters and blockers, in such short supply they too were rapidly bought up, have proved worthless. Industrial and surgeon's masks are also useless. Only the few who somehow have been able to procure chemicals that affect the limbic system, benzodiazepines, for example, can speak to the performance of such pharmaceuticals. To this point these persons have been conspicuously silent.

A short time ago the members of CEC initiated a petitionary process that mandates a referendum on the recall from office of those who bear responsibility for denying, misleading, evading, refusing to act until compelled to, etc. Contrary to what has been bruited about by these officials and their political allies, this action has been taken not just for the well being of the privileged few. It's true that most of those who comprise CEC reside in the West End. But equally true, we West Enders pay the lion's share of taxes that support our municipal government and fund the city's services. Mindful that all citizens, no matter their financial status and where they happen to dwell, are affected, our initiative speaks for the aroused conscience of the entire community.

As our petition, which already bears almost the requisite number of signatures to set the legal process in motion, makes clear, we are aware these officials are not the cause of our affliction. We are not scapegoating or merely venting frustration. Rather our focus is on the dereliction of office holders who are charged to maintain the safety, protect the health, and promote the welfare of the citizenry.

The exodus from our city is difficult to calculate with any exactitude. But the proliferation of For Sale signs on residential properties in the West

End alone is one indicator that an alarming number of citizens have left or are intending to leave if they are able. To be sure, there are no newcomers to our community; no one is purchasing housing. No doubt those who have already gone have widely reported what has struck us. The effect of these demographics has been devastating. Every day we become more of a ghost town. Even the flow of visitors who initially came out of curiosity has trickled virtually to a stop.

Time is running out. To read editorials in our local newspaper almost daily proclaiming we are on the brink of disaster when disaster is already upon us, is ironic, to say the least. And it may well be that something beyond the catastrophe we are presently suffering is looming. Perhaps the rumor that Freising, our twin city in Germany, is likewise in the grip of whatever has assaulted us, is unfounded. But what has taken place under our very noses, to make a grim pun, cannot be explained away or dismissed.

It happened within the past week. A forty-nine year-old old woman, prominent in civic affairs and known to be in excellent health, returned to her home in the West End from Kodiak, Alaska. She'd flown there a couple of months ago, not long before our city had been stricken, to be with her daughter, wife of an army lieutenant, during a difficult pregnancy. The morning after her homecoming as a joyously relieved grandmother, her husband reached over in bed to touch her and found she was lifeless.

With the consent of the husband, CEC demanded an autopsy. Performing it was a West End physician whose professional capacities and personal integrity are beyond question. He it was who completed and signed the Registrar's Certification of Death. Beneath "Immediate Cause" he wrote unknown.

UNCLE OSCAR'S FUNERAL

Oscar's funeral did not commence with the word's first syllable. Located about fifteen miles east of the city from which we live twenty miles west, Beckett's Funeral Home, advertising itself as "A Garden of Peace and Remembrance," turned out to be a good-sized, squat, L-shaped building of blood-red bricks and bright white mortar. The macadam parking lot was almost filled, as were the seats in the chapel, situated in the leg of the L. Gwen and I were ushered to a couple of empties in the middle of the next to last row.

The front of the small auditorium looked like a florist's shop. Somewhere an electronic organ softly was playing a medley of traditional Protestant hymns expressing grief and comfort.

"At least an open coffin's not on display," Gwen—my wife and the niece by marriage of Oscar, the corpse—whispered after we'd settled on straight-backed chairs, thinly upholstered, with leather seats. I assumed they were designed to strike a balance between providing too little and too much comfort. I responded with an appropriate, but I'm afraid sacrilegious, "Thank God."

Shortly after we'd been seated, Gwen's Aunt Bess, Oscar's widow, and her daughter Debbie were led to seats in the middle of the front row, directly in front of the low platform on which a lectern stood. Aunt Bess was dressed in a black velvet suit. The hem of the skirt fell well beneath her knees. On her birdlike legs were black stockings. The veil of the black straw hat she had on was folded up so that her face was bared. Truly, she might have served as a mourner in a Civil War film. I was surprised to see how small and bent she was. It seemed she'd been preparing for her husband's death by growing a widow's hump I hadn't noticed even on the most recent of the infrequent visits Gwen and I had made to Aunt Bess' household.

Though Debbie, Gwen's cousin, was not tall, she stood a full head above her mother. Debbie was clad in a plain gray gown that fell to her ankles. On the back of her head was a white lace cap. She might have passed as a Quaker of even earlier vintage than her mother.

"Notice that Sarah's not with them," I whispered to Gwen.

"I wouldn't expect her to be," Gwen whispered back.

"Not even at their father's funeral?"

Gwen shook her head, expressing either agreement with my implication or disapproval of her absent cousin. Although I scanned the backs of those in the rows in front of us, I couldn't find anyone who might possibly be Sarah. Of course, I told myself, she could be seated in the row behind us. Or standing at the rear of the seats where, turning, I could see there was an overflow of mourners. For some reason even Gwen didn't know, her sister cousins hadn't spoken to each other for some fifteen years. Neither had married, a fact I had no trouble understanding. Debbie, a nurse, lived at home. Where Sarah lived Gwen had never been informed.

Gwen had never felt close to or at all compatible with her cousins or their father, who had died suddenly at eighty-five from a heart attack while running. Still and all, she felt it was necessary for her aunt's sake that she be present at his funeral. To support my wife I'd permitted her to take me in tow.

Pitying her aunt Bess, who we agreed deserved a better spouse and daughters than she had, Gwen and I had dutifully made visits to the Stulls' split-level home, exactly the kind I'd imagined that until his retirement in his late seventies Oscar had constructed and sold. My surmise that, although they'd received a number of invitations, the Stulls had not once visited us was that, without ever having seen it, they suspected our dwelling was a house of sin and corruption, with only secular paintings, prints and drawings, perhaps dancers, even nudes adorning the walls and non-religious books and periodicals lying on tabletops. From their perspective, of course they had our number.

Gwen's distaste for her cousins went back to childhood visits her parents had made to her mother's sister. Although Gwen had never told her mother or father, who had no religious affiliation or convictions, whenever she'd been sent off to play with Debbie, who was exactly her age, and Sarah, two years older, "play" had consisted of inquisition, humiliation, reproach, and even threat.

"Are you saved?" "How old were you when you were baptized?" "Don't you go to Sunday school?" " Is Gwen a name in the Bible, like ours?" "Does your father say a blessing before meals?" "Do you memorize a verse of Scripture every day?" "Do you kneel and say prayers before getting into bed?" "Do you want to be a missionary when you grow up?" And the sockdolager— "If you should die before you wake, Satan to Hell your soul will take, unless you're *saved*... you know that, don't you?"

In defending herself against such bullying, Gwen told monstrous lies, consisting of vague scraps of Protestant beliefs and practices she'd picked up from neighborhood and school friends who had attended mainline Protestant churches. Such answers never satisfied her cousins, who grilled her with the same questions whenever they "played" together. The day she'd revealed to me that what she'd suffered from the tongues of her cousins still brought a sour taste into her mouth just to think of them, let alone to visit the Stulls' household even with Sarah gone, I'd named Aunt Bess' daughters Goneril and Regan.

I too had been in the crosshairs of a Stull, who until he "was called home" had continued to fire away at me whenever we'd make discourtesy that amounted to crude rudeness and, even worse, raw sexism. Gwen took his boorishness in stride. I, as his sole target, came to understand where the genes and behavioral model that had caused her cousins to bully and abuse her as a child had come from.

The ammunition Oscar had pumped into me was of two kinds— athletic and military. The former was fired at me less frequently and did less damage—his prowess as an athlete in high school, scoring the winning basket, hitting the winning home run, catching the winning pass. Whether these stories, told visit after visit, were strict truths, "stretchers," imaginings, or outright lies, I couldn't decide.

Much more offensive were his heroics during WWII. How the 40mm antiaircraft battery he was a member of had hit a bomber he called a "Betty" at Iwo Jima and when two "Japs" had bailed out, had "used the little devils for target practice" as they floated down beneath their parachutes, "scattering "pieces of their cowardly guts all over the Pacific," the "Sea of Peace." How he and his comrades in arms had cheered, backslapped, even hugged on deck the morning they heard on the PA system that a bomb as powerful as 20,000 tons of TNT had been dropped on the city of Hiroshima, which he'd never heard of until it had become world famous.

How a flotilla of battleships, of which his was one, had each rained sixteen-inch shells from nine turrets all night long, first on Hokkaido, then on Honshu, to show the Nips and our own "air boys" what the old battlewagon Navy was still capable of, a demonstration that was given just before the Japs surrendered "because they had nothing left to fight with." Although I too was defenseless, there was no truce or cessation of attack on me.

In fact, the vigor and compulsion with which these war stories were directed at me made me suspect that I was being chastised for not having killed or been killed, or at least wounded, by "gooks" in Viet Nam or Iraq. In fact, it even crossed my mind that Oscar blamed his daughters for not coming out males who could perform heroic feats on the court, diamond, gridiron, as well as on the sea, in the air, or on the battlefield.

As we sat in the bare-walled, bookless living room before lunch or dinner, Oscar would fix his agate eye on me and continue the bombardment until Aunt Bess would announce it was time to reassemble at the dining room table. Once we were seated, only the command "all heads bowed and eyes closed" (given even when his stay-at-home daughter Debbie was a grown woman, invariably followed by the utterance of thanks "to our Lord and Savior Jesus Christ for the food of which we are about to partake, for the nourishment of our bodies and the strengthening of our souls") interrupted the telling of the many-times-told tales. Gwen, I noticed, like me refused to obey the command from second-class petty officer Stull. After a brief silence their eyelids were lifted and the bombardment recommenced.

Oscar, spinning yarns in his native vernacular, was no Joseph Conrad, telling tales in his second language. But his compulsion to narrate and insistence that I must hear, his way of transfixing me with his agate eyes, along with his blatant moralizing, brought to my mind one dinner hour when he was in medias res, not Samuel Taylor Coleridge, but Coleridge's narrator, the Ancient Mariner. Although they were both mariners and compulsive tellers of their own tales, Oscar had not a shred of the Mariner's self-indictment or contrition. Still, I named Oscar the Ancient Mariner.

Appropriate as it was while we were sitting in the mortuary, waiting for the funeral service to begin, to engage in a rehearsal of Gwen's and my relationship with her aunt's family, and to recall how, like Adam and Prospero, I had usurped the privilege of naming, it would be hypocritical to try to convince myself that I was grieving over the death of petty officer second class Oscar Stull.

The review was brought to an end by the presiding minister—

clergyman doesn't seem to be quite the appropriate word for him—as he bestrode the platform and planted himself among the tropical jungle of flowers behind the lectern. He was a middle-aged man with shaggy gray hair and a melancholy air. The black serge suit he was wearing was so ill-fitting—the cuffs of his trousers looked as if he couldn't avoid stepping on them while the cuffs of the coat sleeves covered his hands to the knuckles—it seemed to be a hand-me-down from a much taller man or else a purchase from a hardware store that sold general merchandise.

To the accompaniment of an upright piano played by a gray frizzy-haired woman, who inserted keyboard-length runs between stanzas, we were asked to join in the singing of two hymns whose words struck me as being somewhat contradictory. The first expressed joy at the prospect of crossing to "Beulah Land"; the second lamented what "Adam's curse had visited upon us." Also seemingly in conflict to me was the minister's eulogy, praising "our deceased brother for his willingness to fight and if called upon to die for his country," and his celebration of his virtues as a "devout Christian, a man known for his kindness and gentle ways—the devoted husband of his helpmeet, and the devout father of two daughters he'd raised in the faith." At this point I found myself assailed by doubts that the good man had more than a passing acquaintance with Oscar and the Stull family.

The Scripture we were asked to give our attention to as he read was the rather predictable consolation uttered by the Preacher and recorded in the book of Ecclesiastes, chapter 3: "To everything there is a season…a time to be born and a time to die…a time to kill and a time to heal." From there we leaped to the Epistle of St. Paul (whom he referred to as Paul, as if the saint were his next-door neighbor or a fellow Rotarian) to the Romans: "For the wrath of God is revealed from Heaven against all ungodliness and unrighteousness of men." Then after a generously overweight soprano rendered in a voice with a constant tremolo, all four stanzas of "Abide with Me," the service closed with the minister's pronouncing a benediction that urged us to "fight the good fight and depart in peace."

The service, which I'm certain provided consolation for Aunt Bess but struck me even of its kind as being nothing short of dreadful, having ended, hymn tunes at low volume from an electronic organ again flowed over us. After having searched the chapel for the instrument in vain during the service, I had concluded there was no organ. The hymn melodies were canned.

We sat waiting. While I was more than ready to head for home, I knew that Gwen, as part of the family, wanted to embrace and condole with Aunt Bess, to show our supportive presence by appearing at the customary viewing, and then to join the procession of cars to the cemetery. The protocol being observed, we were aware, was that no one was to leave the chapel before the immediate family, that is, Aunt Bess and Debbie, would plod out. As I sat waiting, I couldn't keep myself from musing over what I'd just experienced. Unable to charge myself with self-righteousness, simply because I hadn't a grain of righteousness in me, I had to own up to my mean-spiritedness. Who was I, in my third marriage after two miserable failures (for which, to be honest, I bore at least an equal share of blame), to pass judgment on the religion Aunt Bess turned to for support and comfort in her time of need? And so far as her daughters were concerned, who was I, a single child, who had neither sired nor raised a child of my own, to condemn them for their bigotry and abuse of my wife when they were children or to assess the responsibility for their estrangement as grown sisters? As I saw Debbie finally rise and help her mother to her feet, I felt sufficiently self-chastened and humbled to vow I'd endure, if not embrace, whatever lay ahead with all the charity and grace I could muster. Little did I know my resolution was to have me headed in a direction it would be impossible for me to follow.

Taking her daughter's arm, Aunt Bess shuffled up the side aisle. Giving her time and distance, the mourners, starting with those in the front row, rose and followed at a respectful distance. Gwen and I were among the last to join the procession. From my vantage point I could see those ahead of us making a ninety-degree turn as they left the chapel, then disappear into the foot of the L of the mortuary. As Gwen prepared herself for what lay ahead, unaware of my self-reproof and new determination, she whispered, "My BMW against your Honda it's open." Rather than accept her bet, I nodded agreement.

It was slow going. By the time we'd turned the corner and were in view of the catafalque, most of those who had been in the rows in front of us had paid their respects to the dead, as well as to Aunt Bess and Debbie, planted at the head of the coffin, and were on their way to the parking lot. The lining of the gaping lid on the mahogany casket was white silk.

A woman posted at the foot of the coffin, six or seven feet from Aunt Bess and Debbie, caught my eye. If wife and daughter of the corpse were costumed quaintly, at least it was with an antique appropriateness. Not so the outrageously got-up woman whom I'd spotted. Her brilliant red hair was beehive-bouffant. In the rather dim light of the place of viewing, which contrasted with the brilliant spotlight illuminating Oscar, her lipstick and cheeks gleamed crimson. Matching, was a dress, with generous décolletage, that fell in flounces well above her knees. Her stockings were the only appropriate color in her ensemble, though their propriety was compromised—no it was rendered imperceptible—by the spike-heeled, gleaming black leather shoes the stockings descended into. So astonished was I to be gazing, if not at a woman of the night or a streetwalker, then at a date-for-hire or a barfly—in such a place at such a time on such an occasion.

"See the lady in red," I muttered to Gwen as we poked along toward Aunt Bess and Debbie. "Looks to be a bit off her beat, doesn't she? Is it possible that the sly old Ancient Mariner…?"

"Shhh," Gwen advised, although we still were not close enough to the casket for Aunt Bess or Debbie to overhear my low-pitched voice. Then she whispered, "That's Sarah."

The shock of this recognition, made by a cousin who surely knew her kin, made me gasp, "Who?" To myself I said "Goneril!"

Gwen nodded confirmation just as we became the next to pay our respects to wife, one daughter, and the dead corpse. Before Gwen could approach Aunt Bess, Debbie had flung her gray-clad arms around Gwen's neck, as if they'd been loving sisters rather than distant cousins. "Oh Gwen," she sobbed on Gwen's throat, "he's gone!"

Gwen bore the burst of emotion tactfully, neither backing off into silent rejection nor clasping and crying out platitudes of comfort. Admirably standing her ground, she murmured, "You have my sympathy."

Before the demonstration of grief had ended, the few remaining mourners behind Gwen and me, bypassing the two women locked in a one-sided embrace, had uttered their condolences to Aunt Bess and said their good-byes to the departed Oscar.

"I'm so glad you and…" groping for my name, then going on "…and your husband came," Aunt Bess declared. While her voice quavered, it had a convincing sincerity. Although the rims of her eyes, behind thick lenses, were red, she wasn't shedding tears. "And Oscar I'm sure would be pleased. He was always fond of both of you, you know. I shouldn't say 'would be,' because where he is now I'm sure he does know." Aunt Bess was a genuine eighty-some-year-old nineteenth-century literalist.

By this time Debbie had turned to the coffin. After bending low enough to kiss the corpse on the lips, I thought, though to be perfectly honest it may have been on the forehead, she commenced a one-way conversation with her father, pitched too low for me to make out any words but "Daddy" and "up there."

"Doesn't he look fine," Aunt Bess told rather than asked us. "Just like himself in life."

The most corroborative response Gwen was able to give was a head nod with a faint smile. Aunt Bess showed not the slightest indication of sensing her niece's least reservation.

Clasping Gwen's free hand, I stood on the other side of her and pressed reassuringly against her. For some obscure yet, I'm certain, perverse reason, I forced myself to look down at Oscar dead. Like the minister and most of the male mourners, he was dressed in a black suit and white shirt. The tie he had on was neatly knotted. In keeping with the event in which he was the center of attention, it should have been a solid dark color; it *was* striped sky-blue and white, colors chosen perhaps to suggest Heaven and innocence. For Oscar, I was sorry there wasn't a stripe of red as well. The black patent leather shoes on feet pointing straight up glistened in the bright light playing on him. Undefiled, their tan soles indicated they'd never been walked on. Comb marks in his coarse gray hair, in which a part of chalky white scalp showed, separated the thick locks, two thirds on the right side, one third on the left. What had been great shaggy eyebrows had been trimmed.

A layer of some sort of powder changed the complexion of his clean-shaven face, which in life had been slate gray, to a sickly hue, some color between tan and candle tallow, suggesting that at the instant of his transformation he'd been afflicted by hepatitis. His pale thin lips had been touched pink, making them look fleshier than they were. As though staring upward, doubtless toward his new home, his marble-gray eyes were wide open. So hollow were his cheeks that he seemed to be sucking them in. The great hump of his nose looked as if it were about to blast out a mighty snort. Yet the cosmetic attempt to disguise the fact that Oscar was now in the state of not being, to present him as still in the world of *is* even as he was about to enter one his Father's mansions, gave me the sense I was beholding a mannequin that had fallen face-upward onto a single bed in the bargain basement of one of those no longer existing department stores.

Given all that to take in and digest, my eye was grabbed and held by Oscar's hands, crossed at the wrists in obvious symbolism, the right on top of the left. Either the sleeves of the coat he had on were too short for his long arms, or the sleeves of the shirt were too long. White broadcloth cuffs covered his hands halfway to the knuckles. Even for a man who still stood a couple of inches over six feet, the hands were the size of ham hocks, with fingers that, despite their length and because of their circumference, had absolutely no taper. Had they been shorter, it would have seemed plausible that the first joint had been chopped off. The knuckles of Oscar's fingers resembled knobs protruding from the limbs of an ancient oak. In what was just visible of the tops of the hands were large purple blotches, suggesting that the skin covering his gigantic appendages had worn thin and that the blood vessels inside were hemorrhaging. As I gazed at those hands, I had no doubt that they could palm a basketball, rounded as it was, could haul in a spiraling football, could grasp and swing the heaviest bat in the rack and knock a baseball on a line drive over the center-field fence. Or for that matter, could squeeze the throat of a "dirty yellow Jap," until his face turned red, white and blue.

"Debbie," Aunt Bess suddenly half-said, half-wept, and now tears were streaming down her cheeks, "I've changed my mind. As I think about it, I believe your father would want me to keep and cherish his wedding ring. If it goes into the ground with him, it won't be seen until we're joined again at the resurrection."

After a pause in which Debbie made no response except to increase the volume of her sobbing, Aunt Bess went on, "Our rings bound us together on this earth."

By this time only the family, including scarleted Sarah in self-imposed exile at the foot of the coffin and niece and nephew-in-law, made captives by the unwritten law of propriety, remained in the space where the coffined corpse was put on display. Thereupon to my astonishment Aunt Bess let go of Gwen's elbow, raised herself on tiptoe—she was a good foot shorter than her husband when he was upright and at least a hundred pounds lighter—placed her left hand on the outer edge of the coffin, leaned over and, taking his wrist, wrestled Oscar's left hand out from under his right, as if she were insistently about to read his pulse.

When she raised the arm, his hand flopped, as would a fish that was being picked up by the tail. The sleeves of his suit coat and shirt went up his arm, and the thick round, silver-plated (I'm sure) old railroad watch he always wore on his left wrist emerged. My guess was that it had been wound and was still running. Aunt Bess pulled the hand, wrist and arm toward her, as though she were tugging him up out of the coffin to bring him back from *isn't* to *is*. A loud sob, so high-pitched it qualified as a screech, issued from Debbie, a sound she might emit if she were watching a strangulation in a horror movie or being choked herself. Still holding on to Gwen's arm, I felt her shudder, whether at what Aunt Bess was about or at her cousin's unearthly outburst I was uncertain.

With the tiny skeletal fingers of her right hand, Aunt Bess seized the fourth finger of Oscar's left hand, which, looking large and heavy, seemed to be resisting. So suggestive was the imagery I couldn't prevent a vulgarity from flashing into my inner eye, though to my credit I immediately censored it by concentrating all my vision and attention on the flesh and blood spectacle exhibiting itself before my outer eye—Aunt Bess' effort to slip off the gold band from the finger she was grasping.

Finding she was unable to pull the ring over the gnarl of the knuckle, she began turning it. Although it moved freely, it wouldn't clear the bony bump. I was watching the struggle in fascination, as I assumed Gwen was too. Muttering something to Debbie that I couldn't make out, all at once Aunt Bess released the finger she'd been at work on. Oscar's hand fell as if it were the iron head of a mallet. Unfortunately, rather than return to the crossed position it had been in, it slammed down on Oscar's chest, landing in a posture that made it seem he was saluting the flag or clutching his inert heart. Aunt Bess took a step aside.

Evidently having been asked to sotto voce, which, given that Gwen's and my eyes were witnessing what was happening and that the Ancient Mariner's ears were no longer admitting sound, seemed unnecessary, Debbie stationed herself in the place Aunt Bess had assumed. After a moment of hesitation, which suggested some reluctance to touch her father's cold still flesh, she took hold of Oscar's limp wrist with her left hand while her right tried to pull off her parent's wedding ring. Enjoying no more success tugging than had her mother, she too resorted to turning, adding the refinement of twisting while the ring revolved. As she went on with these futile maneuvers, I had the urge to whisper to Gwen, "It seems the old bastard insists on holding on to what's his legal possession." Out of a conditioned respect for the corpse, any corpse, and grudging admiration for both wife and daughter in overcoming their squeamishness in working on the lifeless member of their husband and father as he lay in his final resting place, I swallowed the glibly offensive words.

While Debbie went on struggling, out of the corner of my eye I noticed that her scarlet sister was striding down the length of the coffin like a model on the runway as a candidate for Miss Something or Other. When she reached Aunt Bess, to my surprise and I suppose Gwen's too, Sarah, AKA Goneril, flung her silk-covered arms around her mother, pulled her against herself, kissed her on the forehead, and said loud enough for me to hear, "Sorry that Daddy's gone, Mummy, and that you'll have to go on without him." The phrasing of Goneril's consolation definitively dismissed Regan. After she pulled her head back out of her mother's face, I saw that she'd left a crimson print of her lips on Aunt Bess' forehead. Her mother's response was to clutch Sarah's naked shoulders and, with her forehead buried in the cleavage of her wayward daughter, recommence weeping. For what seemed like minutes neither would let go of the other. They resembled two wrestlers at grips with each other, both struggling for the advantage that would allow her to best her opponent.

It was Sarah who finally broke free. Without another word, using her hip, she nudged her sister out of the place where she was at work on her father's fourth finger, bumping her hard enough to make her drop the hand of the finger she was toiling over. It flopped onto the belly of the corpse. Catching her balance, Debbie, AKA Regan, went into a crouch, as might a member of *Felis catus* about to spring. Had Aunt Bess not somehow been able to wedge her meager little body between her daughters, I had no doubt that Goneril and Regan would have gone at it tooth and nail beside the coffin in which the stubborn-knuckled corpse of their father was lying.

"Over your father's dead body!" Aunt Bess wailed through gasping sobs. "For shame!" Her voice, naturally soft, almost a murmur, must have taken on enough volume to send half a dozen black-suited men grouped at the other end of the small room into a hurried retreat into the vestibule, between the leg and boot of the mortuary. The vestibule led to the parking lot.

Her sister bodily out of the way, Sarah began her assault on her father's wedding ring by grabbing and jerking up his left hand. Both of her predecessors had proceeded very much more gingerly. Seizing the targeted finger, she vigorously massaged the obtruding knuckle, apparently in an attempt to smooth the craggy surface and thus eliminate part of the obstruction. This tactic proving ineffective, she separated her feet, which had been placed together as they'd be on a diving board before springing, then lifted Oscar's limp left arm, straightened it, and tugged on the ring as well as the finger that wouldn't yield the band of gold. Using all the strength she could muster, she yanked so hard that her hand came flying off the finger into the air, which sent her careening body crashing into Debbie, still in a crouch behind her.

"Off, woman," Debbie hissed, as she helped her sister comply by giving her a mighty shove. Her command was issued loudly enough, I felt certain, to be heard by the men who had retreated to the vestibule, if they were still assembled there, waiting. Debbie's injunction clearly was suggesting that the offending body of her sister carried a contagious disease, venereal probably, certainly moral, which the recipient believed would contaminate her by mere touch.

Relinquishing her hold on the resistant finger allowed Sarah to grab the side of the casket in order to prevent herself from going down on top of her crouching sister. After regaining her balance, she muttered something I couldn't make out but whose tone let me know it was unacceptable for coffin-side use. Unable to hear any further sound from Sarah, I concluded that the concealed speakers from which canned hymns were flowing had not yet gone dead. On this occasion it was good fortune that Aunt Bess' hearing was failing. And it was certain that, no matter the volume or the degree of depravity of the utterance, the puritanical ear of Goneril and Regan's father, whatever it might surely have been exposed to in his seafaring days, could not possibly be affronted.

Sarah's sudden letting go of her straining hold on the fourth finger allowed the Ancient Mariner's upraised arm to fall heavily. His hand landed protectively on his crotch.

Then occurred one of those frozen instants of time in which, for some reason during a moment of crisis or incredulity, there comes a sudden realization or recognition of what had been ignored. All at once I became aware that Gwen had taken hold of my hand and her fingers were squeezing mine, not tugging on one as if to remove the wedding ring I'd never worn but as if to prevent herself from falling over the deep drop of a cliff on the lip of which she was standing, leaning outward. No wonder. To behold her aunt, of whom she was fond, and two hostile cousins wrestling with their lifeless husband and father in a futile effort to remove a ring he refused to surrender, even in death, would make most sane human beings believe they had gone mad, were not dreaming a nightmare but were conscious and hallucinating. I, a disinterested eyewitness of the unimaginable, found myself imagining I was actually present for the action that would give rise to a primitive myth that an Aeschylus or a Shakespeare centuries later would turn into drama. The only way I could come to terms with the incredible event happening before my eyes was to fall back on vengeance by wishing the schizoid minister—who at one moment offered poetic consolation, at the next a vicious visitation of God's wrath—were coffin-side to witness the effect of his preachings. Then, as time began to move for me again, without realizing I was coping with the unbelievable, I found myself falling back on flippant comedy by turning inside out the well-known, oft-used title of Kaufman and Hart's play as I muttered so softly that even Gwen couldn't hear it, "Who says you can't take it with you?"

The curtain had not yet dropped on the comic-horror drama. From either the vestibule or the parking lot, where it seemed he'd been waiting for a sign the ritual was over, a stocky, strong-looking man, with a suspicious flush of red on his forehead, cheeks and nose, dressed in a black suit and carrying a black derby, came striding toward the little family of mourners. The man looked as if he'd just stepped off a vaudeville stage or left the brass rail of a bar. Without waiting for his arrival, Goneril broke ranks and went sashaying toward him.

"Hi, there, dude," she sang out with remarkable cheer considering the occasion, "how 'bout giving us feeble females a hand?" Then she quickly added as an afterthought, "You are with it, aren't yuh?"

"Sure am," the rosy-faced man replied with a businesslike nod of his head. "Thass whad I'm here for, ta give a hand, so to speak."

"Well, here's the scoop. My mom, like thought she sorta wanted her husband buried with his wedding ring on, but just now like she's changed her mind, a woman's privilege as they say, and kinda decided she wants to keep the ring, sorta in memory of him. We've tried but to save our souls, or whatever, we can't get the damn thing off his finger. Like he doesn't wanna let go. Seein' how yur in the business, I wonder if yuh might bail us out. We're stuck, see."

"You can bet yur kitchen sink I'll give it a try, ma'am," he answered with a jerk of his head that exuded self-confidence. The way his face, with a pug nose and a cleft chin, was set suggested that even when obliging he was forbidden to smile. As he headed for the casket with short brisk steps, Aunt Bess and Debbie moved aside. Sarah, towering over him in her heels, assumed a place beside him at the coffin.

Tucking his derby in his left armpit, without the least hesitation the man snatched Oscar's hand. As Aunt Bess, Debbie and Sarah had done, he tugged on, turned and twisted the ring for a couple of minutes.

"Sorry, ma'am," he murmured, as if to keep the corpse from hearing, and he carefully laid the ring hand back on top of the right, still lying on Oscar's crotch, "but if I yank any harder I'll rip the whole arm outa its socket," making Beowulf's disarming of Grendel pop into my head. "Looks ta me like that ring's really on there ta stay. See, my job's actully not ta handle 'em. I help carry the box and drive the hearse. Tell yuh whad I'll do, though. Mr. Beckett's in his office, so I'll fetch 'im for yuh. See whether he's got some hocus-pocus that'll work. Not a matter of strength.

Anyway, the sooner we can close the box, the sooner we can get off for the cemetery." With that he pivoted and headed for the vestibule. Seen from the back, he waddled like a duck.

The uneasy truce between Goneril and Regan persisted while we waited in a neutral silence. Before long a man dressed in gray-striped trousers and a frock coat emerged from the vestibule and, taking long strides, came heading toward us. Tall and heavy-set as he was, his shiny bald head still looked too large for his body. The furrows in his brow were delved deep and his lips were fleshy. Apparently, as the proprietor of the business, he allowed himself to smile, broadly at us. I decided he was wearing dentures.

"Good afternoon," he sang in a basso profundo that was respectfully modulated while letting you know it could boom when volume was called for. His lips seemed to work mechanically, like a ventriloquist's dummy's. "Guido here tells me you're having a bit of difficulty removing a ring from the deceased. My name is Beckett, Percival Beckett."

As he spoke the name of the stocky man, who was taking two steps to his signeur's one, Guido followed him as would a squire his knight. Blinking his eyes behind the thick lenses of his black plastic-framed glasses, Percival Beckett gave Guido a backhanded flourish that said "halt." "Let's see what we can do."

Taking hold of Oscar's fourth left-hand finger, he gave the ring a single powerful tug. The ring wouldn't come off. Pressing his left palm on Oscar's breast, Mr. Beckett sustained a long pull on the ring. His fat lips were mashed together. The Ancient Mariner refused to surrender his treasure. Seeing Mr. Beckett and him vying for possession of the ring was like watching a big strong human male wrestling with a stone sculpture that was lying prone.

Mr. Beckett signified his capitulation by replacing Oscar's appendage across his groin, fisting his own right hand and coughing into the top of it. Blinking his eyes at the rate of an automatic being fired, he addressed Aunt Bess, whom it would seem he recognized from an earlier transaction, in a voice as soft and gentle as a dove's coo.

"I wonder whether you ladies might mind moving a few steps away from the casket. And turning your backs." It seemed obvious he was sparing the weaker sex exposure to the violent combat he was about to engage in with Oscar.

Without hesitation Gwen and Aunt Bess, followed by a more reluctant Debbie, retreated eight or ten steps from the coffin and turned toward the vestibule. Then after a hesitation that made me believe I was about to witness a battle between the sexes, to my surprise Sarah, who was standing tellingly apart from her sister and mother, also complied. Given that Mr. Beckett obviously entertained Victorian notions about the inability of woman, in contrast to the strength of man, to endure the sight of whatever grisly action he was about to engage in, I concluded that his request-command did not pertain to me and therefore held my ground.

I watched Mr. Beckett's left hand fumble in a pocket of his cutaway, then extract a small black, white and red can with white lettering, which had a spout on top. Instantly I recognized it as the container of Three-in-One oil. After pulling off the cap, Mr. Beckett withdrew a crumpled tissue, which looked like a dried white rose, from the pocket of his striped trousers. Stooping over the coffin and raising Oscar's deadweight left hand in his right, he separated the fourth finger from its fellows and placed the tip of the spout on top of the knuckle, then wormed it under the ring. When he delicately squeezed the can, it spurted oil. After performing the same procedure on the hinged back of Oscar's finger, he reverently laid the hand on Oscar's chest, immense though breathless. Apparently confident of success, he wiggled the red cap back on the spout and, giving the top of the can a swipe with the white blossom of tissue, shoved it back in the pocket of his cutaway.

Again he raised Oscar's hand. Holding the tissue under the fourth finger, Mr. Beckett twirled the ring. With the tips of his own immense fingers, he slid the ring toward the fingernail. Over the tubercle knuckle it went as easily as a quoit that has just made a ringer is removed from the peg it encircles. Then, using the tissue, he meticulously cleansed the defeated member of oil. When he'd finished with the hand, he carefully laid it on top of the right wrist, again forming a cross but with the position of the hands reversed. For some reason the Ancient Mariner's skin looked even more tallowy than it had before Mr. Beckett's assault.

Glancing at me standing just behind him, Mr. Beckett winked, then, leaning toward my ear that was farthest from the quartet of women, he half-whispered, "Just one of the tricks of the trade, sir. You'd be surprised how many of them change their minds when we're about to close it."

"No problem," he then announced to the family in a voice that proclaimed self-satisfaction. As they wheeled around, he beamed a smile at Aunt Bess while striding toward her. Bowing over her from his great height, he pressed the ring into her doll-size palm, which instantly clasped it, as if holding on to a cliff for dear life.

Contrary as it might seem, I'd found myself rooting for the Ancient Mariner, in spite of the bombardments he'd visited upon me. *Then* he was alive. In his present state his means of resistance were severely limited. And Mr. Beckett's falling back on a trick learned through his professional experience struck me as being grossly unfair.

"All set, Guido," Mr. Beckett snapped at the stocky man, who had been permitted to watch his handiwork from a distance. Lowering his voice, he went on, "Now you can close the box, call the boys in, and get going so you beat the late afternoon traffic on your way back."

As Guido closed the door on Oscar's last little sleeping room, so quietly I couldn't hear a sound, Aunt Bess, courageously watching, let out a single great sob. Debbie turned her head with a shriek, while Sarah looked on from a distance without emitting a sound or moving a muscle in her face.

Gwen and I were fourth in the caravan of vehicles heading for the burial ground. In front of us were the hearse, driven by Guido; a black limousine, driven by a black-suited chauffeur, in which Aunt Bess, Debbie and the minister were riding; and a tomato-red convertible sports car, in which Sarah drove herself. On this sunny May afternoon, its roof was down so that, when she went screeching off, her flaming red hair streamed out from her head like a Viking's at sea in a stiff wind. Until Guido had lined us up on the parking lot just inside the gates of the cemetery, I'd been surprised by the number of cars that made up the cortege. In them, I'd assumed, rode fellow members of the flock Uncle Oscar had been a sheep in, fellow Rotarians, neighbors, co-workers in Uncle Oscar's realty company, and business rivals. Death is the finale of all competition. Or it should be.

The graveyard in which the Stulls owned a plot was located beside the highway defining the northern edge of the city, some twenty miles from the town near which Oscar had lived with his wife and daughter. When the cemetery had been established on both sides of what had been a cow path and was now a major artery, it had surely been fields. On the far side of the road stood rows of modest split-level houses, some of which Uncle Oscar might have had built and sold. Next to the cemetery, within the city limits, some planning authority, either ignoring or defying incompatibility, had situated a yellow-brick school building and a macadam-covered playground. Lining the sides of the road winding through the graveyard stood rows of sycamores, very old if their height, spread, and the sparseness of foliage were reliable indicators. The hearse crept along beneath them and finally eased to a stop behind a parked station wagon. As we walked past it on our way to the grave site, I saw some sort of government license plate on the rear bumper. The instant I cut off the engine of my Honda and opened the door, I could hear the high-pitched shouting of children's voices coming from the playground. Glancing at my watch, I saw it was two thirty-five, probably just the beginning of recess.

Guido, "the undertaker's understrapper" (as William Carlos Williams dismissively dubs him in a poem about the proper way to conduct a funeral, which had suddenly popped up in my brain), was carrying the head and three pallbearers were bearing on each side of the coffin as it was conveyed maybe two first downs from the hearse. We followed over grass-covered graves, between weathered gray headstones, to a rectangular hole, over which hovered a crane, on which Guido and his fellow bearers laid the box. Above the crane was a canopy. Given what it was to protect, I concluded the canvas was intended to run up Aunt Bess' account payable to Mr. Beckett. At the foot of the grave was a mound of reddish-brown earth, beside which slabs of sod were piled. The color of the soil suggested that, before serving as a burial ground, the field had been shale, not very fertile farmland.

After the casket had been loaded on the crane, Guido, his derby jammed down on his head, escorted Aunt Bess and Debbie, followed by Gwen and me, as family, to a place at the head of the hole. Bible in hand, the minister was ushered to a place at the foot. He assumed a commanding posture in front of a gray stone, of the size and shape to fill the arch of a chapel window. Inscribed on its surface were the names and birth and death dates of generations of Stulls and their spouses and progeny. After family and the minister were in place, other mourners congregated along the sides of the coffin.

As Aunt Bess confronted the hole, I could see her gasp, then her shoulders danced a little jig. Competing with the shriek and protracted wailing of Debbie were the shouts and laughter of children on the playground, the fence of which was only yards from Oscar's resting place. Although I'd parked directly behind the bumper of Sarah's convertible and watched her get out of her car and start across the lumpy grass, I'd lost sight of her as we'd trekked toward the grave.

When the tail end of the mourners had taken their places, a silence came over the assembly, making the sounds coming from the playground seem all the louder. You might say at that solemn instant a selfishly fearful awe had paralyzed the vocal chords of the gathering, including even

Debbie, who now was smothering sobs in a handkerchief. Aunt Bess' shoulders had stopped jiggling. Suddenly someone coughed, almost surely a man. It was not merely a hm-hm clearing of the throat but a prolonged hacking, coming from ominously deep in the lungs. It was loud enough to compete with the cries and laughter coming through the wire fence separating the land of the living and the land of the dead.

Perhaps it was this memento mori that prodded the minister to clear his throat, take a step forward, and lay one hand on top of the coffin. After fumbling his Bible open, which I could see had a marker in it, with the other hand, he turned his head and cast a forbidding but ineffective glare in the direction of the playground. Finally he commenced reading. Straining to hear, I was able to make out occasional familiar phrases—"them which are asleep"... "rose again"... "shall rise first." Letting his head drop, seemingly conceding he'd fought a losing battle with the children, who he wished would go anywhere else, but not "come unto me," he muttered, "Let us pray." Reinforcing his defeat, he mumbled the prayer so inaudibly that only the final "Amen," which put a seal on his funereal mission, could only possibly be heard even by those who were closest to him.

I suppose they had been standing behind the mourners, with their equipment set to go, waiting for the minister to abdicate in their favor. To my dismay, for I had felt certain that the ceremony graveside had run its dreary course, I heard, holding its own with the shrill voices of the children, a brass rendering of "The Star-Spangled Banner." Since no such band of instruments was anywhere in sight, I concluded I was hearing another recording, at much greater volume than that at which the canned hymns had been played in the mortuary. To compete with the bursts of sound from the playground, whatever mechanism was projecting its sound had to be at full volume. Scanning in the general direction my ear told me the music was coming from, my eyes lit on what had to be a battery-powered machine and two small black speakers, one standing in the grass on each side of the pedestal of the Stull tombstone.

The strains of what would be "home of the brave," if the national anthem were being sung, died into a silence that told me the playground had suddenly emptied of children. Instantly two uniformed Waves, as they had been called during World War II, the insignia on their upper right arm proclaiming they were petty officers, one black, one white, doubtlessly selected to declare the racial blindness of the military, emerged from the front of the gathering along one side of the grave. The black, exercising her authority by taking the lead at each juncture, bore a folded national ensign over her right forearm, which she held high to keep the sacred cloth from dragging on the ground. Given the bigotry I'd heard come from the Ancient Mariner's lips, I confess to feeling some gratification that his country was sweeping aside the prejudice of the veteran it was honoring at his burial.

Marching to an unheard cadence, the two Waves halted graveside as if on command. Together they unfolded the flag. Carrying one end, the black Wave draped the cloth over her arm, which she held high as she marched to the head of the coffin. Carrying the other end in the same way, so that between them not a stitch of the ensign ever touched the ground, the white Wave draped her end over the foot. When they pulled it smooth, the flag neatly covered the casket. The precision with which the Waves carried out their mission bespoke the thoroughness of their discipline and suggested that despite their youthfulness they were old hands at their specialized function.

The black Wave marched to the now silent player, bent over, keeping her knees straight, and threw a switch on the device. The emptiness of sound as the national anthem had ended had come so suddenly that it had produced the aftereffect of a sonic boom. Searching the sky, I half-expected a squadron of fighter planes to come roaring in as they swooped just above the tops of the larger monuments. Or in lieu of air power, I wondered, might a crew of scantily clad cheerleaders, in the youthfulness and with the verve they must have had when they celebrated Oscar's prowess and triumphs on his high school's gridiron, diamond and court, come prancing and dancing across the grass between gravestones, waving their arms as they belted out, "Stull, Stull, Stull"?

What shattered the silence was a bugle playing taps. So sudden and imperative was the first blast of notes that I had to hold my right hand back from rendering a salute, either by snapping it up over my right eyebrow, thumb tucked under the palm, or pressing it flat against my heart. The instant the protracted final notes had died into another silence, the two Waves in lockstep, evidently obeying another unheard command, stripped the flag from the top of the coffin, neatly folded it, taking care again that not a shred be desecrated, and draped it over the forearm of the superior of the military detail. While the inferior in rank stood at attention facing the coffin, the Wave carrying the ensign high marched to the family end of the grave.

As she was extending it, lowering it from shoulder to breast so it was face-high to the widow of the hero who was receiving military honors in death, a figure came breaking through the ranks of those gathered on the far side of the coffin from where Aunt Bess had positioned herself. Glittering scarlet in the bright midafternoon sunlight, she was taking long steps, almost running, a daringly precarious feat given the roughness of the turf and her treacherously frail stiletto heels. The timing was perfect. At the precise instant the black Wave was about to lower the folded flag onto Bess' outstretched arms, Sarah arrived at the family end of the coffin.

"Here," she demanded, throwing out her arms, "I'll take that for her."

The straight-backed Wave snapped her head toward the woman in red, who had not been with the little family group and had come breaking in at a critical instant. Fixing a cold eye on Sarah, she hesitated.

"It's perfectly okay," Sarah went on, modulating her tone from demand to explanation. "She doesn't sort of walk so well like and the grass's so uneven and like I'd hate to have her fall carrying the flag. See, I'm her eldest daughter."

The word *eldest* carried the day. Without replying or even moving a muscle in her military-conditioned face, the Wave surrendered the national ensign, then abruptly pivoted and went marching to the unsounded cadence back toward her sister-in-arms standing at attention beside the equipment they had brought.

Losing interest in the military who, without speaking a word, had executed their prescribed duty with a display of discipline and efficiency that would do the secretary of the navy and even the commander in chief of our armed forces proud, I fixed my eye on Aunt Bess, with her daughter Regan standing on one side of her and her daughter Goneril, with the American flag draped over her arm, on the other. Again Regan had gone into the half crouch that suggested she was about to spring. In fact, I noticed that her fingers were clawed, perhaps unconsciously, or atavistically.

Again Aunt Bess acted quickly, stretching out her bony arm in order to prevent physical contact between her two daughters. On a much smaller scale, and much more fragile in composition, Aunt Bess' arm resembled the bar that confronts the front of a vehicle at a toll gate until the tariff has been paid. Aware that in this instance no toll was to be paid, I held my breath and squeezed Gwen's hand. It felt limp as a shucked oyster, suggesting a dismaying helplessness. Just as an accelerating vehicle might easily go smashing through the inhibiting barrier, Regan could easily have brushed aside her mother's frail little arm. I wondered how Goneril, hands fully engaged by the flag, would counterattack. Would she, heaven help us, allow our national emblem to fall to the ground? To my surprise and relief, Regan unclawed her fingers. Not a word or even a hiss issued from her mashed, bloodlessly pale lips. I found myself puzzled as to whether to ascribe her restraint to cowardice, prudence, respect for her country's flag or for her living mother and dead father. Without wanting to, I found myself admiring Sarah's daring, strategy and perfect timing.

Gwen broke the silent tableau and ended the threat of violence by throwing her arms around Aunt Bess' neck, hugging and kissing her lip-sticked forehead. That took down the barrier and brought Debbie out of her crouch.

"You're a dear soul and I love you," I could just hear Gwen whispering in her aunt's ear as gently she turned her away from the grave site and started her moving slowly back toward the limo that had brought her to the cemetery. Gwen's use of the word *soul*, a term that is foreign to the thinking and absent from the usage of Aunt Bess' niece and her infidel husband, was as graciously received as it was uttered. And her setting her aunt in motion induced Debbie to take her mother by the arm as escort. The most Gwen could give to Debbie was a "good-bye" nod and half-smile.

As Gwen and I ambled across graves, between tombstones, toward the Honda, Sarah pranced by with the flag now tucked in her armpit. A corner of it dragged on the grass. I could sense that Gwen's refusal to acknowledge Goneril's presence declared her conviction that it was possible for her cousin to exist without having any essence.

We watched Sarah climb into her convertible, whiz by the hearse and stately limo in which her mother and sister were being carried away from their husband and father's dead and buried body, miraculously without scraping the side of either vehicle, and streak off on the narrow dirt drive, leaving a trail of dust, like a comet ahead of its tail. When Gwen and I had settled into the Honda, neither of us uttered a word. I drove out of the cemetery with a respectfully meditative slowness.

"Well...?" Gwen finally asked as we turned onto the thoroughfare that would lead to the road that would deliver us to our home.

I gave her a sidelong smile and let out a little laugh.

"I knew it would dreadful, but I never imagined..." Breaking off for want of adequate language, she handed me an apology, then threw the ball back to me. "I'm really sorry I dragged you to it. But what *do* you think was the worst?"

"There's no need to apologize, you know. It's all in the family, as they say. What you're asking me, I take it, is which of the three parts provided me the most entertainment."

"That's a bit perverse. But have it your way. What amused you the most?"

"The Navy damsels were impeccably military. Oscar certainly would have approved."

"You know, I can't imagine Aunt Bess getting the Bureau of Veterans' Affairs involved. Or Debbie either. Are you suspecting what I am?"

"Yep. Sarah. And as well as they did, she outperformed them. I'm surprised she had the… I was going to say feelings or patriotism. Guess though, I'll have to say guts. But what in God's or our president's name will she do with the flag?"

"Maybe use it on her bed. As a spread. In memoriam of her father."

"Whatever other traits she might have, I seriously doubt that sentiment's part of Sarah's sensibility. Besides, the flag isn't the size or shape to fit even a double bed, should Sarah not always be sleeping alone. You've heard of people wrapping themselves in the flag, haven't you? It would be a teasingly dramatic way of disrobing, to use a polite word."

"What an imagination you have!"

"But, you know, Gwen, I have to admit to wishing that rather than coming between Goneril and Regan, Aunt Bess had let them fight it out."

"Physically? Beside their father's bier? Nonsense, although I know you're indulging in hyperbole."

"After the performances we've just seen, how can anything be hyperbolic?"

"Well, then, you're flirting with titillation. But you still haven't answered my question. What *amused* you the most?"

"The way the shouting and laughing of the kids in the school yard drowned out the minister and triumphed over the silence that death asks for was really extraordinary. To be honest, at the risk of also being somewhat blasphemous, I thought it wasn't just happenstance but was divinely ordained. Did you notice how the Bible-thumper went slinking off after the naval show?"

"I did. And also found it gratifying. But you're holding back. What really took the gold, as they say?"

"Well, if I must. Though I sense that you just want to hear me say what you already know. I confess that without a grain of exaggeration never in my life have I had the good fortune to behold anything that measures up to the coffin-side struggle over the ring. In his eighties, lying down in a box, lifeless as he was, the Ancient Mariner fought courageously for what he knew was his by right of possession. That scene will go with me to the grave, so to speak."

"Did you happen to see how the undertaker finally got it off?

"Easily. Three-in-One."

"Those the odds for or against Uncle Oscar?"

"No, no, no. Not odds. Oil."

"What?"

"Lubrication liquidated Oscar's last bastion of defense. His mighty knuckle had to knuckle under. A couple of squirts of Three-in-One oil made it smooth and slick as an eel, a dead eel."

"Good Lord. How crude! Oiling a corpse?"

"Worse than the bad form, it was downright unfair. Oscar was no more able to defend against oil than an eel just pulled from the water. But in my judgment the Ancient Mariner won a battle more magnificent than any of those triumphs on the field or at sea he never tired of describing. Call it a moral victory. You'd give Oscar the gold too, now wouldn't you?"

"Of course. But…"

"No buts about it. It made me hear and understand the f-u-n in 'funeral'."

"You've got it, said the last word: *Fun*-eral. Amen."

ANSWERING FIRE

Lest thou forget the things which thine eyes have seen.
—Deuteronomy 4:9

She was no more than five feet tall. A Walking Stump. Her steps were tiny and brisk. When she'd wiggled her little body into the upholstered chair in the inglenook at the far end of the barroom, the feet on her club legs scarcely touched the floor, although she leaned back, making her look tentative, out of place. Beneath a dull brown skirt that fell halfway between her knees and ankles, she seemed to have a single thigh. Everyone else in the place was part of either a couple or a foursome. She was the only person without a drink.

The bartender, craggy-faced Yorkshireman who was as dour as a highland Scot, paid her no attention. Once situated, she laid her petite hands on her lap, one on top of the other, as if trying to conceal something. Daniel was sitting close enough to see her eyes darting around to take in all they could without turning her head. As they were about to land on Alma and him, he quickly looked away.

"Having another?" he asked.

"Sure, if you are," Alma replied.

Standing at the bar, half-facing the woman while waiting for the bartender to refill their empty glasses, he noticed that the small woman's hands now were squeezed between the of the chair and the outside of her thighs. As he carried the second martinis back to where Alma was sitting, he hoped the woman would notice and come to understand the custom of the inn. He walked slowly, so as not to spill a drop and walked closer to the woman than was necessary. When directly in front of her, he pulled back the corners of his lips and crinkled his eyes ever so slightly. She could decide whether he was or wasn't directing a smile at her. Her face remained as expressionless as a death mask.

The headwaiter dame striding in from the dining room. Tall, broad-shouldered, straight-backed, wearing a black serge suit with gold buttons, he must have appeared intimidating to an ill-at-ease foreigner. He distributed menus, in large maroon covers, to everyone in the bar. When the woman unfolded hers, her faced disappeared behind it. Her hands were chunky, with stubby fingers. She was short-armed.

"Dan, have you noticed the woman sitting alone beside the fireplace?" Alma asked without opening her menu. She must be Japanese or Korean. Maybe even Chinese, now that Nixon opened the country up. His one good deed."

"No," he lied. Why he didn't quite know.

"Well, I've been watching her. She hasn't had a drink."

"Maybe she doesn't want one."

"Why else would she come into the bar?"

"God knows. Perhaps she just blundered in."

"And sat down? When she could see everyone else had a glass in hand? My guess is she can't figure out the procedure. Remember how puzzled we were our first time her. We felt like intruders. I'll bet she doesn't know what to make of the menu."

"Could be she has fluent English."

"I'm going to see whether she needs help."

"How's your Japanese?"

"No better than your Korean, Mandarin, or Cantonese."

As he watched Alma, still slender and straight-backed at seventy five, approach the short squat woman, he sipped his martini. While trying not to, he couldn't help overhearing the verbal thrust and parry as the couple beside him went at it.

"With or without the U. N. the cowboy's going in, with guns blazing."

"But Saddam *is* a threat."

"Not to us or the Americans,"

"He has weapons of mass destruction."

"They're not aimed at us."

"He could ignite the whole Middle East."

"Georgie lad has not more sense of history than does the pony he rides."

"Sadam Hussein's a madman. Suppose his uranium or chemicals land in the hands of terrorists? Remember nine eleven."

"We learned from Afghanistan. Twice. As well as in Iraq after World War I."

"Ancient history."

"What happened to the Russkies in Afghanistan is recent history."

"His father and Maggie ought to have bone all the way in '91."

"Bush will have a tiger by the tail. You'll see."

"Until Saddam's gone there's no hope of cleaning up the Israeli-Palestinian mess."

"Blair ought to know better than to hitch his wagon to a falling star."

"Well, whenever I have a chance I'll wave the dear old Union Jack and now's the time."

This last from a woman in late middle age with a tallowy face and a jaws that swiveled rather than dropped when she spoke, words of the man, presumably her husband, sounded as if they were being ground out by his teeth. To taunt him she broke into the chorus of "Rule, Britannia." Last evening he'd heard them spatting just as vigorously over whether it was more proper to pour tea into the cup before milk, his position, or after, hers.

Back home in the States the drums of war were being beaten so loudly and insistently and dismayingly that Alma and Daniel had cut and run—to be away for a while, settled into a lovely North Yorkshire village, which they visited many times. Yet here "it" was, following them into the bar of their favorite inn, infiltrating his ear—and mind. At least Daniel told himself consolingly, it was being blared out on the evening news. No teleys in the bars here.

"Well, I was right," Alma purred, with a bit of self-satisfaction, as she rejoined him. As if he'd seriously questioned her surmise. "The poor woman is baffled. Sol explained the process, how things work in the bar and that we order dinner here from the menu the headwaiter brings. She does understand and speaks English well enough to be understood. Should we ask her to join us in the lounge after dinner? I forgot to explain that's the convention. I'm rather certain she'd Japanese."

While they were eating he could hear the beating of war drums across thirty-five hundred miles of ocean.

The woman left the dining room while they were eating dessert. On her table he could see an empty win glass.

§

"Have your heard the news on the telly this morning?" The little crown of white lace perched on top of the gray-haired head of their waitress brought back the nineteenth century. A white apron over a black dress constituted the rest of her uniform. Always pleasant and chatty, she was, they'd found out on one of their early stops at the inn, the wife of the sternly laconic bartender. The balance of opposites had held for many a year.

"Why no," Alma replied. "Should we?"

"We've come to get away from the news," Daniel growled, taking care to sound like a good-natured dog awakened from a nap rather than a threatening grizzly.

"Oh, but this is such news as you'll be wanting to know. They've bombed Baghdad, you Americans have, and Saddam and his sons have all been killed. It was fearsome, we're told. Our royal troops have gone in too. God willing, it will soon be over."

As they made their way out of the dining room, they passed the Japanese woman who was sitting at a table just inside the French doors. Facing the rest of the breakfasters, she ate with her head down.

§

"Have you heard the Japs have just bombed Oahu?" My, sister and I are having lunch in a restaurant close to a downtown hospital, in which on the eleventh floor my father is pacing his room like a caged tiger. He's being driven by the anxiety generated by what his doctor has called a nervous breakdown. Why all of a sudden at forty-nine he's been plunged into irrational fear and hopeless despair neither he nor we can understand.

I've never heard of Oahu.

"Our ships and the barracks at Pearl Harbor have been hit by Jap planes," the waitress goes on, "and lots of our sailors and soldiers have been killed."

With doll-like prettiness and blond hair she wears pageboy, like a movie star named June Allyson, she's not much older than I am. If my mother weren't here, I'd try to find the courage to ask her for a date.

When the three of us have gone out onto Broad Street after hurriedly finishing lunch, I buy a newspaper from a boy yelling "Extry Extry! Japs attack Hawaii! Roosevelt declares war!"

"Oh, what this will do to your poor father in the state he's in," my mother half sobs. "The poor man imagines more troubles of his own than he can bear."

The next time I visit him I can see that my father has no emotion to squander on the war.

§

"Early this morning, Near Eastern time, American forces struck Baghdad with three dozen Tomahawk missile carrying one-thousand pound warheads. They were fired from naval units in the Persian Gulf and the Red Sea. A Pentagon spokesman has announced intelligence has learned that senior Iraqi leadership was inside three targeted buildings at the time of the attack. According to a Defense Department official, one identified target was more important than the other two. He went on to report that, after the missiles struck their targets, a pair of F-17 fighter dropped four two-thousand pound bunker-destroying bombs on an underground facility beneath one of the leveled buildings in which Saddam Hussein and two of his sons, Uday and Qusay, were said by a reliable source to be hiding. According to a later Defense Department report, the targets were obliterated and some, if no tall, the Iraqi leadership was Killed. A C .1. A. intelligence report cited witnesses who saw the body of Saddam Hussein being carried from the rubble on a stretcher.

"Subsequent attacks by Tomahawk missiles fired from warships by hundreds of U. S. planes have delivered a staggering blow to the Iraqi regime. According to White House officials, the coordinated operation is intended to shock and awe the government and war machine of Saddam Hussein into a state of collapse. 'Shock and Awe' is the phrase we keep hearing his morning out of Washington.

"Meanwhile here in London the War Department has reported that Royal Army troops, including the famed Desert Rats, along with four thousand Royal Marines and units of the First Armoured Division, have joined the U. S. Marines' First Expeditionary Force. Landing from the Persian Gulf, they are rapidly closing in on the strategically important city of Basra in southeast Iraq. Major General Robin Brims, in command of all Her Majesty's forces in the region, including the First Amoured Division, had announced..."

"Do you mind?" Daniel asked as he clicked off the television set in their room. Considering that Alma had tuned into BBC news despite the mutually agreed upon reason for their being in this Yorkshire inn at this time, he felt that his mild irony along with his unilateral action was justified.

"I was hoping the Brits might hold out, along with France and Germany, and insist on U. N. inspectors go back..."

"Not a chance. Look, we knew the dogs of war were about to be unleashed. Since there's nothing we can do about it, let's not let it get to us. No more TV news, what say?"

"Of course you're right. No point having out noses in what we've already sniffed. No more television for the duration of...our temporary escape."

"Agreed. Here's hoping BBC will take time out from the destruction of Baghdad to offer some footage of the test match in Melbourne."

§

When they entered the bar before dinner that evening, the Japanese woman was sitting in the same chair she had the evening before. She had a drink in her hand. Noticing Alma smile at her, he nodded at the woman noncommittally. The woman, lifting herself by pushing on the chair arms, responded by half rising and bowing, then holding up her drink like the torch of the statue of liberty.

"Don't you find it rather strange," Daniel began after they'd in with their martinis, "an Far Eastern woman halfway around the world from home, alone?"

While watching the dance of the dance of the gas-fed flame in the fireplace beside the woman's chair, the choreography of whose programmed flares he'd studied and diagrammed in his head, he was forcing himself not to hear what he knew would be the conversation of his near neighbors.

"On the face of it, yes," Alma agreed. "Though when you consider how the world has changed since the end of World War II, maybe not so strange. Not only women in the West have been liberated, you know."

"True enough. But what can she be doing in a village on the edge of the North Yorkshire moors, where we're hiding out, you might say? It's not exactly London or Stratford-upon-Avon. Or Paris or Rome. Remember the hordes of Japanese we ran into in Stratford? Clicking their cameras and flashing light bulbs and posing. What on earth can they do with all those photographs and slides? Send them to friends and relatives who toss them away, as we do? Have slide show evenings, which we find excuses not to go to?"

" 'Hordes'? Of Japanese? Genghis Khan was a Mongol."

"Touché."

"They have a right to revere Shakespeare in their own way."

"Still, I think I'm on the right track. With Stratford-upon-Avon."

"Not sure what you mean."

"Our little friend's a teacher. No matter where she's from, you see a woman traveling alone, wearing sad-looking clothes, skirt halfway down her calf, hair in a double knot, you can be pretty damn certain you're looking at a schoolteacher."

"Oh my! More stereotyping. Every bit as bad as 'hordes.' Your notion of schoolmarms must be a carry-over from your childhood, which was, let me see, rather a few decades ago."

"Okay. I'm benighted. Hopelessly. No point in trying to enlighten me. Still, I'm convinced the lady *is* a teacher. Forget about her being an old maid because she's traveling alone. And about her self-presentation. Something emanates from her that says 'Japanese schoolteacher.'"

"From bad to worse. You've gone from stereotyping and fixation to clairvoyance."

"What'll you bet?"

"Though I have no strong feelings about her national origin, I'll take the bet. She's not a Japanese schoolteacher. For you, with your self-assurance, to win, she must be both. Winner chooses the restaurant in London the evening before we fly home. Price, no consideration. The tab goes on your credit card."

"No. On yours."

"You are sure. But actually I meant the generic 'your.' Whatever, how to find out? We can't just go up to her and ask. And she seems rather ill-at-ease to be forthcoming about herself."

"Leave it to me."

He was puzzled by his own certainty. And couldn't account for the attention he was giving the woman.

She'd finished her drink and, having ordered from the menu, had gone into the dining room before he and Alma had started on their second martini.

§

As they were passing through the hallway outside the bar, Daniel said, "Why not ask the lonely lady to have coffee with us, after dinner in the lounge, as you suggested last evening. You can explain the way it's done here, which you forgot to then. Remember? Maybe she's already figured it out. She seems to have caught on to procedures quite quickly. For an old maid schoolteacher from Japan."

"So, you're really determined to prove you're right. More to yourself than to me, it seems. Or maybe there's a glitzy restaurant in London you've had a secret hankering to dine in. Though you just might find yourself taking me to the Indonesian place near the Marble Arch that you dislike and I love. But why should I do the inviting? Why not you?"

"It was your idea to make her feel cozy in the first place. And if it's a woman thing, she'll feel more comfortable. She might think I'm coming on to her."

"No doubt, no doubt. A middle-aged schoolteacher young enough to be your daughter."

"Okay then. I'll ask her." He was surprised by his ready capitulation.

After entering the dining room, he broke away from Alma and went up to the table just inside the doorway.

"Good evening, madam." To address her formally and bow slightly seemed called for. Still he felt as if he were playacting. "May I invite you to join my wife and me for coffee in the lounge after dinner?"

The little start she gave as she looked up from the bowl of soup her spoon was going into let him know she hadn't seen him approaching. Spoon in midair, she hesitated, then relaxed into a smile. Her teeth were discolored.

"I am honored to accept the kind invitation," she replied, jerking her head into a nod. But she didn't scoot back her chair and half rise, as he'd expected. On his way to join Alma it occurred to him that he ought to have added "or tea" after "coffee."

§

She did ask for tea. While sitting around a coffee table in the lounge, waiting for her pot and their French press to arrive, they exchanged names. Hers was Yuko Miyataka. Even though he and Alma had engaged in mock battle, primarily over his insistence that she was a schoolteacher, the fact that she was Japanese *was* of greater significance to him than her profession.

As Alma chatted her up about the loveliness of the village and the attractiveness and comforts of the inn, he studied her face, as if scrutiny might reveal what lay behind it. Her skin, the color of sun-baked mud, was slightly pitted. Narrowed by the plumpness of her cheeks, lumpy, like roughly molded clay, her eye sockets seemed to toe in. Making it appear you were looking at her, or she at you, from a distance, her black pupils were small. The top of her nose was flattened, widening her nostrils. In her upper lip was a deep indentation. She wore no makeup. She didn't exactly fit his picture of a geisha.

After the waiter had served them, Alma made the first thrust.

"I cannot help wondering what has brought you to Yorkshire."

He was pleased that she hadn't used the first person plural.

"Oh, well, the great writers of this place."

He had to check an impulse to shoot a quick smile of triumph at Alma.

"Then I believe you are a teacher." Alma put it bluntly to confirm that she'd lost the bet.

"Oh sure. I teach the literature of English novel."

"Why are you not teaching now?" Given that she was conversing with a non-native speaker of English, Alma obviously found it appropriate to avoid contractions. "Is March not a school month in your country?"

"In March we are having school in Japan. You see, I have been given the leave of absence."

"So, you are engaged in research?"

"Oh no. Not the research. I am only the teacher."

They seemed to have reached a dead end. While they sat sipping in what he felt was a strained silence, he told himself the fact that Yuko Miyataka understood a word like "engaged" indicated that, despite some uncertainties in idiom, she was capable of keeping a conversation in English going. Which suddenly she did.

"You have read the novels of the famous Brontë sisters?" The question was directed to Alma.

"Yes. I have read *Jane Eyre* and *Wuthering Heights*. Many years ago. When I was a student in college." Alma was making her English sound as if she'd learned it from a book.

"Today I ride the bus to Scarborough. About one hour. I wish to respect the grave of the youngest, named Anne Brontë. But I am not able to find it. Scarborough is a big city with many burial places."

"That must be a disappointment. When you have traveled so far. I have never read anything Anne Brontë has written. Have you, Dan?"

There was no way to escape Alma's ploy to involve him in the conversation.

"*The Tenant of Wildfell Hall.* That too was years ago. Anne wrote at least one other novel, it does seem to me." He heard his own idiom as unnatural.

Yoko Miyataka clapped her hands, smiled and nodded. There was a sweetness to her smile that eclipsed her lack of beauty. "The gentleman is very learned. Only one other. It has the title of *Agnes Grey*. Anne Brontë" not so famous as her sisters."

"Will you pay your respects to them also?" Alma asked, to show her interest.

"Of course I must do that. But before, I must respect the grave of one other great writer. Not many miles from this village."

"Who is that?"

"Laurence Sterne, a fellow of infinite jest."

"A fellow of infinite jest?" Dan echoed before he could stop his tongue. "But that's Shakespeare. Yorick, in 'Hamlet.'" Sensing he was being rude to correct a woman from another culture so bluntly, especially a teacher of English, he wished he could unsay the words the instant they were out.

Again Yuko Miyataka clapped her plump hands, nodded and smiled. "Very good. And there is Yorick also in Laurence Sterne's novel *Tristram Shandy*. Very difficult to read for Japanese people."

Realizing Yuko Miyataka had tried to help him save face, Daniel felt a little flush of humiliation. And hearing her manage the l's and r's in "Laurence Sterne," "fellow," "Shakespeare," and "Yorick," usually so treacherous for Far Easterners, he had to admire her mastery of spoken English.

"I have never heard of it," Alma confessed. "Have you, Dan?"

"Yes, but I haven't read it. You say Sterne is buried near here?"

"Oh sure. Tomorrow I will ride the taxi to Coxwold village. It is fifteen minutes. That is where Laurence Sterne wrote and where is his grave."

"But the Brontës lived in Haworth," Alma put in. "We have been there. It is quite a distance."

"Then in two days more I will ride the bus to York city. One half hour when I came to here. Then I will ride the train to Leeds city. There I will ride the taxi to Haworth village. I will respect the graves of Charlotte and Emily Brontë and I will see into the museum. It was the home where they did their writings. These are important for me to teach the Japanese students their greatness."

"I have very much admiration for you," Alma said reverently. "For your commitment and your courage."

Daniel wondered whether Yuko Miyataka had understood "commitment." But again she nodded and beamed her sweet smile.

Back in their room neither Daniel nor Alma mentioned their bet. Now that he'd been proved right on both counts, he'd persuade her, when they'd reach London, that his choice was the Indonesian restaurant he didn't care for. To counter the condescension she'd be certain to feel, he'd insist the tab go on her credit card.

§

A chronic insomniac, he awakened in the grip of depression. The red numbers on the face of the digital clock said 1:22. If he'd been dreaming, he couldn't recall what. He knew the martinis were a component of the chemistry that was keeping him from sleep. As he confronted the prospect of hours of restlessness, he heard Alma breathing with a regularity indicative of a state of blessed unconsciousness. He was lying on his right side. After rolling onto his left, dropping onto his back, flipping onto his belly, squirming onto his right side again, stretching full-length, then doubling his knees and hunching over them, he found himself saying to himself the names of the international code of flags at sea.

*A*ble, *B*aker, *C*harlie, *D...*, *E*asy, *F*ox, *G*eorge, *H*ow, *I*tem, *J*ig, *King, L...*, *Mike, Nan, O..., Peter, Queen, Roger, S... Tare, Uncle, V*ictor, *W...*, *X*-ray, *Y*oke, *Z*ebra. Five flag names he couldn't remember. When he ran back through, he came up with "Love," "Oboe," and "Sugar." Without succeeding, struggle as he might, in dredging up the words for "D" and "*W*," he drowsed off.

Reawakening at a few minutes past four, he flattened himself on his back. When he closed his eyes, the darkness of the room became a blank slate. Gradually it dawned on him that the two letters whose code names he hadn't been able to come up with were the initials of his name.

§

"Have...one...suburb...of...Pittsburgh...in...tow...fullstop... awaiting... instructions... end of transmission.

Dean, signalman first class, is reading flashing light from the *Hornet,* two or three miles off our port bow. I take the words down on a clipboard. The message is addressed to the admiral aboard. It's dated Je 9, '45. We've just ridden out a four-day typhoon off the coast of Kyushu. This morning the sea is smooth enough to deserve its name—Pacific.

"What in Christ's name does that mean?" Dean growls. "I'm going to ask for a repeat. Whitlock, read the son of a bitch with me."

" 'Have one suburb of Pittsburgh in tow.' That's what he's saying, Dean."

"Don't make no Goddamn sense," Dean grumbles as he carries the message off to the admiral's chief of staff in flag plot.

At chow Dean fills me in. "The fucking storm split the bow off the *Pittsburgh* and her watertight doors kept it afloat. The *Hornet* spotted it, pulled alongside, put a man aboard that secured a hawser on a bollard and they took the fucker in tow. Their captain's asking Old Ironsides what the fuck to do with it. Nobody don't know where the hell the rest of the fucking cruiser is."

§

Waiting to see a crack of light between the draperies across the bedroom window, he recalled how welcome the wit of the *Hornet's* captain had been during a harrowing time and how remarkable the recovery and repair of the *Pittsburgh.* Both parts were towed back to Pearl Harbor, where, after being welded together, she became seaworthy again. Yet the severity of that typhoon was eclipsed, he remembered, by the destructiveness of the typhoon they'd gone through, literally, the previous December in the South China Sea, off the coast of Luzon in the Philippines.

And the kamikazes. At first our command had construed the planes' plunging into ships as unintentional, the result of the pilot's inability to control his aircraft after it had been hit by antiaircraft fire. Gradually it dawned on those at the top that these were planned suicide missions, not even instantaneous decisions, like that of Captain Colin Kelly, the first U.S. hero in the Pacific theater, where in the early months of the war we were suffering one defeat after another. Rather than bail out, he'd guided his stricken fighter plane into the superstructure of a Japanese battleship. What irony—the first kamikaze was an American.

The admiral aboard his ship, Annapolis '07, appropriately nicknamed Old Ironsides, came up with a counter to the devastating new Japanese tactic. In addition to our twelve-inch signaling lamps, we carried four thirty-six inch carbon-arc searchlights. Their function was to locate enemy aircraft at night and illuminate them as targets for our twenty and forty-millimeter antiaircraft batteries. After Pearl Harbor we'd quickly learned that, logical as the theory was, its use was both futile and self-defeating. Guided by hand, the lights couldn't locate and track fast-moving aircraft in the dark, while they made the ships that were showing them visible targets for high flying bombers and skimming torpedo planes. From that time on, no light aboard ship was permitted to be visible between sunset and sunrise.

Old Ironsides, with enough gold braid on his uniform to change a designated procedure, concluded we could defeat the kamikazes by picking them up visually, after radar had located and fixed on them, with our thirty-six inch lamps' powerful beams, which would confuse and blind the pilots as they made their dive or run. The Japanese rode the streams of light we provided smack into their targets. After two ships were hit in rapid succession, that tactic was abandoned. Old Ironsides remained in command of our task group.

§

Water-borne armadillos, we're prowling the South China Sea for prey—whatever remnants of the battered Japanese fleet might be foolhardy enough to show themselves. Or a freighter, slow and low in the water, her lading meant for lands that the Japs have taken, a sitting duck for the guns of a man-of-war—you might say an albatross if freighters had wings and ships still carried crossbows.

A brilliant sun. On the signal bridge I'm scouring the space just above the horizon, a seam between the paler blue of sky and the darker blue of ocean. In the lens of a long glass my eye picks up a black speck. Its blip on the radar screen, I hear through the earphones of the headset I'm wearing, is too small to identify.

I push the button that brings to life the speaker my lips are almost touching. "Small craft at four o'clock. Distance approximately two miles. Looks dead in the water. Probably fishing boat."

Target confirmed by my eye, I'm blinded for an instant by a flash as the five-inch mount only feet from my right eardrum blasts off. In the glass I see a straddling of waterspouts a pod of whales might jet around the speck which has disappeared.

They never knew what hit them. No need to expend main-battery sixteen-inch shells on such small game. In these waters it couldn't possibly have been Japanese, was most likely Vietnamese or Filipino. Still, even the humblest native craft might radio our presence and position. We can't afford to take chances. Or prisoners. Think of it as baptism, of water and fire at once.

§

It came back to him in the dark—the first war crime in which he'd been a participant. Next time there had been less anguish. And the next and the next, diminishing. He closed his eyes and shuddered. In the still darker dark a circle of blue shone brightly enough to make his inner eye want to look away. If only his bodily eyes would open. The lids refused to go up. Within the blue, either sea or sky, he saw the ribbed hull of a scallop-shaped fishing boat. Inside was a cargo of white bones. Above it hovered a host of human shapes—children, wives, parents, he knew they were, heads bowed in submission or prayer, arms flung up in horror or supplication, mouths rounded as if moaning or exclaiming, eyes lowered in grief or despair.

Summoning all his will, he lifted his eyelids and stared into the less dense dark of the room. "Unfortunately we had to," they'd told themselves while doing. "Had to" now was his story, a memory for himself, a record for posterity that provides justifications. What the boy-sailor, a moral virgin until then, had done, his necessity, carrying out the commands of Old Ironsides, he'd buried in his mind as many fathoms deep as the little boat lay in the gulf of oblivion. Sooner or later it had to have happened—some outside force was bound to shatter the concealment of time and distance, the waters of the grave would part, and the boat with its cargo of bones would rise into his consciousness.

Guilt can't be bought off, satisfied by remorse. He knew he harbored no retroactive willingness to swap his billet aboard a man-of-war, fifty-five thousand displacement tons of armor and weapons, for a nameless fisherman's berth on a timbered unarmed boat. What penance then is an unmanned man to do when it's generations too late for reparation?

Ought he pay the *New York Times* to make public his *mea culpa* and a plea for forgiveness in a full-page spread, with one photograph of him then in uniform, another of him now in sackcloth and ashes? Would a home-page on the Internet provide greater exposure?

Ought he fly to Vietnam, with an exaction of its own, make a barefoot pilgrimage, stumping the final mile on his knees, to the village of My Lai, first land west of the fishing boat's watery grave, prostrate himself in whatever the burial ground there, and fast until he'd be nothing but skeleton?

Ought he make his way to the leper colony on Culion, Isle of the Living Dead, a dab of arid earth off Palawan in the Philippines, due east of the unmarked sea in which the fishing boat had vanished, and like San Juan de Cruz press lips against the lesions of "the living dead"?

Why shift it off to someone somewhere else? What better time and place than here and now, where and when the cover of distance and time have been breached? Come morning he could present himself to the rector of the parish church, hand him a document that would commit him to give all he had to the parish poor, the widowed, the orphaned, and to spend the remainder of his days celibate, praying and fasting.

If only he could love the souls of six—or were there nine or a dozen or more who had been aboard that boat—men he never knew. Oh, the futility of babbling lamentations!

§

Scout planes have radioed that we're steaming directly toward a powerful typhoon. A quartermaster lets it leak that by altering course twenty degrees to the north we can skirt what for us will not be a divine wind.

"Damn the typhoon," I hear Old Ironsides, striking an original heroic phrase, bark at his chief of staff in the passageway between flag plot and the shelter on the signal bridge. "We'll steam between her thighs and break into her cunt at the center, then batter our way out of her arms. Engines to thirty knots."

As surprised as I am that a man I consider scarcely literary can strike a metaphor, I'm shocked to hear an admiral use the word "cunt."

"All hands on deck," blares over the PA system.

The wind has begun to roar. Water becomes a gargle of sea and rain. Spray, thick and heavy as waves, stings what's exposed of my face, cowled by oilskin gear. On deck we've slung lines between railings and stanchions. Clinging to them, as I make my way hand over hand against gusts, burns the skin on my palms. When I measure the wind's force by leaning full weight against it, it holds me up. At first it's exciting.

From time to time I poke my head into the signal shelter. Eyes bugging, I watch the swinging of the pendulum of the clinometer—27° starboard, 26° port, 28° starboard we're rolling. At thirty, hull over stacks we go, Dean, who's mocked me by saying he's worn out more sea bags than I have socks, has told me. Maybe he's yarning, maybe not. When I check the log, I find the anemometer reads 157m.p.h.

Hearing over TBS that the storm's breath has blown a seaman off the flight deck of the *Intrepid,* I make out through the swirl of sea and rain a destroyer, the *Monaghan,* more shark-like than savior-like, prowling the circle that describes his liquid grave. Now sea heaves itself as high as the captain's bridge. Everyone hugs inboard bulkheads. Although even old salts, including Dean, are seasick, it hasn't come nigh me.

Word seeps out from flag plot we're battling the worst blow Old Ironsides has run afoul of since he was a midshipman. When he shows himself on deck, gold-braided cap off so his thinning gray hair is swept back by the wind, as I imagine Ahab's or an Old Testament prophet's would be, it's evident he's relishing the encounter. For the old bastard or the task unit he commands, except the ship I'm on, I wouldn't give a rusty piss. Fear has shriveled my prick to an earthworm. Nobody jokes. I realize I'm a born coward.

During what should be daylight, visibility is less than at dusk. When neither she nor us is dropped in a trough, I can barely make out the ghostly silhouette of the *Monaghan.* Since Old Ironsides has ordered the formation to tighten up, I judge she can't be more than the length of a football field at two o'clock off our starboard bow, rolling and pitching like a whale in its death throes. We plummet into a deep gorge. Then when we're flung on top of a mountain that would take eons to form on land, I look and wait for the *Monaghan* to reappear. She never does. Swamped, she's turned into a submarine who's made her final plunge.

Over TBS comes a report her sister destroyers, the *Hull* and the *Spence,* have also been swallowed, hundreds of unwitting kamikazes aboard. Unfathomable. Piloted by the unmalleable will of Old Ironsides, we blunder through to deal more death.

I imagine the three armor-plated coffins. Inside each is a contortion of bodies, which moments ago were snapping and obeying commands and performing assigned duties. Their resting place is the bottom of the South China Sea. In the ear of my mind I hear the descending voice of Lawrence Tibbett, which I'd listened to as a child when the needle clutched by the hand of the tone arm went spinning through the grooves of a seventy-eight r.p.m. bakelite record on the rosewood victrola in the parlor of my family home:

"Rocked in the cradle
of the
deep"

At this moment I'd give an arm, literally, yes, a leg, to be back there. Because of the wind's roar I don't have to stifle the childish sob I feel rifling up my throat.

§

He was having a bad night of it, very bad. The bed was a ping-pong table and he was being batted from awakenedness to sleep to awakenedness, from present to past to present, from where he was to where he'd been to where he was. Having fallen into a doze at a few minutes past four, after having gone through the South China Sea typhoon, he awoke at a few minutes past six to find himself tapping numbers in Morse code on his thigh: dot dot dot dot dash—four; dot dot dot dot dot—five; dash dot dot dot dot—six...

When he reached ten he made himself stop tapping, but went on counting, slowly. Carrier planes. One of his duties had been to record the number of aircraft in a strike as, bomb-laden, they were catapulted off the flight deck of one of the carriers their task unit was protecting. Hours later he'd record the number that returned. Then subtract.

Off Luzon, during the retaking of the Philippines, the kamikazes had struck erratically. During the invasion of Iwo Jima, where the invading troops desperately needed naval and air support, the suicide attacks accelerated to a steady flow. In mid-March, off Kyushu, Japan's southernmost island, the Franklin, the closest carrier in the task unit formation, her flight deck filled with loaded planes about to take off, was hit. Her bombs, ammunition and fuel exploded into flames that lit up the sky like a Fourth of July fireworks display. To watch with irresistible fascination human torches leaping from the hell of the flight deck into the sea brought tears salted with fear that scalded his cheeks. For eight hours the Franklin committed slow suicide. Next morning she was a smoldering hulk.

Some of the roasted bodies still alive enough to writhe and scream with pain, plucked from the sea by destroyers, were ferried to his ship, hoisted by boom, block and tackle onto the forecastle, then carried below to sick bay for whatever immediate treatment and relief the medical staff could administer. The metal stretchers on which they'd been transported were returned to the forecastle. There powerful hoses were played on their steel mesh to flush off shreds of scorched skin and charred flesh, morsels of beef cleaned from the grille of a hibachi.

During the month-long battle for Okinawa in April '45, kamikazes sank twenty destroyers on the picket line. More than a hundred and fifty other ships were severely damaged.

On the signal bridge a grim joke was going the rounds. He'd heard the format in junior high school.

"Knock, knock."

"Who's there?"

"Chicken."

"Chicken who?"

"Chicken Teriyaki."

"Who the hell is Chicken Teriyaki?"

"The only kamikaze pilot who'll survive this fucking war."

The laughter was hollow. When Blessington relayed the joke to Gallup, Gallup responded by grabbing Blessington by the shirt front, slamming him against a bulkhead, and twisting the chambray cloth so tight that Blessington squealed for help. It took Pettinghill, Mirski, and Catherman to pry Blessington, gasping and red-faced, loose. "It's a joke, for Chrissake," he whimpered as he went slinking off.

One afternoon our antiaircraft batteries, stressed, frightened, edgy, took down two U.S. fighters engaged in a dogfight with some Zekes, probably kamikazes. Neither pilot survived the friendly fire. Two replicas of the Stars and Stripes were not painted on the outside bulkhead of the captain's bridge to join the line of Rising Suns that served to keep score of the enemy we'd killed.

It trickled down the chain of command that, after the first beachhead had been established, it was touch and go on Okinawa. To provide stronger air support, the bomb loads carried by the carriers' TBF's were increased. On one memorable morning one out of every half dozen or so aircraft catapulted from the carrier he was keeping track of failed to get the necessary lift as it left the flight deck and went plunging nose-down into the drink. For hours destroyers circled, searching for those who'd managed to extricate themselves from their harness and wriggle out of the cockpit of their submerged planes. He estimated that less than half were rescued.

With chilled awe he remembered those airmen on the carriers. Knowing whose and how many seats at mess in the wardroom and bunks in their sleeping quarters were empty, they'd watched the plane ahead of them in line take off, nose down, and disappear. Then they'd taxi their own plane into position to be catapulted to potential death by drowning. How could they do it? Were they too not kamikazes, willing to give up their own lives for a chance to kill the enemy? If they were, along with the pilots shot down by their own guns and those burned to death from their own explosives aboard the stricken Franklin and those buried inside the *Monaghan, Spence* and *Hull*, was every airman, soldier, marine, and sailor, including him, also a breath of the death-dealing Divine Wind?

But at least our "kamikazes" had a chance, he reminded himself, not for the first time. Only eight or nine hundred men needlessly went down in the typhoon, ironic as "only" and shameful as "needlessly" were. Our guns destroyed many fewer of our own planes than Japanese. Most of our pilots lifted off the flight deck and flew into the blue to deliver their loads of killing fire without being taken down by Japanese antiaircraft batteries or gunners on Japanese planes, their opposite comrades-in-arms. Those who failed to get airborne at least had about a fifty-fifty chance of freeing themselves and being fished from the sea by a searching destroyer.

But the Japanese kamikaze took off knowing he was not to return. He recalled a night when he was stretched out, frightened and weary, expecting general quarters to sound at any second, commanding him to leap out of his bunk, scoot up the ladder from his compartment, race across the forecastle, and climb to the signal bridge. Night after night, to work their nerves and deprive them of sleep when they were already worn down by repeatedly alternating five hours on and off watch, Japanese planes, flying above the range of their antiaircraft fire, would drop tinfoil that showed up on the radar screen as flocks of bogeys. That night, while waiting, he'd tried to imagine himself as a Japanese kamikaze, about to take off on what was certainly his last mission, perhaps his first. "Duty is heavier than a mountain," he still remembered reading somewhere, could be the imperial rescript written on his brain, "while death is light as a feather." He hadn't been able to put himself inside his enemy.

§

A gorgeous morning. On the surface of the water you can track the wake of flying fish for yards. Sea and sky are vying for the purity of ail blues. Clarity of air means unlimited vision to the horizon. Sun is a wafer dipped in red wine. "Red in the morning, sailors take warning." Our carrier planes are off striking Japanese ground installations on Kyushu.

All at once the peace is broken by the popping of ack-acks. Glasses to eyes, I'm scanning the quadrant from zero to ninety degrees starboard. On the way back to zero, I pick up a plane, skimming the water to stay beneath the waves of our radar.

"Zeke approaching at two o'clock," I shout into the mouthpiece of my headset. "Closing fast."

Undeterred by the swarms of twenty and forty-millimeter shells our antiaircraft batteries let fly, the plane keeps coming. It's close enough for me to see its nose, targeted on the signal bridge, on me.

"Still closing fast!" I yell.

All at once I've been shot headfirst from the mouth of a five-inch gun. Zooming toward the plane, along with a stream of red tracers, I can make out a goggled and helmeted head behind a Plexiglas windshield. Suddenly over the racket of the twenties and forties, I hear the blast of five-inch guns. I know I'm on the bridge, paralyzed, but I can't feel the deck beneath my feet, I know I'm screaming "still close..." but I can't hear my voice.

Now there's nothing to see but endless blue and the red sun, nothing to hear but silence.

§

Now as he lay hopelessly awake, sleep-deprived not by dropped Japanese foil but by gin-fueling and history-feeding machinery in his brain he couldn't switch off, he found himself trying again, six decades later, to imagine what would have been his state of mind on the morning just before, had he been the one to take off on a death flight. Quietly, careful not to disturb Alma, whose brain had no such machinery and contained no such pernicious material, he slipped from bed. Fumbling at the night stand, he felt out his glasses and the tablet and pen the inn provided beside the telephone. Then he tiptoed into the bathroom, slowly closed the door to keep it from creaking, turned on the light, and slipped on his glasses. After relieving himself, he sat down on the toilet seat. Making use of his scant, romantically clichéd notion of things Japanese, he began writing. The words were waiting to spill out.

"After three days inform my father, gem merchant in Kyoto: 'In the month of the ripening plum he answered the summons of the Rising Sun without sorrow.' To my mother convey this empty urn, enameled with gulls on the wing. Speak no word. Bow three times and retire. Do not search for the girl with oval hands and lustrous eyes.

"Here in moonlight, ahead of dawn, stands the raven-winged plane that will burst into flame. May the birds on the back of the giant eagle it is my duty to destroy be pregnant with eggs that will consume their mothers and the father eagle with them.

"Sometimes when you light the ceremonial tapers and scatter incense before your sons, remember, my friend, how we locked fingers here, last human touch. Not yet twenty, I fly to greet the sun and dive."

"At last," he murmured to himself as he crawled back into bed. Within minutes he fell into sleep.

§

Reveille has sounded over the PA system. Minutes later, in the light of false dawn, I'm standing in ranks on the signal bridge, still groggy with sleep. Ensign Farnham is calling muster in a voice shrill as a bosun's whistle.

"Argersinger... Blessington... Dean... Gallup... Mirski... Pettingill ... Vincenti... Webster... Whitlock..."

Hearing my name jars me fully awake. "Ho, sir," I sing out. The top of a fireball, which is either the sun or an aircraft carrier bursting into flames, is just becoming visible on the eastern horizon.

§

He awoke to a sliver of light between the draperies. When he and Alma entered the dining room for breakfast, he immediately looked at her table. Empty. Most likely she was already off to "respect" Laurence Sterne's grave. Sometime he'd have to read *Tristram Shandy*.

Craving a shot of caffeine to counter sleep deprivation and, he hoped, rally him to contend with the despair that had him by the throat, he pushed down on the plunger of the French press the instant the waitress let go of the handle, poured Alma, then himself a full cup of coffee.

"Have a rough night?" Alma asked, as he took a long swig even though the liquid was burning his tongue. "You should give it a couple of minutes to mix. That'll make it stronger."

"No need to let it stand. That's the mystery of a French press. Brews in an instant. Thoroughly." He swilled more coffee.

"Doesn't seem possible. Think of the time it takes a percolator. Or a drip."

From the nearest tables he could hear what for the English, who had a tendency to mumble and who in the dining room at breakfast would pitch their conversation almost to a whisper, were perfectly audible voices. Certain he knew what was inciting them, he refused to allow his brain to process their words. To hold his own in a skirmish with Alma over the virtues of various methods of brewing coffee was beyond his power. Bruised, shaky, paralyzed, he gave in to silence.

"I suppose Yuko's had early breakfast and already's off to 'respect' the tomb, wherever it is, of that writer whose name I can't seem to remember who wrote a novel I've never heard of. Don't you find me a perfect blend of ignorance and loss of short-term memory?"

The sound of the name "Yuko" gave him a shake. Well-intentioned as Alma was in trying to divert him from himself by making what she believed was small talk, she was asking him to address a subject which, so early in the morning after a dreadful night, he'd prefer not to. Yet he hadn't the heart not to respond.

"That writer's Laurence Sterne. The title of his novel is *Tristram Shandy*. It's a classic. The name of the village, I think, is Cock's Wold. You know how eccentric English place names seem to us."

"Oh the blessed fortune to be hitched to a star that displays learning like a shower of meteorites. How does that blazing metaphor strike you, Mr. Luminary?" Coming on as though he were a literary historian did make him an inviting target. "What say we drive to Cock's Wold and respect Laurence Sterne's grave? Could be that would seduce me into reading... *Tristram Shandy*. That's not quite right, is it? Whatever, we might run into Yuko and we could lunch with her in the local pub."

He had no intention of seeming to be following Yuko Miyataka and traipsing through the parish churchyard, searching for the grave of Laurence Sterne. The reason was ... well, the reason had to be akin to why he'd lied when Alma had asked whether he'd noticed the woman sitting alone in the bar without a drink the previous evening.

"To be honest, I've been looking forward to watching the delayed tape of the test match between Australia and Sri Lanka on the telly. If it's on."

§

Alma was ensconced in the window seat, reading the *Guardian*. He'd vowed not to look at a newspaper for the duration of their A.W.O.L. Unable to get his mind off what he imagined was going on in Iraq, he was slumped in a Chippendale wing chair, only his eye attending to the match on the TV screen. Suddenly his full attention was grabbed by a powerful stroke from a Sri Lankan batsman. The camera was following the flight of the ball toward the boundary. Then it shifted onto the Aussie at long-leg racing toward it. Leaping like a grasshopper, he thrust out his right arm and snatched in his palm what surely would have been a six.

Still stretched out, he crashed onto the green, doubled up, rolled over three times, and lay still. The downed man's teammates raced into the frame and surrounded the player motionless on the grass. In their whites they looked like a team of doctors consulting over a patient. As the camera withdrew, in a long perspective they blurred to a single white shape, a fallen parachute ballooning above the surface of a body of water.

§

General quarters has sounded. I race from my compartment, where I've been folding wash on my sack, up the ladder, out the hatch, across the forecastle, up the ladders to the signal bridge. Sky is an endless prairie of blue, sea a field of deeper blue. Manning a long glass on a swivel, I slip on my headset and commence scanning a quadrant off the starboard beam, air space that's my responsibility. My eye picks up and focuses on a bomber at low altitude.

"Betty four o'clock starboard, elevation 30°, approximate distance a half miles" I shout into the mike hanging around my neck. "Betty closing fast at four o'clock. .." My voice is drowned out even to my own ear by the chattering of two twenty-millimeter antiaircraft guns directly below me.

All the forties on the starboard side are also crackling.

Suddenly a puff of black smoke trails from the tail of the Betty. Two parachutes, white handkerchiefs signaling "we surrender," open behind the plane. Letting the doomed aircraft pass out of the lens of my long glass, I focus on the body dangling from one of the parachutes. Guns are still spitting out shells. All of a sudden there is no body, just dangling shreds. The firing doesn't stop as the unmanned chute continues its slow descent. Nor does it end when the chute softly kisses the water and collapses to a small white mushroom bobbing like a patch of plankton. Shells are being pumped into a man who no longer is, is not even a corpse. They're riddling mere fabric. Then silence.

§

Even though he felt vomit about to rifle up his throat, still he couldn't help re-experiencing a giddy elation over the destruction of a plane and its crew whose mission had been to bomb his ship, intending to kill him.

Then he recollected that full recognition of the war crime he'd abetted by discharging his duty hadn't come until a year later. War over, honorably discharged, he was being rewarded for his services by a grateful government with the benefits of the G.I. Bill of Rights. He'd returned to the university in which he'd been a freshman when, prompted by conscience to fight against the Nazis, not the Japanese, he'd enlisted in the Navy and after a stint in communications school had found himself in the Western Pacific.

For a class in world literature he'd been reading the *Iliad*. At the desk in his room, light thrown by a gooseneck lamp, he'd come to Homer's account of the behavior and emotions of Achilles during the killing of Hector. Daniel's eye could still see Achilles stripping the armor from his enemy's lifeless body, repeatedly stabbing the corpse with the point of his spear, tying the carcass to the axle of his chariot, then dragging what had been Hector around the walls of Troy for the eyes of the dead man's mother and father to behold.

Etched in Daniel's brain were the words with which Homer had had Achilles reveal to the dying Hector his impulse to revert to cannibalism: "Would that my heart's desire could so bid me to carve and eat your raw flesh." Sitting before a television screen in a room in an inn in Yorkshire fifty-seven years later, he felt again the shudder of horror that had come over him in his dormitory room that night as the connection suddenly had sparked.

§

The Aussie at long-leg who had made the amazing catch was hobbling on one foot, arms around the shoulders of two teammates, toward the pavilion. Shaking his head to bring himself back to here and now, Daniel turned toward Alma, immersed in the *Guardian*, and stared at her for reassurance—reassurance for what, he couldn't say. Just reassurance. Then while waiting for play to be resumed, he leaned his head back on the top of the chair and shut his eyes. Within seconds he heard a loud cheer. Raising his eyelids, he saw the hand on the right arm of the injured player raise itself from the shoulder of one of his teammates and wave. This heroic gesture increased the cheer to a roar.

§

"Now hear this, now hear this. At eight zero one five this morning, a 4.5 ton device with the unprecedented force of 20,000 tons of TNT was dropped on the city of Hiroshima on the island of Honshu. Preliminary reports indicate that massive damage was inflicted on the target."

A roar of exultation explodes from every man of us on deck, from lieutenant commander to seaman. Someone claps me on the back, hard. Wheeling around, I look into the grinning blubbery face of Gallup, who hails from Frog Pond, Tennessee, and had once called me, not a damn Yankee, but a "Goddamn mother-fucking Yankee." Catherman, so fat he huffs and puffs and turns beet-red climbing a ladder, and Vincenti, the smallest and oldest inductee in the division, who shamelessly weeps every evening over his wife and daughter back in Perth Amboy, are jitterbugging together. Thompson and Zelinski, who, glutted with warm beer, had bloodied and battered the features of each other's face with their fists on the coral reef island named Mog Mog, Ulithi, during a three-hour liberty we'd been granted between Iwo Jima and Okinawa, are embracing like eleven-year-old girls. Cragg, who had never been out of Flat Rock, Alabama, before he'd been drafted, snatches off his white hat, flings it onto the deck, as if to say, I'm done with you forever, then, letting out a rebel whoop of jubilation, tramples it as he dances an impish jig.

Sounding like a grand pipe organ, the ship's horn blasts three short and one long peal of triumph. Body feeling light enough to fly, I let go a full-throated cry of joy and playfully poke Gallup, whom I loathe, in the ribs.

§

He recalled the controversy in 1995 over displaying the Enola Gay, named with what would be an oedipal pathos, were it not so bitterly ironic, for the mother of the pilot of the plane that had dropped the bomb, called Little Boy— litotes to beat all litotes—as part of the exhibition mounted by the Smithsonian Institution to commemorate the fiftieth anniversary of the destruction of Hiroshima. Above the mellow tones of the commentators when the cricket match was resumed in Melbourne, fifty-eight years after how many mothers and little boys had been incinerated and doomed and disfigured in the blink of an eye, he heard a jumble of voices in his head clamoring for his attention.

Still immersed in the *Guardian*, Alma seemed not to notice that he got up, crossed to his night stand, again picked up tablet and pen, and returned to his chair. He supposed she supposed he was still watching and listening to the match. Neither the images of the game nor the commentary on it distracted him. After many false starts, much crossing out and rewriting, he managed to sort out the voices he still was hearing.

I turned to a clinker that burned ten years
before consuming itself.

Still simmering, I have scoriae for fingers, a
blister where my left breast ought to be.

We, the lucky ones, flashed and burned out,
Roman candles, sparklers, Catherine wheels,
celebrating your Fourth of July a month and
two days late.

I, pilot of the weather plane that scouted the
skies over Hiroshima and gave the all clear to
the Enola Gay for letting Little Boy fall—beyond
forgiveness, denied rest, haunted, drifting, an outcast,
cashiered, committed, all those charred and radiant
bones lashed to my back, the lament of a ghostly
choir of a hundred thousand souls humming in my ear.

In unison we cry: bury the bird that dropped
the egg of fire. Exhibit us.

§

As the cricket players became no more than moving images on a screen, he knew his eye was losing interest in the match. Shame and remorse were carrying his mind back to his effort to contend with the accelerating guilt he' d felt while reading John Hersey's *Hiroshima* after returning from the war, anything but a conquering hero. He remembered telling himself that at that moment of spontaneous celebration he'd really had no way of comprehending the enormity of what had happened.

Besides, his own life, he'd been convinced then, had been at stake. He'd experienced the ferocity of the Japanese resistance, had witnessed the sinking of destroyers, the kamikaze attacks that had killed and burned and maimed his comrades-in-arms on carriers, cruisers and battleships. Reports of the cruelty of the Japanese military to those they'd conquered and of their barbarous treatment of prisoners of war he'd believed were more than propaganda churned out by the films he'd been exposed to, which heavy-handedly divided the globe into two worlds, the light and the dark, the good and the evil, the Allies and the Axis. Hadn't the Japanese allied themselves with Hitler and treacherously attacked Pearl Harbor?

In the "pony" editions of *Time*, which were passed from hand to hand, he'd read that the Japanese had held countless planes back from combat, had stockpiled ammunition along the entire coast of its home islands with an unbroken line of shore batteries, that a million ground troops, some battle-hardened, some fresh, as well as every able-bodied old man and boy, and thousands of women had dedicated themselves to fight to the death against the invasion of their homeland, scheduled to commence in November. The forces he was a part of were still depleted and exhausted from the battles of the Philippines, Iwo Jima and Okinawa.

According to *Time*, reliable intelligence estimated the number of casualties the American people were being prepared to expect ranged from hundreds of thousands to a million. Feeding in the luck he'd enjoyed so far, he'd calculated the odds on his survival were less than even. Any wonder he'd shouted with joy and clowned in exultation when he'd heard the flat-toned voice on the PA system announce that a device of unprecedented destructive power had been dropped on a Japanese city named Hiroshima?

§

He clicked off the TV and pushed himself out of his chair. From the corner of his eye he could see Alma looking up from the *Guardian*, toward him.

"I should get some pounds from the ATM. It's my turn. No need for two of us to go out. Finish the newspaper. Just don't tell me a word of what you've read."

Throwing her a quick glance, he saw that she was staring at him quizzically. Unused to practicing little deceptions on her, he lacked the touch to be successful.

"Okay. Though I hate to see you leave the cricket. I have enough cash."

"The truth," he winced inwardly as he uttered the word, "is I can't seem to get into the match. A walk will do me good." So pathetically feeble was his rejoinder that he felt a rush of gratitude for her consideration in ignoring it.

The sky was lowering, the air chill.

After withdrawing two hundred pounds from the ATM outside the bank, directly across from the inn, he started to saunter around the square. His feet carried him through the lychgate of the graveyard beside the parish church at the far end of the village. Immediately inside, on opposite sides of the slate path stood two war memorials, a gritstone obelisk for those who'd died in World War I, a lighter, perhaps limestone, slab for the dead of World War II. On both monoliths were two long columns of names.

So many from a single village cut off before their time, most in their prime. He couldn't estimate the sum he'd get by multiplying the number buried here by a like proportion from all the hamlets, villages, towns, and cities in all the homelands of those who had fought and been killed. And then he thought of the unnumbered who'd died unburied, those swallowed by the sea and those blown to debris or burned to ashes. To say nothing of the countless civilians.

A gray melancholy infiltrated his depression, mist thickening to fog. Beyond the demographic and moral lurked the cultural, anthropological and biological. How feeble the sunlight of civilization in such darkness, how cold and remote the moonlight of art, how rarefied the beams of saintliness! Had not a sudden rage at the silent conspiracy of avoidance, at the hypocrisy, pretense, and self-deception surged through him, he'd have had to weep his grief on the spot.

His feet, about to carry him along the slate path through the mass of gravestones of the village dead, centuries of them, were stopped by the thought of a possibility that darted into his brain as might a fragment of an exploding shell. Here he was, having reached a ripe old age by the merest of chances, sound of body and mind, with a loving and beloved wife, three children, and five grandchildren to carry on his seed, and he'd witnessed and played a part in the murder of the airmen whom, surrendering, he'd seen blown to bits, and in the death of the kamikaze pilot who, trying to kill him, had been obliterated by a five-inch shell. Although he couldn't do the calculus of years and chances, mathematically astronomical as such coincidence had to be, the age he'd approximated for Yuko Miyataka made it possible she could be the daughter of one of the two Japanese airmen. For that matter, she could even be the child of the kamikaze pilot he'd imagined as little more than a boy, who had got a young wife or girlfriend pregnant, perhaps deliberately, with her agreement, as a token of his love and a way to continue his bloodline, before taking off on his sacrificial though futile mission. What of the life none of the three had ever had? Here he was, alive to wonder.

Approaching the parish church, ancient enough, despite obvious extensive renovation, for him to make out traces of Norman architecture, he told himself that in this landscape of tombs and the stones of the past he was clouding his mind with morbidity. As he entered the edifice and slid into a pew near the narthex, an afternoon during a visit to this village in late summer of 2001 came breaking into his mind. Hemmed in by the architectural reminder surrounding him and held by the strength of the memory, he was trapped in a time of no time.

§

After torching the bed in our room in late afternoon, we stroll the village. We're still simmering, fingers locked, too wedded to separate. With a will of their own, feet take us into the graveyard of the parish church, then usher us through a portal. Damp as a bog inside. Sidling into a pew, we settle rib to rib, to prevent the gloom of the place from seeping between us. Still living in you, my seed will perish there.

Between two massive pillars, the Lady Chapel tells of generations who, laboring for Mary's sake, hewed, lugged, dressed, carved, and piled these stones in cruciform.

A sudden shaft from the sun illuminates the Virgin and Child in glass—sapphire, ruby, emerald, amethyst, gold. Inwardly I vow, two unbelievers, we'll make a sanctum, not of rock by faith, but of ourselves with love.

In the afterglow of passion, the radiance of the jewels of the Madonna obscures the blood that's stigmatized these stones.

A hundred years of carnage across the Channel. Henry's murderous lusts. His daughters' righteous slaughters. Harvests of opium, cotton and slaves. Gifts of Bibles and smallpox.

We breathe in silent harmony until the bells of evensong clang out of tune.

A few weeks later we're back in the U.S., just in time to reprise Babel on a screen. Watch the genius of engineered architecture, twin towers, which prove more vulnerable than caves, crumbling in slow motion. The height of civilization collapsing on itself. A cathedral of modernity settling into a tomb for melted flesh. The slow-motion picture confounds our brain, ties our tongue, and shrivels what we can only call the heart.

No more than it can consecrate those bones and ashes or resurrect the lives I've buried in you, can love make bombs fall skyward, guide missiles to open sea, keep kitchens from turning to ovens for roasting children, bedrooms to burial chambers for brides and grooms, mosques and synagogues and churches to morgues for corpses and dismembered parts of bodies.

There are no sanctuaries for the *sanctum sanctorum* of love.

§

The clang of the hour brought the present back. Gnawing on his soul was the ache of memory, a spurious relic, born during after-love in this Yorkshire church.

§

As they were finishing lunch in the dining room of the inn, he tendered a suggestion. No way Alma could know it was against his will, which was overpowered by the grotesque though improbable possibility that had struck him in the graveyard.

"What say we invite the Japanese schoolteacher to have dinner with us this evening? Tomorrow morning she'll be leaving to respect the graves of Charlotte and Emily Brontë." He hoped his echo of her quaint idiom conveyed a kinship he wished to feel, rather than any mockery.

"A lovely idea. Except for our after-dinner coffee with her, she's been alone."

"This time you do the inviting. Since it's for dinner. You know, more formal. And the Japanese have such a sense of propriety."

"You're a bit retrograde, as I suggested before. The fact is Yuko has been traveling without a male to escort or help her. And she's had to be in contact with many men. Besides, she's every bit as easy with you as with me."

"All true. Yet somehow I think she'd be more comfortable if a dinner invitation came from you."

"Meaning you'd be more comfortable."

Not much got past Alma. Though she couldn't possibly know the reason for his reluctance after he'd made the suggestion, she sensed some ambivalence in him.

"Oh, I really don't mind," she conceded in the face of his unyielding silence. "I suppose she's still in Cock's Wold, trying to find the grave of the fellow of infinite jest. See, I remember. Wonder where in Japan she comes from." "Using some clever discretion maybe you can find out." "Just idle curiosity. I really know so little about Japan." Japan. As they climbed the staircase and he moseyed down the hallway to their room behind Alma, the sound echoed in his head like a gong.

§

Alma was about to drive to Thyrsk with a woman of the village they'd come to know during their previous visits, to poke around in the secondhand bookshop. He'd begged off, pleading an incipient headache. More deception. Alma had sniffed that out too, though, again, not the reason.

"Come on, Dan, you know you never get headaches. They're all mine. Migraines. And I won't give a single one up to you. More likely your interest in the cricket match has been rekindled. Or maybe it's just that you prefer not to listen to a couple of jabbering women, the girl thing I haven't had with Yuko."

"You're as right as our government's intelligence is. I want to give you two dames the chance to hatch a conspiracy I'm not privy to. Better check Aurelia's automobile for bugs. I'd love to inform on you to MI6."

No sooner had she closed the door, after holding it open a crack to throw at him, "Ta-ta—hope the headache doesn't hit full force while you're watching cricket," than he sat down at the Queen Anne desk, a centennial piece, he was certain, on the inside wall of the room. On inn stationery he began to write. Struggling to find words, at first he seemed to have to squeeze them out of the tip of the ballpoint pen.

Slowly, so gradually he was only vaguely aware it was happening, the words started to flow. Then they were streaming out. In an effort to keep up with what he was reliving as if it were happening for the first time, his handwriting became scarcely legible. Gobs of language were pouring from his brain. As he went on at a breathless pace, his history became the words.

§

It's been three days since through binoculars I watched the launch flying the ensign of the Rising Sun pull alongside the *Missouri*, our sister ship. We were anchored so close I was able to see with my naked eye a corps of Japanese diplomats climb the ladder that had been dropped for them, march across the quarterdeck to where General Mac Arthur, Admiral Nimitz, and a cluster of army and navy brass stood waiting, and salute. Wearing swallowtail coats and top hats, the Japanese looked so much like a troop of clowns in mock full dress I could scarcely believe that they were the enemy, that I was witnessing a historical drama. As were all those on every ship anchored in Tokyo Bay, all our guns were loaded and primed, just in case. Pearl Harbor had proved that for the Japanese deceit was a cardinal virtue. Apparently they'd abandoned that *modus operandi* and were meekly surrendering.

As the ceremony proceeded, I imagined what lay ahead for the Japanese leaders. It would be no comedy. They'd strung themselves a necklace of atrocities, with which in the name of justice we, the victors, would choke them black.

Crammed with the liberty party I'm part of, one of the first to set foot on Japanese soil after the surrender, the landing craft makes for waterside Yokohama. As I scramble up the remains of a series of docks, I come on stacks of rifles, evidence of total capitulation. Ahead of me there is no city, only devastation and debris. The charred earth is pocked with craters in every direction. As I move away from the waterfront, I see that pieces of tin, wood and cardboard cover the larger craters.

Without the least idea of where I'm heading, I break off from a couple of shipmates and keep walking beyond what I conjecture is the ruin of the center of the city. I'm surprised that I'm only shocked, not afraid.

The few Japanese who appear veer off when they see me. It's silent as death. As I go on, the size and material of the debris lead me to believe I'm now passing through a residential section. Suddenly, close to my feet, a piece of tin slides. The skull of a skeleton rises from a crater. Brown wrapping paper covers the face of the skull. Rags hang on the bones.

I guess the ears on the skull have heard my footsteps in the silence of the upper world. Is this assemblage of bones living in that pit alone? I wonder. Might it be the head of a family of skeletons? Down there at this very instant might whatever of strength and breath is left be forsaking another such creature? Might it even be that the one I'm face to face with is inhabiting this grave-home with what already has become its own remains? Hot as the cloudless morning is, I shiver.

The creature confronting me casts the foreshortened shadow of a stickman. All at once I become aware its bony hand is extending a figurine to me, insistently. Hesitating, I make myself accept it, taking care not to touch the proffering claw. While I stand holding the figurine, two twiglike fingers form a V. It can't be Churchill's celebrated sign for victory, that's certain. The fingers touch, then move away from bloodless lips. Spreading its five fingers wide, the skeleton raises its other claw, like a policeman stopping traffic. The porcelain figurine feels cool.

I stare at it—a statue of a woman a few inches taller than my hand is long. She's wrapped in a midnight blue robe, with a hood that cowls her head, except for a thick braid of black hair curled on her brow. Gilt-edged and flowing in folds, the robe is brocaded with floral figures—red, orange, yellow, green, brown, all fringed with gold. Lustrous skin is exposed on her toes, peeping beneath the hem of the robe, on her wrists, around the left of which is a gold bracelet, on her hands and fingers, the right clasping a gold scroll, the left lying across her right palm, on her breast, upon which inside a deep décolletage hangs a gold necklace, and on her throat and face. Wing-shaped eyebrows and birdlike pupils are coal black. Consonant with the repose of the woman's hands is the otherworldly serenity in her face.

I'm astonished that a piece of porcelain should survive intact the bombing that has utterly destroyed a city. And I'm stunned that it's been thrust into my hands by hands emerging from a crater dug by a bomb dropped from a plane I may have tallied as it lifted off from, and, if lucky, destruction accomplished, landed back on the flight deck of one of the carriers my ship was protecting.

After gazing with rapt attention and, I hope, evident admiration, I shift my eyes to the eyes in the pits of the skull. They seem no more alive than the eyes of the porcelain woman. Uncertain what this skeleton, who is doubtless exhibiting a, perhaps *the* only, valuable he still possesses, is asking of me, I smile with all the good will I can project without words, then extend the figurine back to its owner. Instead of accepting it, he points his forefinger at his mouth, and, after returning the V-ed fingers to his lips, draws hard on an imagined cigarette and blows imagined smoke from puckered lips. Again he holds up the five fingers of his other hand.

"Now I get you," I mutter to myself, nodding to acknowledge I've caught on and at the same time shooting up three fingers of my left hand. Still the skeleton holds up five fingers. Tucking my thumb against my palm, I counter by showing him four fingers.

"Ho-geh," comes from the gray lips in a high-pitched voice, more a retch than a moan. I'm surprised this foreign apparition, my vanquished enemy, knows what those two syllables of English mean, can roughly approximate their sound, and has already learned the protocols of trafficking with the conquerors. The realization that what might well be a precious heirloom is being bartered for cigarettes suddenly hits me.

Bending over, I work three packs of Lucky Strikes out of the inside of my left sock, one from inside my right. All are sealed. I don't smoke. Following the lead of my shipmates, I've bought a carton of cigarettes at the canteen in the fantail and stowed inside my socks, for use as illegal tender, six packs, the limit the duty officer inspecting the liberty party of enlisted men mustered on the quarterdeck will pretend not to know I'm concealing. Looting and trading for booty are being winked at.

Hands that form a stone-like begging bowl receive eighty Lucky Strikes in exchange for the figurine. Seconds after the bony torso and skull have descended into their underworld home, the tin scrapes its way across the open top of the crater. As I wander on through the wasteland, feeling less guilt than I know I ought, I can't prevent myself from wondering about the value of my plunder in U.S. dollars.

Noticing some jagged remains of walls off in the distance, I steer myself toward them. It seems I'm on a lane through a suburb, heading out of the city. As I draw close, I can see the walls are yellow brick, unexpected in that to this point I've happened on no brick debris. Across from what's the shattered remains of this building of considerable size, stands a frame house, more like a cottage than a shanty. It looks intact. In front of it is a knee-high bamboo fence with a gate. Behind the fence, as though prisoners of war, five emaciated human beings, clearly parents and children, are lined up.

As I approach they don't retreat but stare at me silently. The father finally nods. Lifting the front of the jumper of my whites, I slip from the pocket of my bell-bottoms a thin bar of Hershey's milk chocolate, which, also bought at the ship's canteen, I've brought along as a pick-me-up. Over the fence I offer the candy to the father, who, bowing as he accepts it, hands it to the mother. Carefully she tears off the wrapper, breaking the bar into squares two at a time, and gives them to each of the three children. She holds onto the two left over. The way the children devour the chocolate makes me wish I had the power to turn one Hershey's bar into five thousand.

Bending again, I remove one of the two packs of Lucky Strikes that remain in my right sock and hand the cigarettes to the father, who accepts them with another bow. At that instant the terrible irony that resides in the brand name hits me. For three or four seconds I close my eyes, an involuntary expression of gratitude that the man I'm offering the "Luckies" to won't understand. Remembering that I've stowed a book of matches I carried off from the bar of a cocktail lounge named Lou Yee Chai's in Wakiki, when we'd been moored in Pearl Harbor for a few days on our way to the battle zone, I pull it from the pocket of my bell-bottoms. The matchbook had replaced a condom, which I'd used losing my virginity to a prostitute I'd picked up with the matches. She'd told me she was Japanese-Hawaiian.

Seeing the matches, the man breaks open the pack, pounds out a cigarette and offers it to me. When I shake my head, he tenders it to his wife, who also shakes her head. I strike a match, cup my hands over it, and carry the fire to the tip of the cigarette the man is holding between his lips. The formality being observed on both sides gives me the feeling I'm participating in a ceremony.

"I have much gratitude to you," the man says after exhaling a cloud of smoke. His voice is surprisingly deep for so small a body, his accent more British than American.

Astonished at hearing the man's words, I blurt out, "Do you speak English?"

"A little, badly."

"Your pronunciation is fine." Trying not to sound condescending while wondering whether the man would know the word "pronunciation," I translate my compliment. "You speak very well."

The man shakes his head and smiles between deep draws on his cigarette. When he hands the Lucky Strike pack back to me, I hold up my hand and say, "No, no. You please keep it."

The mother, I notice, gives the two remaining squares of the chocolate bar to the youngest, a girl of five or six.

I'm feeling ill at ease. Turning toward the city behind me, I sweep my eyes along the line where the rain meets the horizon. As I return to the man, I see his face in a cloud of smoke he's just exhaling.

"Very bad," I say. Trying to look and sound somber, sincere and apologetic, I slowly shake my head.

"Americans are so big," the man says quickly. He's no more than five feet three or four, very slight.

"I'm not one of the big ones. I'm five feet eight and a well-fed hundred and sixty pounds," I reply. "Is Yokohama a very large city?" It's an honest question in that all I know of the place we've destroyed is its name. While waiting for an answer, I realize that to be scrupulous I ought to have used the past tense.

"Well, yes," the man answers. "Very big city."

"Your home has not been damaged."

"Oh no. Very lucky." So he knows the word after all. But he couldn't possibly comprehend the ironic meaning of "strike." "Many times the bombs are falling near."

"That building across the road, it was large?" I spread my arms wide, then turn my palms in, as if trying to encompass it.

The man nods, blowing smoke.

"Made of bricks." I point to the closest section of the remains of a wall.

Again the man nods.

"Was it a factory?"

The man shakes his head.

"What was it?"

The man hesitates. Then with what seems to me to be obvious reluctance says, "This was school. There I teach students English. But I speak badly. I read more better."

"Was anyone inside? Were children killed when..." Coward that I am, I trail off.

"No, no. Children all gone." As I breathe a sigh of relief, he adds, "But many people killed "

"Who? What kind of people?"

The man draws hard on his cigarette, holds the smoke in his lungs for what seems minutes, then slowly lets it out. It's evident he's loath to go on. I try to encourage him by lifting my eyebrows inquisitively.

"Was hospital people. Sick from bombs and fires. Too, doctors and nurses."

"Why was the school..." I break off, realizing the question I've begun has an evident answer. "Because more hospitals were needed."

Slowly the man nods. "No more hospitals in Yokohama."

I become aware I'm biting my lip, uncertain whether to prevent myself from crying sorrow or shouting anger. I've no more chocolate to sweeten what can't be sweetened. The man's pinching the stub of his cigarette. Get out of here, I tell myself. As I'm about to say good-bye, the mother speaks to her husband. To me her hoarse voice seems to be chanting. When the man replies sharply, pointing to the ruin of the building, she raises her voice to a shout.

"Forgive, please. She is my wife and cannot know how is the war."

The woman begins to shriek. Her husband jerks up his free hand, palm close to her face. She stops as if her throat had been cut.

"What is she saying?"

The man throws down his cigarette butt, grinds it into the ground with his toe, and stares at it.

"Tell me, please, I want to know."

"She say I must say to you the bombs come during the sunlight. Three times. Many people die." Raising his eyes, he looks directly into mine.

Silence. I close my eyes and drop my head as in prayer, and something between a sigh and a soft whistle escapes me. A scream from the woman makes me open my eyes and snap up my head. As the man slowly nods his head, the woman stops screaming.

"She say I must tell very big red crosses were painted on the roof."

I reach down, extract the remaining pack of Lucky Strikes from my right sock and thrust it into the man's hand. Bowing again, he accepts it.

Without a good-bye I turn and start walking back down the lane, then strike out across the pitted and debris-strewn landscape that had been Yokohama, in the direction I think will lead me to the waterfront. I keep altering my course and twice I have to backtrack. There are no vertical landmarks.

While waiting on the shattered dock for the arrival of the landing craft that will ferry the congregating liberty party back to our ship, I survey the devastation along the coastline. I can identify nothing intact enough to serve as functioning shore batteries or antiaircraft installations. Between us and the armada anchored in the bay, a dozen or so battered and burned warships, some capsized, some half-submerged, remind me of the wrecks of eight battleships and some smaller vessels I'd seen when we lay moored in Pearl Harbor.

All at once a brawny bosun's mate grabs a rifle from the top of a stack and slings it over his shoulder by its leather strap.

" 'Tain't loot. No way. Just a souvenir for my boys back home," he drawls in a deep-South voice. "What the fuck, we beat the shit out of the little bastards, didn't we?"

Shoving and pushing hands commence grabbing rifles that are theirs by the ancient right of conquest and sling them over their shoulders. I edge my way in, seize one, and yank it out. It's heavy, a good twelve pounds, I judge, and looks as if its kick would dislocate your shoulder. Certain it's antiquated compared to the nine-pound Garands the marines aboard ship carry, I guess it's modeled on the German Mauser of World War I vintage.

Burdened with what I've plundered, an obsolescent rifle slung over my left shoulder and a porcelain figurine clutched in my left hand, I shuffle into the landing craft, which ferries me across the bay on what appears to be much the same course that carried the Japanese diplomats to sign the document of their surrender. After climbing the ladder affixed to the hull of my ship, I report myself back aboard. The duty officer on the quarterdeck looks the other way as he returns my sloppy salute.

§

After reliving his "liberty" (the grotesquerie of the unintentional irony of military nomenclature!) in what had been the city of Yokohama, he felt as though he'd walked across the desolate surface of the moon. Or through the vestibule of Hell.

§

When they entered the bar for their before-dinner cocktails, Yuko Miyataka was sitting alone in the inglenook, drinking whatever she'd ordered from the bartender. She looked to be perfectly comfortable with the procedures of the inn. Alma immediately went up to her while he requested two martinis.

"She'd be pleased to," Alma reported as she sat down across the low table from him. "Really, Dan, she's a very sociable person. With poise and self-assurance. You wouldn't have discomposed her, I'm sure."

Contrary to their custom of sipping, he gulped down his martini. Ordered another, for both of them. When he'd finished his second, Alma's was standing on the table beside her still unfinished first drink.

"Alma, what say we have a third this evening?" Occasionally they did what they knew was imprudent—certain to increase his insomnia and leave both of them hung over the next morning. Usually there was a celebratory pretext. Or one of them was feeling depressed. The amount of gin they'd indulge in to elevate their spirits, he well knew, would depress him hours later.

"You have the blahs?"

"Not at all." He wasn't lying, just being deceptive. Again. With Alma. What he did have was quite different and far worse than the blahs. "We're here on a lark to avoid, aren't we? Seems to me to justify a bit of self-indulgence. Since now we know the worst, we might as well live it up."

"You're right. It's worse to be a hypocrite than own up to opting out, going fugitive."

"Would you mind ordering? I want to run back up to the room and change shirts," he explained. This was an outright lie. At the sound of the word "fugitive" he'd winced inwardly. That Alma wasn't aware of the immense difference between the context and significance that prompted her to use the word *hypocrite* and the place where and the force with which it hit him, made him feel cowardly as well as hypocritical. "There's a tab inside the back of the collar of this shirt that's rubbing my neck and annoying the hell out of me. Give me a few minutes. Why not sit with Yuko Miyataka and I'll join you in the dining room? We can drink the third martini at our table. Order soup and fish of the day for me."

To his ear the excuse he'd invented carried little plausibility. Even over a seeming trifle Alma gave him all the ground he asked for.

Once he'd turned the corner of the barroom, he hurried to the stairwell, ascended two steps at a time, and raced down the hallway to their bedroom. Unbuckling his briefcase, he drew out a sheaf of graying pulpy sheets. He hadn't let Alma know that, compelled as he'd recently become to revisit his life during World War n, before they'd taken off for Yorkshire he'd crawled into the eaves of their home and removed the seven-page history of the ship he'd served on, from the bottom drawer of a mahogany sea chest that had been in his father's family for generations.

The document was entitled

DEPARTMENT OF THE NAVY, OFFICE OF NAVAL RECORDS AND HISTORY, SHIPS' HISTORIES BRANCH

Stenciled 28 March 1949, it had been compiled and signed by one Howard Sigler, Officer in Charge, Journalist, USN. Driven by an urgency to read again— the first and only time had been more than half a century ago, when he'd begun to write, then had quickly given up on, a novel tentatively entitled "The Battle for the Sea of Peace"—a factual account of what he'd participated in, he'd marked passages and underlined sentences. Although rereading had done nothing for his peace of mind, he'd stashed the mimeographed typescript in his briefcase the morning they'd left home, for... he really didn't know why.

Thumbing through to locate his markings, he stopped in the middle of the last paragraph on page four.

Operations were resumed on 8 June with a final assault on Kyushu, but *Japanese air strength was so depleted that only 29 planes were located and destroyed.*

He flipped the page. His eye jumped to the second paragraph.

Admiral Halsey's Third Fleet carrier forces, *now the greatest mass of sea power ever assembled, steamed northward on 1 July to wage a tremendous pre-invasion campaign of destruction against every Japanese facility which could be used for prolonging the war.... No attempt was made to conceal the location of the fleet. On the 15th we participated in the bombardment of Muroranu Hokaido,* wrecking steel mills and oil facilities in the city. On the 17th, our *sixteen-inch guns blasted the Hitachi Mito area on the Honshu coast, northeast of Tokyo.* In this bombardment British battleships joined those of our fleet, *all units shelling the Japanese homeland at will without opposition.*

The underscored passage ended with

The Yokosuka Naval Base in Tokyo Bay received the carrier planes' attention [a chilling euphemism, he thought] next day and *one of two remaining Jap battleships, NAGATO, was placed out of action.* On 24 and 25 July the Inland Sea area between the main islands of Honshu, Kyushu and Shikoku was visited with special attention to the Kure Naval Base, where six major fleet units were badly damaged and 258,000 tons of naval shipping were either sunk or put out of action. *This was the end of Japanese sea power.*

Up from somewhere in his brain leaped the fact that the destroyer *Callaghan*, the last ship to be sunk by a kamikaze, was hit during the night of July 28, nine days before Little Boy was dropped on Hiroshima. Perhaps this perversely celebratory event had been niched in his memory because *that* July the 28th was his twentieth birthday.

Dropping the pages, he sat with his head in his hands. In his mind he added to the resume of what he'd been part of, the unimaginable death and destruction dealt to Japanese military personnel and facilities, factories, and cities, with their civilian population, by B-29's, to say nothing of the losses in air and at sea, including planes and airmen suicidally gone.

With their navy and air force destroyed, he asked himself, would a fleet of fishing boats have stood off "the greatest mass of sea power ever assembled," as it bombarded the coast of Japan in preparation for the massive invasion the Japanese knew was coming? Or would the shark-cleaned bones of drowned sailors have grown new flesh, repaired the blasted and burned-out wrecks of their ships lying on the sea bottom and brought them up from the deep to drive off the attacking naval and air forces?

Would the Japanese pilots, five thousand of whom were kamikazes, whose ashes and body parts were scattered, have reassembled and resurrected themselves to re-commit suicide by diving into U.S. naval units? Or, with the supply of able-bodied young men almost depleted, would willing and able young women have climbed into the cockpits of planes that had reconstructed themselves from their own debris and as dedicated kamikazes have wreaked havoc on the naval forces supporting the invasion? Who in what planes would have intercepted and destroyed flock after flock of our fighters and bombers?

Would the millions of corpses rotting in jungles and caves and those devoured by raptors on beaches of the islands that dot the Pacific have come back to life and joined the reported million ground troops and the vast home guard and the hordes composed of civilians, like the skeleton and the little teacher of English, who had survived the bombings of their homes, schools, hospitals, and factories, and armed with the World War I vintage rifles stacked on the battered docks of Yokohama, have driven off the amphibious legions spewed from LST's, LCT's, LCI's, and LSM's, bearing Garands, Browning automatic rifles, and grenades, supported by field guns, howitzers, mortars, armored personnel carriers, and tanks, that were invading their homeland?

Would the untold dead in Yokohama, where his own eyes had witnessed the utter devastation, in Muroran and Mito, whose destruction he'd participated in, to say nothing of Tokyo and Kobe, Osaka, Nagoya, and Sapporo, have produced the necessary armaments and munitions? Were these the components of the mighty fearsome force that would have taken the life of an American soldier, sailor, airman, or marine for every foot of Japanese soil they fought over? Perhaps the Divine Wind, with an unimaginably exponential strength of the typhoons his ship had gone through, would have blasted the attacking planes out of the sky, swamped the approaching naval force, drowning every last man of the invaders, while sparing the sacred soil of those who had summoned it.

Such was the "reality" the military had projected, a reality that compelled and justified the dropping of the first weapon of mass destruction ever used. And the only, except for the second.

With trembling hands, he returned the document to his briefcase. Despite his urge to hurry in order to account for the length of time he'd been gone, he shambled into the dining room where his third martini was waiting for him. As was his wife.

§

And Yuko Miyataka, who was sitting at their table chatting with Alma. A glass with a couple of fingers of red wine stood in front of her. Untouched martinis were at Alma's place and his.

"Welcome to the gentleman," Yuko Miyataka said, bowing over the table as he sat down across from her.

"Sorry to take so long," he muttered. Then, giving no ear to the conversation in progress, he began slugging down his third martini. Neither woman seemed to care about, or even notice, his aloofness, as he carried on the dialogue with himself.

Oh, the hoax of history! For two generations the myth had persisted, until it had become fact in the mind and conscience of a nation. Reliving at this late date what his eyes had seen, his ears had heard, his hand had done exposed the grand lie. It also had compelled a self-judgment. And now that guilt had been confirmed, finally and convincingly, wasn't he therefore bound, like Dante's sinners, to administer his own punishment? Interfused with that still-living past, doubling its horror, was the abomination of the ongoing present, which was blighting what was left of his life.

It *was* between himself and himself. He wouldn't declare it, even to Alma. Like what lurked behind the black veil of Hawthorne's minister, it was a scene from his life over which a curtain was drawn, concealing complicity, cowardice, shame, and guilt. Was extending his silence all the way to his wife meant to protect and prevent her, a citizen who'd lived through World War II, from having to face a monstrosity? An easy rationalization. What then was inhibiting him from confiding in and confessing to her he couldn't articulate, except to acknowledge it was everything he despised. He could smell its rottenness, taste it.

And what of the obligation he had to the world at large, to future generations, to the misguided and naive, and especially to those victims and their descendants who were still alive, one of whom might well be Yuko Miyataka? He couldn't take it on. He was no polemicist, not a trained historian, even though in his head he was correcting and rewriting history. Was just a second-rate writer of fiction. And his story was fact, not fiction. So with his responsibility unmet, he'd have to bear the burden of his knowledge. Himself death's spy and messenger, his conscience unclean, what gave him the right to indict those, some unwittingly, some cynically aware, who were creating a new myth to serve as the history that would justify the devastation of their declared enemies, the slaughter of the innocent, the corruption of the humanity of their own people by dropping bombs and firing missiles of mass destruction?

The loop of the rope on the load he'd have to carry was slung around his neck. The knot might still be tightened.

§

"So, how did you like Cock's Wold?" he began when a gap in the women's conversation invited him to enter.

"Well, very beautiful village. All stones are light, the color of honey, I read in the guide's book."

"Is it the size of this village?"

"Oh no. So little, no shops. Just pub and houses with gardens. Very beautiful flowers. And the church. Eight sides to its tower. An octave

"And did you find the grave you went to visit?" Alma put in.

"Oh sure." Yuko Miyataka flashed her smile. "Not big like Scarborough graveyards. Laurence Sterne has grave close against church wall. With much writing on it. Some too hard for me. He was the rectum there, I respected his grave."

"So Sterne was a clergyman?" Alma half-asked, unfazed by Yuko Miyataka's malapropism

"Oh yes. But I read in the biography the people in the church will turn backs to him when he preaches the sermons sometimes."

"How strange! I wonder why. Did you know that, Dan?"

"No. But I do know *Tristram Shandy* is seriously comic. An anti-novel long before there was such a thing."

Yuko Miyataka clapped her chubby little hands and trilled a laugh. "This gentleman is the scholar."

"Afraid not. Just a hack writer." At Rutgers he'd completed all the course work and passed his generals for a Ph.D. but had never finished his dissertation on Jonathan Edwards' influence on the American Renaissance.

"Hack writer? What is hack? Some kind of writing?"

"Yes, bad writing."

As if her right hand were a fan, Yuko Miyataka touched the tips of all five fingers to her lips, then giggled. "Pornographies?"

"Worse than that. Hack writing is writing no one will buy." He laughed in a way that would let Alma know he wasn't spewing bitterness, just being drolly realistic.

When Yuko Miyataka shook her head, he couldn't decide whether she was indicating she didn't understand or was suggesting he was being modest.

"I know too that Sterne's novel is bawdy. 'Bawdy' means it's pornographic *and* literary. Which makes it okay. Maybe because he was living in the rectumry while writing it, his parishioners turned their backs on him after they'd read it."

How much of his playfulness was going past Yuko Miyataka he couldn't tell. At least he was letting Alma know he was trying to be agreeable and entertaining. But he wasn't getting on with "it" and time was running out.

They'd had their starter, a crab bisque, and were eating their entrees. Having downed his third martini, he was keeping all three wine glasses filled with a Medoc, which Alma said had been recommended by the headwaiter, who also served as sommelier.

"Please charge everything to my account," he whispered, while Alma was explaining to Yuko that "bawdy" didn't really mean pornographic.

Well aware of the looming hours of sleeplessness and depression, he felt energized at the moment by a welcome buzz.

With Sterne exhausted, Alma had kept things going by throwing questions at Yuko Miyataka about the Brontës. While trying to come up with a verbal primer for starting Yuko Miyataka to pump out what he was driven to have her reveal, he withdrew. All at once she provided him with the handle.

"Has the gentleman ever been to Japan?" As she asked she cocked her head, almost coyly.

"No," he answered without hesitation. Glancing at Alma, he saw she was staring at him for responding to an inconsequential question with another lie that seemed pointless. She knew how come the figurine stood on a shelf in his studio and a Japanese rifle was stored with old furniture in the eaves of their home in a village in Pennsylvania. To allay her fear that he might have sounded abrupt with Yuko Miyataka, he quickly went on. "Do you live in Tokyo?"

"Oh yes. The college which in I am teaching locates itself in Tokyo."

"Have you always lived in that city?" He was trying to make his tone casual, his manner congenial.

"Oh no. Before, I have gone to study in the University of Tokyo. Not the same which I teach. This is very much smaller, with lesser importance. All students are girls. A Christian college."

"Where were you before you went to the University of Tokyo?" He feared he was beginning to sound like a prosecuting attorney, but now that he'd started he couldn't stop himself. "Where did you grow up? Where were you born?"

"In a city on the island of Honshu. Born and grow up."

"Near Tokyo?"

"Well, it takes the speed train one half hour. Fifty kilometers distance."

"Is it inland, west of Tokyo?"

"Oh no. Direction north. Near to the sea."

"What is the name of the city?" It was if he had her under oath.

"If you have not been the visitor of Japan you would never hear it. It is not very famous. Name of Mito."

He was stunned. Stunned silent. After what seemed minutes, Alma moved things along, innocently staying on the same track.

"Is Mito a very large city, Yuko?"

"A little large but not very. Not like London. Maybe I will say size like York, where I left from train to take the bus to here. Mito could have a little more people."

"Have you been teaching for a long time, many years?" As he took over again, he hoped he was coming off as nothing more than a boorish male, not the Grand Inquisitor putting words in her mouth.

"Well, I would say... thirty years. After seven more years I am retired."

"You must have been very young when you began."

"Oh, not very. You see, I married when a young girl. Then too soon my husband died. So at that time I left Mito and have gone to the University of Tokyo. Not many women then."

He knew he ought to slow down and seem less pointedly intense. To ask what her husband had died of would never do. So on sped his brain, recklessly improvising, single-minded as he was.

"I have a friend who was a visiting scholar at the University of Tokyo. In 1966 and '67, I'm quite sure it was. His field was the English novel. Might you have been one of his students? His name was Clayborn Weeks. Does Professor Clayborn Weeks sound at all familiar to you?"

Stealing a quick look at Alma, he saw that again her eyes were fixed on him in wonder. Had she been less self-possessed her mouth would have been hanging open. Clay Weeks was their slightly retarded handyman, who had no more visited Japan than he'd read *Tristram Shandy*.

"Oh no, I regret I must say. You see, I received my graduating degree when I was older student. Twenty-seven years. No Professor Weeks. Then I started to teach."

The gin and wine forced him to calculate with slow deliberateness, as if his mind were a slate and he was chalking numbers on it. She'd begun teaching when she was twenty-seven. She'd been teaching thirty years. So now she was fifty-seven. It was 2003. Two thousand and three minus fifty-seven equaled 1946, the year of her birth. In Mito. Which his ship had been bombarding on July 17, 1945. Beneath the table, he flicked out all his fingers except his left thumb. Nine. Nine months from July 1945 to April 1946.

"I am sorry to hear that your husband died so young," Alma said just as he'd finished his calculation, and she reached over and patted Yuko Miyataka's left wrist, which was lying on the table. So obsessed was he now that when the glint of a diamond on the middle finger of Yuko Miyataka's right hand caught his eye, he thrust Alma's expression of sympathy aside.

"I've been admiring your ring." Another lie. "Is it your birthstone?"

"The gentleman is very kind. It is a ring my mother has given me at her death. What is 'birthstone'?"

Yuko Miyataka's curiosity was an unwitting ally.

"A birthstone is a gem, a precious stone," Alma explained, providing him an opportunity to let up without allowing the conversation to veer off course. "A diamond is one. An emerald, which is green, is another. Whichever month you were born in, the stone connected with that month becomes what we call your birthstone. Many people wear rings with their birthstones in them."

"My birthstone, for example, is a sapphire, which is blue." He hoped uttering still another lie would encourage Yuko Miyataka to reveal what he was after. He kept himself from glancing at Alma. Yuko Miyataka failed to respond. But Alma, who couldn't possibly fathom why what would appear to be small talk was making him so compulsive, came to his rescue.

"If you happened to be born in April, Yuko, your mother's ring would also be your birthstone. The stone for April is a diamond."

Yuko Miyataka clapped her hands and trilled her little laugh. "Oh yes. It is so. April is the month for my birth. Now I will always remember the birthstone I have." She punctuated her delight with a nod, then held up her ring and touched it with her lips.

"That is a happy coincidence!" Paying no heed to the fact that Yuko Miyataka might not be able to grasp a spoken English word of four syllables, he heard himself shouting confirmation. And he couldn't stop his tongue from uttering more lies, necessary lies.

"Alma and I have a coincidence also—of birthdays. We were born in different months and years. To look at her you would have to believe she is at least ten years younger than I. But I am certain she will not be displeased that I tell you—will you, Alma, my beautifully preserved wife—people cannot believe she is only three years younger than I am. The coincidence is that we were born on the same day of the month. So we can have a double celebration each seventeenth of July, her birthday, and of September, mine. She is ruby, I am sapphire. Might your birthday be the same—the seventeenth of April? That would make a triple coincidence."

Not only was he fabricating, he was spouting nonsense, when cleverness and adroitness were called for, at a speed that gave Alma no opportunity to interrupt with a humorous correction of more lies she didn't know the reason for. He never forgot her birthday, the fourth of February, she his, July twenty-eighth. Although he did know the birthstone for July was ruby, he had no idea what the stone for February was, let alone September.

"Oh no. In Japan, you see, all persons celebrate birthday on the day of the New Year, a great holiday. For month and day we do not care. All birthdays come on one same day."

"But if by chance," he persisted, "you happened to be born on the seventeenth of April, Alma and I could include you in our minds when we celebrate our birthdays. We would be remembering you."

Again Yuko Miyataka made no reply, either because she failed to understand what he was trying to say or she found it absurd.

"What Dan means, Yuko, is that if you happened to be born on the seventeenth of April, that would remind us of the pleasure we've had with you here. Do you know which day of the month you were born on, Yuko?"

While blessing Alma for her help, he couldn't imagine why she was going along with what to her had to be a ridiculous direction for mere table talk.

Yuko Miyataka looked down at her nearly empty plate, as if studying it. At first he thought she was feigning pensiveness, either to be polite or to seem to be playing along with a game she couldn't understand. Then he wondered whether she might be straining to remember a fact that had no significance for her, or perhaps be calculating in order to come up with the day and month of her birth. He'd eaten all he could, not much more than half of the Dover sole on his plate, and was squeezing his hands, their fingers interlocked, beneath the table.

"Oh no," Yuko Miyataka finally sighed. "You cannot celebrate me with you. Twenty-one of April is my born day."

Nine months and four days after he'd spent an anxious night on watch, waiting for return fire from Japanese shore batteries or whatever naval units might be within range, or for a dreaded kamikaze to plunge into the battleship he was on as for hours it bombarded Mito with sixteen-inch shells, each weighing more than a ton. *There* Yuko Miyataka had been brought into this hellish world. That night no answering fire or planes had come.

He took a large gulp of wine. Feeling tears that swelled in his eyes about to spill over and stream down his cheeks, he feigned a spasm of coughing. While pretending to be catching an explosion of germs that might contaminate Yuko Miyataka, his wife, diners at neighboring tables, he managed to dab his eyes as he covered his mouth with his napkin. A coincidence, far more remote and wrenching than any of the improbable notions he'd begun broodingly entertaining not long after he'd laid eyes on Yuko Miyataka in the inglenook of the bar, was proving to be history.

He might take it as the final judgment, judgment with a vengeance. This middle-aged Japanese schoolteacher, sitting at table with him and his wife in the dining room of an inn in a pastoral village in Yorkshire, must have been conceived close to or at the very time his ship had been bombarding the city her parents were living in. If it had been on that terrible night, when could they have made love, she being the love they'd made? Most likely it had to have been before the first shell had hit. Had it been after, how could they have had the heart? As for during the shelling, inconceivable as it might seem, it was not outside the realm of possibility that while the world the parents lived in was being destroyed and their lives were a hostage to each moment of chance, an egg of fear in the mother was receiving a spurt of woe from the father, and Yuko Miyataka had begun to be. And it could well have happened that at the instant her father had projected his gush of love into the womb of her mother, where its fate was to hit and unite with the target it sought, a shell fired from his American battleship would have blown the lovers to gobs of flesh, shards of bone, splatters of blood, ending the life of Yuko Miyataka before it had begun.

Was there ever a more bitterly ironic drama, not in a play on a stage or in words on paper, but in life? And to think, the Enola Gay had been waiting in the wings.

After he'd won a brisk but polite skirmish about paying Yuko Miyataka's share of the bill, Alma said brightly, "Let's finish our last supper by having coffee and tea in the lounge."

Given that Yuko Miyataka taught in a Christian college, he thought it possible she might catch Alma's allusion.

"Afraid I must ask you to excuse me. Something I've eaten seems not to be agreeing with me." Hearing still another improbable pretext issue from her husband's lips within six hours would let Alma know he wasn't expecting her to believe it. "But don't let me break up the party. You two have your after-dinner coffee and tea together."

Alma, who, he suddenly noticed, had not drunk a measurable amount of her third martini, raised her eyebrows and shook her head just enough to be sure he saw it Actually, however, not the whole truth and nothing but the truth, but a metaphorical truth was embedded in what she took for total falsification. Although the full force of three martinis and more than a third of a bottle of wine wouldn't hit him until he'd be lying awake in the small hours of the morning, he was experiencing an ache, an ache of sorrow. And afflicting him still more fiercely than his mythical headache earlier in the day or his supposed present indigestion was the pain of rage.

Neither the sorrow nor rage was located only in his head or stomach. Commingled, they surged through every part of him—flesh, bone, blood, brain, heart, lungs, stomach, bowels, liver, balls, prick, all of which as one we call the self. Had he also a soul to add to the catalog?

Nor were the ache and pain brought on by the constriction of arteries, a reflux of acid, inflammation, or a pinched nerve. The pathology, rather, was anguish, the anguish of discovering what he'd brought himself to believe was Yuko Miyataka's history, as well as of unwriting, then rewriting history, his history and, he was convinced, while it never would be acknowledged in his lifetime, the true history of the final phase of the war against Japan. In the document he possessed, compiled and distributed by the Department of the Navy, as well as what he himself had seen and done, these interwoven histories had their sanction. What had provided the impetus for his sorrow and fueled the rage that had driven his search and anguished rewriting was that, even while the pain and slaughter and destruction on a massive scale were being perpetrated again, a history that was a fraud was being written and believed. He wouldn't be here to rewrite that.

"So sorry the gentleman is having the disagreeable digestion," said Yuko Miyataka, as they paused in the hallway outside the lounge.

"I suppose you will be leaving on the early bus to York. On your way to pay your respect to the Brontës. I am certain you must know that their father was also a rectum." He used the malapropism not for the fun of it, but to cement the unbreakable though unacknowledged bond that would join him to Yuko Miyataka for life.

"Oh yes. The revered Patrick Brontë. Bus will come at seven o'clock. Sharp." The last word demonstrated her growing proficiency in *l'usage du monde*.

"You two must say your good-byes," Alma put in.

"Well, I thank you too much... Dan." The sweetest of smiles appeared on Yuko Miyataka's homely face. He was no longer "the gentleman."

Only half realizing what he was about, he took a step forward, threw his arms around her, and pressed her to him. Her head was on his chest, ear to his heart, as if she were listening to its beat. Yet he could feel her body stiffen.

As he freed her, she stepped back. Dismissing her resistance, he leaned toward her, bowing, and kissed her forehead. Even had her skin been parchment, his lips been coated with ink that was not subject to the fading of time, it wouldn't have been enough, would have been far far from enough.

Before any of the three could utter another word, he turned and went slouching toward the staircase. He hadn't let his eyes meet Yuko's.

THE NOVICE

As that Christmas season approached, I was still struggling to climb out of the black hole I'd been in since I'd been discharged from the Navy and had returned home. My parents had no idea why I didn't go on to college and why I declined to pal around with my old friends. My mother, though, I was quite sure, wasn't sorry I was unable to strike up a conversation with one of the two sisters whose family had moved into a house just beyond ours while I was in the Pacific, finishing off Japan. In their late teens or early twenties, both were appealingly pretty.

I knew I wanted to go to college, which, thanks to the G. I. Bill of Rights, I'd be able to do without taking money from my father. I knew I wanted to get together with the boys, now young men—all but two of us had survived the war—with whom I'd played baseball, football and basketball and gone on double dates. I knew I wanted to make a move on either of the two pretty sisters. In short, I knew I wanted to repair the broken line of my life and with it, pull myself out of the pit I was in.

But I couldn't. Instead, I kept to my father's house as though I were a Trappist in a monastery. I read, not books about the war I'd recently been a part of, which I couldn't face, but exclusively fiction, especially Russian novels, the longer the better. In between I listened to old 78 RPM Bakelite records on the wind-up rosewood Victrola that still stood in our parlor. And to help consume more of the empty time in which I skulked, paralyzed, I read the daily and Sunday newspapers front to back. Fully aware I was regressing to the preadolescent boy I'd been before going into the Navy, I couldn't help it.

I *did* know why I was unable to do what I wanted to, why I was incapacitated, why I was hiding out at home like someone on the lam, to shift the simile from the severely religious to the guilt-ridden criminal. You'll come to understand too, if you go on reading this piece.

It wasn't the urging of my parents that I make something of myself by going to college that finally ended my self-imprisonment. This I assented to without acting on. Nor was it telephone calls from old friends proposing that we get together. About this I expressed a feigned enthusiasm, without having any intention of reuniting. Nor was it the sidelong but not-to-be-doubted smiles from the prettier of the two sisters

I would occasionally pass when she returned, from work, I assumed, as I was walking to the nearby trolley line, out of boredom and for a bit of exercise. I'd wait for my father's arrival at the stop two blocks from the street our houses stood on. He'd be returning from the arsenal, where he was still working, even though the war was over. Complying with gas rationing and his own necessary thrift, my father never drove our old Studebaker to work. He'd be carrying the daily newspaper, rolled up and tucked in his armpit like a giant thermometer taking his temperature. None of these served to get me moving back into the larger world.

Rather it was a squib on the last page of the newspaper that caught my eye one evening. It announced that the U. S. Postal Service would be hiring returned veterans to serve as temporary deliverers during the holiday season. With hundreds of thousands of soldiers, sailors and marines back home, celebrating victory, as well as Christmas, the amount of domestic mail would be record-breaking. My motivation for signing on was in no way festive. It was purely pecuniary. I forced myself to face the fact that the twenty dollars a week which, without my father's knowing it, I was slipping to my mother, who quietly accepted it, would soon exhaust the fund I'd accumulated from what I'd saved of the scant pay I'd received for my service in the Navy. What I'd earn during three weeks of December, I calculated, would allow me to continue providing the small amount I thought of as covering my room and board for another six months. And all I'd have to do would be put mail in slots or boxes, I told myself.

On the afternoon of the thirtieth of November, I was hired to begin delivering mail from our local post office on Monday, December 1. Each veteran was assigned to a regular mailman. "Call me Mitch," was the way my carrier introduced himself to me that morning as he squeezed the hand I offered in response to the extension of his. He had a bone-crushing grip. What his given name was I never learned. Mitch, I assumed, was clipped from the surname Mitchell. The voice in which he communicated whatever instruction, advice, greeting, or good-bye he offered had the texture of the foghorn on the battleship I'd been aboard. But what he had to say was always punctuated with a hearty laugh. Even in the ear-and-nose-nipping wind and bone-chilling cold of gray December mornings, he exuded cheer.

Mitch had been around for quite a while. Even physically he was quite a contrast to my gentle and reserved father, whose long narrow face was shaped like and smooth as a crescent moon. Although my father's thinning hair had turned silver during my absence, his eyebrows were still blond. Under a lumpy bald head, with a ragged fringe of gray hair, Mitch's face was blubbery round, with purple cheeks. Also purple, his knob of a nose was covered with tiny holes that made it look as if it had been used as a target on a dart board. Beneath shaggy black eyebrows, behind lenses the thickness of those of the binoculars I'd used to spot planes for our gunners to shoot down, the pupils of his eyes looked like agate marbles. The irises were red-veined. Without appearing athletic, because of a potato-sack belly that lapped over the belt on his gray postal service trousers, Mitch looked to be strong as a Clydesdale.

On a street map tacked to the wall behind the swivel chair at the kneehole of his battered desk, Mitch's route was marked in faded purple ink. "Nothin to it, kid," he assured me after tracing the part of the route he was assigning to me. The stubby forefinger of his right hand was so short and plump it looked as if a joint had been chopped off and the end sewn up. "Yuh jus stash the packets the boys here ready in order inside the pouches of yur bag. The house numbers'll be scrawled on a slip of paper under the rubber band. If thur's anything people hand yuh to be mailed or thur's anything in thur box to mail, see that yuh stick it in outgoin when yuh get back here. Some a the dames might hear yuh comin and show up in thur nightgown, so don't act surprised or take it as somethin that's special juss fur you." As he growled a laugh, he jabbed me in the ribs with his elbow.

Winking his right eye at me, he clapped me on the back, so hard I staggered forward, weighed down by the leather bag I'd hoisted onto my left shoulder. Not once in the weeks I was assisting Mitch was he anything but jolly and helpful to the "kid." After the Navy, in which I, as a petty officer, was taking curt commands from chiefs, ensigns, lieutenants, and occasionally commanders, once even an admiral, and was having to give orders to seamen old enough to be my father, who understandably expressed their resentment by ornamenting their responses to me with such epithets as "son of a bitch," "bastard," and a certain male body part, I found Mitch to be a genial guardian angel. So warm was he under his rough exterior that daily contact with him kept me from minding the freezing weather outside and the load of the leather bag I had to lug.

Our branch post office was situated in a section of the city that had once been the home of the relatively well-off white-collar middle class. Now the rows of brick houses were occupied by working class people. I had been born in one of these houses, as had my father. Our family fortunes had declined since my grandfather's time. My father had been "contributing to the war effort," while earning a barely sufficient wage to keep my mother and himself modestly comfortable, by working on the other side of the city in an arsenal, where shell casings were being manufactured. As I'd seen our guns spewing out twenty and forty millimeter shells at Japanese fighters, torpedo planes, bombers, and kamikazes, and from five-inch guns at military installations, ships, and fishing craft, and from our sixteen-inch batteries at cities the Japanese could no longer protect, I often wondered whether the casings holding the deadly powder had passed under my father's certifying eye. "You and your father are in this war together," my mother once proudly wrote to me when, unknown to her, we were in the throes of the battle for Iwo Jima.

Just as Mitch and I were to go our separate ways on that first morning I was on the job, he thumped me on the back and growled, "If thur's anybody there waitin for thur mail, give em a big smile and sing out 'good mornin,'" for which two words he changed his range and tone to a surprisingly sweet tenor. He accented the 'good' hard. "Make 'um feel yur not bringin um bills to pay or bad reports from thur doctor, but Christmas cards from old friends or a piece a good news thur not expectin. And somethin else I should uv told yuh, kid. When yuh come to St. Maggie's, don't stuff the mail in the big box they got out on the stoop. Ring the bell and one of the novices'll come to the door and take the bundle from yuh. The holy sisters like to get a little touch of the outside world, I guess, even if it's juss us bringin um a Christmas card from thur dentist."

"St. Maggie's?" "novice?" "holy sister?" "touch of the outside world?" Although I knew the meanings of these words, I hadn't the least idea they could possibly have to do with my delivering mail.

As I started on my assigned round, wearing my pea jacket and watch cap, parting gifts from the Navy, and a pair of ugly yellow gloves, with elastic cuffs that covered my wrists, pressed on me by my mother, I was dressed against the cold of the sunless morning. For the first time since

I'd got home I felt glad to be outside the house, doing something, even if it was just delivering mail. Mitch's good will, I realized, had injected me with a shot of confidence that was beginning to heal the psychic wound that had been open and festering. He made me believe there was *some* good will in the world after all.

In the middle of the second block of my route, I pulled out an extra thick packet of envelopes along with a few small packages of the size that were carried on foot. Large packages were delivered by truck. The address on the slip of paper under the rubber band was "St. Margaret's," without a street and number.

Sure enough, in the transom above the marble lintel of the arched doors at the top of the brownstone steps of the house at which I stood looking up were Gothic gilt letters on ebony, which read "St. Margaret's Convent." On the stoop in front of the right-hand door was the large metal mailbox, which was not to be used.

As Mitch had instructed me, I pushed the button of the door-bell. Within seconds the door on the left-hand side opened inward. I found myself looking into a pair of deep-set eyes, green gems embedded in creamy white ovals beneath crescent-shaped black brows. Before I could smile or get out a "good morning," I heard a liltingly sweet voice sing a little tune.

The postman, the postman,
We always welcome the postman,
The postman, the postman,
The postman is bringing us mail.

The melody sounded familiar, but on the instant I couldn't identify it, coming as it did so suddenly from such an unexpected source. Just inside the closed back door of the vestibule stood a bucket of water and a scrub brush with its gray-yellow bristles up. Ah ha, I said to myself, a novice performing a menial duty.

The face in which those eyes were set was oval. Her skin, the color of a ripe peach, tawny, with a flush of pink on the cheeks, looked to be stretched so vulnerably tight a pinprick might cause a hemorrhage. Full-fleshed, her lips were the color of not quite ripe cherries. Her nose would have been a perfect little triangle except that it was saucily turned up at the very end. What was she, I asked myself, doing in a convent? I was stunned by her beauty.

We stared at each other for countable seconds, she with her head slightly cocked, before I was able to reply, "Good morning," as Mitch had advised me. What came out was a husky whisper, with the accent falling on the "morn," rather than on the "good" I'd heard in Mitch's advice. To my ear it sounded as if I were recommending that she give herself up to mourning rather than celebrate what was good.

"Come in, mister postman, and warm yourself for a spell. The morning air carries such a chill." Her speaking voice had a resonance suggesting that simple statement was a poem set to music. My ear imagined the sweetness of her saying a prayer or chanting the litany. Reaching behind me, I pulled the heavy door closed as quietly as I could. There we were, alone in the vestibule, a space scarcely larger than a telephone booth. When she smiled, I spotted a dimple in her chin.

Extraordinary as was the beauty of her features, I sensed a quality beyond that. Perhaps it was the harmony of the fleshly shapes and dimensions. Yet, absolute materialist that I am now and was by the time I'd come back from the war, I recall that at that moment I believed that she had a soul and that somehow it glowed.

Spiritual as she might be, at the same time she radiated a vibrancy, an overflow of life, despite the drab brown apron over the gray garment that reached to her ankles, allowing me barely to make out the worsted black stockings between the hem of her dress and the high tops of the battered brogans she was wearing. Exposed by rolled-up sleeves were slender forearms and wrists, dripping wet, as were her hands. Struggle against it as I might, at that instant I couldn't help wondering about the breasts, the waist, the thighs beneath the concealment of her flowing clothing. As a kid I'd heard that nuns shaved their heads bald. Still I imagined that, were I to snatch off the slate-gray hood the novice was wearing, locks of shining black hair would come cascading down over her shoulders.

Jolted as by the firing of a 16" gun, suddenly I felt that, despite those somber-colored work clothes, which covered her from chin to toes, and declared her renunciation of the flesh, I was enclosed with the most feminine, yes, the most sexual woman I had ever been in the presence of, or had ever seen. Yet even while my sexual inclinations were asserting themselves, her self-evident purity deflated them, in fact, made me wish I could undo the dissatisfactions of the always brief, quite passionless encounters I had experienced during my years in the Navy. In these, my partners had been a scattering of romantic girls, a few patriotic and lonely women and a couple of prostitutes. These had first occurred before I'd been shipped to the seas and skies and lands of slaughter and then, killing accomplished, had been resumed after my return to the States, in the interval before receiving the honorable discharge I'd been presented with as a reward, and my return home, innocence lost. Yet even while this novice provoked a powerful arousal in me, I could no more have touched her flesh than I could have my mother's.

That melodiously sung greeting, that smile, even the invitation to warm myself in the vestibule, fully as sexless as her clothing, couldn't have been more innocent. What had prompted the surge of desire in me and, at the same time, an equally strong inhibition I could no more account for than I could for the physics and device which, contained in a single bomb, had destroyed Hiroshima, then three days later Nagasaki, killing almost two hundred thousand human beings in two bursts of light. And what had propelled such physical beauty to renounce its own fleshly fulfillment and embrace a life of denial I had no more understanding of than I do now of the structure and significance of the double helix. What I did know then, with unqualified certainty, was that, having forced myself to venture out of my father's house, to which, psychically disabled, I'd retreated and fallen into a deep pit, now having taken on an undemanding temporary job, I, at that instant, was being called back to life by of all people a nun-to-be.

Without daring to keep my eyes on her, even to get out a mumbled 'I better be off on my route,' I extended the packet of mail, being careful to keep the awful yellow-gloved fingers clasped on one end of it. She received the packet, taking it by the other end in her slender pink fingers. Then I deposited a few small packages on the floor where she had not yet scrubbed. Imagining how Paul of Tarsus must have felt when he could see again, I shouldered my bag, shambled out the door and, after closing it softly, descended the brownstone steps. As I went on my way, I pondered over why a convent was located in a row of houses on a city street. I had, though, gained some comprehension of the puzzling advice Mitch had given me about St. Margaret's.

Lying in bed that night, unable to fall asleep, my wide-awake inner eye saw the novice down on her knees, not praying with a rosary in her hand, but on the floor of the vestibule holding a scrub brush. Performing that humble chore seemed to enhance her beauty.

Next morning my excitement rose as I approached St. Margaret's with my burden over my shoulder. I waited on the stoop at the top of the steps for maybe half a minute, holding my breath in expectation, before pushing the button of the doorbell. A full minute passed before the door opened slowly. Feet astride in the frame, filling it in fact, dressed exactly as yesterday's novice had been, an immense, dough-faced young woman, with brawny forearms and hands the size of a slab of bacon, was posted. Behind her were the pail and scrub brush. She wiped her hands on her apron.

Since I just stood there in stunned disappointment, she finally said, "Here, let me have the mail." There was no melody in what I heard as a brusque command. Drawing the packet and a few packages out of my bag and extending them to her with my still gloved hand, I felt no apprehension about touching. From this stern-seeming potential mother superior came no invitation to step into the vestibule to warm myself for a few seconds against the near-zero cold that had set in.

The following morning a third novice, as nondescript in appearance as the first and third were striking, halfway between the size of her two holy sisters, was performing the morning chore of scrubbing the floor of the vestibule. We exchanged polite smiles but no words. So the rotation went on until Sunday, December 7, an ominous anniversary, on which of course no mail was delivered.

Breaking what had been a family tradition, a ritual, say, maintained even during my period of withdrawal, I announced at the breakfast table on that Sunday that I'd not be attending morning service in the Methodist church, to which congregation our family had belonged, going back that I knew of to my great grandfather. To my bombshell, my father, a member of the Board of Deacons and a financial supporter to the full extent of his tithing, which modest as his earnings were, he scrupulously practiced, reacted by pouring himself a second cup of coffee.

As I'd been expecting, my mother, who sang in the choir, taught a young women's Bible class, and held some office in the Women's Christian Temperance Union, demanded to be told why. Rather than confront and do battle, which I well knew she was better armed for and would prove stronger in waging than I would—God, not Satan, was all that she feared in the universe—I compounded my sin of resolved-upon absence by offering what I knew, given her rigid code of Christian conduct, she would sniff out to be the additional sin of lying.

"I have a headache and an upset stomach," I whined, hoping the feebleness, with which I couldn't help declaring such a falsehood, would support the assertion. It didn't satisfy my mother, a spry little woman, not much more than five feet tall and a hundred pounds. Her strong-mindedness, which was quick to assert itself, more than compensated for her physical slightness. Quite a contrast to my lanky, languid, self-effacing father. Tall, skinny, full of self-doubt and hesitant, I was a mismated blending of my parents' genes.

When pressed for more particulars, I shrugged my shoulders, shook my head, and retreated into silence. If my father had his doubts and suspicions, the only indication was the raising of his blond eye-brows.

If truth, the whole truth, and nothing but the truth were to be told (as I had once sworn to tell it and had—my mother's gene at work—at a captain's mast, in which a seaman, a member of the watch I was in charge of, had been shamefully accused of insubordination, by a warrant officer, for whom in my presence he'd refused to fetch a cup of coffee while we were at general quarters under kamikaze attack), I did have some compelling reasons for refusing to attend church.

First and foremost was self-honesty. Going off to war at seventeen as a nominal Christian, I never had examined myself about what as a Methodist I did and didn't believe. Seeing men burn and drown, imagining thousands of civilians dying and suffering from shells and bombs in whose launching I had been complicit, culminating in the triumphant report of the killing, burning and maiming of hundreds of thousands of innocents in two bursts of light when our enemy was no longer capable of fending us off and defending his homeland—these had bled from my conscience every drop of the faith that had been my birthright. You might call it unconversion.

Then, too, meeting the exotic novice as I'd emerged from deep depression had set me to thinking about intolerance in the religion that, seemingly like a genetic trait, had been embedded in me. Some particular memories had come flashing back as I'd lain in bed, unable to fall asleep, bone-weary as I'd been after my first day of carrying the mailbag.

The first two went far back in my childhood, when I'd been too young to comprehend the significance of what I was hearing from good Methodist guests, husband and wife, at our dinner table one evening. During the 1928 presidential election it had been. Republican, Protestant, as were my parents and my forebears, Herbert Hoover, the incumbent, was running against Democratic, Catholic Al Smith. The first remark I remember came from the wife of the visiting couple, a woman named Phyllis, who was a close friend of my mother's. Why her name and the exact words, half-whispered, on that occasion have remained in the memory sack in my brain all these years, I haven't the least idea.

"They say, you know, his wife eats her peas from her knife," her being, of course, the wife of low, common, Catholic, Democratic Al Smith. Were he to be elected, this woman without even proper table manners would occupy the position of First Lady in the land.

I never have been able to call back the exact phrasing of a loud assertion her husband had made at that memorable dinner, but I have held onto the gist of it—the day that fellow takes over as president a telephone line will be connected from the Vatican to the White House and you know who will be running this country. Although so far as I can recall, no response came from either of my parents, the memory of those childishly but viciously prejudicial charges against Al Smith and his wife planted the seed which blossomed into a recognition that my parents, who considered themselves decent folks, and were good Methodist Christians, were also anti-Catholic bigots.

The black flower of prejudice was watered, to carry on the organic metaphor, while I was home on leave just before being shipped to the Pacific. My father having gone off to work at the arsenal, assuring that the ammunition we'd be using met specifications which made it safe for us to handle and deadly for our enemies to receive, my mother and I prolonged our breakfast together by having a second cup of tea, her, and coffee, me. For some reason she was glowingly, yes, I'm afraid gloatingly telling me about a new friend of hers who had recently joined the Methodists and had become a member of the church I would decline to attend the first Sunday after I'd begun my temporary career as a mailman. This incident is so strikingly absurd, so comically revelatory that I've also remembered what was said word for word.

"Teresa was a Catholic, but she became a Christian," my mother announced.

My impulse was to erupt into laughter. Somehow I managed to suppress it. Yet the part of my brain in which some facts of history, however scattered, were stored, lit up as if a switch had been thrown in a dark attic. I let out a gasped "What! What are you saying?"

"It's true," my mother insisted, as if her veracity, not recorded history were at stake. "And she's given up drinking, smoking and card-playing."

"Mother," I urgently went on, unable to fall back on silence, as I ought were I to obey the Fifth Commandment, "you *are* aware that before there were Methodists, Baptists, Presbyterians, Congregationalists, Episcopalians, and Lutherans, every Christian was what you're now calling a non-Christian, that is a Catholic. Why do you think it's called Mother Church?"

"Well, *we* don't call it that," my mother countered, dismissing the existence of a millennium and a half of the Christian Church, as if it were the lifetime of a fly or mosquito, with a sweep of her hand. "Anyway, you know what I mean." Then she calmly went on to narrate the conversion of

Teresa as if she'd come out from among voodooists.

Yes, I was aware that the crowning reason for my decision not to attend church with my parents was the delivery of mail into the hand of the beautiful young novice in the vestibule of St. Margaret's two days before. She, I realized, would already have gone to morning prayers, and at the time I was supposed to be at the Methodist service would be attending mass, if not inside the convent, then probably at St. Boniface's, just two blocks away.

Still and all, it was mystifying to me that she had chosen to live her life confined within the narrow walls of the Church, renouncing all the outside world had to offer, for meditation, prayer and ritual. Instead of continuing her education, she would be scrubbing floors and performing who knows what other acts of humiliation. The waste, indeed the sacrifice of her beauty was visible in the very clothing she was required to wear while still a novice.

Spirited, vital and sociable to the point where, if it hadn't been for my imagining an invisible halo around her covered head, she might almost have seemed flirtatious, with a stranger no less suggested. Then how *could* she divert passion and sexual gratification to the love of a fleshless Father, Mother and Son? How *could* she abjure love, marriage, motherhood, friendship outside her order by narrowing the breadth and depth of human possibility to the thinness of the wafer that was dipped in blood-colored wine?

Startling myself, suddenly I realized that the recoil from the horror of war, guilt for collective participation in the killing and maiming of countless masses of human beings, and the attendant loss of faith had made my home a refuge, yes a monastery. My parents, a hierarchy of superiors. My routine, canonical hours. The music I was filling my ears with, my mass. The novels I was devoting myself to, my breviary. Until I'd summoned the energy and determination, in short, the will to take the step of delivering Christmas mail, I'd been even more of a recluse than the beautiful novice. Exempt from the humiliation of scrubbing floors, I lacked the comforting recompense of what she had to believe in and, along with her sisterhood, give herself to with all her heart.

The shudder that this recognition produced brought me back to the Sunday morning breakfast table. The bare white cloth I was staring down at made me aware the table had been cleared, my own dishes and flatware, as well as my half-full mug of coffee, taken from under my nose. From the silence I heard I knew that my father had washed, my mother had dried plates, bowls, utensils, cups and saucers and had then retired upstairs to dress for attending service. I was sitting alone. During the remainder of that Sunday, family communion gave way to sterile formality.

Not until Wednesday would the rotation have her back in the vestibule, scrubbing. That morning I climbed the five brownstone steps of St. Margaret's with the mailbag on my shoulder. Crammed with Christmas cards, and packages, it felt as if it were filled with cobblestones. Almost the instant the tip of my yellow-gloved forefinger left the button of the door bell, the brass knob turned and the door swung inward, suggesting to me that the hand which had done the twisting had not been scrubbing the floor but had been poised to seize the knob. Even before I felt the flutter of wings in my chest, as if my heart were a fledgling testing its wings before daring its first flight, I dismissed such a gratifying possibility as a self-serving illusion. Yet just inside the door stood the lovely novice.

"It's the postman, the postman," she sang again, "bringing us Christmas mail." Light as her voice was, without anything like the power of the soprano singing on our recording of Haydn's "Mass in Time of War"—ironically that had become my favorite piece of music— and banal as was the melody, to my ear the song of the novice was exquisitely musical.

As again I wondered where the melody, familiar as it was, came from, suddenly I recognized it—the last lines of a song from the eighteen-nineties my father occasionally would sing, to the tch-tch-ing of my mother over its worldliness. "The Bowery, the Bowery, / They do such strange things in the Bowery, / The Bowery, the Bowery, / I'll never go there any more." It had to be the novice had heard the song in her home and had accommodated words of her own to it. Secular as the source of the tune was, her willingness, perhaps desire to sing it for me suggested that, whatever the differences of our heritages, her family and mine must have had *some* traditions in common. One thing I could be certain of— the place she was in and her coloring declared she could not be the WASP that I was.

Although in preparation I'd had the fingers of my gloved right hand on the packet of mail labeled "St. Margaret's,' I withdrew them from the pouch they were in, then unslung the bag and let it fall gently to the floor, clear of the bucket, scrub brush and pool of water close to the inside door. After pretending to have to fumble and fish for mail addressed to the convent, with my head down I took time extracting it. Again I extended the packet to her lengthwise, to keep our fingers from even brushing. This time, as she received the mail as circumspectly as I was offering it, I took notice that now she was drying her hands thoroughly on her apron. When she smiled at me, seeing her lips part was like being privileged to watch a pink tulip opening itself in sped-up motion to the morning sun.

Then, bending over my bag, I fumbled out from the bottom the half dozen packages addressed to St. Margaret's. I wondered whether her name were on any of them. It wasn't. The game I was playing, devising ways of extending the time to minutes while taking care not to touch, was a delicate one. If she were aware of my ploy, she in no way resisted it.

So it went on every third day—the door always opening as soon as my finger had left the button that rang the bell, her little song always greeting me. Both of us were circumspect in positioning our fingers on the packet of mail I handed her. And I kept those loathsome yellow gloves on. In bed one night during my second week on the job, I couldn't fall asleep as I pondered her behavior. Was it possible that her cheerful demeanor, her self-composed acceptance concealed a raging civil war within? After all, was I not in a similar trying circumstance with my mother and father, with limited success? Might it be that when the novice had entered the convent she'd left behind forever a lover for whom she still harbored a powerful passion? Aware that, having taken vows of chastity, she was constantly committing sin in her heart, might she be using the new young mailman as a substitute, someone she could be attracted to, could even wish were attracted to her, without sinning by desiring to love in the flesh?

All at once, lying in my narrow bed, I felt a rush of jealousy, insane jealousy, jealousy of someone I'd never laid eyes on, jealousy of someone who might not even exist. Yet if he did, I might well be an agent delivering love letters, perhaps pleas from him to her. Madness, I hissed. In an effort to relieve myself of the torment such a problematic, foolish but very real emotion had provoked, I told myself that were she using me as a vicarious and chaste lover, or even as a pander, she was being compelled by an impulse stronger than giving in to a bit of coquetry could account for, something deeper, a longing, a desire, a need she couldn't control, perhaps without being aware it was governing her behavior. In one way or another, I concluded, as certainly as entering the convent established the fact that she was determined to give up the flesh for her soul's sake, at the same time her conduct suggested that she had come to the holy altar with the feelings of a never-to-be fleshly bride.

One morning during the third week in December, I pretended to be rearranging the packets in my bag, after she'd opened the door of the vestibule that led to a hallway. I'd placed the day's mail on the table. So long did I fuss that she went back to work. Dropping to her knees as gracefully as a ballerina doing a pliè, she plunged her left hand into the soapy water in the bucket, then commenced scrubbing the marble floor so vigorously it seemed she was scouring off the film generated by the traffic and factories of the city, including the arsenal in which my father still was inspecting shell casings, and the filth sin leaves at night. So hard was she bearing down that I imagined she was trying to make the marble floor white as the alabaster her Lord and Savior's body was often carved in, rubbing determinedly, as if that would highlight the barely visible blood in His veins. Crestfallen, I couldn't help wondering whether such a dive into activity were intended to be a rebuke of or at least a check on me, for lingering.

On Friday of the week before Christmas, the door opened, as it always had on her day to scrub, the instant I let up on the bell button. When that interval was measured against what occurred with her sister novices, I still clung to the possibility that she was waiting for me, despite the rebuff I feared I'd received for loitering. So short was the interval it almost seemed that, even though she couldn't walk through a wall, she could see through a thick walnut door. Since the age of miracles had passed, I settled for the explanation that, estimating the time of the arrival of the mail, she would stop scrubbing, rise from the floor, begin to dry her hands as she'd cross the vestibule, and post herself with her ear, which I'd never seen but imagined was small and pink as a cherry blossom, against the door to listen for footsteps outside. The sloshing of the galoshes I was wearing against the cold and slush the recent snow had turned to made such a conjecture plausible. Certainly it was a possibility that gratified me.

As always she sang the little song, which I chose to believe she'd composed and sang only for me, though the spontaneity with which it had come out the first time our lives had touched forced me to entertain the possibility she had been singing it playfully to Mitch, who was old enough to be her grandfather, a disconcerting thought. Then, fixing her emerald eyes on mine, something she'd never done before, without smiling, she asked, "And what might your name be, Mr. Postman?"

So taken aback was I that, instead of first producing the packet of mail from my bag, I rooted around and brought out three small packages, no doubt Christmas gifts for nuns and novices, perhaps one for her, a present from the lover my tortured imagination had created, and placed them on the dry floor at her feet. I didn't dare to look. And so slow was I to reply to her straightforward question that when I did manage to get out the single syllable, I thought she might have concluded that I didn't have a name or couldn't remember it. Only afterward I realized that what had seemed like minutes to me actually must have been mere seconds.

"John," I finally managed to mutter. To my ear, in contrast to her melodious voice, the sound I produced was a grunt, like that coming from a man in the late stages of emphysema. Then I brought out and circumspectly handed her the packet of St. Margaret's mail. Her face opened into a full-blooming smile.

"John," she echoed, though it was mellifluously pitched a full octave above my growl. "John, the bringer of good news. So right it is for a postman!" Although I'd never much taken to Sunday school, I was grateful to whichever of the maiden lady teachers I'd been exposed to for having informed me of John the Baptist's role.

As with her left hand she accepted the mail and clasped it against her chest, the contour of which I never had been able to make out beneath her thick loosely-fitting woolen gown, I was reminded of how the girls when I was in high school—that seemed to me to be in another time and place—had carried their books, proudly swelling out their young breasts. Then she pivoted, again reminding me of a dancer, twisted the knob with her free right hand, and delicately pushed open the inside door of the vestibule with the toe of her left foot. How mysterious the darkness of the long hallway I took in with one quick glance before she pulled the door closed behind her! So abrupt was her departure that I'd have thought somehow I'd offended her if I had done any more than reply to her question by muttering the monosyllable of my name. The only alternative I could come up with, tormenting as it was to entertain, was that she was frantically anxious to carry the message or package, if there were one, from the lover I'd imagined for her to the privacy of her cell-like room and open it.

Since the stern brawny novice had been scrubbing the vestibule the next day, Saturday, I expected that the taciturn novice would be performing the obligation on Monday. Which she was. That meant that the rotation had the beautiful novice in the vestibule on Tuesday, the day before Christmas, my final day as a substitute mailman.

On that Tuesday, protected by my pea jacket and watch cap, which I'd kept after my discharge as a reminder of the war I couldn't get over, rather than as a souvenir of victory, the knit cap pulled down to cover my ears and eyebrows, and of course wearing the ugly yellow gloves, I slogged through the foot or so of snow that had fallen over night. Pellets the ice flakes had turned into by morning, propelled like antiaircraft shells by a gale-force wind driving in from the northeast, thwacked my cheeks and chin. I kept my eyes slitted. Slung over my left shoulder, so my gloved right hand was free to brush off the ice that was forming on my eyelids, the mailbag was loaded with last minute Christmas cards and packages. The effort to lift each foot through the deep snow and to shove my body against the wind seemed to add to the weight of the bag I was carrying, a physical correspondent to the heaviness of heart, which I believed was more than metaphorical. I'd be delivering mail to the beautiful novice for the last time.

The closer I came to St. Margaret's, the more apprehensive I became that I'd be denied even this melancholy gratification. It might well be that the rotation would be disrupted for some reason and that I'd find the brawny or the pallid novice behind the door. Or might it be that when the bell was rung, a nun or the mother superior herself would respond, all chores for the novices being suspended on the day of Christmas Eve? Maybe I'd have to leave the packet in the mailbox outside and carry the packages back to the post office for delivery by Mitch the following Monday.

My gloved finger went ahead and pushed the button in the hope that the well-known legend, "neither snow nor rain nor ice nor gloom of night..."—the last of which I found myself in although it was half past nine in the morning—was believed by the nuns and that the someone appointed to receive the mail would be the beautiful novice.

Instantly the door opened and there she was, pail and scrub brush on the floor behind her. Fearing she might quickly take the packet of mail, then shut the door immediately to keep out the wind and pellets of ice I'd allowed in, I dared to pull the door closed behind me. Brief as it would be, I cherished this last occasion we'd be enclosed together alone in the vestibule, a space I'd come to consider a sanctuary, a place of escape from the narrowly regulated life practiced behind one door and the seemingly limitless freedom of life that went on outside the other. Now, after all the years that have passed I still think of that entryway as a shrine.

"I was worrited you might not be coming this morning, the storm being sent surely by the Devil himself on the eve of the birth of our Lord," she said, forgoing her little song. Even so, I could hear the lilt in her voice. And my ear had picked up the fact that she had a manner of phrasing somehow different from Mitch's, my parents', that of others in our city, and mine too. And where had the word "worrited," which I distinctly heard have come from? It had to be her way of saying "worried." "Yet here you are, John the postman, on this bitter cold day, bringing us the mail despite."

Confounded by the reverence in what she'd said to me and unable to come up with an appropriate response, I blurted out "And what's your name?" As I dared to keep my eyes fixed on hers, shining green in the dusky vestibule, to my disgust again I heard my voice come out hoarse as that of the ragpicker who when I was a boy would come by in his horse-drawn wagon chanting, "Eny rags, eny bones, eny boddils tuday/ They's a puh ole ragpicka comin yuh way."

"Deirdre I was christened, but when I'm no longer a probationer, I will then be Sister Lucia."

"Deirdre?" I echoed, changing the intonation and ignoring the Lucia to be. "I've never heard that name." Even as I spoke, I was reprimanding myself for revealing the naiveté I was exposing by responding with what sounded prejudicially dismissive.

"Why it's a Gaelic name, to be sure! Deirdre is a heroine in our old Irish stories. Yet sure I'm sorry to have to be telling it turns bad for her at the end. That's why when I take the holy veil I'll give up 'Deirdre' in favor of the name of a blessed saint."

Irish, of course, I told myself, while she was speaking. The lilt, the phrasing, the use of such a word as "worrited." And in retrospect I realize her eyes and dark coloring had not been infiltrated genetically by the reddish blond of the Scandinavian raiders and invaders but were pure Celtic. "Blacks" the highlanders are called in one old border ballad to distinguish them from the fair "bonnies" of the lowlands.

"And who might you be named for, John? One of the Popes? Or a saint? Perhaps for the apostle who wrote the Gospel? Or the John who sees the end before it has come to pass? So many Johns have there been. As well, the John who washed our blessed Savior's body in the river, baptizing Him."

"None of them, I'm afraid. I was named for my grandfather." She tinkled a laugh and scrunched up her piquant nose. "Well, it just could be your grandfather was named for one of those Johns, going back some years in time it might be. Which then would come down to you. Do you know what I am thinking, John?"

"What are you thinking, Deirdre?" That we were addressing each other by name, which I wouldn't have dared had she not taken the lead, made me aware of the excitement my blood was charged with.

"Even though John the water man was a bringer of good news as are you, which I said a time ago, I've thought it for the best if you were named after the John who was the apostle our Savior loved, as the Scripture tells us. Yet whichever John it be your name has come from, you *are* John the postman, who brings the mail to St. Margaret's. For which I say may God bless you, John, and may you celebrate the birth of Jesus our Lord and Savior with a deal of happiness."

During the silence that set in I stared at my galoshes. A little puddle had formed around them. For me to acknowledge that I was not a Catholic, not even a believing Methodist, was impossible. I felt at once like a hypocrite and a coward. Though I could think of no pretext for lingering, I couldn't bring myself to go. We were down to our final minutes alone together. Scarcely knowing I was doing it, I wriggled the yellow glove from my right hand and, peeling my fingers free, tucked the glove in my left armpit.

"I'm afraid I've brought the storm in on the floor you're scrubbing clean," finally I managed to get out to fill the emptiness. For falling back on such a prosaic phrase as "scrubbing clean" at such a moment, I reproached myself again. Even "washing" wouldn't have been so crude.

She let out another bell-like laugh. "That's no care," she said. "You're John the Postman." Then she sang her little song, modifying the final line from "The postman is bringing us mail" to "It's John who brings us our mail." And that made all the difference.

Although I found it hard to credit, at that instant I did believe she too wanted to prolong our time together, motivated by something more than not wishing me to venture out in the storm so soon again. Something passionate, if not sexual. Could it be that she *was* reluctant to renounce her womanhood?

"Well," I said breaking another bewildering silence, "guess I'd better get back on the route. People will be wanting their last mail before Christmas."

She was standing just inches from me, perfectly rigid, not much taller than my mother. How I longed, even if it would be only to say good-bye, good-bye forever, to throw my arms around her shoulders, to draw her against me, to bend and press my closed lips against her sealed lips! Not only did I know I didn't dare. I also knew that, even if she wouldn't cry out in protest or push me off with her little hands as she uttered "no, no, no!" I'd be doing her a great wrong, perhaps irreparable harm.

I forced myself to stoop, draw the packet of mail labeled St. Margaret's from the pouch in my bag, which was leaning against my calf beside the puddle I'd made on the floor. And I settled for holding the packet not by the end between the tips of my fingers but across the middle, well inside my bare hand.

When her little hand came up to accept it, I felt her fingers against the flesh of my palm. It was, I swear to this day, more than a grazing touch. Remaining in that posture for countable seconds, I closed my eyes and lowered my head, as in prayer, while, perversely, I felt blood swelling my manhood.

"I'll light a candle for you, John, and again I say, may our Lord bless you on the day of His birth," I heard her say. As she whispered the words, her voice seemed to be coming from faraway, from wherever it was her eyes sometimes appeared to be. When, surrendering the packet and feeling her take it and withdraw her touch, I opened my eyes to see her turn toward the inner door of the vestibule. I heard a screech from the turning knob, a sound I at the moment convinced myself was coming from her, a soft scream of protest, though surely it was the latch wanting oil. Watching the door opening toward whatever mysteries lay behind it, I found just enough voice for her to hear me say, I hoped, "And may you have a *wonderful* Christmas, Deirdre." It wasn't enough. I should have but couldn't add a blessing. That it would occur to her I was using "wonder " in its literal sense, "full of marvels," I couldn't deny doubting.

After the door had closed softly behind her, I found myself in the vestibule with her bucket of gray water and scrub brush and my mailbag. Bending, I picked up the brush and, soggy wet as the bristles were and covered with who knows what, I rubbed them across my lips. They tasted roughly bitter.

"Soon to be Sister Lucia," I added aloud, not as a reproach but as a sigh of grief. As I gathered up my burden of mail, opened the front door of the vestibule, descended the brownstone steps, and, facing the storm of ice pellets, tugged on the obscene yellow gloves, I wondered whether she was fully, partially, or not at all aware of what had happened, to her, I felt certain, as well as to me.

By mid-afternoon I'd finished my route. The storm had ended. An overcast sky was just giving way to a Madonna blue. Suddenly, bouncing off the pristine whiteness of the world around me, brilliant sunlight almost blinded me.

After surrendering my mailbag to Mitch, I vigorously shook his thick hand, which responded with a crunch that would have cracked open a walnut. He had the strength to move huge boulders.

"Thanks for everything, Mitch," I said, "and merry Christmas."

"Hey, yuh wuz a big help, not like one a these college deadbeats wur sometimes stuck with. Yu'd make a helluva good mailman. Yuh ever wanaply fur permanent, I'll put in a good word fur yuh with the man. It ain't the wors job in the world, if yur dogs and gams don give out. With a pension that ain't too bad either that I'll be collectin in a cupla years. Hey, don swig too much anjul juice, yuh know whad I mean. 'N have a murry Chrismas. See yuh 'round, kid." All this was bellowed in his spooky foghorn voice and was punctuated by his jaunty laugh. When he punched me between the shoulders as an expression of our camaraderie, his hand felt like a hunk of lead. The punch turned into a caress.

Carrying a voucher for what I'd earned, which sum would arrive by mail on a check I'd be receiving in a week or so, instead of for home I headed for the trolley-line avenue with its rows of shops, all decorated for Christmas and crowded with mobs of late shoppers. As I was certain I would, I came across a reliable-looking jewelry store. In my pocket was all the cash I had to my name.

"Just a plain cross on a chain," I told the clerk who asked whether he could help me. "Real gold, solid not plated."

As he dangled in front of me precisely what I had in mind and assured me it was twenty-four carat, he looked me up and down. Conspicuously displaying the bills extracted from the pocket of my slacks, I instructed him to wrap it in white paper, "nothing Christmasy," and to put it in a simple white box, then to use heavy brown paper for mailing.

"No, thanks, no card inside." I said when he produced one. As he went on wrapping, he raised his pale eyebrows. In the bright fluorescent light his slick black hair with comb marks shone. The cross cost more than I'd earned delivering mail the past three weeks.

Back at the post office, which was scheduled to stay open until six o'clock, instead of the usual five, this being Christmas Eve, before joining the long line at the stamp and mail window, I wrote "Deirdre, St Margaret's Convent," followed by the street address I knew so well. The place for a return address, the upper left-hand corner, I left blank. Then, as an afterthought, just in case there was more than one novice named Deirdre, I squeezed "Soon to be Sister Lucia" between her name and the convent's. For having revealed the fact to me, I hoped Deirdre wouldn't be violating any rule of the convent's discipline. Although I knew she wouldn't receive it until after Christmas, I sent the package Special Delivery.

At Christmas dinner I informed my parents that I'd applied for admission to a liberal arts college in the center of the state and had been accepted, to begin the spring semester in mid-January. This concession had been made, I supposed, because I was a veteran.

"Thank the dear Lord!" my mother cried out, as she clasped her hands and jerked her head up at the chandelier hanging over the dining room table. I couldn't help interpreting her gratitude to "the Lord" as a rebuke of me, for not having acted sooner, quite a contrast to the communal and beseeching of "our Lord" by novice Deirdre. My father arose from the table, walked to a station behind my chair, squeezed my shoulder, and murmured "Atta boy, John."

As our three-member family—I was an only child, as was my father—was eating mince pie, not bought but baked by my mother, I thought it a propitious time to inform them of another development that would serve as evidence I was emerging from my self-imposed seclusion. After breakfast, returning from a solitary walk in the little park nearby, still gorgeously decorated with snow, I'd run into one of the two young women living just up the street from us. She happened to be the one I'd fastened on as the prettier of the two.

Her smiling "hello" had propelled us into conversation. Although it turned out she was two years younger than I, we discovered that, having attended the same high school, we had a number of acquaintances in common. Also we'd had many of the same teachers. As we'd evaluated them, we discovered we pretty much agreed on their competences and qualities.

Before excusing myself from the table, I revealed that I'd asked our neighbor whether she'd care to see a film showing in a cinema a few miles away, "The Big Sleep," with Humphrey Bogart and Lauren Bacall, it happened to be.

This announcement produced a profound silence, during which I caught sight of my mother fixing a Medusa stare on my father. Blinking as he cleared his throat, my father smiled at me. "It *is* Christmas night," he said gently, " your first home from the war and… "

"We're planning to sing carols around the piano," my mother broke in, "and then I'll make hot chocolate to sip while we listen to our favorite excerpts from Handel's *Messiah* on the phonograph. As we've always done. Your father and I carried on the tradition while you were gone, of course."

"Oh…afraid I hadn't…." 'Remembered' was on the tip of my tongue, but, hearing the cruelty of pronouncing that word at this moment, I was able to suck it back in. "…hadn't been thinking," I managed to get out. Then realizing that explanation was scarcely a softener, I felt a surge of pity come rifling up my throat, shot from my metaphorical heart, pity not only for my father, whose skin was thin as a butterfly's wing, but even for my armadillo mother. My head went down, as if I were praying, yet wretched as I felt over the hurt I was causing, I had no intention of capitulating to the urge to redress it. I had to get out. Now.

More silence, a really fearsome weapon of my mother's. I ended it with what I intended to be a sincere apology, lie though it was, while still making clear that I was resolving the conflict on my terms. "Oh, I'm really sorry I asked her, but now it's done, I'm afraid."

A third still longer, and therefore more threatening silence. My mother's pale lips were pinched so tightly together that the Inquisition couldn't have forced out a syllable.

"John…" She finally broke the silence by pronouncing my name, then pausing as she was poised to strike. "Before you go any further in encouraging this young woman, who for all I know might be perfectly respectable otherwise, I think there's something you ought to be aware of." She made a strategic pause, to which I declined to respond to with an inquiry.

"The family of that person, and, mind you, I have nothing else against her…," another measurable pause, "well, they're Catholics."

Calling up strength generated by my recent, perhaps imagined, almost romance with Deirdre, soon to be Sister Lucia, I blurted out in an unquavering voice, "Maybe I'll be able to persuade her not to enter St. Margaret's Convent, you know, on the other side of the post office. So she'll avoid Hell by finding her way onto the straight and narrow Methodist road to Heaven." How cruelly flip I was after my liberation!

Hearing my mother gasp, I saw my father jump up from the table and rush to the opposite end, near to the kitchen. He threw his arm across his wife's heaving shoulders as she sobbed, "I don't know what's got into that boy. He doesn't seem to be our son any longer."

I had to bite my tongue to keep from shouting, 'the war, it's the war! And a beautiful little novice in St. Margaret's Convent.' In order not to cause any additional splintering of the trinity of our family on this Christmas night, I began carrying dessert plates and flatware into the kitchen. Soon my father joined me. After we'd cleared the table and headed back toward the dining room, he slipped the key to our Studebaker into my pocket. There was no need to be stealthy. My mother, remaining at her place at the table, chin on her breast as though in prayer, dabbed her eyes with her lace handkerchief. No sound was coming from her, but her shoulders were bobbing like a motor whaleboat in a rough sea.

The date wasn't worth the price. In fact, it was a debit. The doll-like prettiness of the girl of the neighborhood, Mary Jo, who with her fur coat off was more plump than I'd judged her to be, paled beside the dark beauty of Deirdre. And some acne was all too obviously covered with pancake makeup. No sooner had she settled in the Studebaker, her right shoulder close to the door on her side, leaving a space on the seat between us that suggested I was infected with a contagious disease, than she informed me she was waiting for the return of a marine. A running back on the football team, he'd left high school at the end of his junior year, just as the war was ending.

The night before he'd embarked on a tour of duty in the occupation of Japan, which I'd helped bring about by my participation in taking lives and shedding blood, he and Mary Joe had pledged to be faithful to each other. As she solemnly announced the inaccessibility their commitment to be chaste had imposed on her, I, with considerable experience in the mores of the military, had to choke back a laugh of scorn. "Though we aren't exactly engaged, we're as good as," she explained. Which pronouncement brought a derisive but undelivered 'congratulations!' to the tip of my tongue.

On she chattered about the prowess of her beloved on the gridiron, his patriotism in leaving school to enlist, all the manly virtues that complemented his handsomeness. How could I possibly measure up to, let alone supplant, such a paragon? In the cinema we both took care to keep our elbows off the armrest between our seats. The instant the lights dimmed, despite the blare of music and flashing of the Pathé news on the screen, in my mind I relived to the point of feeling tactilely the tips of a beauty's slender fingers on the side of my hand.

Additionally I was put off by noticing that during the feature film Mary Jo fished a stick of chewing gum out of the handbag she held in her lap as if it were a fumbled football she'd recovered. It occurred to me she might consider the bag a crucial component of a chastity belt. When she said goodnight, as she emerged from the car, whose door I was holding open in front of her house, she was still working away on the gum. Had the conventional thanks for the date been offered, a chaste touching of lips, or only her lips on my cheek, somehow I would have declined it.

Consoling myself for spending an ungratifying, to say the least, evening as I drove home, I realized I'd kept my mind, my inner eye and ear, and, as well, my desire fixed so intently on Deirdre, the novice, soon to be Sister Lucia, that I had only the haziest idea of what was happening on the screen, except that the plot seemed hopelessly tangled to an inattentive mind. Later I somewhere read, or was told, that the film was based on a novel by Raymond Chandler and that William Faulkner had come up with the screenplay, both of whom it seemed likely had been soused while they were writing.

In early January off to college I went, with hundreds of thousands of other veterans, to secure an education, which before the war had been reserved for the privileged few. It would enable us to become professionals, earning unheard of salaries, as well as turn us into enlightened citizens who would commit ourselves to a morality that within our country would eliminate prejudice and poverty and, spreading to the nations of the world, would serve their peoples as models. And above all it would lead to the abolition of war. If reading this manifesto six decades later, you detect a heavily ironic undertone, you can trust your ear.

The identity of the college I attended has no bearing on this narrative. I was not, I confess, a dedicated student. Yet it went well enough for me to feel I'd been released from the self-imprisonment I'd imposed on myself, after having had to submit to those years of discipline, often pointless, sometimes sadistic, that had provided the man-and-woman-power to engage in the slaughter of war.

How frequently during those college days I saw the beautiful Deirdre, still a novice, in my inner eye, lived again those preciously few minutes we'd been enclosed together in the vestibule-shrine of St. Margaret's, heard in my inner ear her sing her little John the postman ditty, felt again the touch of her fingers on the side of my bare hand, and puzzled over what her impulse and intention had been! Such a gratifying yet problematic inner life did not motivate me as a student or prompt me to socialize to any significant extent with my fellow students, even with, or perhaps I should say, especially with the vets, athletes, or cheer-leader types among them. I did though meet and court my first wife.

Home for the spring break of my freshman year, while sauntering one morning along my mail delivery route of a few months before, under a Pacific-blue sky in March sunshine, with its promise of warmth and resurrection, I found myself approaching St. Margaret's, just to see the door to the hallowed place and pass by. Although I could feel the hard leather button of the doorbell in the tip of my forefinger, I didn't dare to mount the brownstone steps. Just having finished descending them was a familiar figure, his leather bag slung over his left shoulder, plodding along the sidewalk. Back in December unknowingly he had begun my liberation from myself.

"Mitch!" I shouted. Glancing back but not stopping, he turned around. Then I went racing toward him, intending to embrace him. "How's it going, Mitch?"

The blank look my presence and greeting drew as he stared at me face to face, warned me not to follow my impulse.

"Okay, how 'bout you?" He sang out in his deep raspy voice, then trailed off into that hearty laugh I remembered so well. For a couple of seconds I stared into the eyes behind the thick lenses of his glasses, muddy stones in oval-shaped scoops of cloudy water.

"Don't remember me, do you, Mitch?" I responded, trying to make my interrogative sound matter-of-fact, not reproachful. As I listened to my words reverberate in a moment of silence along the street, I heard the quivering resonance of a plea. I had to forbid my voice to identify myself as 'your helper during the Christmas rush.' There was a considerable pause as Mitch narrowed his eyes, then broke into a broad smile. I'd never noticed how yellow his teeth were. "Wull, I seen yuh 'round." Again that gush of good-will laughter as he winked.

A question that I'd sorely, jealously wanted to put to Mitch while I'd been doing part of his route but never had had the courage to, came leaping into my head. In the months between then and now the possibility had haunted me. As I held back the words, 'has one of the novices ever sung a little song to you when you deliver the mail to St. Margaret's?' I almost choked on them. Emitting a sound that must have been inexplicable to Mitch, I could do nothing but turn it to bitter laughter, which, joined with Mitch's hearty guffaw formed a dissonant duet Bartók might have written for a violin and bass viol.

"Well, take it easy, kid," Mitch called over his shoulder as he veered onto the walk leading to the steps of the house next to the convent. "'N keep yur pecker up." Although no doubt he meant it as a conventional good-bye, I took it as bitterly ironic advice.

"So long, Mitch," was all that I could get out in response. And that was that.

§

Reader I advise you to stop reading here. Sorry that I've had to go on.

A Meditation on My Own Story

As I write this narrative, not because I want to but because I must, I'm in the ninth decade of my life—in my eighties, that is, of course. It's more of a grope and suppose than a confession, a grope in the darkness of my past to grab hold of something that happened to me sixty-some years ago, something that, while seemingly insignificant, has stayed with me and has played a part in determining who I am and why I am what I am. I'm not deluding myself into believing that getting it out, into words on paper, will bring justification or acceptance or purgation, a term that merges the religious and the psychological. Certainly it won't bring consolation or peace of mind or conscience. It demands to be done not for what it will produce or lead to, but for its own sake. If a few incidental sparks of light should be struck, certainly not the blinding flash that, it's recorded, converted Paul of Tarsus into St. Paul, transforming his being and his life—a negatively pertinent allusion—those glimmers will be a bonus, a gratuitous reward.

Some spare but relevant details of my life between then and now. If I haven't fallen back into the depths of the bottomless pit you found me in at the beginning of this narrative, neither have I managed to lift myself all the way out of it, never near enough to the top of the abyss to live with joy in the sunlit world. Rather, from time to time I've just been able to get myself, by scrambling, to a level where briefly in the flesh, and from time to time in glows of memory, I have been able to see and find joy in the beauty that harks back to Deirdre the novice.

Three times I've tried marriage. Three times I've failed. And there have been, I must confess—perhaps acknowledge would serve while being a less damaging word—a number of other relationships, each of which ended either badly or sadly. That bare bones summary should make clear who is the cause of those failures.

I do consider it fortunate for myself, and for all my partners, let's call them, and certainly for those potential human beings who have never come into being, that I've not imposed this world on a single child. Or, to turn it around, the world hasn't been burdened with any offspring of mine. Just consider the blood with which we fuel and lubricate the death-dealing machines that run what we call civilization. Consider the massive abattoirs we construct in which to carve up flesh to satisfy our nation's appetite. Consider the deep valleys we dig in, in order to bury the scorched and fleshless bones, skeletons of what once were women, men and children. The collaborative intelligence of the brightest and best of those we educate should relieve us of pain, give us health and longevity, generate enlightenment, cultivate sensitivity, make us hunger for and be satisfied by beauty, tenderly care for our earthly home, produce equality, nurture goodness, and foster love of all living creatures. Just think of the horrors it *has* given birth to. Father a child to fuel and feed, to be shaped and destroyed by such monstrosities? That lets me out.

End of jeremiad. Which might strike you as a brief and outrageously presumptuous attempt to emulate the last forty or so pages of *War and Peace*. Not so. This narrative is not a lesson that elucidates a theory of history. Nor is it a homily or cautionary tale. As you should and I do know, stories neither have nor need morals, usable or useless. They are just what they are.

Well, I'm an old man, now facing what's left and then what isn't, alone. My salt and pepper hair is thinning, my face is a dried prune, I'm a bit stoop-shouldered and slightly bowlegged, not from lugging an overloaded mailbag, I can assure you. Yet my heart and lungs are sound enough for someone my age. As for my brain, having read this narrative you be the judge. My second wife did have a daughter and a son by a former husband. When she and I married, they were grown and had families of their own. Although there were no conflicts, even hard feelings over their mother's divorce from their father, her marriage to me, then our divorce, her children and I never became close. The last time I saw and spoke to either of them—it was the daughter—was at her mother's funeral, some twenty years ago. I know nothing of her or her brother's whereabouts, even whether either of the two is still breathing. I have no known relatives on either my mother's or father's side. I do, however, have reason to believe that my mother's only sister, my aunt, of course, who died when I was in my teens, was read out of the family for producing an illegitimate child. He or she was not embraced by our family. Nor ever mentioned. What may have happened to her or him I haven't the least idea of or interest in.

Never have I regained a mustard seed of any faith. Nor have I managed to escape from the pit of guilt that was dug by a never-sleeping conscience, a conscience that, without knowing how to do penance or how to petition for forgiveness, gropes and grieves over the collective part I played in the gratuitous mass killing of innocents at the end of the war against already vanquished Japan. I'm afraid the candle Deirdre the novice lighted for me that long ago Christmas Eve has failed to illuminate the darkness in which I've lived.

I'd be overstating to no purpose were I to assert that Deirdre has constantly been living in my consciousness, determining my every choice, decision and action. On the other side, I'd be pointlessly denying were I to contend that, buried alive in my mind, she never resurrects herself. Or do *I* summon her back? I'm not being in the least sentimental, only stating a cold fact, of which the narrative I've just written is, I hope, sufficient corroboration. Isn't life defeat, loss and bitterness, with rare small triumphs, bits of sweetness, glimmers of light?

What I do find strange, unaccountable, is that so far as I've ever been able to recall, Deirdre has never appeared, as have and still do the blood-chilling horrors of war, in a dream. Might it be that she's all dream, that she never happened as I imagine, that it's mostly, if not completely, invention? That I've embellished a triviality into a private myth? I must concede that from time to time I do have doubts about how much I've made of those few minutes I spent alone in the vestibule of St. Margaret's Convent with a novice named Deirdre. The wondering, though, is real.

Had I in particular, a young man, little more than a boy, even though an initiated veteran, actually aroused in a beautiful novice the womanhood she was denying for a life of chastity? Had I caused her deep pain? Or is it possible that what I'd sensed emanating from her, an urge deep in the flesh, might have been brought to the surface, if not by Mitch, her jolly middle-aged mail carrier, then by any other passably congenial, eligible, and, yes, sexual young man?

And might it actually have come to pass that she never had become Sister Lucia, had remained Deirdre, renouncing whatever vows she'd made before her probationary period had expired, gone back into the world she'd left, and become wife and mother? On the other side, the chance, fanciful as it might be, of her giving up the regulated life and embracing the world invites so many possibilities that I can understand her choosing to choose to not do so. Though I go back and forth on my conjecture of the path she took, my suppose is that the choice she made was to submit, rendering all other choosing moot. Give up your life to whatever, then choices are made for you. It's the easier road to take.

As for me, with certainty impossible, "suppose" haunts me. Suppose I had been an unwitting pander between her and an existent lover, inadvertently determining that she renounce her preliminary vows, that she return to the world, marry for love, have children and grandchildren, all of whom turned out well, and that she be happily still alive in good health. In other words that inadvertently and unwittingly I was the instrument of a miracle. Given the abomination of the world we live in, that would have been the one good I'd have done in my life. On the other side, suppose the presumptive marriage would have turned out to be a disaster. We do live in a place of darkness, in which presumptions are mere will-o'-the-wisps.

Then again, suppose there were no lover and she had become Sister Lucia. Then at least the Deirdre she was, to whom I'd delivered mail, whom I'd touched and sent a gold cross during that long ago Christmas season, has been a preserved lighthouse, providing some gleams of beauty in the darkness, a lighthouse that I, like Virginia Woolf's Mr. Ramsay, glimpsed and never was able to reach.

Or suppose I'd never encountered what I still believe is 'pure,' in more than one sense of the word, had never found beauty in a convent on a city street when I was in a state of despair, just emerging from the lower depths to deliver mail as a substitute during the Christmas season? Would my life, devoid of the fleeting fact and long memory of her, have been even more wanting than it has? Suppose I, after closing the book on Protestantism, from the wailing of snake handlers and the jabbering of those who speak in tongues to the chanting of divines in the High Church of England, had eventually returned to Mother Church, even as a nonbeliever, and had taken the Sacraments as merely symbolic wafer and wine—are they any closer to flesh and blood than the Methodist's bread and grape juice?—and had said prayers with my fingers crossed, and had renounced and retreated from the world of my fellowmen and women. What if I'd dedicated my life to serving the poor, needy and disabled as penance for the bloodshed, suffering and killing I'd been complicit in during my youth—would I then have found atonement? peace of mind? Would my life have been worth something? Would I have justified my existence? Would I have given some purpose to the purposelessness of being?

Or, the most tormenting question that dogs me from the chance touching of my life and the life of the beautiful novice—suppose during our final encounter, with Eloise and Abelard in mind, I had shrugged off the mailbag I'd been carrying, had gathered up Deirdre in my pea jacket-covered-arms, and, crowning her with my watch cap and tossing the hideous yellow gloves onto the floor of the vestibule, had carried her, with her consent, given or tacit, from the convent out into the raging storm—what then would have been our lives?

Suppose leads to wonder. Reluctantly because fearfully I wonder whether Deirdre is still in the land of the living. If not, I fervently hope the end of her story did not in any way correspond to Celtic Deirdre's, her mythic namesake, who died of a broken heart on her lover's grave. When I think she might still be breathing the air you and I breathe, I refuse to let myself try to picture what she must be now, wherever and whatever her lot. The deceitful eye of my imagination, not my brain, insists that she is a constant, immune to the ravages of time and change, unaffected by the rottenness of the world, that she is still Deirdre, the beautiful novice.

I sometimes wonder too whether, if she be on this our earth, she ever remembers there was a John the postman, to whom she sang and smiled, whose flesh she touched once, more than glancingly. Might she ever wonder what I am and look like as I record this suppose, while memory, probably glossed-up, the gnaw of that rat time, and the fumble to find words are exerting conflicting claims? Most probably if she does retain a fleeting remembrance of John the postman, it's just a shape in the dust supposedly we're made of, or the waning crescent that can be seen in the sky after the full moon has drowned in the sea of darkness.

Yes, even the seemingly inconsequential suppose always comes down to never-to-be-satisfied wonder. What did she make of the cross of gold? Did she know or suspect from whom it came. Did she ever wear it? Not even once? Did she sell it to a pawnshop for money to give to the Little Sisters of the Poor? Might she, while fingering it during the silence of regulated hours, on her knees with her head bowed, ever have sung so only her inner ear could hear,

He's coming, he's coming,
Named for the beloved disciple,
John the postman is coming,
As sure as our Savior's love?

Because after the war never was I able to bend my knees and I've refused to bow my head, hours of silence have not been *appointed* for me, though they have been plentiful and these days are even more so. From time to time during silences my inner ear has heard the parlor-song melody and the substitute words sung not by the croaking contralto of a fat old nun, perhaps now a mother superior, but by the lilting virginal soprano of a truly beautiful young novice.

To fill in and give up on my story. As I've suggested, I was graduated from college as a B-minus student. I did succeed in earning a Master's Degree in Education. And I did manage to become a high school teacher of... you guessed it...English. As a teacher, I'd grade myself C-plus.

The best I can do to conclude this narrative I don't know how to end, in fact I can't even find the words with which to take a proper leave, is to fall back on some appropriate lines of poetry by the seventeenth-century Welsh poet Henry Vaughan in the hope they will convey something of how a few moments of confluence in the lives of Deirdre the novice and a temporary mailman have affected, or should I say have infected me.

> If a star were confined into a tomb,
>   Her captive flames must needs burn there;
> But when the hand that locked her up gives room,
>   She'll shine through all the sphere.

Substitute "can't prevent a touch" for "gives room" and, though it's at the cost of losing the poet's meter and rhyme, you'll understand.

RIVER LOVE: PROLOGUE

I came across the following poems quite by accident. They'd been stored in a barn beside the house my wife and I live in. The property has belonged to her family for generations. In the cornerstone of the limestone foundation, 1832 has been chiseled.

My wife and I had gone into the loft of the barn to show some guests a historical curiosity—an Old Towne canoe that had belonged to Woodrow Wilson. It happened to be there because "Woody," a notorious penny pincher, had taken a fancy to an oil landscape, a piece of early American Impressionism. Unwilling to shell out the modest amount the painter, who happened to be my wife's first husband's father, had put on it, Woody had induced the artist to swap the painting for his canoe. The painting went into the White House, the canoe into the barn.

After lifting the sheet from the pedigreed object, my wife was reciting for our guests the oft-repeated scrap of history that accounted for the boat's having landing there. While they were gawking at the relic, my roving eye happened to light on a Saratoga trunk, standing in a nearby bay. I'd never noticed it before.

Pointing to it, I asked my wife, "What's in that trunk?" She had just finished her brief tale of a tub. "I haven't the slightest idea," she answered. "Most likely nothing. Why it's here I haven't a clue."

"Mind if I take a peek?"

"Of course not," she replied.

After lifting the rounded lid, I began fussing with garments that almost surely had been in the wardrobe of some nineteenth-century female member of my wife's family.

"What's this?" I suddenly exclaimed, as I lifted a brown paper packet, unmarked, from the cincture of a hoopskirt. "May I open it to see what's inside?"

Although my wife is a thoroughly liberated woman, she does have some residual family pride and can be a bit touchy about any denigration of her genteel ancestry.

"Help yourself," she replied offhandedly.

When we returned to the house, I carried in the packet and laid it on my desk. Later that evening, after dinner and the departure of our guests, I retired to my study and opened the parcel. Imagine my surprise when I extracted a slim sheaf of gray paper, with blue-green lines that time had made almost invisible. The rough edge at the top of the sheets suggested they'd been torn from a tablet or pad. On them, written in pencil, were what looked to be verses of varying lengths. After leafing through, I decided to read them, not because I was expecting to make an earthshaking literary discovery, but just because...well, because I'm a curious person. I counted the pages. On ten of the eleven sheets what certainly had to be poems had been printed in block letters. So faint were the words that it was difficult, though possible to make them out under the light from the halogen lamp on my desk. The letters had been so neatly drawn that, if they hadn't been badly faded, they could almost be taken for typefaces. At the bottom of these sheets, across the blue-green lines at varying angles, cursively written phrases, also in pencil, had been scrawled.

One sheet, the eighth, however, was vellum-like ivory. It had scarcely deteriorated. What was on it had been written in black ink, which, though slightly faded, had not given in to—how many years? The slanting strokes and stylized flourishes would seem to indicate that the inscribing hand had had some training in penmanship.

What had been written toward the bottom of the ten sheets, I came to conclude, indicated the occasions that had called forth the poems. These phrases appeared to have been hastily scribbled at varying times in varying states of emotion, presumably after the poems had been composed and painstakingly printed. So meticulous was the care with which the poetry had been set down and so careless had been the recording of the occasion that it would seem the composition and transcribing of the poems were acts of love, while the scrawl was an afterthought. On the vellum-like page there was no such scribbling.

As I read the contents of the packet a second time, more closely, I came to understand that the ten printed poems purported to have been written by a river man sometime in the distant past. If so, I considered it remarkable that, limited as his knowledge of poetry must have been, he'd felt compelled and had been able to commit his comings and goings, along with a powerful passion, to paper. Presumably uneducated and isolated from literary culture as he must have been, it seemed unlikely he'd ever read a poem by Wordsworth or Longfellow, let alone Keats or Emerson.

Nor do the poems resemble the poetry of the sentimental poets of the nineteenth century. In fact, they struck me as being quite original. Clearly they were not a substitute for love notes or letters. The beloved, never named, is mostly a feminine pronoun. Only twice is she directly addressed. All we see of her is "a flounce behind a tree." Yet these poems are both intimate and passionate. And unliterary as they might be, they have a convincing integrity. In the boatman's poetic endeavors I also find surprising sensitivity, an ear for language, some diction you wouldn't expect from such a man, an eye for the river and sky, light and dark. And yet you can be certain that these poems never will become part of the canon of literary poetry.

The presumptive date for the building of the barn, 1832, more than a decade before the first railroad tracks were laid in this region, a period when boats, barges and log rafts, carrying lumber, freight, grain, and passengers, were still plying the Susquehanna and its adjunct canals, seems likely to be the approximate time in which the poems were written and during which the events they present happened—if they weren't just by-products of someone's imagining.

Arguing against the poems' being fiction is poem number eight, written from a woman's perspective, in a woman's voice. This poem does suggest that the writer had some familiarity with the Lancelot-Elaine of Astolat love story in Arthurian narrative, perhaps by way of Tennyson's *Idylls of the King*. Like the quality of the paper it's written on and its calligraphy, it almost surely indicates a class difference between the protagonist and the woman he loves. Such a surmise is supported by the ladies' garments, with their frippery of hoops, hooks and eyes, ruffles, flounces and furbelows, within which the packet had been hidden in the trunk. Quite a contrast to the rugged dress of a river man.

Although the events recorded, if they did happen, are cryptically fragmented, with huge gaps, the sequence of poems does seem to tell the story of the river man's falling in love with a woman living in a house situated close to the shore, which he passes as he makes his runs down and back up the river. At first the woman rejects his advances, then comes to accept and return his love. It appears there was a consummation, without marriage, culminating in the woman's premonition that she was soon to die, followed by her death in fact, or in her lover's imagination. If my supposition about what happened is correct, it's quite possible that a difference in class was an impregnable barrier between the lovers. From what I know of my wife's genealogy, a number of beautiful and stylish women might serve as plausible prototypes for the beloved. For the river man there is no candidate.

Concluding that these pieces might be of some local historical interest, I decided to edit and transcribe them. In so doing I've not altered the diction, with the exception of a single word I couldn't resist (see whether it jumps out at you)—or tampered with the figurative language—obviously the river is the dominant metaphor—nor have I modified the original rhythms in any way. But I have supplied punctuation where it seems helpful and regularized spelling where it's eccentric. Also, I've taken the liberty of changing the format of some poems by indenting lines that are metrically short. Neither the poems nor the pages of the original are numbered, but I have preserved the order in which they lay in the packet. This arrangement seems to be compatible with the sketchy narrative I've constructed.

The poems are without titles. So I've used the scribbled occasion as a title for each of the ten printed poems. Since there is no such notation on the vellum-like sheet, I invented a title for that poem, enclosing the words in a parenthesis to signify that the title had not been provided by the writer. I've also given the entire set of poems its straightforward title.

It would seem that these poems, secured in a trunk as they have been, were not meant for the eyes of any of the living save the two who were involved. Might their preservation suggest that the one who wrote ten love poems did not, perhaps could not bear to destroy them? After all, our ancestors did have matches, lucifers they were then called, and the river was running by, waiting to spirit off shreds of paper that were tossed into it.

Somehow the ten poems must fallen into the hands of the one who seemingly had called them forth. Placing it where it significantly belongs, she then had added a poem of her own to the cache. Could it be that, with every intention of doing away with all the poems at some future time, she had hidden them in the trunk with her clothing? Were that the case, it seems unlikely she would forget they were there. Perhaps death, *her* sudden death saved the life of the poems. Or might it be she hadn't the heart to destroy her lover's poems? Could this be the reason her trunk had been stored in the loft of the barn like an exile or a castaway, rather than in the capacious attic with its hoard of Victoriana? There are mysteries that will never be solved.

Still another possibility is that the lady, if there really was one, when she was no longer a maiden, however short or long her life, didn't want the poems to be destroyed, after all. Rather, perhaps, she wished them to be preserved for her familial posterity, some one of whom, after she was no more, she wanted to find and read them as evidence of her having lived, having been loved, and having given her love in return. Whatever the circumstance or intention that preserved them and however slight their literary quality, as I've worked over them I've come to believe that these pieces of poetry, which serve as a cultural or poetic curiosity, maybe also be a bequest, a last will and testament.

I should add that my speculations and conjectures about this trove of love poems raises a genealogical/biological question. Whether such a possibility has also occurred to my wife since I exposed the poems to her, or her to the poems, I have no idea. In fact, I've made a pact with myself never to put the question to her. When you've read the poems, you'll know, I'm sure, what the hazardous, unmentioned and unanswerable question is.

RIVER LOVE

i. The Night After the First Morning I Dared Speak to Her

Three times I put the name I love
In one great question to the night,
While near the shore I stood against
The running of a powerful tide.

The current would not let me stand,
Three times it heeled my stern around.
Three times I spoke out through the dark,
Three times the hills returned the sound.

And after that a silence came,
Giving her ungiven answer.
Three times I called the name I loved,
Then gave myself up to the river.

ii. Another Rejection

There were no lights along the river,
      None in the sky,
There was no sound upon the water
      As I ran by.

Tonight her answer has been given,
      My promise kept.
Tonight I passed along the river
      While she slept.

Swift flowed the current down to Winfield,
      Silent her door.
There was no light upon the water.
      None on the shore.

iii. My Futile Persistence

Now clouds eclipse the eastern headland
And night obscures the sky.
Strong runs the river on through darkness
In which I tethered lie.

Oh, I've stood along the shore till evening.
From her window, not a gleam.
Untying the knot, I let the current
Carry my boat downstream.

iv. A Glimmer of Hope

One morn as I ran to Liverpool—
    a flounce behind a tree!
Was she looking for me going past,
    Secretly?

When I came up from Liverpool
    As sun slid down the sky,
Was she waiting there again to watch
    Me passing by?

Might it be I'll run to Harris Ferry
    And seal a bargain there?
A gown I'd buy of virgin color,
Stockings of silk and shoes of leather,
    And a comb for auburn hair!

v. A Miracle

Came days when joy like Jesus walked
Upon the tide that bears my soul.
All fair that time, no storms, nor night,
    Nor cold.

The bush of Moses burned in me,
Night glowed when there was not a moon,
And even the distant shore shone bright
    As sunny noon.

A powerful current carried joy
With strength enough to wrest me free
From time to temporize to now
    Eternity.

vi. How Much I Dread the End of Summer

It's coming, love,
Blood's in the leaf,
Bright shoots of crimson
Before October's hemorrhage.

I saw white this morning
Curl off the river, love,
First shroud skeins,
Twisted up north.

See that high field where flowers
And weeds embroidered summer
With robes of color, love?
Now turning brown.

Come, be white beneath my fingers,
For most I jealous death.
Keep me in you green always,
Always alive.

Let the blood I feel be blood
Surging to bring us joy, not rue.
Love, then let it come, love,
Oh, let it come.

vii. Sorrowing

But once you let me have my way
  And then our life was done.
And I, I could not yet believe
  Your love turned cold as stone.

Dark flowed the current, black hung the night,
  And not a breeze was sighing,
While you, no longer blood and flesh,
  From loving turned toward dying.

viii. (Song of the Riparian Maiden)

Somber as with some mournful purpose,
Silent as with a private grief,
The clouds toward Winfield make an evening
        Retreat, retreat.

The one I love rides on the river
As far as the seabirds venture in,
Where the shadows of spires float long on the water
        And boatmen sing.

Oh, I sit by the far-flowing Susquehanna
And I watch while the current flows off into time
And I dream of the maid long ago on the river.
        Who died, who died.

ix. A Dream

Last night I lay by Harris Ferry
    And dreamed my love was dead.
Dark hung the night upon the river,
The night hung heavy on a lover
    And starless overhead.

I saw my love all dressed in white,
    A gown of white she wore.
White hands upon her breast lay crossed,
Her eyes like bluebells touched by frost,
    White lilies in her hair.

From her cold cheek I raised the veil.
    I spoke, she made no answer.
My lips I touched to her cold breath,
Then seeing how she'd chosen death,
    I gave her to the river.

My love lies sixty miles upstream,
    Last night I dreamed she died.
This morn I saw a ghostly sight,
I saw a maid laid all in white,
All cold and still and lily white,
    Come floating down the tide.

x. Pain and Loss

And comes there bleeding from the mountain,
    Blood rays from the sun,
Have clouds dispersed, exhausted,
    Does thunder say, "it's done"?

Do the cliffs all echo moaning?
    Have the fields all turned to stone?
Have I lost all life within me
    Since love has gone?

xi. Last Words

While I lay still a bedrock moved,
The angry river thundered by,
And blood-red stars rolled down the sky.

Had I not known, had I not loved,
Had I not once pure passion proved
And calmed her fears to quietude
And kissed the pearly tears she cried,
While bedding with an unwed bride,
Had we not loved would she have died?

EMILY'S ROSE

Beckoning, her fingers were thin as chicken bones. He wobbled to her side of the bed on his cane, a cypress stick, sanded and bent into a crook. Five or six years ago he'd bought it at Clemm's, with his own money, to help him when he toted the market basket, holding what she'd told him to buy, back to the house. Now, he was using the cane most of the time.

Two days ago she'd lost the strength to reach for her cane, leaning against the night table so she could knock on the rail of the bed to summon him from the back kitchen. Her cane was black, straight and smooth as the barrel of the deer rifle hanging above the mantel in the kitchen. Its gold handle, which she hadn't instructed him to polish for years now, was shaped like a bird.

The cane had belonged to her father. Before he'd taken to bed, he'd carried the cane whenever he left the house, even in former days when, straight-backed and spring-stepped, he'd had no need of a walking stick. When he'd died, she wouldn't let anyone near him for three days.

Now that she couldn't raise an arm, could only waggle her fingers, he felt certain it had come, was perched on the tester above the headboard, waiting, watching down inside the drapery. It would be seeing her as he saw her—a pillow and two bolsters arranged like a body and legs beneath the sheet, above them a face yellow as the pillow slip the back of her head lay on. For the past week he hadn't bothered to run the comb through her coarse gray hair, now a snarl of whipcords. She paid no heed.

Until a year or so ago her face had been full-fleshed, its skin smooth as a ripe peach. Since she'd shrunk, the skin had wrinkled until she looked like a new-born baby about to cry. Except for her eyes—bigger than they'd ever been, they glowed like hot coals.

Low and thin as her voice had become, he could feel her breath inside his ear. And he could just make out her words. Smelling and feeling were the best parts he himself had left, though he still could see and hear middling.

What now it was time for, she'd told him yesterday morning. After he'd slid a few spoonfuls of corn meal between her lips, colorless and thin as the edges of the spoons, and past her teeth, still there, where he had only three bottom and two top left, she'd shaken her head, "No more." As if saving what little voice she had left.

He'd picked up the bowl from the night table and turned to go. "Wait," she'd whispered. "There are some things I must tell you to do."

Putting the bowl on the table beside her watch, he'd bent over her. Her breath smelled like sour milk.

What she'd told him hadn't surprised him. Long ago as it had been, he knew she hadn't finished with it up there. In spite of what had gone on between her and him all these years. Beginning the night he'd heard her enter his room beneath the cupola. Without knocking. She'd reached over to where he was lying in the rope-bed, wide-eyed. Without a word, she'd taken his hand, not gnarled as it was now, and raised him.

He'd let her lead him down the attic steps. Past the closed door of her father's bedroom, where, he knew, it was lying in the four-poster her father had died in and he'd heard she'd been born in. Down the front staircase. Into the room across from the parlor, once her father's library, into which she'd had him move the big walnut bed with its feather mattress, so different from the canvas of the rope-bed he'd been sleeping in that it had taken him many nights to get used to its softness.

She'd come for him the night after the night and early morning the sobbing in her father's bedroom had turned into screaming, the screaming to moaning, the moaning had died into silence.

Never again had he slept in the narrow bed in the attic room. Not even after they'd given it up between them, nine or ten years ago now that had been. Before that it had dwindled from at first every night, often in the first years more than once, to two or three times a week, to once, to every other week, to every once in while. Always without any talk or false starts. As if each silently read the other's mind, or whatever part tells when and when not to begin.

It had never been the occasion for many words between them. Not one, not even his name as they'd begin. None during, though at a point she'd always start to moan. Then to scream. Afterward she'd sob until she'd become still as a statue. Just the reverse of what he'd heard in her father's bedroom that time. From her breathing he could always tell when she'd fallen asleep.

During the years they'd lived together alone in the big old house, both of them graying as it had grayed from weathering, the most frequent words between them were her "Buy cornmeal, flour, eggs, milk, broad beans, cowpeas, apples, mangoes, musk melons, breast of chicken, lamb or pork chops." Or do this or that. And his "yes'um" and sometimes in answer to a question "no'um."

If what she'd told him yesterday hadn't surprised him, that she'd dared to put it off so long, almost until it would have been too late, did make him wonder. Yet it turned out that when she'd no longer had strength to use the cane to knock or do more than signal with her fingers and gesture with her head, she'd known it was time and had just enough breath left to tell him to do it. Yes, she'd been a good calculator.

Because his head shook on his turkey neck all the time now, he wasn't sure she'd known he'd been nodding as she'd instructed him a step at a time. In fact, in the dimness of that room, where the blinds hadn't been opened since the night she'd fetched him, he couldn't be sure she was able to see him at all, what with her sight so far gone as it was.

"When you've done precisely as I've told you, come back here and inform me. Even though you think I shan't hear you, I will. And I shall know whether you've done just as I say."

"Yes'um," he'd replied.

Then as if shooing a mosquito, she'd waved him off.

Now a day later, in the quiet that had presided over the house for many years, her voice was less than a whisper, a mere hiss of air. Yet he knew it was telling him the time had come.

Leaning his cane next to hers against the night table, he bent over the bed. When he lifted her head from the pillow, she felt limp as a sack of grain. The fingers of his other hand groped for the chain he knew was hanging around her neck.

In the sparse daylight that seeped into the house, he'd grown so accustomed to seeing the long gold chain on her person that he noticed it no more than if it were a part of her body, like the brown mole with black hair growing in it on the left side of her chin or the curve of her hairline high on her forehead. She hadn't taken off the chain since the night she'd gone to the attic for him. When she was dressed, a gold watch, which she'd always carried in the pocket of her skirt, was fastened to it. He'd never seen her consult the watch, even when she'd remove it each night and lay it on the night table, where it was lying now.

In bed he'd felt the small links of the chain against his flesh. Also something else that was hooked on. Not a locket, he could tell. Maybe a Cross, he'd thought, which some people wore, though since the day her father had been buried in the churchyard, beneath a tall gray granite stone bearing the family names and dates, on which her name and birth date were carved beneath her father's, she hadn't set foot inside the church.

When he tried to slip the chain over the back of her head, as she'd told him, a link caught in her hair at the nape. While he untangled it by feel, her head didn't move. It took two more tries before he got all the fine links clear and slipped the chain over her ears, which looked to have grown larger in the last few years. Dangling, the key came out from beneath the sheet. He slid the chain and key into the pocket of his trousers.

Without using his cane, he limped around the foot of the bed and up the side where his pillow lay. Stretching over it, he reached for her head again, felt out a strand of hair using the balls of his forefinger and thumb.

"Watch me closely," she'd told him yesterday. Her small hand had slowly lifted itself, as if it were being hoisted on invisible wires. The sudden energy with which she'd jerked her hand away from her head surprised him. "When you pull on the hair," she'd said, "you must not be afraid you will hurt me."

Now he was studying her face, to see whether he could make out a wince of pain when he pulled. By their glow he could tell her eyes were fixed on his. He felt the strand of hair, coarse as darning thread, slip from between his fingers.

After feeling out another strand, he wrapped it around his forefinger three times. As he yanked, he saw her eyelids close, as if she'd blinked involuntarily. Then her eyes were riveted back on his. The long strand of hair came out, he could tell. Although he thought he saw her lips quiver, he heard no sound.

There was no need for him to make a dent in his pillow with his fist, as yesterday she'd summoned the strength to show him to. From where his head had been resting a few hours before there was still an indentation. In it he laid the hair.

As she'd told him, he placed one hand on top of the strand, slid the other beneath his pillow. Lifting it, he carried it gingerly, as he would poison he feared he might spill.

Without the cane to lean on, it was a slow scuffle. Especially up the staircase when he didn't have a hand free to grasp the railing. He laid the pillow on the linen chest, right beside the door. When he wiggled the key out of the pocket of his trousers, there was enough light in the hallway for him to see the key was brass, tinged with green, small but appropriately heavy for the lock on the oak door. It took some jiggling before he got the key in the scutcheon.

The lock didn't want to turn. Before he heard it give, he had to muster all the strength he could. While holding the porcelain doorknob with its tongue withdrawn, he bumped the door a couple of times with his shoulder. At last the door swung in, groaning on its hinges. He felt bruised.

The valanced curtains on the three windows were drawn so there was just a crack of light between them. As he shuffled in, after picking up the pillow from the top of the linen chest, something smacked his nostrils so as almost to take his breath. Not the smell, he knew, from years before when they'd come sneaking onto the lawn after midnight and sprinkled lime around the foundation of the house and on the sills of the cellar door and windows. That smell had died years ago.

What hit him was the dust, acrid dust, so thick that as he shambled through it, carrying the pillow, he had to narrow his eyes to slits. On the gray-brown carpet, under a Morris chair, he saw a pair of shoes. They had been white buck, he recalled, but now looked like two dead rats.

Above them, draped over the rung of the chair, were two yellow rags. From there his eyes went onto the linen suit he'd seen at the kitchen door those many years ago. In the dusk that evening it had been bright white, like the dress a bride would wear. Now folded neatly over the back of the chair, it was yellow as the pages of the books he'd used to dust. When he reached the bed, he kept his eyes down. Yet he had to see what was on the pillow on the other side and what below the pillow was covered with moldy rags on top of the mildewed sheet. There was enough room on the side he was standing on for him to place the pillow just as she'd said to. He felt for the strand of hair. He could feel it in the hollow of the pillow.

Before leaving, he lowered his stiff bones until he was on his knees, as if kneeling in prayer at the bedside. Scraping up a handful of dust from the carpet, he scattered it over his pillow and the strand of hair, as she'd told him. Then he ratcheted himself onto his feet.

As he scuffed back toward the door, he spied his sole prints in the dust, as if the floor he'd hobbled across were sand. Their eyes, he guessed, would go somewhere else when they'd break down the door to see what was in the room. And when they'd enter, the prints they'd make would mingle with his. To turn the key as he left, locking the door, took less strength.

After he'd said, with his lips almost touching her ear, "Ah done done whad ya tole me to up theyah, evythin xactly," he saw her eyes flutter. That meant it was still perched on the tester above the headboard. Her eyes were glowing cinders.

Taking his cane from where it was leaning against the night table, he was about to shuffle off to the back kitchen to wait. In all the years they'd slept in the same bed, he'd never eaten a morsel in her presence. She'd take the velvet-covered chair, with brass finials on its shoulders, at the head of the mahogany table in the dining room. When he'd cleared her meal, he'd eat leftovers of the same food he'd prepared for her, at the deal table in the back kitchen.

That's where he always sat during those long evenings too, while she sat in the parlor, in a chair with cracked leather, facing a gilt easel that stood in front of the fireplace. On the canvas it held was a portrait of her father, dark-toned except for the great mane and thick mustache of bright white hair. His coal-black eyes were fixed on where she sat.

Just before turning from the bedside, he sensed something had happened. First he realized he wasn't feeling her eyes on his face. Then he noticed that her lids had closed.

He didn't leave. Stood there, leaning on his cane, looking down at her. Now he heard rasping snores with silences between. As he waited, he realized the silences were getting longer as the snores sounded louder.

He never heard it. No flapping of wings, as he'd expected. Just before the last great snore her eyes opened wide. They looked like two holes burned by the red tip of a cigar in the yellowed linen covering a feather pillow.

He laid his hand on her breast. When he didn't feel it rise, he knew.

Still he let time pass to be sure it had carried her off. After a spell he poked and pushed until he'd nudged the lumps of flesh to the middle of the bed, as she'd told him. Without touching her face, he plumped the pillow so her head was propped. She'd told him not to close her eyes.

Then, as she'd told him, he took the gold watch from the night table and stuffed it into the pocket on his trousers, on top of the key and chain, which like the watch she'd told him he was to keep. He touched nothing else in the room, as she'd said he was not to.

"Afterward you will have no further responsibilities here," she'd told him yesterday.

Leaving her bedside without a backward look, he traipsed through the house, opening all the jalousies, draperies and blinds, except those in the two rooms it had come into, as she'd told him. Then, dragging himself up to the attic, he stowed his own belongings, none of which he'd ever moved down into the house, in a carped-bag.

Just as he arrived at the bottom of the staircase, he heard them on the porch.

Plodding to the front door, he turned the key, twisted the brass knob, molded to the shape of a rose, and tugged open the massive front door, as she'd told him, so they'd know it was permitted the ladies of the town to enter. Just as years before she'd told him to admit four men dressed in linen suits and pastel neckties, holding palmetto hats over their parts as if covering themselves. They'd come to collect taxes but had never got to take chairs in the parlor before she'd told him to show them out.

And as still longer ago for some years he'd received young ladies of the town, in bright floral dresses with pleats and flounces who'd come to have her teach them to paint flowers on vases and pitchers and creamers and teacups. And as before that time, not long after her father had died and she'd cut her hair short, he'd ushered in the preacher, dressed in his black suit, starched white shirt with a high collar, and shoestring tie, who'd started in on her for buggy-riding on Sunday afternoon, but who'd left right quick, looking like a whipped hound.

Taking the handles of the carpetbag in one hand, wrapping the palm of the other around the crook of his cane, he scuffled past the closed door of the room he'd been sleeping in all those years. Behind him he heard them heading for the staircase.

He shambled through the kitchen. Out through the door he'd opened to see the red tip of a cigar, clamped between teeth behind fat red lips, glowing in the dusk all those years ago.

A TALE TOLD

I do not want to tell this tale. For a number of reasons. Any one of which I consider justification for refusing to go on with it. Because overkill is a self-defeating tactic, I won't go into all of them. A man who takes his obligations seriously, I try to fulfill them even when I'm inclined not to. Yes, I do try to be true to myself and act honorably and effectively, though sometimes these intentions do get in one another's way.

Of course it's up to you to decide what you do or don't want to do about the story, should I go on and tell it. You can always say, "Not my cup of tea." Or, "I'm not going to let him dump this on me." Or, "Who gives a damn?" Frankly I don't care one way or another. What you choose to do or not do is your affair. I have the weight of my own decisions to bear, without taking on any of yours.

At any rate, I will give you three among my numerous reasons for not wanting to tell the story. First, I know little about the man who claims it's his story, except that seemingly he's familiar with the opening four notes of Beethoven's Fifth Symphony—it was also the rhythmic code for victory during World War II. Heroism and triumph, I confess, are not my familiars. And that the man's persistent, or I should say insistent to the point of rudeness. Oh yes, I can add that he told me his name is Fels, though I'm not sure I believe him.

Second reason. I don't want to get to know him. If I do try to tell his story, necessarily I'll have to learn some things about him. Let me assure you it will be as little as possible. I have enough trouble with myself let alone dealing with some kind of nut case. Such a serious reservation in itself is justification enough for not going on.

Reason three. I'm finding myself rather weary these days, and telling a story, anybody's story, takes one hell of a lot of energy. That might surprise you. When you tell a story, you're not lifting dumbbells or running, even necessarily standing. Although some story tellers do claim that standing at a lectern circulates the blood more freely, making their brain work more efficiently, most prefer to work sitting down. Either way, you don't have to push anything heavier than a pen, which is almost light as a feather—an apt comparison in that, as I'm certain you know, feathers are what pens, from the *Latin penna,* for feather, used to be—across a smooth surface. Which it would seem does not demand much energy. But even if you should have reservations about my character or find me a failure as a storyteller, give me the benefit of your doubt in the matter of energy. Believe that just the little I've been doing before the story, if there is to be one, gets started, takes a lot of energy out of someone who's wrung out to begin with.

What's put me into such a state, I'm not going to tell you. To do so would amount to special pleading. Besides, it's none of your business.

I can only hope you're fair-minded enough to agree that these three reasons alone are sufficient for my not wanting to tell this story. Yet though I myself find them convincing and compelling, here I am, still moving a pen across the blue-green lines on yellow sheets. Because there's only one reason for that, I'll tell you what it is. That bastard Fels. He won't go away and let me languish in peace. So at this very moment I'm in my study at my desk right after breakfast, sipping a second cup of coffee, as I always do.

But I'm not telling a story, anybody's story. What I am making myself do is try to balance my checkbook. Doing so is necessary because, I admit, I'm careless and inexact, where I should be scrupulous and precise if I'm to reach an accommodation between my record of the money I've spent and have available and the statement of my financial status the bank sends each month. I find this a hateful, perplexing, painful, and finally futile ordeal. Yet I consider submitting to it preferable, infinitely, to having to tell a story.

Thus, lost in gaps, confused by my own notations, and baffled by my own arithmetic, I'm here are my desk, heroically struggling with the lesser of two evils involving paper and pen, when I hear four knocks on the door of my study—three light and quick, followed by one hard and sustained.

"Go away," I shout, "I'm busy."

Though I listen intently, turning my head so my left ear is toward the door—my right ear isn't all it used to be—I can't pick up the sound of footsteps in the hallway, just as I'd not heard the approach of anyone before I was interrupted. There's no more knocking.

Next morning, same time, I'm back at my desk with a pen in the fingers of one hand, the handle of a coffee cup between the fingers of the other. Fagged as I've been for months now—or is it already years, my perception of time is that unreliable—the last thing I want to do again this morning is tell a story. So thrusting aside whatever claim storytelling might have on me, I'm on the point, so to speak, of writing a difficult-to-compose letter to someone with whom over a period of time—again I have to be approximate—I was rather intimate. As was the case with balancing my checkbook, I've compelled myself to face up to and embark on what ought not be avoided.

The moment that, assuring myself the adjective at the beginning of the salutation in a letter is nothing more than a convention, not necessarily an expression of affection, I get down the word *dear,* followed by the given name of the addressee and a comma—I'd prefer to use the formal colon but realize that too would be overkill—I hear a loud rap rap rap on the door. Perhaps it's because I'm concentrating the meager amount of energy I can summon in order to proceed with the letter I don't want to write that I fail instantly to connect the rhythm of the knock I've just heard with that of the knocking yesterday morning.

"Whoever you are and whatever you want," I yell, making myself sound as irritable as I feel irritated. "I'm not here." Then I take a long swig of coffee.

All at once recalling having heard some knocking in the same rhythm twenty-four hours before, I lift my pen and point it at the ceiling. Again I listen for footsteps withdrawing and again no sound reaches my ear. Rather than return to the letter I don't know how to begin, I wait. Maybe half a minute passes before whoever is on the other side of the door knocks again, same pattern of sound.

Irritation rising to anger, I scream, "Bugger off!" and I jab the point of my pen at the door as if I were throwing a dart. Although I wait to hear either another knock or footsteps in retreat, neither happens.

Irrelevant as it might seem, I must confess that just as I'd failed to balance my checkbook, I never wrote the letter. I might well plead that the unexpected knocking for a second time was a sufficiently distracting interruption to inhibit me. But that's not the whole story. Why I gave up on the second endeavor I'm not going to tell you.

Now for day three. Nine o'clock sharp—I'm a creature of habit and promptitude—I'm in my study. Against a July sun so bright it's almost blinding, I draw the curtain on the single small window facing my desk. Already the temperature must be close to ninety. After a long gulp of coffee, I pick up the damnable pen. Incidentally, I'm left-handed, which bit of information might help you to visualize what I'm telling you. In front of me is an accursed blank sheet of paper. Pen point again raised toward the ceiling, which in case you care to know is oyster gray, I'm staring into space. No need to tell you what I'm struggling to mount the energy to do but can't. As you've probably guessed—knocking again, same rhythmic pattern. Connecting it with Beethoven and "V for victory" this time, I conclude whoever the knocker might be, the knock is mocking me. Achievement? Victory? God, no.

Rather than howl "Fuck off!" my impulse on the instant, I manage to swallow the words and hold my tongue by taking another gulp of coffee. Deciding to let silence answer for me, I stare at the door and wait. Within seconds another knock of triumph. Again I manage to restrain myself. After no more than ten seconds, a third knock. Before I can decide how to respond, I see the white porcelain doorknob—I've converted one of the two rooms in the Victorian house in which I rent an apartment into a study—turn.

You might be interested to know that after rising in the morning I keep the door of my flat unlocked until I retire for the night. The neighborhood I'm living in at the present is perfectly safe and I have no acquaintances who might pay me a surprise visit. I confess I have a touch of *agoraphilia*. For some reason I feel more comfortable, actually more secure behind an unlocked door. A corollary to this sense, irrational as it might seem, is that being located inside, the real threat ought not be contained, that is, locked in, but should be provided the readiest egress. Whenever I go into my study, I do close the unlocked door, however, in order to separate the self in there from the self that eats, sleeps, urinates, defecates, what have you.

Hearing the screech of the doorknob, I swivel the seat of my desk chair around to see the door swing creakingly open. Posted just outside the frame is a short, stoop-shouldered, barrel-chested, bowlegged man, with an orange-white, tobacco-stained mustache, which droops on the same parabola as his shoulders. His bald head, the size and shape of a large honeydew melon, mottled like an overripe cantaloupe, is fringed with wads of cotton. The small thick lenses of his wire-frame glasses are oval. Sunny and hot as the day is—it's the twenty- fourth of July—he's wearing a raincoat, black. A couple of sizes too long for his short-legged, dumpy body, it almost touches the floor. Without causing his elbows to bend, his hands are plunged into the pockets. He doesn't come in or go away.

"Well?" I snap, after taking a swallow of coffee, "what is it?"

Disregarding my question, legitimate if one ever was, he slowly crosses the threshold. As he shuffles toward me, he leans so far forward it seems he might trip on the front hem of the raincoat and pitch forward onto the oak floor, smashing his parrot-beak nose. When he's close enough for me to smell his foul breath, also to punch him in the mouth as I've a mind to, he stops, stands swaying, as if about to flop onto the yellow pad on my desk top. He doesn't utter a word of explanation for his appearance.

"Can't you see I'm at work?" I demand to be told.

"Not true, governor," he shoots back. His gravelly voice seems to be coming from the depths of a cave. "You're caught doing nothing."

"Impudent fellow!" I shout, when he's just inches from my face. "Whatever your business is, don't presume to tell me mine. To come barging in on me like this. ..."

"I've come knocking twice before, and you told me to scram." Beneath his mustache his fleshy lips are purple, as are his cheeks and nose. Ah ha, I say to myself, he's an alchie. "When I knocked again this morning, you didn't' respond."

"How did you know I wasn't out...somewhere?"

"Because I was sure you were here."

Below shaggy white eyebrows and behind the thick lenses of his glasses, his eyeballs look like those of a trout that swims in whiskey.

"Isn't your logic rather circular," I sneer. "Anyhow, when you've entered my premises uninvited, I could have you arrested for trespass, you know. Breaking and entering would put you in the slammer for a spell."

"The door to your apartment and this door were unlocked. What did I break, governor?"

"Look here, I'm not going to argue with you. Just get out. Decamp. Vamoose. Before I call the police."

"Do you no good. You don't have a leg to stand on, legally."

"It *is* my dwelling. A man's home is his castle."

"But you summoned me."

"What! Are you out of your mind, man? I don't even know your name."

"The name is Fels."

"As in 'I do not like thee, Dr. Fell.' And the fact is I don't.

"Just change the second *l* to an *s* and you've got it, governor."

"You say I've invited…what was the word you used?"

"Summoned."

"Nonsense. I've never laid eyes on you before."

"Before what?"

"Before you entered my apartment uninvited and opened the door of my study. Why it was literally a *tour de force*!"

"Be that as it may. I received a summons and I've answered it."

"A summons, huh? Summons for what?"

"I shouldn't have to tell you, because deep down, governor, you know as well as I do. You summoned me so you can do what you have to do. Namely, me."

"What in the name of God does that mean? I must do you?"

"You've said it. You must tell my story."

"Well, it just so happens I know your story as little as I know you. Which is not at all."

"Sorry, that won't wash. Matter of fact, it's the reason you must. To prove you're wrong, to prove you do know my story."

"Now listen to what I'm telling you. Listen carefully, digest what I'm saying and end all this poppycock. Even if I did know your story, which I don't, I don't want to tell it. I don't want to tell any story. Yours or anybody else's. Not even my own."

"Of course you don't, governor. And I can't blame you. But what you want to do and what you must do are two different things. That's the way it is. Want to or not, you have to tell my story."

"Do you mind telling me why I must tell your story?"

"Because you're a storyteller, governor. At least that's how you present yourself."

"Look here, there are lots of storytellers. Far too many, if you ask me. Find yourself on the Ross Ice Shelf or on one of the Svalbard islands and you're sure to run into a storyteller."

"But they didn't summon me. You did."

"Good heavens, man, must I tell you again—I've never even heard of you and I haven't the faintest idea what your story is about. What's more, I don't want to know. You or your story."

"Forget about me. But the story…well, the story is about the book."

"The book?"

"That's right, the book. Is there anything wrong or extraordinary about a person's having a connection with a book"

"Well, no. But what book are you referring to?"

"Revealing that now, governor, would be taking the heart out of the story before it gets told."

"Even if I were to agree, for some insane reason, I wouldn't have the least idea where to start."

"You're right about that. Starting, that is the hardest part. My advice is, don't try to find the beginning. Doing that keeps you from getting started. And most often it turns out to be a waste of time and energy. Has to be trashed in the end. Which proves it's not really a part of the story. You've heard the phrase 'false start'? The way to go about it, governor, is to plunge right in, as a smart Greek once advised. Or to use an analogy—it's like getting into cold water."

"Suppose I refuse?"

"Look here, governor, I don't mean to threaten you. But believe me, now that you've summoned me and I'm here, I'm not leaving with my story untold. Like a certain infamous raven I'm here till the end."

"Raven? With that nose you look more like a…"

"I know, I know, It does look like a parrot's beak. But to be blunt, governor, you have a hell of a lot more in common with an American poet manqué than with a truly great French writer of fiction. Fact is, I have no more choice in this whole business than you. Were it up to me, I certainly wouldn't have alighted—to keep the metaphor running—here. But unfortunately you and I…well, to shift the figure from Aves to Reptilia, are intertwined like a pair of copulating cobras."

"I can disentangle us by throwing you out. You don't look to be in the best of shape for a brawl."

"True. But I'll just come back."

"I can lock my doors, you know."

"But you won't, you know."

"What makes you so certain I won't?"

"Because, as you and I are fully aware, governor, you're scared to death of locked doors."

"Even though all that you say, preposterous as you and I know it is, were to be so, I'm not…"

"Preposterous? Of course it's preposterous. That's the nature of the beast in the jungle we find ourselves in. Look at it this way, governor. When I received this summons, in the early hours of the morning it was, I knew I had to respond. No way not to. So here I am. To stay until you've told my story. It's as simple as that."

"By stay, do you mean the whole time? You here in my study? Until it's done?"

"Until the story's been told. To the end. *Fini*, as you might elegantly put it."

"Wait a minute. You don't just snap your fingers and have a finished story. It takes time."

"Depends, largely on how long or short the story is. This one, my guess is…well, a matter of hours, not days. Should be finished by lunchtime if you put yourself to it."

"In one morning? It can't be much of a story."

"Oh, I don't know about that. I have no doubt it's a necessary story. Dickens, remember, had a story told in one Christmas Eve. One of his most widely read. And it's still around."

"Well, I'm no Dickens."

"Glad to hear you say that, governor. Something we can agree on. A storyteller's reach shouldn't exceed his grasp. But you should feel flattered that, with it all, I've enough confi—"

"Hold on. You've got it backwards. Browning said..."

"—dence in you, I was going to say, before you so rudely interrupted me. But let it pass. Forget about Browning. The story'll determine its own shape and be just as long or short as it needs to be. The thing to do is get started, move that ball point across those empty blue-green lines that are just waiting to be written on. Ready to begin?"

"I am not. The more I think about it, the more outrageous I find your intrusion and the more absurd your demand. I won't, no, I can't allow myself to be imposed on in this way. There is a right to privacy, you know. This is my place and it's my time and it's *your* story, not mine."

"None of that holds true or applies, governor, when someone's been summoned to do it. Here and now."

"Back to that, huh. Necessity. Listen, for the sake of argument, I'll grant that you have a story, a great story, a story that has to be told. I'll even grant that you have, or believe you have, received some kind of a summons from someone to tell your story. But that doesn't mean that I've summoned you. No by a long shot." "Well, I have had some false leads and made missteps, have tried a few others. Couldn't even get my foot inside the places where they dwelled, let alone the rooms they worked in. When I found your doors open, I knew I'd come to the very spot from where the summons had been issued. And there was the dude who had issued it."

"So we're at an impasse. Great God, I feel a migraine coming on.

You can't believe what they do to me. Totally incapacitate. And the pain. It's exquisite. Have to lie down—the rest of the day. Listen, I'll tell you what. Compromise. I agree to tell your story, just to get rid of you. But not today. Not just because of the migraine. Already weary, now I'm exhausted, worn to a frazzle, whatever that is, trying to reason with you. Later. Say, tomorrow. The migraine will be gone. Tomorrow morning. Even though I don't know you and haven't an inkling of what your story…"

"An inkling. Just the right word in the right place. I can tell you'll do just fine."

"…I'll give it some thought as soon as the pain in my brain has gone and I can think. Try to come up with something. But you have to agree not to harass me any more. After I've finished, done all I can for you, you can come back to pick it up. Then disappear from my life forever. Promise?"

"Good try, governor, but no cigar. Just won't do. Even though I do trust your intention. Because you strike me as being a man of your word, as well as a man of words. But intentions have short lives, give up quickly, vanish as soon as they run into difficulty. As I've said, I'll be here when you tell my story. Because you'll need me."

"Despite your offensive manner, a certain crudeness in your speech, and a preposterousness in your reasoning, I can see you're not a stupid fellow."

"Appreciate the compliment, even though it does come from that left hand of yours. The one still holding the pen."

"But there are limits."

"That there are, governor. But who sets them is one question. And who enforces is another."

"In this instance, since you're asking *me* to tell *your* story, it's only reasonable that I set and I enforce."

"Reasonable? Well, maybe. But certainly wrong. Why, governor, if you were given the authority to set and the power to enforce, there would be no limits. And it follows as the night the day, no story. See what I mean?'

"So that, I suppose, puts limits—incidentally, again you've got the quotation backward—and enforcement in your disinterested hands."

"Now you're getting into the quicksand of metaphysics, a place I refuse to venture anywhere near. Let's keep our feet planted in the real world, which gives us more than enough to contend with. Here and now, seeing that it's my story, I have the right to see that it's properly told, at least as properly as is possible, given the person who's summoned me to tell it. Isn't what I say self-evident, governor?"

"Just how will your being here, when your presence oppresses me, assure that your story is properly told. Are you going to read over my shoulder? take my pen in hand?"

"We'll get to that, governor. But first let me tell you that all the while I've been here, standing over you, I've been eyeing that easy chair over in the corner. That's where I'll be sitting. Starting, say, about nine a.m. tomorrow. Staying till you've finished. About lunchtime, it should be, if all goes well."

"You make it sound as though I'm a common laborer and you're the overseer, the big boss."

"That's the long and short of it, all right. *Es muss sein*, to quote from the notation on the score of a string quartet that came from the heart, or the gut, of a certain heroic composer."

"I have no idea what the hell you're talking about. But, to be practical, keeping our feet planted in the real world, as you so elegantly and originally put it, apart from making sure I hold to our agreement, that I give it a go, and you've conceded I'm a man of my word, what's the point of having you here, sitting in the chair I read in, with a whip in your hand, so to speak, while I'm at work? Doing my Goddamn best to tell *your* story."

"You have m*y* word, as long as you're moving on the right track at a reasonable speed, you won't hear a peep out of me. Nor even know I'm here. But just suppose you get stuck. Find you've switched off onto the wrong track. Not knowing where you are or what comes next. What if you come to a dead-end, land in a cul-de-sac? Or have a failure of nerve? Or your energy plumb gives out and you up and quit? Well, here I'll be. To reroute you, give you a shove, get you going. Fact is, governor, you read me all wrong. Imagining that I'm your enemy, your oppressor, an obstacle, when I'm making myself available as your little friend. To get you started, keep you moving, see that you finish, ready to help with whatever along the way."

"Well if you stay off my back, maybe we can get on, after all. Despite your intrusion on my privacy and the abrasiveness of your manner. At nine tomorrow morning, then. Will you need a cup of coffee? I always carry a second cup when I come in here to start work. On whatever. Caffeine helps me overcome inertia and move into gear. A quick shot of energy."

"Never touch the stuff. Now if you happen to have a snort or so of bourbon…"

"At nine a.m.? Bourbon? No way. A drink comes after I leave my study and quit work. It's a reward. As for me, it's a couple of martinis. As for you, if you'll forgive my saying so, I can't help noticing the purple blotches of broken blood vessels covering your cheeks and nose, and... well, I don't want to be insulting, but I find myself wondering what you've done to your liver, as well as to your brain. Maybe that's the reason you can't tell your own story and have come up with this fantasy about being summoned. No, no. No bourbon first thing in the morning. I don't want to be responsible for your self-destruction."

"Afraid you've guessed me about right, governor, as the old cowboy song goes. I thank you for your concern about my vital organs. Do you mind, though, if I smoke? Confess I'm a bit addicted to nicotine too."

"Absolutely no smoking in this room, where I spend most of my day. It's a proven fact that secondhand smoke can damage the lungs. Even though I myself enjoy a Brazilian cigar, deep brown leaf, tightly wrapped, after dinner, there's no smoking in my work place."

"Can't deny a word you say. Tough as it'll be I'll give up the weed too tomorrow morning. Fair enough?"

"*Entente cordiale*." Nine o'clock sharp tomorrow morning."

"So, you're a disciplined dude, after all. Way you were sitting there with a blank sheet of paper in front of you, pen in the air, staring into space, had me wondering. But to be honest about myself again, nights sometimes are right mean for me. Takes me a while to get it together next morning. So I may be a couple of minutes late. Don't worry, though, I'll show up. Want you to know this so you don't try to get started before I arrive. You well might get off on the wrong foot. Besides, something else important I have to let you know. Then."

"Uh oh. Sounds ominous. Better let me have it right now. To forestall anxiety. And allow me to sleep. You see I am an insomniac."

"A dose of anxiety never hurts, really. Revs up the nerves, in fact. Believe me, I know. See you tomorrow at nine or thereabouts."

If Fels—a name I'm now convinced isn't his but is one that for some reason he's assumed for the occasion—doesn't smile, I sense he's trying to. The walrus mustache makes it difficult to tell. Yet I do believe he parts his blubbery purple lips and draws back the corners of his mouth before he turns and goes wobbling toward the door. The back of his raincoat drops to what look to be a pair of brogans, badly run-down at the heels.

As he's passing out through the doorway, I find sufficient vocal strength—rehearing my words in the silence that's set in, I suddenly realize my voice has become progressively more bodiless—to rasp out, "Close the door as you leave." Then add "Please," as an afterthought.

The soundlessness with which he complies I construe as an indicator of respect. Or, on second thought, self-satisfaction. That he's conned me. Like the smile. If there was one.

During what remains of the morning, I sit at my desk, pen in air. After lunch I prowl the streets of the once genteel neighborhood I'm living in, on the lookout for I don't know what. Certainly not for "Fels." I have dinner in a nearby Indonesian restaurant and spend the rest of the evening listening to Couperin's "Lecon de Tenebros" on my obsolete stereo. Three times.

Before going to bed at midnight, as I always do, I lock the door to my flat. I can't fall asleep. A voice in my brain keeps repeating "something else important." The tinnitus I'm subject to serves as a continuo. When finally I drift off, sleep is fitful and shallow. During periods of wakefulness and drowse, the voice keeps chanting.

Sometime after five, according to the luminescent face of the clock on my bedside table, I do lose consciousness. When I come awake, it's quarter past eight. Following my morning routine, I raise the blinds and unlock the door, then shave while I'm waiting for coffee to heat on the stove. During breakfast—a banana, which I eat, holding it like a monkey, with its skin peeled back, an English muffin, well-done, black coffee, without sugar—I'm aware I'm in such a stupor my brain is effectively shut down. It's a minute before nine—I'm fastidious about time—when, carrying a second mugful of coffee, I head for my studio.

§

After depositing my mug on the pull-out leaf of my desk and plopping myself in my swivel chair, I hear myself growl "Fels." The sound, involuntary, is prompted by a recollection of disgust. It's the first time I've uttered the name aloud to myself.

"Nice to hear your voice this morning, governor. Hope you're in fine fettle. Sleep that migraine off, did you?"

Not being aware that anyone had entered my flat while I was engaged in my morning routine, I hadn't thought to look toward the corner to my left. There he is, ensconced in my reading chair as though he owns it. Recalling his advising me he might be late and why, I conclude he's had a less wretched night than I had. To let him know I'm in no mood to put up with any more of his taunting and bullying, I fix a hard stare on him.

As if in expectation, or from languor, he's leaning forward. He looks for all the world like a tramp on pharaoh's throne, except that in- instead of his fingers overlapping the ends of the arms, his hands are in the pockets of his raincoat, which he's wearing on another sunny day.

"Will you *kindly* stop addressing me as 'governor'?" I accentuate the "kindly" to make certain my annoyance, which I hope will finesse yesterday's ploy of an imminent migraine, gets through. Turning with a jerk, intended to express repugnance, I stare at my ball-point pen, which, top off, is lying askew on the blank page of a legal pad confronting me from my desk top, as if the pen were a lit stick of dynamite and the paper the top of a strongbox, its key lost, which I need to get into.

"Can't."

"Why not?"

"Because that's what you are. Governor, from the Latin *gubernare,* to steer, as no doubt you know. In your case, to steer not a trireme across the Tyrrhenian Sea but a pen across a yellow sheet of paper."

"Well, then, recognize that a governor is in a position of authority."

"True enough. Within limits, as I thought we agreed yesterday."

"I never did. But I get it. Limits are set by an emperor. Or a dictator."

"Righto. Your choice."

"Dictator Fels," I grunt, provoked to sneer the title and name. Then add, "If it's not an alias."

"Self-doubt if I ever heard it, governor. But let that be. Fact that you're able to get out my name, however distasteful, indicates a bit of familiarity, if not cozy acceptance. And makes it easier to acquaint you with something else—the necessary condition I thought it best not to put to you yesterday. Our initial meeting, you know, getting to feel each other out, as they say of boxers in the first round."

"How could I forget? Your announcement that something was coming, after I'd been led to believe the compromise we'd reached had settled everything, to your, not my satisfaction, let me point out, has kept me awake for hours. You'll have to admit, if not readily, I did submit to your demand."

"That you did. And it was gracious of you, governor, even though you really had no choice. But we never came to terms on your actual telling of the story. The how of it, you might say. What I'm obliged to bring up now, not whimsically or arbitrarily, is not negotiable. It's a means, the only means, that must be used. An inescapable implication of the word *tell.*"

"I'm not following you."

"Of course you're not. How could you when it's never even crossed your mind? Because it's not the way you're used to doing. We all prefer to do things in our own way, don't we? But in this instance, sorry to say, you can't. So objectionable as you're going to find it, I have to spell out what *tell* means and what it demands of you."

"However you're trying to manipulate me, I don't like it. Not one bit. But go ahead, let me know the worst. That's not saying I'll comply."

"Oh, it's not that bad. No threat to your life or welfare. At first you'll be reluctant, no doubt. But after some serious consideration you'll grant the necessity and give in. And once you've got used to this way of doing, you'll find it actually makes the doing easier. Believe me, governor, this is not just catering to a whim of mine. It's for you too."

"I'm grateful for your benevolent concern."

"Okey dokey. Here goes. You know, as you compose a tale you jogtrot along. Getting down a page or so in a sitting. If you're lucky. More likely a paragraph that you're satisfied with. Maybe only a single sentence. Or like that Frenchman who had a thing about a parrot, putting in just one comma during a morning, that afternoon taking the comma out. However much or little, before pushing on you stop. Not only to consider where to go from where you've got to. Also to find the courage to go on. And if not always, sometimes, in fact often, you'll read back over what you've managed to get down. A perilous practice, governor, really treacherous. A *ruse de guerre,* as you might say, self against self in the battle in which words are weapons. Am I right?"

"Well...I guess you are."

"No, you know I am."

"Even so, I don't know what business of yours it is. You've been insisting *I* must tell the tale, *your* story. And you just conceded that all of us have our individual ways of doing, our idiosyncrasies. Everybody..."

"Idiosyncrasies. Right, governor. From the Latin for *idiot.* Sorry to interrupt you, But the buried origin of the word got to me."

"Everybody has her or his own method. With whims and tics. A great German poet kept rotten apples under his desk while he wrote. Needed their smell to work."

"Righto. That's it. Whatever works. And don't get me wrong, I'm not faulting your way. 'Tain't easy,' as the dummy used to say to the ventriloquist. On the radio, remember? As I've assured you, whatever's necessary for this arrangement to work, strange as it might seem to you at first, will serve both our purposes in the long run. Not hinder, I swear. Cross my heart and hope to die."

"Don't tempt me. But get to the point. You're beating around the bush."

"To the point, governor. When the matter first came up between us, you might remember, I had insisted you had to tell my story. Because you'd summoned me. After a song and dance of denial, you finally, if tacitly, agreed. Now mind you, the stipulation was that you tell. Not just write. *Manu scriptum*, from the Latin, of course, is not the only way to tell a story. *Tell*, so that I can take it in as you go. And we agreed that, sitting in this wonderfully comfortable chair while you did the telling, I'd be listening. Christ, governor, I'm not going to stand behind you, short or long as it takes, reading over your shoulder what's running out of your pen. And my guess is your handwriting is every bit at bad as mine. Almost illegible. Hell, the last thing you care about as you push on is penmanship. All you care about is getting it down. So you, not somebody else, can make out the words later. Fair enough? I haven't the least desire to read what you write, as you write it. Or ever. What I was summoned for was to hear you *tell* my story.

"Now look here, Fels, or whatever your real name might be, obviously you don't know the least thing about...about giving birth, to use a pertinent metaphor, to a story. Why, what you're asking is utterly impossible. Unheard of. Never..."

"Hold it, right there, governor. Not so fast with your absolutes. As an educated man, a literary fellow no less, you must know that before such a distinctively human activity as writing was, before the implements—computers, word processors, typewriters, pencils, pens, quills, chisels, paper, screens, papyrus, bark—existed as such, stories were chanted, sung, and told by bards, skalds, scops, gleeman, jongleurs, troubadours, prophets. Think of the early scriptures of all religions. The myths and epics—The Pentateuch, the prophets, *The Mahabharata*, *Gilgamesh*, *Iliad*, *Odyssey*, *Beowulf*. Matter of fact, there are some impressive precedents after quill, ink and paper came along. Eyes giving out in his late fifties, Milton dictated his three monumental poems to his daughters. As Flaubert, the perfectionist, wrought his beautifully crafted sentences, he belted them out. Closer to home and our time, fastidious Henry James, a master from who, or as you'd say whom, you can learn a lesson or two, chose to dictate his last three great novels, long and complex as they are. Not to mention such a diverse crew as Thomas Aquinas, Wordsworth, Stendhal, Wallace Stevens, and James

Joyce, all of whom used their tongue as their pen. Rather than turn your nose up at such a practice, you should think of the company you'll be in."

"You're a master of sleight of hand. Or to throw back at you, the organ you're using to torment me, a wizard with an adder's tongue."

"Though it's not meant to be, I take the epithet as a compliment. But what you're confronting here, governor, isn't a matter of choice. Just like the reason for your being the one to tell the story, delivering it aloud is a necessity."

"Are you taking into account how much faster I can write a story I'm making up than I can tell it, groping for words as I'll be to make certain they're the ones I need. Rewriting, even crossing out and moving things around."

"There you go. You've got the point of it, governor. Not the point of the pen but the tip of the tongue. You just can't think a story. You also have to hear it. As for speed, you can set the rate and go at your own. It doesn't want to be easy, telling a tale doesn't. You don't want to just let the words run out of your pen into ink on paper. You have to find them in your gut—a more polite word is heart—then breathe them out and hear them, pacing yourself to keep up with your invention and your writing it down. I won't rush you, I promise. Okay? Now, no more pointless insistence and resistance, needing and pleading. 'Harpier cries, 'Tis time, 'tis time.' Begin telling my story. Now."

Before complying, I finish my second cup of coffee with deliberate slowness.

§

He'd come across the bookstall by the merest of chances. On his way to the Indonesian restaurant where occasionally he ate dinner, something made him saunter in. Skimming along a shelf, his eye was caught by black letters on the crimson…

§

"Stop! Hold it. Right there. Wrong, all wrong."

He was sitting so far forward on the cushion of my easy chair that I thought he was about to topple over and land face-first on the floor. On the words *stop* and *wrong* he pounded the air with the clenched fist of his left hand.

"What can possibly be wrong? I've scarcely begun. Haven't even finished the second sentence."

"Exactly why I stopped you, governor. So you wouldn't pursue the wrong road. What you've said is based on a mistaken premise."

"Which is?"

"Which is, he doesn't just happen on the book, the direction you're taking. No, no. Not by a long shot. He's been actively looking for it. To use a word you and I have worked our way toward understanding, the book has been *summoning* him. That's why he's been traveling from city to city, town to town in search of it in plausible places. Already he's found twelve copies."

"What then does he want with a thirteenth?"

"Although that seems to be a reasonable question, it's out of place. As you go on, in the right direction, you'll see why. Now forget the misconception you've begun with and start again."

Warthog, I say to myself.

§

As he'd done many a time before, in city after city, town after town, he moved slowly along the cobblestone alley dividing the shelves, on one side of the outdoor bookstall, from the troughs, overflowing with books, on the other. The stall was attached to a bookstore.

This evening he was doing the top shelf, scanning methodically. Because he had to straighten to his full height—he was a short man—while keeping his left hand on the outer edge of the shelf for balance, and because he had to get a satisfying look at the spine of every book that was undersized and slim, his progress was slow. In light now growing dimmer by the minute, he was squinting. The summer afternoon had been quite warm and bright. But with the top floors of the apartment building, in which the bookstore was housed at street level, blocking the sun, he was gratified to have the falling temperature as a plausible explanation for wearing the raincoat. In no way was he concerned with appearance for appearance sake.

All at once his eye stopped...

§

"Sorry to break in on your thought. But you've been sitting there silently with your pen motionless, as though you're considering writing on air, for nigh on five minutes. If we're to finish by lunchtime, as we agreed was both possible and desirable, you need to start spitting out words and getting that pen moving across the lines of your legal pad. Word, words, words, governor. Start producing words again."

"Can't."

"What? I thought you summoned me because you are a writer."

"I am. But I'm stuck. It happens, you know. I got to 'his eye' and I didn't know *what* his eye."

"You're stuck, governor! Why you haven't even got into the first act. All you've done is ramble your way into a prologue. Can it be because those long Latinate sentences of yours are impossible for you, let alone a listener or a reader, to follow. As a hermit manqué once advised, 'Simplify, simplify, simplify!'"

"Sorry you don't take to my style. But that's the way it is. You didn't have to answer my summons, as you call it, you know. Anyway, that's not the reason I'm stuck."

"What in God's name has you stuck, then, governor?

"Some necessaries. I can't go on without some necessaries."

"Necessaries? You have a brain, a voice, a pen and paper, haven't you? What necessaries?"

"For one, I have to know where I ...I mean you...I mean the man in the story...let's just say *he* is."

"Why you know perfectly well where he is. You've got him in a bookstall. Exactly where he belongs."

"Look...I mean, listen. If the story is going to be believed, there must be the illusion of reality. I have to provide convincing details and particulars. Density creates realism. What's the architecture of the building the bookstall is attached to? Are there trees along the sidewalk? Are they plane trees, maples, oaks? Any shrubs in tubs? Flowers? What section of the city are we in? or is it a town, which makes a difference in the ambience. Is there litter? Are there trash baskets? Any odors? Buses? Traffic noise? How about pedestri..."

"Whoa there, Governor. Rein it in, rein it in. Your imagination's got the bit between his teeth and is running away with you. None of that sort of horse...well, to use a polite term, hogwash, matters in this story. I know, I know. You consider it part of your craft. But keep in mind and fix your eye and ear on what this tale's about. The book. It's not a travelogue or a costume drama. What you have to make believable is the existence of the book. Nothing more."

"Thanks. Thanks a hell of a lot. It's a good thing you're here, all right. Your support and advice are exceeded only by your presumption. But so be it. It's your tale, asshole, to make an appropriate pun."

"Don't take it so hard, governor."

"Well, I have to warn you. Given the circumscriptions and restraints you're putting on me, the story won't amount to much."

"Whatever 'amount to much' means, I take responsibility for. As is only fair. After all, it's my story."

"You're both a grateful and a generous...bastard."

"Be that as it may, on with the tale."

§

...on a book. In the gathering dusk he was unable to make out the faded letters on the spine of the dust jacket. Yet the size of the little volume sent his arm up, told his left hand to reach for it. Feeling himself on the verge of falling forward into the shelves, he threw back his head, counterbalancing, then turned it and looked over his right shoulder. No one in sight. When he swung his trunk and glanced to his left, he caught sight of a woman in a bright green dress. Back to him, head down, she was picking up a book from the trough on the other side of the alley. His quick impression was that she was tall.

When he returned to the shelf in front of him, he hooked his left forefinger...

§

"What are you stopping for now? When you were cantering along at a nice clip."

"Take your hands out of the pockets of your raincoat."

"What? For God's sake, why?"

"Hold them out toward me. I want to see your fingers."

"Oh no, you don't. Sorry, governor. If we start down that road, well, it could be endless. Fact is, those descriptive details you're convinced are necessary to make a story realistic and believable would put both of us to sleep with boredom, if not drive us to suicide. Also they keep you from getting on with the story, something it seems you're having trouble doing."

"But to go on I have to see the fingers grasping the book, the particular fingers."

"Nonsense. Fingers are fingers. All you need is something that can grasp. Prehensile."

"But these are not fingers generically. They're somebody's fingers and therefore are distinctive."

"Whose fingers are they then, may I ask?"

"Why yours, of course."

"Oh ho. How can you be so sure?"

"Didn't you persuade me that you were summoned by me to tell *your* story?"

"Just because it's my story, governor, you can't assume the fingers about to pull the book from the shelf by its spine are mine. Or that I'm the man in the bookstall. Seems to me he's a character in a story that happens to be mine."

"You're splitting hairs. Maybe trying to worm out of it is a more fitting phrase."

"Now, now, governor. Those are right nasty remarks. Though we may have our differences, let's stay focused on story-telling and forswear character assassination."

"Even granting you the point on which you're weaseling, trying to have it both ways, still and all the fingers that are acting in the story I'm telling, if not unique, do belong to a recognizable category of fingers. Are they stubby, as if they've been chopped off? long and slender, like a concert pianist's? hairy? smooth? knobby and gnarled with swollen joints, that is, arthritic?"

"Doesn't matter in the least. Story's not about what fingers look like. It's about what fingers do. You want to embroider. What you need to do is get on with plain-stitching."

"I hereby place on record my disagreement and reluctance to proceed as you stipulate. Yours is not the proper way to compose a story—yours, mine of anybody else's."

"Wrong-minded as you are, your objection has been noted. Now enough of your childish grumbling. On with the story."

§

...inside the top of the binding. Just in case the woman in the green dress should be eyeing him, he hummed a tuneless ti ti ti dum, as if to himself. So tightly packed on the shelf were the books that the slim little volume didn't want to come out. Wiggling it from between its closest neighbors, he heard his humming turn to a grunt, which he feared might be audible in the canyon the two tall surrounding buildings made of the alley. All at once the book tumbled free, with such force it fell, smashing his no....

§

"Cut! as they say, or used to, in film-making. Don't finish that word."

"What in heaven is the matter now? I was just getting into gear."

"The matter is, and it's no small one, you're starting to tell a story you're inventing. It may be your story, but it's not mine."

"Haven't I got the book in hand, so to speak? Literally, as well as figuratively. At this very instant it's tumbling..."

"You've got the book off the shelf, governor, and that's all well and good. But the point is, how?"

"How what?

"How you're coloring it."

"Honestly, I haven't the least idea what you're talking about, what your objection is. How does my coloring the telling, as you call it, make it my story, instead of yours?"

"I'll tell you how, Goddamnit. My story is not slapstick. With the 'he' humming to himself and grunting as he's about to smacked on the schnozzola by a book he's trying to remove. The man in the story is not a buffoon. And my story is not slapstick. I'm a serious man, governor, and this is a serious story."

"Oh my God! I try to provide a little humor. To lighten up what strikes me as a rather dull tale. And you explode with anger. And, while I'm being candid, I must say you're not only touchy and waspish. You're also an ungrateful fellow. After all I've done to oblige . . ."

"Wait just a minute, if you please. Aren't you forgetting something? Though tacitly and reluctantly, you did agree."

"Agree to what?"

"Agree that you had no choice. When you've been appointed to tell my story, you can't claim grace or your part. So put it in reverse, governor and, proceeding with a touch of humility and a tone of high seriousness, to use the self-descriptive phrase of a solemn nineteenth-century poet and essayist, give my story the dignity it asks for."

§

Wiggling the book, he wrenched it free. While clutching it in his left hand, again he checked behind him. The woman in the green dress was holding the oversize volume open, presumably reading. Quick as a reflex he slipped the little book into the left-hand pocket of his raincoat.

§

"Mind if I interrupt again?"

"What in the name of Christ is it now? I've got through only four new sentences. If you keep sticking in your big nose, how in hell am I supposed to finish the story by lunchtime?"

"Figured it would help your morale, governor. Which I worry might begin to flag. It commonly does at about this point."

"In case you didn't happen to notice, I was getting on with it."

"Though I wouldn't exactly call it highballing, you were moving, I grant you that."

"Then why make me slam on the brake?"

"To congratulate you, provide en-courage-ment. Courage is what's needed now. Slipping the book into the pocket of the raincoat 'quick as a reflex'—that's not too bad, not bad at all."

"Well, well, well. At last I've done something you approve of. Are you aware this is the first time you've expressed an iota…"

"*Iota*—ninth letter and the smallest in the Greek alphabet, in case you didn't know."

"…of satisfaction with my craftsmanship. All you've done to this point is chastise me and complain. And, I might add, try to impress me with your learning. Pretty shallow, I'd be willing to bet."

"Now that's ad hominem. From the Latin. But the fact of it is you're misreading, or I should say, mishearing me, governor. Only trying to keep you on the straight and narrow, the road every story has to hold to, as Mr. Bunyan knew, if it's to arrive at its destination and ring true. Fact is, you're doing quite well, now."

"So you *are* capable of feeling gratitude, it seems."

"Glad you see it that way. But let's stop exchanging posies and get on with the story."

§

He opened the front cover of the little book. On the flyleaf he read

To Leslie,
with my love,
Felix

As he quickly clapped the book shut, his heart leaped up. What a…

§

"No, no, no, governor. That will never do."

"What won't?"

"The heart leaping up. It's ruinous. Hearts don't leap. They beat. Unless you're a stiff. And as a metaphor it's stolen. What do you think you are, doing what—a poet beholding a rainbow?"

"It seems you're an educated fellow after all. Passing yourself off as an autodidact, a Jackie-Come-Lately London or Kerouac, you had me believing the reason you weren't venturing to tell your own story was, not having read much in the way of literature and not feeling comfortable with words, as the idiom of your conversation sometimes suggests—look, I'm not trying to insult or demean you. Perhaps you present yourself that way for self-protection, as a disguise. Increasingly it's become evident that actually you're a well-read man. Not inarticulate by a long shot. Maybe you're inhibited by what's called 'the anxiety of influence.' Perhaps you've read *too* much."

"I take no offense. But your speculating's far off the mark. Since you raise the question, I'll tell you why. Distance, governor. When a story takes you over, possesses you, you can't split yourself in two—the one it's happening to and the one who's telling it. So it has to be turned over to someone else, the somebody who summons you to prod him, or her, to tell the story for you. In this instance, for better or worse, you're the one. *Verstehst du?*"

"Could it be you've misidentified the person you were summoned by, as you call it? Samuel, you might remember, in the Old Testament book that bears his name, was deceived about who was calling him. Maybe you ought to find someone else and ask that person whether you were summoned to hear her, or him, tell your story. Someone who would tell it as you want it told. Exactly."

"Now don't sulk, governor. Or go into a funk under pressure. You're too thin-skinned. What you're going through happens to the storyteller all the time—finding it hard to get started, stopping, running out of energy, doubting whether it's worth going on even if you can, digging deep inside yourself to find a reason to, as well as to tap a source for more energy. Look it's time for a break. We've made more progress by midmorning than you, not having the whole story in your head yet, as I have, can measure. And, as we've agreed, the first part is the hardest. Soon the tale will being telling itself. You'll merely be speaking and putting down words. Believe me, I've been through this before. Now go fix yourself a fresh pot of mocha that'll put another shot of caffeine in your system. Since you've designated this place a hootch-free zone, I've stashed a couple of Granola bars in the pocket of my raincoat. Quick energy. I need a pop as badly at you do. You ought to try high protein, governor."

§

When I force myself to reenter my study after a lunch that's anything but re-energizing, I see his head has dropped onto the top of my reading chair. Which has been transformed into a listening chair. His glasses lie on the lamp table beside him, and his eyes are closed. Presuming he's fallen asleep, I tiptoe to my desk. As I ease myself into my swivel chair, being as quiet as I can, he suddenly starts, then slowly tilts forward, dangerously so, it seems to me.

Spotting no Granola bar wrappings on the table or in the wastebasket beside my desk, I realize it *is* possible he's stuffed them into one of the deep pockets of his raincoat. That leads me to ask myself two questions. Can this grungy piece of flotsam be the soul of neatness? And why is he wearing a raincoat when it's sunny and warm outside? As it was yesterday. The blue-green-lined yellow sheets on which I've been scribbling away haltingly have not been disturbed.

"There now, governor," he rasps, after clearing his throat so audibly and crudely, I wouldn't be in the least surprised were he to disgorge onto the floor of my study what he's hawked up. Disgustingly fascinated, I watch him fit his glasses back on his cauliflower ears and dart-board nose.

"Sounds as if whatever you happened to have in the pocket of your raincoat has done more for you than caffeine has for me."

"I catch your insinuation. No, it's an outright accusation. But don't you recall, governor, when I asked you yesterday whether you might have a splash of prairie juice to help a man get through, you declared this room off-limits. And I didn't protest, did I?"

"What better way to throw me off ... the scent."

"Come now, do I strike you as being a devious fellow?"

"The crookedest and trickiest it's ever been my misfortune to have got myself involved with."

"But as one hapless human being to another, surely you'd understand if...well, best let it rest. Now while I was providing myself with a tad of sustenance, my brain roamed back over what we've done so far. Reluctantly but realistically I've concluded it's not possible to persuade you to give up your embellishing. Lord, governor, I implore you, out of deference to that great Southern novelist who pointed out there are no adjectives in nature, to control your predilection for what's decorative but damagingly extraneous. What say you set a limit on your transgressions—like half a dozen details and particulars, a dozen modifiers, per every five hundred words. Not only will the story be cleaner, purer, but you, the storyteller, will too."

"Well, it just so happens that, while I was waiting for my coffee to brew, I too was thinking things over. I became certain that, given our irreconcilable differences, I was right in my conviction that the summons you claim you received did not come from me. So I've decided I'm not..."

"Please, governor, please. Recognize this is a time of testing. What's needed at this crucial moment is determination, the will to persevere. Even though we agree we're not altogether on the same page, perhaps wavelength is a more apt metaphor, be resolved that somehow we can muddle through. Think what we've already accomplished, even while still working out an accommodation. Don't go stumbling into the Slough of Despond or, worse, fall into the hands of Giant Despair and land in Doubting, really in our case it should be called Self-Doubting, Castle."

"Ah ha. I had your number, all right. You *are* sailing under false colors. Or I should say you're putting an antic disposition on."

"No matter. Just cross out those four worn words we stopped on before our little pick-up. Whatever you want to say about the emotional response to finding the inscription, which is incidental anyway, will be in there if it needs to be. Without your pilfering from Willie Wordsworth. Now onward, if not upward."

§

...what an ironic happenstance! After working his way through scores of secondhand bookshops and stalls dotting the face of our nation, like pustules of chicken pox, and finding only twelve copies, none of them inscribed or signed, out of, what was it, a couple of hundred printed...to come across the Leslie book. To think, with all the others moldering in somebody's attic or basement or gone to the dump, he'd just about resigned himself to give up on what was beyond his reach. However many remained, he'd done his best.

But the Leslie book! To stumble on that. With Leslie, the last he knew, which was what? a decade or so now, still alive somewhere on Madagascar, how in the whole wide world did that, the first complimentary copy of the seven the publisher had provided, land in this bookstall in this Midwestern town? With all contact broken, could it be...

§

"Glad you stopped, even though you're just barrel-assing along. I was on the point of breaking in on you."

"To proceed, I need a pronoun. For stylistic reasons. I can't go on using a given name time after time. I need a gender pronoun. Immediately."

"Gotcha, governor. Not knowing whether Leslie's a hot dog or a doughnut, you're not sure whether you ought to use the boy or the girl pronoun."

"Exactly."

"Well, you go right ahead and use whichever you feel comfortable with. If you like you can even use the hot dog pronoun in one instance and the doughnut in another. Won't make a damn bit of difference. I can guarantee you sex won't rear its ugly head in this tale."

"What? It has to matter, man. The reader has to know whether the character in focus is a male or a female."

"Have it your way—in any other story you might tell. But in this one the woman in the green dress might just as well be a man in a jockstrap, the two males who are coming up, women in the raw. Trouble is, governor, you're wandering by the wayside. That's why if you hadn't drawn up just where you did, I'd have had to bring you to a halt. Fact is, you've been misled into thinking the inscription 'with love' is a pyrotechnic at the heart of the story when it's nothing but a zit on the skin. What with the conditioning imposed and the expectations raised by the stories that get told these days, yours is an understandable mistake. Sex sex and more sex.

Implicit and explicit. Discreetly clothed or nakedly revealed. In pairs or in a daisy chain. Single-sexed, double-sexed or triple-sexed. Making use of every orifice, including the ear and the big toe. Exclusively involving Homo sapiens or embracing other physiologically capable species. But it just so happens in the tale you've summoned me to hear told, in my story, sex and love are both unspoken, off the page. Unless a book can make love and have sex."

"Quite a rant. Why you're a purer puritan than Cotton Mather. Or his father, Increase. You know, it's becoming more and more evident that I'm nothing but your scribe and mouthpiece. You led, I should say *mis*led, me into believing I summoned you because *I* was to tell your story."

"Drop the 'nothing but' and you say true. Yet consider, without your telling there wouldn't be any story."

"Okay, let's get it over with. Forget the gender question, though I raised it merely for a literary reason. The way it set you off makes me suspect your smoke and mirror act is just…well, never mind. I'll manage somehow. And will back up and get off the primrose path. But I must say, a story about a little book with a liver-colored dust jacket isn't likely to win…"

"Of course it isn't. But that's the story you're stuck with. Before you pick it up, governor, let me tell you you're doing better and better. I do believe we're getting to the place where you can proceed on your own. Wrong-minded as it might seem to you, just keep your focus on the book, which in fact does have a liver-covered jacket."

§

After checking and finding the woman in the green dress still facing away from him, her nose buried in the volume she'd removed from the trough, he turned over some pages of the book he was holding. They'd yellowed to the color of straw. Yet when he tested the paper by rubbing it with his forefinger and thumb, it didn't seem to be deteriorating. Another glance behind him. There she was. All at once…

§

"Look, governor, as I just said, you've done pretty well getting to this juncture in the story. But now you're rowing with one oar, going around in a circle, protracting and wasting time, trying to tease your listener into attending, your reader into going on. Forget about those 'all at onces' and 'suddenlys' to keep it going and trigger surprise. Just get on with it."

"You couldn't be more wrong. If dramatic moments, climaxes, epiphanies are to be effective, you must approach them craftily, as if nothing unexpected is coming. Then you spring them, like a trap, so they come as shock."

"Effect is dreck. You're not telling a story to morons. Show some respect for your audience. Preserve the good faith necessary for a tale to be properly told. Give up the clichés and gamesmanship."

"Scrupulous and pure as you present yourself, the truth is you're a supercilious, self-righteous, know-it-all son of a bitch."

"Please, governor, please. By this time you at least ought to know *my* character's not at stake. Doesn't matter in the least, has nothing to do with the story. Think of the personal depravity of Villon, de Sade, and Genet, to cite three Frenchies who just happen to pop into my head. You didn't summon me to evaluate the me outside the tale as a moral or immoral being or to commend me for my sweetness and light or to reproach me for my sourness and darkness. 'I yam what I yam,' as the man who's invisible pronounces after breaking the skin of a street-roasted yam with his teeth and savoring its juicy pulp. The story, the tale of the book is what you have to tell. Now get on with it."

§

...he slipped the slender volume into the left-hand pocket of his raincoat. Having turned the trick a dozen of times before, he knew better than to go darting off. Instead, he plucked a standard-size book from the shelf at eye level and broke it open. Although he hadn't the least interest in the text, whatever it might happen to be, he couldn't help noticing the indentations of lines and the spaces between stanzas. Without taking in a single word, he stood staring at the page for what he judged was close to five minutes, sufficient time, in case any eyes were on him, to make it seem the book was commanding his intense interest. Before replacing the volume on the shelf, he turned the page and a few seconds later faked a fit of coughing as...

§

"Just want to compliment you, governor. Well done. The coughing fit's a deft touch at this moment. Never would have occurred to me to use it."

"Much obliged. But don't imagine for a minute your few and far between expressions of approval compensate for all you fault-finding, chastising, bullying, nagging, meddling, obstructing, instructing, demeaning...well, let's just call it what it is, crude riding herd on me when, for Christ's sake it's your story I'm trying to tell."

"My, oh my. Seems you've stored up a chamber pot full of black bile when I'm only doing what I must to make it a mite easier for you to do properly what you're obliged to. Best way to relieve yourself—trust me on this, governor—is to go on telling the tale."

§

...a way of attracting the attention of the woman in the green dress. That would make it seem he had nothing to hide. While sliding the volume of poetry back in place, he prolonged the coughing. When he looked around, the woman in the green dress was gone. Sauntering out to where the alley met the sidewalk of the avenue on which the bookstall and bookstore were situated, he nonchalantly fell in with the flow of pedestrians. He hadn't taken but half a dozen steps before he heard a shout.

"Officer, stop that man! He's just committed a theft."

Coming toward him, as chance would have it, was a hulking man in a dark blue uniform. Above the peak of the blue cap he was wearing was a silver badge. A nightstick hung from his belt. Strapped to his thigh was a pistol in a holster.

The policeman planted himself astride the sidewalk. As pedestrians flowed by on either side, the burly blue body blocked his path. To prevent a collision he had to stop short.

"That's the man, officer," he heard in a trumpetlike voice from behind him. "The one in the black raincoat"

"Whoa there, big daddy," the policeman sang out, extending his huge arms as if to embrace him. Even while realizing the words were ominous, he heard a mellifluousness in the policeman's voice.

Finding himself staring eye level at the top brass button of his coat let him know the policeman was of a height to ram his icebreaker of a jaw into his forehead. Quickly he swung his head around and spotted the woman in the green dress. She was pointing an index finger at him as she approached. With a narrow face that gave her a horsey look, she reminded him of someone he'd had to do with many years ago, someone with whom he'd had some trouble. She was taking long loping strides as she came on.

Scurrying behind her was a gnome with the face of a cherub and pure white hair, fluffy as a Bichon's. He was wearing glasses with heavy black frames and had on a vanilla-colored smock, white shirt and a peacock blue and green bow tie. The woman in the green dress towered over the gnome as the policeman did over him.

"What's this all about?" the policeman asked to be told as the woman in the green dress and the gnome arrived.

"He stole a book," the woman in the green dress proclaimed. Her *j'accuse* was stentorian. "He took it from a shelf in the bookstall and slipped it into the pocket of his raincoat, then shuffled off without paying inside." Although her corrugated face suggested she was beyond her middle years, she held herself as though she had an I beam for a spine. A small crowd was collecting around the foursome.

"Did you walk off with a book without paying?" the policeman asked, frowning so that his forehead which had been smooth as polished bronze looked like brown corduroy. For such a big man to have a voice that might have sung countertenor was disconcerting.

"I did not steal a book," he proclaimed emphatically. His own voice came out more hollow than he wished.

"What!" the woman in the green dress exclaimed with feigned surprise. "I suppose I was hallucinating."

Seizing his elbow in his powerful fingers, the policeman declared, "You're going to have to come along with me to the station…"

§

"No, no, no. You've got it all mixed up. That's another story. Happened at a bookshop in Oshkosh, Wisconsin. The gendarme in this tale is a gentle, compassionate human being."

"But if you remove the center of conflict, you drain all the drama out of the denouement."

"We're not after drama, governor, we're telling truth. The way it happened. Without pepper or spice. No buts about it, you've got the wrong ending."

"You know, you're not really a pest, like a fly. Nor even a mosquito. You're a cobra. Striking with venom on your tongue."

"Not very nice. Not nice at all. What you still don't seem to grasp is that when I give you no choice, it's because I have no choice. No ill will or malice is intended. There are dictates that must be obeyed. Now be an agreeable fellow and back up to 'I suppose I was hallucinating.'"

"If I had any guts, at this point I'd draw the line, say 'step over it one more time and you're out of here.' But having let myself be used and abused to this point, I'll be a coward and capitulate again. March to the beat of your drum. Besides, I have to admit, grudgingly, now I'm rather curious to see how it turns out."

"Good boy. Just remember, governor, there's comfort in surrender. In discipline you find your freedom, as a philosopher once put it."

§

"Afraid I'm going to have to ask whether you might happen to have a book in your raincoat pocket, sir," the policeman said apologetically.

"I do. But it's not a stolen book."

"Could be there is some sort of mix-up?" the gnome suggested. "This gentleman here does not look like a thief. Or act like one. He was not running away."

"Well then, just ask him whether he took the book that's in his pocket from a shelf in the stall," the woman in the green dress put in.

"Well, did you, sir?" the policeman inquired.

"I did."

"Now ask the proprietor standing here next to me whether he came into the bookstore and paid for the book," the woman, who seemed to be the director of the little drama, went on insistently.

"No," the gnome conceded after a considerable silence. His *no* made the woman in the green dress nod her head in agreement. For his part the gnome sounded as if he were reluctant to admit to a wrong *he'd* done. With a chest the size of a wrestler's, his voice was surprisingly deep, full and rich, like the sound of a contrabassoon. For no apparent reason his face went into a dimpled smile.

"Sir, can I have a look at the book…in question?" Pausing and adding "in question" made the policeman sound very official.

"Certainly, officer."

Extracting the volume from the left-hand pocket of his raincoat, he extended it to the policeman, whose gigantic hand made the book seem even smaller than it was. Letting it fall open, the policeman glanced at the inside of the dust…

§

"May I?"

"What polite irony. To ask permission when you've already done what you pretend to be asking my consent to do."

"Such pat phrases are an accepted convention, as you well know, governor. Keep things civil on the surface to avoid provoking the hostility lurking beneath to snarl and show its fangs."

"Between us, it seems to me, civility has never shown itself. But proceed. Whatever it may be this time, get it over with."

"Not at all what you're imagining. Fact is, you're doing so well, moving straight ahead, you ought to be able to finish up without my being all over you. Now you're getting it right. Resisting impulse. Letting it have its way. Without flummery. No excess. Eye on the book. Assuming you don't eat lunch before one, you should have it finished with time to throw some water on your face. Relax with a beer or whatever. Congratulations."

For a good thirty seconds I stare at him. Speechless. When I do reply, I try to keep all irony from my voice.

"Why, here's a sea change. By so tactfully withdrawing you make me realize, full of irritation, resentment, yes, downright hostility as I confess I've been, it may be I've misjudged you. The confidence you've just expressed in me gives me confidence in myself. After all that doubt. You know, when I've wound it up, so to speak, maybe you and I can part as friends, after all."

Friends? Afraid you're pushing it. Asking too much of both of us. We do have widely different intentions and goals. Not bitter enemies, perhaps. But let that pass. What will be, will be. From here on in, I'm leaving it in your hands. Now really, it wasn't so hard once you knew what was being asked of you, was it, governor?"

"It was gut-wrenching. I'm back at it."

§

...jacket and squinted.

"Is this your book, sir," he asked clapping the volume closed and handing it to the gnome.

"To be truthful," the gnome replied, "so many books come and go in the stall, I cannot keep them all in my head." He had very small white hands, which had no hair on them. In his pronounced Germanic accent "books" came out as a rhyme with "spooks." Opening the front cover, he paused. "I do see one dollar ninety-five cents here on the flyleaf. This *is* where I mark the price. In pencil, as here."

"Do you remember writing a buck ninety-five there?" The policeman asked. "On the flap of the jacket it says four ninety-five. It's printed there."

"I cannot say I do," the gnome replied, narrowing his eyes behind the thick lenses of his glasses so they seemed almost closed. "Though it could be my writing. To be priced so low, the book must had been on the shelf for a long time. Probably years. Maybe going back to the previous owner."

"So I guess you're not willing to swear it's your book. In court, I mean. Under oath."

"Well," the gnome responded, with hesitation in his voice and manner as he handed the book back to the policeman, "although in line with what this lady says, it appears the book was taken from my bookstall. But I am not going to press charges against anyone for a dollar and ninety-nine cents when the book has not sold for many years. Added to this, it is not worth my time."

Shaking his head slowly and breaking into a smile, the gnome washed his hands with air, as if cleansing them of the touch of the book. Having no option but to receive what was thrust back upon him, the policeman mashed his lips together and shrugged his shoulders.

"Still and all, the man did steal the book," the woman in the green dress insisted. Her face was white marble. "He thought I didn't see him behind me while I was rooting around in a trough. But I had been keeping my eye on him, over my shoulder. Because he was....was acting suspiciously."

"What do you have to say to what the lady here says?" the policeman wanted to know.

"What she says is true. But I didn't commit a theft."

The woman in the green dress let go a trilling laugh of derision. Knocking his cap askew with the formidable knuckles of his right hand, the policeman scratched his right temple with the fingertips of his left hand.

"I *honestly* don't understand." While maintaining an attitude of respect and a tone of politeness, the policeman did stress "honestly." "If you admit you took the book from the shelf as the lady here says and you didn't pay the owner of the bookstore there for it, how can you claim you didn't steal the book. I don't want to make a big thing out of a buck ninety-five, either. But stealing..."

"I didn't steal the book. The book is mine."

"Yours?" the woman in the green dress hooted. "I find it strange that a book you agree you stole from the shelf of the stall is yours."

"Maybe he does not have a dollar and ninety-five cents to spare," the gnome ventured to say, as he looked the accused up and down, seeming to assess his jeans and brogans, both of which, along with his raincoat, showed considerable wear. "And maybe he wants the book so badly he really believes it is his. Such things do happen." He frowned and cocked his head philosophically.

"Whether I have a dollar and nine-five cents or not has nothing to do with it. I don't want the book at all. That's why I removed it from this man's shelf."

"But why would you take the book if you don't want it? And how can you claim a book the owner of the bookstore is trying to sell is yours?" the policeman, throwing the gnome a nod, asked patiently.

"Because I wrote it."

A moment of silence. The little crowd that had collected, finding they were audience to nothing more exciting than a verbal confrontation about a book, had gradually been drifting off. Straightening his cap, the policeman cocked his head and pinched his bushy eyebrows together. The gnome was still smiling, enigmatically. Vigorously the woman in the green dress shook her head. The way she was holding her face suggested she was about to stamp her foot on somebody's face.

"May I have the book," she demanded of the policeman, then grudgingly added "please."

"Of course, madam," he replied, handing her the little volume that now had been passed around the little circle.

The woman in the green dress studied the back of the dust jacket, then stared at the man in the black raincoat.

"Here's a photograph of the author," she announced. "He's clean-shaven, dressed in a suit and a tie, looking like a professional man—a doctor or lawyer or maybe a college professor. Now I ask you," she went on, making her case by holding the volume so first the policeman, then the gnome could see the photograph, "can that possibly be the man who stole the book?"

"Guess I must agree," the policeman answered slowly, as if deliberating with himself, "there's no resemblance that I can see. What do you say, sir?" he then asked, turning to the gnome.

"True, it does not look much like him. But in my trade I've learned that dust jacket photographs are not to be trusted. If you could see some of the pictures of gorgeous women and handsome men that in the flesh are downright ugly…"

"Of course it's not me. It *is* who I was. Then."

Turning the book over and holding it high, close to her face, to keep what was on the front of the dust jacket from being visible, the woman in the green dress snapped, "What's your name?"

"Call me Fels."

Narrowing her eyes to slits and puckering her lips as she lowered the book, the woman in the green dress smiled. "Ah ha. It just so happens that's not the name printed on the dust jacket or," she went slowly, as she opened the volume, "on the title page. This book was written by one Felix Els." The smile made her satisfaction apparent.

"The author might be using a pen name," the gnome suggested hopefully, making clear which side of the split jury he was on.

"It's not a pen name. My name, madam, when the book was published and I was another person, did happen to be Felix Els. The name Felix, which either suggests a cartoon cat or, when translated back into Latin, from which it comes, means fortunate or lucky, was imposed on infant me. It was the Christian name of my paternal grandfather, whom, though no longer winning with us, lo these many years, I still despise. By ridding myself of the "elix' of my loathsome given name and prefixing the remaining "f" to my surname, thus collapsing three syllables into one, I became another person. Fels. That's my name."

"Implausible as it sounds to me, you're certainly quick to come up with an explanation for the discrepancy. Be that as it may, everyone must have a given name and a surname. By law. In our society. Am I correct, officer?"

Although the policeman dipped his chin once, rather ambiguously, the woman in the green dress proceeded with her cross-examination without waiting for a verbal affirmation of her point. "And the publisher? If you wrote the book, as you claim, tell us who published it."

"It was long ago and I can't quite recall the name of the publisher. Although it really doesn't matter, what I can tell you is it was a small press, as they're called. Something like 'A Finger up Yours Press.'"

"Hmmm," the woman in the green dress whinnied, lips pressed together to show she wasn't to be thrown off by a scrap of smut.

"How about the title?" the gnome asked brightly. "Surely you will know the title." Then he added with tardy reluctance, "If it is your book."

"That's right," the policeman agreed, seemingly inclined to aid the defense against the prosecution.

Another measurable silence.

"Well?" the woman in the green dress broke it by demanding she be answered, "what *is* the title of what you say is your book?"

It came slowly, a word at a time, as if each syllable were resisting utterance.

"*A ... Tale... Told.*"

"That is what it is," the gnome cheerfully confirmed while the policeman energetically nodded his head. "Just that."

"Still, it proves nothing," the woman in the green dress flung at the policeman, proddingly. "The fellow had every opportunity to read—"

Abruptly she broke off. Her stony features collapsed into dough. Then, as she knowingly nodded her head, they slowly reconstructed themselves into a slight smile.

"You know," the policeman said, removing his cap and running his fingers through his wavy black hair, "I can't make anything out of this. Man here says it's his book because he wrote it, which it does look like he might have, but the lady saw him take it from the shelf and stick it in the pocket of his raincoat, which he agrees he did, and you do have to wonder why he's wearing a raincoat on a hot sunny day, yet the owner of the bookstore isn't sure it's his book and doesn't want to prefer charges... besides, the book's only worth a buck ninety-five, which is hardly grand larceny...all of which adds up to I can't see enough evidence to take the man into custody. Do you agree, sir?"

"I do agree," the gnome almost purred. He was still beaming a cherubic smile. "And even if it were my book, it's been standing in the bookstall so long...well, I say, if he wants it that badly the gentleman is welcome to it."

"All well and good," the woman in the green dress pronounced, then went on in a surprisingly softened tone, "still I'd like to ask a few questions." She waved the book she was still holding at the man who had and hadn't stolen it.

"That's between you and him. Nothing more for me to do here." The policeman put his cap back on and nodded his head to indicate he agreed with himself. "I got a beat to cover and you never know." Touching the peak of his cap with the tips of his sausage fingers, he began whistling as he sauntered off.

"Think I should return to the shop. I would not want anyone to pocket one of the books in there whether he had written it or not. Out here," the gnome gestured toward the stall as his smile altered from cherubic to that of a clown who's just discovered the joke is on him, "I just have to trust people over what is really only peanuts."

The few passersby who had remained until the policeman had gone his way had gone on theirs, leaving only the woman in the green dress and the man she'd accused of theft standing on the sidewalk.

"Do you mind, Mr. Els? I only want to..."

"Fels is the name."

"I'm sorry. Mister Fels.... I merely want to satisfy my curiosity. You see, I too am a writer of books. I've written quite a few, in fact."

"Shoot. But drop the 'mister.'"

"Just what is your book about?"

"Wrong question. What the book's about doesn't matter."

"Well, perhaps then you *will* tell me what kind of book it is. To what genre does it belong—fiction, poetry, biography, memoir, trav..."

"It doesn't belong to a genre. It is what it is."

The woman stroked her long chin and pursed her lips.

"May I ask whether you've written any other books."

"No."

"No I may not ask or no you haven't."

"Take it whichever way you want."

"I should think you'd be gratified, maybe a bit proud, to have come across a copy of your book, even though it was in a secondhand bookstall."

"No to *prou*d, yes to *gratified*."

"I'm afraid I don't quite understand the distinction you're making. Is the reason you stole..."

"I didn't steal anything. Paying for my own book would be an absurdity."

"...you *took* the book be that you don't have a copy. Or have very few. Might the book be out of print?"

"Wrong. Last thing in the world I want is a copy of the book."

"But you're the author. It's your book. And you do have a copy of it in your raincoat pocket."

"I was and I have. That I've acknowledged."

"And it has been published. Small press or not, it's in print."

"That too is undeniable."

"You make it sound like a crime. Or a sin. Forgive me for saying your reasoning just doesn't make sense. To me, at least."

"It's not supposed to."

"Just because my curiosity's been aroused, let me see whether I understand what's going on. You don't want a copy of the book you wrote yet you went out of your way to get your hands on a copy. If it hadn't been for that easygoing policeman and the soft-hearted owner of the bookstore, at this very moment you could be under arrest for theft."

"Right."

"Then why *did* you slip the book into the pocket of your raincoat, which you must be wearing for that express purpose, and carry it off?"

"The answer's obvious."

"Not to me it isn't."

"Then I'll spell it out. I want to d. e. s. t. r. o. y. the book."

"But even if you shred the pages of the copy I'm holding, the book will still exist. It has been written and published. By you."

"Unfortunately you're right. In the abstract. The material fact is I can and will destroy this copy. As I've destroyed every other copy I've managed to lay my hands on in bookstores and bookstalls I've come across as I travel around the country."

"And how do you destroy your books?"

"I burn them."

"You what! Burn them—that's what the Nazi's did. May I ask how many copies you've succeeded in locating and have burned?"

"This makes thirteen."

"But surely there are other copies. In the hands of individuals who bought them, perhaps some in libraries, unsold ones in bookstalls and shops in other cities and towns, as well."

"Mighty few. I do what I can."

"Although I hesitate to ask this question, I must. Why do you want to burn your own book?"

"I'm not going to tell you."

"I'm averse to burning books, the woman declared, shaking her head in obvious disapproval. "Because of the association."

"Because of the association," he echoed under his breath.

Quite a long silence. In it he suddenly realized that the woman in the green dress bore a striking resemblance to the English teacher he'd had as a sophomore in high school many years ago. They hadn't got along. One afternoon she'd summoned him to her office when classes were over for the day and had accused him of plagiarizing a story he'd written about a boy killing his first deer. When she'd asked him whether he'd ever shot a deer, he'd told her he hadn't and never would. Then she'd insisted he'd stolen his story from a published story, by a famous author, he'd never read, about a boy killing his first bear.

Instantaneously with that recognition, it dawned on him why, against all his principles and his inclination, he was permitting the woman in the green dress to cross-examine him, to probe his inmost being. That long ago afternoon the accusing teacher had been wearing a green dress. Because he despised her, he needed to vindicate himself.

"You know," the woman said, breaking the silence, "I'm interested in your book. One writer to another." Now she was pressing the volume against her chest with her arms folded over it. "Will you sell me this copy? At the original price."

"No."

"Even if I give you my word I'll destroy it by some other means than burning as soon as I've finished reading?"

"No."

"Why not?"

"I'll give you only the most superficial reason. Allowing you to read the book would defeat my purpose in coming to this town, where I had the luck to find a copy. Since I wrote the book it's my responsibility to destroy it. By burning."

"Given that you and I have been having such an honest and open conversation, will you concede, just between the two of us, that I was right? The truth is you did steal the book."

"Technical truth is not *the* truth. You can't steal your own book. Not even a copy of it."

"Look, I know where you got the title. Just as you pretended to have a coughing spell to make me believe you were absorbed by the second book you took from the shelf, so I wouldn't suspect you'd slipped the first book into the pocket of your raincoat…in the same way you dropped the last three words of a memorable phrase written by one the great greats to make it seem you hadn't stolen your title."

"Wrong again. I had no doubt that almost all of the very few into whose hands the book would find its way would instantly identify the source the title was taken from and would supply the omitted words for themselves. Besides, if you really are a writer, you have to know it's an accepted practice to use well-known phrases for titles. In fact, a great Southern writer swiped three words from the very sentence my title is lifted from for the title of his greatest novel.

During another long silence the woman allowed another smile, this one a full smile to take over her face.

"You're right," she finally got out, "I've misjudged you. Will you accept my apology for calling you a thief?"

"No. It's hypocrisy for you to apologize when you still believe I stole the book. You can't help it. But I don't need your exoneration."

"Since I've taken an interest in you—a writer's interest, though I should say it has its human dimension as well—I hope you won't think me presumptuous for asking whether you've ever considered…well, getting help for what has to be a terrible compulsion—a kind of infanticide it is—to steal and burn your own book."

"No. Now you'll have to excuse me, madam. I must get on with it."

"It turns out you've been graciously responsive even though you…"

"Thank you. Good-bye."

"Good-bye. Do you know what that word means?"

"Of course. Fat chance of that."

He cut the final moment of silence between himself and the woman in the green dress with a chilling laugh.

"The book, please. It's mine."

"Oh. I almost forgot. I hope you won't think it was trying to…to steal it."

As she unfolded her arms and handed him the small volume, she sighed. With polish on their nails, the color of fresh blood, her fingers, he noticed, were long, slender, beautifully tapered.

Slipping the book into the left-hand pocket of his raincoat, he shambled off in the direction opposite from that he'd taken when he'd left the bookstall.

§

"Well, governor, seems you've done it. Stumbled your way through. My taste buds, or I should say thirst buds, tell me it's just about time for you know what."

"So, how'd I do? Be honest."

"Couldn't be anything else. Sorry to have to say I have some reservations."

"Let's have them. And get it over with between us."

"Now don't be bitter. You asked for them."

"Okay, okay. Shoot."

"It's not life, you know. It's a tale."

"What then are your reservations?"

"Well, the ending, denouement, as you'd style it. It's a bit flat and far too drawn out. The dialogue between the woman in the green dress and... let's just call him the man...is anticlimactic, a transparent device to wrap things up for the reader. It's not just unnecessary, it's condescending. And, as I was afraid you were going to, you dragged it out with all those accursed details and particulars of yours."

"Such as...?"

"Such as the policeman's cap, the smile of the proprietor of the bookstore, the fingers of the woman in the green dress. Adjectives, adjectives, adjectives. Even some adverbs. That 'suddenly', when the man makes the connection with the teacher who'd accused him spoils everything after you've quite nicely prepared the reader by the echoing of the word 'association.'"

"You're wrong. What you're finding fault with is necessary for realism. To enable, no, to *compel* the reader to believe."

"I, though perhaps mistaken, am of another opinion, as a wily Greek once said. But hell, getting the tale told, like making it through life, is one long compromise. Comes with the territory, as Willy Loman's neighbor Charlie says."

"I can't pass up the opportunity to observe your use just then of the adjectives—verboten parts of speech—'wily' and 'long.' Anyway, to turn your doctrine of necessity back on you, I did it the way I had to."

"Touché, governor. That you did."

"Which leads me to the question you've never answered to *my* satisfaction. How can you be so sure *I* summoned, as you call it, you to have your story told?"

"The answer's now self-evident, isn't it? Because you've done it. You had to tell my story. Otherwise it wouldn't be told."

"Your reasoning makes time run backward. Which is an absurdity."

"So absurd physicists these days are proving it's possible. Don't read very widely, do you, governor."

"Such stuff is beyond my down-to-earth brain. But there's another unanswered question."

"The light's still green."

"Don't you think after I've done my part to the best of what you consider my limited ability, I have a right to know what the book's about?"

"My, oh my. Question shows you don't understand the tale even though you've told it."

At this point, after he's been sitting in my reading chair still as a dummy all morning, I see him stir.

"Wait! Before you leave. There's one last piece of unfinished business between us."

"You do find it necessary to wrap up the package and tie the ends in a neat bow, don't you, governor. Closure, as you'd call it.

Well, let's have it, and be quick to the point. Time for me to be out of here."

"Now that the tale's not only been told but also has been inscribed on these sheets of paper, which you've noticed are yellow with blue-green lines, what am I to do with it?" I wave the thin sheaf at him. "Incidentally I've come to hate these pages."

"Sorry you asked that question, governor, really sorry. And mighty disappointed."

"What in God's name is wrong with my asking? Since it's your tale, obviously you're the one to address the question to."

"All I can say, and I deeply regret having to say it, is if after having put my story down in your hand, at the same time you were rendering it with your lips, you don't know what to do with it, I'm not going to tell you."

On that sour note he draws his hands from the pockets of his raincoat and plops them on the arms of my reading chair so his stubby fingers overlap the ends. At that instant he does indeed look like Ramses II. Then, grunting, he pulls himself up onto his feet. Hands in front of him, fingers clawed, he's bent over an invisible walker. Wearily, as though *he'd* exhausted *himself* telling the tale, he shuffles across the room, passing so close to me, pen still in my left hand, now pointing in the air at nothing, that I can't help wondering how long it's been since he's bathed. Phew!

"Have anything in the pocket of your raincoat? You know, to pick you up." I fling it at him, sounding as brutal as I know how.

Ignoring me, as if I weren't there, he grasps the doorknob with his left hand.

"Haven't you the decency, the common decency, to thank me?" Though I try to make my voice sternly reproachful, it comes out shrill, even more sepulchral than his bodiless tone. "I *did* tell your story, for Christ's sake. Leaving me exhausted while consuming one whole morning of my life. Of which I don't know how many I have left." The note of pleading I hear in my final words gives rise to an intense feeling of self-disgust.

"Thank you?" he echoes, changing the tone from entreaty to

contempt. When he turns his head around toward me, the scowl on his face bespeaks the darkest scorn. “I prefer not to.”

As he twists the doorknob, it screeches, the head on a neck being wrung. The door swings slowly open, hinges creaking. When it closes behind him, I can’t hear a sound.

§

To get back to you, should you still be with me. Now you know why I had to tell this tale. As I’ve done.

The Wessex Collective Books in Print

Good fiction does more than tell a story. It gives the gift of experience.

Sandra Shwayder Sanchez. *Stillbird.* From the strangling of a midwife perceived to be a witch in Scotland in the 1880s to thwarted love and the tragedy of incest in West Virginia during the depression, thence to Denver on the eve of the sixties, accurate history is enhanced by elements of magical realism in this tale of five generations that is as ancient as the Greek tragedies and as modern as the daily news. $9.50, paper

R. P. Burnham. *"Envious Shadows* is a deftly crafted, engrossing contemporary novel, one of those works that is not afraid to face the grim realities of life and the cruelties of society as well as the redeeming power of love....A beautiful work that depicts life in all its grim realities, *Envious Shadows* is a rewarding read." —Mayra Calvani, *Bloomsbury Review.* $11.50

Ita Willen. *The Gift.* Meditating upon the seasons in her garden, the author describes in poetic language and penetrating insight how the study and understanding of Buddhism helped her come to terms with the inescapable legacy of the Holocaust. Touches of surrealism give this memoir the feel of a novel. $9.50

William Davey. *The Angry Dust* tells the story of Prescott Barnes and his family leaving the dust bowl for California. The grandson of a wealthy preacher who disinherited Prescott's father, Barnes, despite his cynical black humor, hostility to religion, and illiteracy, possesses a fierce integrity and passions that make him larger than life at the same time he is perfectly human. $24.95, hardback

Brian Backstrand's stories from rural America chronicle often small but important moments in the lives of ordinary people. Memories—healing or disruptive, constant or denied—often play an important role in the stories of *Little Bluestem* which link together rural people from various generations caught in the midst of struggle or in a moment of recognition or healing. $12.95

R. P. Burnham, *On a Darkling Plain*: Samuel Jellerson, 56 and forced into early retirement, is walking in the woods behind the family farm in Maine one fall day when he witnesses a priest molesting a boy. From this one event all the action in the novel follows and draws a wide cross section of the town into a theme that explores the nature of evil and its antidote, empathy, the force that creates community, fellow feeling and a sense of responsibility to others. $12.95

Paul Johnson, *The Marble Orchard.* "...A deep, sweet story of accidental enlightenment... an optimistic coming-of-middle-age novel that will resonate loud and strong with those of us struggling to stay hopeful as we deal with aging, loss, and regrets." —Nancy Cardozo. $18.95

Margaret Guthrie. *The Return.* In this sequel to her 2003 novel, *Silent Truth*, two orphaned sisters return thirty years after their parents' deaths to find out what really happened. The perpetrator is dead, but will those who were with him talk? $15.00

Paul Johnson. *City of Kings.* "Paul Johnson's comic imagination takes the reader on a great ride through Brooklyn in this provocative sequel to the critically praised *Killing the Blues.* His anti-hero Casey is back, a character close to the author's heart, and it shows in his wit and intelligence. – Anthony Tripi. $15.00

R. P. Burnham. *The Many Change and Pass* is the third novel set in the same small town in Maine that explores the serious issues of the day. "Fully realized characters gain, lose, triumph and show themselves capable of life-transforming change. Small-town Maine has never been more vividly drawn."–Laurel Speer, poet and retired reviewer for **The Small Press Review.** $18.00

Sandra Shwayder Sanchez. *Three Novellas*. Each of these three novellas describes a journey. Noah Brown, a complete innocent, trusts the people he encounters along the roads who tell him their stories, until he comes to another port city, New Orleans, where he rescues people from a flood forty years later. *The King and the Clockmaker* takes up where an old legend leaves off about the maker of the astronomical clock in the 15th-century town hall of Prague. In *The Vast Darkness*, a young woman student of anthropology learns about the effect of isolated mountain living on her backwoods neighbors. $15.00

William Davey's *Brother of Cloud in the Water* is an amazingly imaginative first-person narrative of the life and exploits of the protagonist, a leader of a tribe of headhunters. "The book is very wise and has a great deal to say about what it means to be human." $24.95, hardback

Bob Sommer, *Where the Wind Blew*. After years of living a conventional middle-class life, Peter Howell's secret past as an anti-war radical involved in a bombing is suddenly revealed and forces him to flee. "Emotionally taut and historically intriguing…engrossing and heartfelt."–Ron Jacobs. $27.95, hardback

Gloria DeVidas Kirchheimer, *Amalie in Orbit*—an insightful and hilarious tale of one woman's miraculous conversion. What *Booklist* said of her previous collection of short fiction is equally true of *Amalie in Orbit*: "Like honey and lemon, each page mingles sweet and sour." $15.00

Helen Hudson. A seemingly peaceful village at the edge of Oxford seethes with the unspoken tensions and frustrations of a group of neighbors. A disparate group of women including a visiting American professor's wife, a school head mistress, a young recluse, a hairdresser and a fanatic churchgoer, react in wildly different ways to their enigmatic young male neighbor. As in all her novels, Hudson's theme in *Night Voices* is about the tragedy that befalls the most vulnerable among us when good people lack the courage to reach out to them. "A superior writer...Miss Hudson has Charlie Chaplin's magic way of provoking derision, sympathy, exasperation and curiosity all with the same gesture." -*The New Yorker*

R. P. Burnham. *A Robin Redbreast in a Cage* is a novel about a teenaged girl taken from her alcoholic and promiscuous mother and sent to live with her uncle, a fundamentalist minister. The only non-Christian she befriends in high school is Jeremy Lawrence; years later they serendipitously meet again. "As he does with his earlier novels, Burnham takes his time in skillfully creating his characters so that by the end, the readers know them inside out, down to their raw hearts."—Mayra Calvani, *blogcritics.org*, 2010 $15.00

Sandra Shwayder Sanchez. *A Mile in These Shoes*. These nine stories describe people who live on the margins of society, people who are often oppressed and always ignored. These stories give them voice and let the reader into their worlds on the edge. $14.00

Wessex books are available from BookLink Distribution (944 Broad Street/ Camden, SC 29020/ Tele: 803-432-5169). Visit them online at the The Book-Link Online Store (http://www.thebooklink.com), and under publishers choose The Wessex Collective. Also available at amazon.com.